Honoré de Balzac

The Jealousies of a Country Town

Les Rivalites, etc.

Honoré de Balzac

The Jealousies of a Country Town
Les Rivalites, etc.

ISBN/EAN: 9783337291709

Printed in Europe, USA, Canada, Australia, Japan

Cover: Foto ©Andreas Hilbeck / pixelio.de

More available books at **www.hansebooks.com**

H. DE BALZAC

THE COMÉDIE HUMAINE

HE LISTENED PATIENTLY-— TO TALES OF THE LITTLE WOES
OF LIFE IN A COUNTRY TOWN

THE
JEALOUSIES OF A COUNTRY TOWN

(LES RIVALITÉS)

ETC.

TRANSLATED BY

ELLEN MARRIAGE

WITH A PREFACE BY

GEORGE SAINTSBURY

PHILADELPHIA

THE GEBBIE PUBLISHING CO., Ltd.

1899

CONTENTS

LIST OF ILLUSTRATIONS

PREFACE.

THE two stories of " Les Rivalités" are more closely connected than it was always Balzac's habit to connect the tales which he united under a common heading. Not only are both devoted to the society of Alençon—a town and neighborhood to which he had evidently strong, though it is not clearly known what, attractions—not only is the Chevalier de Valois a notable figure in each; but the community, imparted by the elaborate study of the old *noblesse* in each case, is even greater than either of these ties could give. Indeed, if instead of " Les Rivalités" the author had chosen some label indicating the study of the *noblesse qui s'en va*, it might almost have been preferable. He did not, however; and though in a man who so constantly changed his titles and his arrangements the actual ones are not excessively authoritative, they have authority.

" La Vieille Fille," despite a certain tone of levity—which, to do Balzac justice, is not common with him, and which is rather hard upon the poor heroine—is one of the best and liveliest things he ever did. The opening picture of the chevalier, though, like other things of its author's, especially in his overtures, liable to the charge of being elaborated a little too much, is one of the very best things of its kind, and is a sort of *locus classicus* for its subject. The whole picture of country town society is about as good as it can be; and the only blot that I know is to be found in the sentimental Athanase, who was not quite within Balzac's province, extensive as that province is. If we compare Mr. Augustus Moddle, we shall see one of the not too numerous instances in which Dickens has a clear advantage over Balzac; and if it be retorted that Balzac's object was not to present a merely ridiculous object, the rejoinder is

not very far to seek. Such a character, with such a fate as
Balzac has assigned to him, must be either humorously gro-
tesque or unfeignedly pathetic, and Balzac has not quite made
Athanase either.

He is, however, if he is a failure, about the only failure in
the book, and he is atoned for by a whole bundle of successes.
Of the chevalier, little more need be said. Balzac, it must be
remembered, was the oldest novelist of distinct genius who
had the opportunity of delineating the survivors of the *ancien
régime* from the life, and directly. It is certain—even if we
hesitate at believing him quite so familiar with all the classes
of higher society from the *Faubourg* downward, as he would
have us believe him—that he saw something of most of them,
and his genius was unquestionably of the kind to which a mere
thumbnail study, a mere passing view, suffices for the acquisition of a thorough working knowledge of the object. In this
case the chevalier has served, and not improperly served, as
the original of a thousand after-studies. His rival, less carefully projected, is also perhaps a little less alive. Again,
Balzac was old enough to have foregathered with many men of
the Revolution. But the most characteristic of them were not
long lived, the "little window" and other things having had
a bad effect on them ; and most of those who survived had, by
the time he was old enough to take much notice, gone through
metamorphoses of Bonapartism, Constitutional Liberalism, and
what not. But still du Bosquier *is* alive, as well as all the
minor assistants and spectators in the battle for the old maid's
hand. Suzanne, that tactful and graceless Suzanne to whom
we are introduced first of all, is very much alive ; and for all
her gracelessness not at all disagreeable. I am only sorry that
she sold the counterfeit presentment of the Princess Goritza
after all.

"Le Cabinet des Antiques," in its Alençon scenes, is a
worthy pendant to "La Vieille Fille." The old-world honor
of the Marquis d'Esgrignon, the thankless sacrifices of Ar-

mande, the *prisca fides* of Maître Chesnel, present pictures for which, out of Balzac, we can look only in Jules Sandeau, and which in Sandeau, though they are presented with a more poetical touch, have less masterly outline than here. One takes—or, at least, I take—less interest in the ignoble intrigues of the other side, except in so far as they menace the fortunes of a worthy house unworthily represented. Victurnien d'Es-grignon, like his companion, Savinien de Portenduère (who, however, is, in every respect, a very much better fellow), does not argue in Balzac any high opinion of the *fils de famille*. He is, in fact, an extremely feeble youth, who does not seem to have got much real satisfaction out of the escapades, for which he risked not merely his family's fortune, but his own honor, and who would seem to have been a rake, not from natural taste and spirit and relish, but because it seemed to him to be the proper thing to be. But the beginnings of the fortune of the aspiring and intriguing Camusots are admirably painted; and Madame de Maufrigneuse, that rather doubtful divinity, who appears so frequently in Balzac, here acts the *dea ex machina* with considerable effect. And we end well (as we generally do when Blondet, whom Balzac seems more than once to adopt as mask, is the narrator), in the last glimpse of Mlle. Armande left alone with the remains of her beauty, the ruins of everything dear to her—and God.

These two stories were written at no long interval, yet, for some reason or other, Balzac did not at once unite them. "La Vieille Fille" first appeared in November and December, 1836, in the "Presse," and was inserted next year in the Scènes de la Vie de Province. It had three chapter divisions. The second part did not appear all at once. Its first install-ment, under the general title, came out in the "Chronique de Paris" even before the "Vieille Fille" appeared in March, 1836; the completion was not published (under the title of "Les Rivalités en Province") till the autumn of 1838, when the "Constitutionnel" served as its vehicle. There were eight chapter divisions in this latter. The whole of the "Cabinet" was published in book form (with "Gambara" to follow it) in 1839. There were some changes here; and the divisions were abolished when the whole book in 1844 entered the Comédie. One of the greatest mistakes which, in my humble judgment, the organizers of the *édition définitive* have made, is their adoption of Balzac's never executed separation of the pair and deletion of the excellent joint-title "Les Rivalités."

If Balzac had been acquainted with the works of Chaucer (which would have been extremely surprising) he might have called "Le Contrat de Mariage" "A Legend of Bad Women." He has not been exactly sparing of studies in that particular kind; but he has surpassed himself here. Mme. de Maufrigneuse redeems herself by her character, however imperfectly supported, of *grande dame*, Beatrix de Rochefide by a certain naturalness and weakness, Flore Brazier by circumstances and education, others by other things. But Madame Evangelista and her daughter Natalie may be said to be bad all through—thoroughly poisonous persons who, much more than the actual Milady of "Les Trois Mousquetaires" (there was some charm in her), deserved to be taken and "justified" by lynch law. If the "Thirteen" (who were rather interested in the matter) had descended upon both in the fashion of d'Artagnan and his friends, I do not know that any one would have had much right to complain. How far the picture is exaggerated must be a question to be decided partly by individual experience, partly by other arguments. Although I am not always disposed to defend Balzac from the charge of exaggeration, I think he is fairly free from it here.

Madame Evangelista, beside the usual womanly desire to make a figure in the capital, has (not to excuse, but to explain her) the equally natural tendency to regard everybody outside her own family as an at least possible enemy to be "exploited" pitilessly, together with bad blood which, though luckily not common, is by no means impossible nor even extremely rare. Her daughter, as Balzac has acutely suggested, both here and elsewhere, is, like not a few women, destitute of that sense of abiding gratitude for pleasure mutually enjoyed which tempers the evil tendencies of the male sex to no inconsiderable extent. She has never cared for her husband; she has no morals; and (as in another book and subject, her letter to Félix de Vandenesse, well deserved as it is in the particular instance, shows) she has the fortunately not universal but excessively dangerous combination of utter selfishness with very clear-sighted commonsense.

The men are equally true, and much more agreeable. It is noteworthy that here only does Balzac's pattern Byronic dandy Marsay cut a distinctly agreeable figure. He is still something of a coxcomb, but he is, as he is not very often, a gentleman; he is, as he is scarcely ever, a good fellow; and he deserves his character as *un homme très fort*, to say the least, better than he does in some places. The two family lawyers are excellent. As for Paul de Manerville, the unfortunate *fleur des pois* (the title for some time of the book) himself, he is one of the profoundest of Balzac's studies, and it was perhaps rather unkind of his creator to call him a *niais*. At any rate, he was not more so than that very creator when he committed slow suicide by waiting and working till a woman, who cannot have been worth the trouble, at last made up her mind to "derogate" a little, and, without any pecuniary sacrifice, to exchange the position of widow of a member of a second-rate aristocracy for that of wife of one of the foremost living men of letters in Europe, who was himself technically a gentleman. Marsay's letters to Paul only put pointedly what the whole story puts suggestively, the great truth that you may "see life" without knowing it, and that for a certain kind of respectable person the sowing of wild oats is a far more dangerous kind of husbandry than for the wildest profligate. It is true that Paul has exceedingly bad luck, and that in countries other than France he might have subsided into a most respectable and comfortable country gentleman. But as a great authority, whom he probably knew, Paul de Florac, his namesake and contemporary, remarked, "Do not adopt our institutions *à demi*," so it would seem to be a maxim that the two kinds of life cannot be combined—at least, that seems to be Balzac's moral.

The first titles of the two main stories have been given above. "La Fleur des pois," as such, appeared in no newspaper, but in the "Scènes de la Vie Privée" of 1834–35. It had three divisions, which disappeared in the first edition of the Comédie, when also the title was changed. Its companion was printed under its first title, and with fourteen chapter divisions, in a paper called "La Législature," between July and September, 1842. Balzac at first meant to call it "Les Jeunes Gens,"* but changed this to "Le Danger des Mystifications," and that again to the present form, when it appeared (with "La fausse Maîtresse") as a book in 1844. Next year it was classed in the Comédie, undergoing the usual process of deletion of the chapter divisions and headings.

G. S.

* This refers to "A Start in Life."

THE JEALOUSIES OF A COUNTRY TOWN.

THE OLD MAID
(*La Vieille Fille*).

To M. Eugène Auguste Georges Louis Midy de la Greneraye Surville, Civil Engineer of the Corps-Royal, a token of affection from his brother-in-law.

DE BALZAC.

PLENTY of people must have come across at least one Chevalier de Valois in the provinces; there was one in Normandy, another was extant at Bourges, a third flourished at Alençon in the year 1816, and the South very likely possessed one of its own. But we are not here concerned with the numbering of the Valois tribe. Some of them, no doubt, were about as much of Valois as Louis XIV. was a Bourbon; and every chevalier was so slightly acquainted with the rest that it was anything but politic to mention one of them when speaking to another. All of them, however, agreed to leave the Bourbons in perfect tranquillity on the throne of France, for it is a little too well proven that Henri IV. succeeded to the crown in default of heirs male in the Orléans, otherwise the Valois branch; so that if any Valois exist at all, they must be descendants of Charles of Valois, Duke of Angoulême, and Marie Touchet; and even there the direct line was extinct (unless proof to the contrary is forthcoming) in the person of the Abbé de Rothelin. As for the Valois Saint-Remy, descended from Henri II., they likewise came to an end with the too famous Lamothe-Valois of the Diamond Necklace affair.

(1)

Every one of the chevaliers, if information is correct, was, like the chevalier of Alençon, an elderly noble, tall, lean, and without fortune. The Bourges chevalier had emigrated, the Touraine Valois went into hiding during the Revolution, and the Alençon chevalier was mixed up in the Vendean war, and implicated to some extent in Chouannerie.* The last-named gentleman spent the most part of his youth in Paris, where, at the age of thirty, the Revolution broke in upon his career of conquests. Accepted as a true Valois by persons of the highest quality in his province, the Chevalier de Valois d'Alençon (like his namesakes) was remarkable for his fine manners, and had evidently been accustomed to move in the best society.

He dined out every day, and played cards of an evening, and, thanks to one of his weaknesses, was regarded as a great wit ; he had a habit of relating a host of anecdotes of the times of Louis Quinze, and those who heard his stories for the first time thought them passably well narrated. The Chevalier de Valois, moreover, had one virtue : he refrained from repeating his own good sayings, and never alluded to his conquests, albeit his smiles and airs were delightfully indiscreet. The old gentleman took full advantage of the old-fashioned Voltairean noble's privilege of staying away from mass, but his irreligion was very tenderly dealt with out of regard for his devotion to the Royalist cause.

One of his most remarked graces (Molé must have learned it of him) was his way of taking snuff from an old-fashioned snuff-box with a portrait of a lady on the lid. The Princess Goritza, a lovely Hungarian, had been famous for her beauty toward the end of the reign of Louis XV. ; and the chevalier could never speak without emotion of the foreign great lady whom he loved in his youth, for whom he had fought a duel with M. de Lauzun.

But by this time the chevalier had lived fifty-eight years,

* The Royalist rising in Vendée.

and if he owned to but fifty of them, he might safely indulge himself in that harmless deceit. Thin, fair-complexioned men, among other privileges, retain their youthfulness of shape which in men, as in women, contributes as much as anything to stave off any appearance of age. And, indeed, it is a fact that all the life, or rather, all the grace, which is the expression of life, lies in the figure. Among the chevalier's personal traits, mention must be made of the portentous nose with which nature had endowed him. It cut a pallid countenance sharply into two sections which seemed to have nothing to do with each other; so much so, indeed, that only one-half of his face would flush with the exertion of digestion after dinner; all the glow being confined to the left side, a phenomenon worthy of note in times when physiology is so much occupied with the human heart. M. de Valois' health was not apparently robust, judging by his long, thin legs, lean frame, and sallow complexion; but he ate like an ogre, alleging, doubtless by way of excuse for his voracity, that he suffered from a complaint known in the provinces as a "hot liver." The flush on his left cheek confirmed the story; but in a land where meals are developed on the lines of thirty or forty dishes, and last for four hours at a stretch, the chevalier's abnormal appetite might well seem to be a special mark of the favor of Providence vouchsafed to the good town. That flush on the left cheek, according to divers medical authorities, is a sign of prodigality of heart; and, indeed, the chevalier's past record of gallantry might seem to confirm a professional dictum for which the present chronicler (most fortunately) is in nowise responsible. But in spite of these symptoms, M. de Valois was of nervous temperament, and in consequence long-lived; and if his liver was hot, to use the old-fashioned phrase, his heart was not a whit less inflammable. If there was a line worn here and there in his face, and a silver thread or so in his hair, an experienced eye would have discerned in these signs and tokens the stigmata of desire, the furrows traced by past pleasure. And, in fact, in his face, the unmistakable marks of the crow's foot and the serpent's tooth took the shape of the delicate wrinkles so prized at the court of Cytherea.

Everything about the gallant chevalier revealed the "ladies' man." So minutely careful was he over his ablutions that it was a pleasure to see his cheeks; they might have been brushed over with some miraculous water. That portion of his head which the hair refused to hide from view shone like ivory. His eyebrows, like his hair, had a youthful look, so carefully was their growth trained and regulated by the comb. A naturally fair skin seemed to be yet further whitened by some mysterious preparation; and while the chevalier never used scent, there was about him, as it were, a perfume of youth which enhanced the freshness of his looks. His hands, that told of race, were as carefully kept as if they belonged to some coxcomb of the gentler sex; you could not help noticing those rose-pink neatly-trimmed finger-nails. Indeed, but for his lordly superlative nose, the chevalier would have looked like a doll.

It takes some resolution to spoil this portrait with the admission of a foible; the chevalier put cotton wool in his ears, and still continued to wear earrings—two tiny negroes' heads set with brilliants. They were of admirable workmanship, it is true, and their owner was so far attached to the singular appendages that he used to justify his fancy by saying that his "sick headaches had left him since his ears were pierced." He used to suffer from sick headaches. The chevalier is not held up as a flawless character; but even if an old bachelor's heart sends too much blood to his face, is he never therefore to be forgiven for his adorable absurdities? Perhaps (who knows?) there are sublime secrets hidden away beneath them. And beside, the Chevalier de Valois made amends for his negroes' heads with such a variety of other and different charms that society ought to have felt itself sufficiently compensated. He really was at great pains to conceal his age and to make himself agreeable.

First and foremost, witness the extreme care which he gave to his linen, the one distinction in dress which a gentleman may permit himself in modern days. The chevalier's linen was invariably fine and white, as befitted a noble. His coat, though remarkably neat, was always somewhat worn, but spotless and uncreased. The preservation of this garment bordered on the miraculous in the opinion of those who noticed the chevalier's elegant indifference on this head; not that he went so far as to scrape his clothes with broken glass (a refinement invented by the Prince of Wales), but he set himself to carry out the first principles of dress as laid down by Englishmen of the very highest and finest fashion, and this with a personal element of coxcombry which Alençon was scarcely capable of appreciating. Does the world owe no esteem to those that take such pains for it? And what was all this labor but the fulfillment of that very hardest of sayings in the Gospel, which bids us return good for evil? The freshness of the toilet, the care for dress, suited well with the chevalier's blue eyes, ivory teeth, and bland personality; still, the superannuated Adonis had nothing masculine in his appearance, and it would seem that he employed the illusion of the toilet to hide the ravages of other than military campaigns.

To tell the whole truth, the chevalier had a voice singularly at variance with his delicate fairness. So full was it and sonorous, that you would have been startled by the sound of it unless, with certain observers of human nature, you held the theory that the voice was only what might be expected of such a nose. With something less of volume than a giant double-bass, it was a full, pleasant baritone, reminding you of the hautboy among musical instruments, sweet and resonant, deep and rich.

M. de Valois had discarded the absurd costume still worn by a few antiquated Royalists, and frankly modernized his dress. He always appeared in a maroon coat with gilt buttons, loosely-fitting breeches with gold buckles at the knees, a white sprigged vest, a tight stock, and a collarless shirt; this being a last vestige of eighteenth-century costume, which its wearer was the less willing to relinquish because it enabled him to display a throat not unworthy of a lay abbé. Square gold buckles of a kind unknown to the present generation shone conspicuous upon his patent-leather shoes. Two watch chains hung in view in parallel lines from a couple of fobs, another survival of an eighteenth-century mode which the old boy did not disdain to copy in the time of the Directory. This costume of a transition period, reuniting two centuries, was worn by the chevalier with the grace of an old-world marquis, a grace lost to the French stage since Molé's last pupil, Fleury, retired from the boards and took his secret with him.

The old bachelor's private life, seemingly open to all eyes, was in reality inscrutable. He lived in a modest lodging (to say the least of it) up two sets of stairs in a house in the Rue du Cours, his landlady being the laundress most in request in Alençon—which fact explains the extreme elegance of the chevalier's linen. Ill luck was so to order it that Alençon one day could actually believe that he had not always conducted himself as befitted a man of his quality, and that in his old age he privately married one Césarine, the mother of an infant which had the impertinence to come without being called.

"He gave his hand to her who for so long had lent her hand to iron his linen," said a certain M. du Bousquier.

The sensitive noble's last days were the more vexed by this unpleasant scandal, because, as shall be shown in the course of this present Scene, he had already lost a long-cherished hope for which he had made many a sacrifice.

Mme. Lardot's two rooms were let to M. le Chevalier de Valois at the moderate rent of a hundred francs per annum.

The worthy gentleman dined out every night, and only came home to sleep; he was therefore at charges for nothing but his breakfast, which always consisted of a cup of chocolate with butter and fruit, according to the season. A fire was never lighted in his rooms except in the very coldest winters, and then only while he was dressing. Between the hours of eleven and four M. de Valois took his walks abroad, read the news-papers, and paid calls.

When the chevalier first settled in Alençon, he magnan-imously owned that he had nothing but an annuity of six hun-dred livres paid in quarterly installments by his old man of business, with whom the certificates were deposited. This was all that remained of his former wealth. And every three months, in fact, a banker in the town paid him a hundred and fifty francs remitted by one M. Bordin of Paris, the last of the *procureurs du Châtelet.** These particulars everybody knew, for the chevalier had taken care to ask his confidant to keep the matter a profound secret. He reaped the fruits of his misfortunes. A cover was laid for him in all the best houses in Alençon; he was asked to every evening party. His talents as a card-player, a teller of anecdotes, a pleasant and well-bred man of the world were so thoroughly appreci-ated that an evening was spoiled if the connoisseur of the town was not present. The host and hostess and all the ladies pres-ent missed his little approving grimace. " You are adorably well dressed," from the old bachelor's lips, was sweeter to a young woman in a ballroom than the sight of her rival's de-spair.

There were certain old-world expressions which no one could pronounce so well. "My heart," "my jewel," "my little love," "my queen," and all the dear diminutives of the year 1770 took an irresistible charm from M. de Valois' lips; in short, the privilege of superlatives was his. His compli-ments, of which, moreover, he was chary, won him the good-

* Fiduciary agent.

will of the elderly ladies; he flattered every one down to the officials of whom he had no need.

He was so fine a gentleman at the card-table that his behavior would have marked him out anywhere. He never complained; when his opponents lost he praised their play; he never undertook the education of his partners by showing them what they ought to have done. If a nauseating discussion of this kind began while the cards were making, the chevalier brought out his snuff-box with a gesture worthy of Molé, looked at the Princess Goritza's portrait, took off the lid in a stately manner, heaped up a pinch, rubbed it to a fine powder between finger and thumb, blew off the light particles, shaped a little cone in his hand, and by the time the cards were dealt he had replenished the cavities in his nostrils and replaced the princess in his waistcoat pocket—always on the left-hand side.

None but a noble of the Gracious as distinguished from the Great Century could have invented such a compromise between a disdainful silence and an epigram which would have passed over the heads of his company. The chevalier took dull minds as he found them, and knew how to turn them to account. His irresistible evenness of temper caused many a one to say: "I admire the Chevalier de Valois!" Everything about him, his conversation and his manner, seemed in keeping with his mild appearance. He was careful to come into collision with no one, man or woman. Indulgent with deformity as with defects of intellect, he listened patiently (with the help of the Princess Goritza) to tales of the little woes of life in a country town; to anecdotes of the undercooked egg at breakfast, or the sour cream in the coffee; to small grotesque details of physical ailments; to tales of dreams and visitations and wakings with a start. The chevalier was an exquisite listener. He had a languishing glance, a stock attitude to denote compassion; he put in his "Ohs" and "Poohs" and "What-did-you-dos?" with charming appropriateness. Till his dying day no one ever suspected that while these avalanches of nonsense lasted, the chevalier in his own mind was rehearsing the warmest passages of an old romance, of which the Princess Goritza was the heroine. Has any one ever given a thought to the social uses of extinct sentiment?—or guessed in how many indirect ways love benefits humanity?

Possibly this listener's faculty sufficiently explains the chevalier's popularity; he was always the spoiled child of the town, although he never quitted a drawing-room without carrying off about five livres in his pocket. Sometimes he lost, and he made the most of his losses, but it very seldom happened. All those who knew him say with one accord that never in any place have they met with so agreeable a mummy, not even in the Egyptian museum at Turin. Surely in no known country of the globe did parasite appear in such a benignant shape. Never did selfishness in its most concentrated form show itself so inoffensive, so full of good offices, as in this gentleman; the chevalier's egoism was as good as another man's devoted friendship. If any person went to ask M. de Valois to do some trifling service which the worthy chevalier could not perform without inconvenience, that person never went away without conceiving a great liking for him, and departed fully convinced that the chevalier could do nothing in the matter, or might do harm if he meddled with it.

To explain this problematical existence the chronicler is bound to admit, while Truth—that ruthless debauchee—has caught him by the throat, that latterly, after the three sad, glorious Days of July, Alençon discovered that M. de Valois' winnings at cards amounted to something like a hundred and fifty crowns every quarter, which amount the ingenious chevalier intrepidly remitted to himself as an annuity, so that he might not appear to be without resources in a country with a great turn for practical details. Plenty of his friends—he was

dead by that time, please to remark—plenty of his friends denied this *in toto;* they maintained that the stories were fables
and slanders set in circulation by the Liberal party, and that
M. de Valois was an honorable and worthy gentleman. Luckily
for clever gamblers, there will always be champions of this
sort for them among the onlookers. Feeling ashamed to
excuse wrongdoing, they stoutly deny that wrong has been
done. Do not accuse them of wrong-headedness; they have
their own sense of self-respect, and the Government sets
them an example of the virtue which consists in burying its
dead by night without chanting a Te Deum over a defeat.
And suppose that M. de Valois permitted himself a neat
stratagem that would have won Gramont's esteem, a smile from
Baron de Fœneste, and a shake of the hand from the Marquis
de Moncade, was he any the less the pleasant dinner guest, the
wit, the unvarying card-player, the charming retailer of anecdotes, the delight of Alençon? In what, moreover, does the
action, lying, as it does, outside the laws of right and wrong,
offend against the elegant code of a man of birth and breeding? When so many people are obliged to give pensions to
others, what more natural than of one's own accord to allow
an annuity to one's own best friend? But Laïus is dead.

After some fifteen years of this kind of life, the chevalier
had amassed ten thousand and some odd hundred francs.
When the Bourbons returned, he said that an old friend of
his, M. le Marquis de Pombreton, late a lieutenant in the
Black Musketeers, had returned a loan of twelve hundred
pistoles with which he emigrated. The incident made a sensation. It was quoted afterward as a set-off against droll
stories in the "Constitutionnel" of the ways in which some
émigrés paid their debts. The poor chevalier used to blush
all over the right side of his face whenever this noble trait in
the Marquis de Pombreton came up in conversation. At the
time every one rejoiced with M. de Valois; he used to consult capitalists as to the best way of investing this wreck of

his former fortune; and, putting faith in the Restoration, invested it all in Government stock when the Funds had fallen to fifty-six francs twenty-five centimes. MM. de Lenoncourt, de Navarreins, de Verneuil, de Fontaine, and La Billardière, to whom he was known, had obtained a pension of a hundred crowns for him from the privy purse, he said, and the cross of St. Louis. By what means the old chevalier obtained the two solemn confirmations of his title and quality, no one ever knew; but this much is certain, the cross of St. Louis gave him brevet rank as a colonel on a retiring pension, by reason of his services with the Catholic army in the West.

Beside the fiction of the annuity, to which no one gave a thought, the chevalier was now actually possessed of a genuine income of a thousand francs. But with this improvement in his circumstances he made no change in his life or manners; only—the red ribbon looked wondrous well on his maroon coat; it was a finishing touch, as it were, to this portrait of a gentleman. Ever since the year 1802 the chevalier had sealed his letters with an ancient gold seal, engraved roughly enough, but not so badly but that the Castérans, d'Esgrignons, and Troisvilles might see that he bore the arms of France impaled with his own, to wit, *France per pale, gules two bars gemelles, a cross of five mascles conjoined or, on a chief sable a cross pattee argent over all;* with a knight's casquet for crest and the motto—VALEO. With these noble arms the so-called bastard Valois was entitled to ride in all the royal coaches in the world.

Plenty of people envied the old bachelor his easy life, made up of boston, trictrac, reversis, whist, and piquet; of good play, dinners well digested, pinches of snuff gracefully taken, and quiet walks abroad. Almost all Alençon thought that his existence was empty alike of ambitions and cares; but where is the man whose life is quite as simple as they suppose who envy him?

In the remotest country village you shall find human molluscs, rotifers inanimate to all appearance, which cherish a passion for lepidoptera or conchology, and are at infinite pains to acquire some new butterfly, or a specimen of *Concha Veneris.*   And the chevalier had not merely shells and butter-flies of his own, he cherished an ambitious desire with a perti-nacity and profound strategy worthy of a Sixtus V.   He meant to marry a rich old maid ; in all probability because a wealthy marriage would be a stepping-stone to the high spheres of the Court.   *This* was the secret of his royal bearing and prolonged abode in Alençon.

Very early one Tuesday morning in the middle of spring in the year '16 (to use his own expression), the chevalier was just slipping on his dressing-gown, an old-fashioned green silk damask of a flowered pattern, when, in spite of the cotton in his ears, he heard a girl's light footstep on the stairs.   In another moment some one tapped discreetly three times on the door, and then, without waiting for an answer, a very handsome damsel slipped like a snake into the old bachelor's apartment.

"Ah, Suzanne, is that you?" said the Chevalier de Valois, continuing to strop his razor.   "What are you here for, dear little jewel of mischief?"

"I have come to tell you something which perhaps will give you as much pleasure as annoyance."

"Is it something about Césarine?"

"Much I trouble myself about your Césarine," pouted she, half careless, half in earnest.

The charming Suzanne, whose escapade was to exercise so great an influence on the lives of all the principal characters in this story, was one of Mme. Lardot's laundry girls.   And now for a few topographical details:

The whole first floor of the house was given up to the laundry.   The little yard was a drying ground where em-broidered handkerchiefs, collarettes, lawn slips, cuffs, frilled shirts, cravats, laces, embroidered petticoats, all the fine washing of the best houses in the town, in short, hung out along the lines of hair rope. The chevalier used to say that he was kept informed of the progress of the receiver-general's wife's flirtations by the number of slips thus brought to light; and the amount of frilled shirts and cambric cravats varied directly with the petticoats and collarettes. By this system of double entry, as it were, he detected all the assignations in the town; but the chevalier was always discreet, he never let fall an epigram that might have closed a house to him. And yet he was a witty talker! For which reason you may be sure that M. de Valois' manners were of the finest, while his talents, as so often happens, were thrown away upon a narrow circle. Still, for he was only human after all, he sometimes could not resist the pleasure of a searching side-glance which made women tremble, and nevertheless they liked him when they found out how profoundly discreet he was, how full of sympathy for their pretty frailties.

Mme. Lardot's forewoman and factotum, an alarmingly ugly spinster of five-and-forty, occupied the rest of the third floor with the chevalier. Her door on the landing was exactly opposite his; and her apartments, like his own, consisted of two rooms, looking respectively upon the street and the yard. Above, there was nothing but the attics where the linen was dried in winter. Below lodged Mme. Lardot's grandfather. The old man, Grévin by name, had been a privateer in his time, and had served under Admiral Simeuse in the Indies; now he was paralyzed and stone deaf. Mme. Lardot herself occupied the rooms beneath her forewoman, and so great was her weakness for people of condition that she might be said to be blind where the chevalier was concerned. In her eyes, M. de Valois was an absolute monarch, a king that could do no wrong; even if one of her own work-girls had been said to be guilty of finding favor in his sight, she would have said, "He is so amiable!"

And so, if M. de Valois, like most people in the provinces,

lived in a glass house, it was secret as a robber's cave so far as he at least was concerned. A born confidant of the little intrigues of the laundry, he never passed the door—which always stood ajar—without bringing something for his pets—chocolate, bonbons, ribbons, laces, a gilt cross, and the jokes that grisettes love. Wherefore the little girls adored the chevalier. Women can tell by instinct whether a man is attracted to anything that wears a petticoat; they know at once the kind of man who enjoys the mere sense of their presence, who never thinks of making blundering demands of repayment for his gallantry. In this respect womankind has a canine faculty; a dog in any company goes straight to the man who respects animals. The Chevalier de Valois in his poverty preserved something of his former life; he was as unable to live without some fair one under his protection as any great lord of a bygone age. He clung to the traditions of the *petite maison.** He loved to give to women, and women alone can receive gracefully, perhaps because it is always in their power to repay.

In these days, when every lad on leaving school tries his hand at unearthing symbols or sifting legends, is it not extraordinary that no one has explained that portent, the Courtesan of the Eighteenth Century. What was she but the tournament of the Sixteenth in another shape? In 1550 the knights displayed their prowess for their ladies; in 1750 they displayed their mistresses at Longchamps; to-day they run their horses over the course. The noble of every age has done his best to invent a life which he, and he only, can live. The pointed shoes of the Fourteenth Century are the red heels of the Eighteenth; the parade of a mistress was one fashion in ostentation; the sentiment of chivalry and the knight-errant was another.

The Chevalier de Valois could no longer ruin himself for a mistress, so for bonbons wrapped in bank-bills he politely offered a bag of genuine cracknels; and to the credit of

* Little house: place of a mistress' installment.

Alençon, be it said, the cracknels caused far more pleasure to the recipients than M. d'Artois' presents of carriages or silver-gilt toilet sets ever gave to the fair Duthé.　There was not a girl in the laundry but recognized the chevalier's fallen great-ness, and kept his familiarities in the house a profound secret.

In answer to questions, they always spoke gravely of the Chevalier de Valois ; they watched over him.　For others he became a venerable gentleman, his life was a flower of sanctity. But at home they would have lighted on his shoulders like paroquets.

The chevalier liked to know the intimate aspects of family life which laundresses learn ; they used to go up to his room of a morning to retail the gossip of the town ; he called them his "gazettes in petticoats," his "living feuilletons."　M. Sartine himself had not such intelligent spies at so cheap a rate, nor yet so loyal in their rascality.　Remark, moreover, that the chevalier thoroughly enjoyed his breakfasts.

Suzanne was one of his favorites.　A clever and ambitious girl with the stuff of a Sophie Arnould in her, she was beside as beautiful as the loveliest courtesan that Titian ever prayed to pose against a background of dark velvet as a model for his Venus.　Her forehead and all the upper part of her face about the eyes were delicately moulded ; but the contours of the lower half were cast in a commoner mould.　Hers was the beauty of a Norman, fresh, plump, and brilliant-complexioned, with that Rubens fleshiness which should be combined with the muscular development of the Farnese Hercules.　This was no Venus dei Me ici, the graceful feminine counterpart of Apollo.

"Well, child," said the chevalier, "tell me your adventures little or big."

The chevalier's fatherly benignity with these grisettes would have marked him out anywhere between Paris and Pekin. The girls put him in mind of the courtesans of another age, of the illustrious queens of opera of European fame during a good third of the eighteenth century. Certain it is that he who had lived for so long in a world of women now as dead and forgotten as the jesuits, the buccaneers, the abbés, and the farmers-general, and all great things generally—certain it is that the chevalier had acquired an irresistible good-humor, a gracious ease, an unconcern, with no trace of egoism discernible in it. So might Jupiter have appeared to Alcmena—a king that chooses to be a woman's dupe, and flings majesty and its thunderbolts to the winds, that he may squander Olympus in follies, and "little suppers," and feminine extravagance; wishful, of all things, to be far enough away from Juno.

The room in which the chevalier received company was bare enough, with its shabby bit of tapestry to do duty as a carpet, and very dirty, old-fashioned easy-chairs; the walls were covered with a cheap paper, on which the countenances of Louis XVI. and his family, framed in weeping willow, appeared at intervals among funeral urns, bearing the *sublime testament* by way of inscription, amid a whole host of sentimental emblems invented by royalism under the Terror; but in spite of all this, in spite of the old, flowered green silk dressing-gown, in spite of its owner's air of dilapidation, a certain fragrance of the eighteenth century clung about the Chevalier de Valois as he shaved himself before the old-fashioned toilet glass, covered with cheap lace. All the graceless graces of his youth seemed to reappear; he might have had three hundred thousand francs' worth of debts to his name and a chariot at his door. He looked a great man, great as Berthier in the Retreat from Moscow issuing the order of the day to battalions which were no more.

" Monsieur le Chevalier," Suzanne replied archly, "it seems to me that I have nothing to tell you—you have only to look!"

So saying, she turned and stood sideways to prove her words by ocular demonstration; and the chevalier, deep old gentleman, still holding his razor across his chin, cast his right eye downward upon the damsel, and pretended to understand.

"Very good, my little pet, we will have a little talk together presently. But you come first, it seems to me."

"But, Monsieur le Chevalier, am I to wait till my mother beats me and Madame Lardot turns me away? If I do not go to Paris at once, I shall never get married here, where the men are so ridiculous."

"These things cannot be helped, child! Society changes, and women suffer just as much as the nobles from the shocking confusion which ensues. Topsy-turvydom in politics ends in topsy-turvy manners. Alas! woman soon will cease to be woman" (here he took the cotton-wool out of his ears to continue his toilet). "Women will lose a great deal by plunging into sentiment; they will torture their nerves, and there will be an end of the good old ways of our time, when a little pleasure was desired without blushes, and accepted without more ado, and the vapors" (he polished the earrings with the negroes' heads)—"the vapors were only known as a means of getting one's way; before long they will take the proportions of a complaint only to be cured by an infusion of orange-blossoms." (The chevalier burst out laughing.) "Marriage, in short," he resumed, taking a pair of tweezers to pluck out a gray hair, "marriage will come to be a very dull institution indeed, and it was so joyous in my time. The reign of Louis Quatorze and Louis Quinze (bear this in mind, my child) saw the last of the finest manners in the world."

"But, Monsieur le Chevalier," urged the girl, "it is your little Suzanne's character and reputation that is at stake, and you are not going to forsake her, I hope!"

"What is all this?" cried the chevalier, with a finishing touch to his hair; "I would sooner lose my name!"

"Ah!" said Suzanne.

2

"Listen to me, little masquerader." He sat down in a large, low chair, a *duchesse*, as it used to be called, which Mme. Lardot had picked up somewhere for her lodger. Then he drew the magnificent Suzanne to him till she stood between his knees; and Suzanne submitted—Suzanne who held her head so high in the streets, and had refused a score of overtures from admirers in Alençon, not so much from self-respect as in disdain of their pettiness. Suzanne so brazenly made the most of the supposed consequences of her errors that the old sinner, who had fathomed so many mysteries in persons far more astute than Suzanne, saw the real state of affairs at once. He knew well enough that a grisette does not laugh when disgrace is really in question, but he scorned to throw down the scaffolding of an engaging fib with a touch.

"We are slandering ourselves," said he, and there was an inimitable subtlety in his smile. "We are as well conducted as the fair one whose name we bear; we can marry without fear. But we do not want to vegetate here; we long for Paris, where charming creatures can be rich if they are clever, and we are not a fool. So we should like to find out whether the City of Pleasure has young Chevaliers de Valois in store for us, and a carriage and diamonds and an opera box. There are Russians and English and Austrians that are bringing millions to spend in Paris, and some of that money mamma settled on us as a marriage-portion when she gave us our good looks. And beside, we are patriotic; we should like to help France to find her own money in these gentlemen's pockets. Eh! eh! my dear little devil's lamb, all this is not bad. The neighbors will cry out upon you a little at first, perhaps, but success will make everything right. The real crime, my child, is poverty; and you and I both suffer for it. As we are not lacking in intelligence, we thought we might turn our dear little reputation to account to take in an old bachelor, but the old bachelor, sweetheart, knows the alpha and omega of

woman's wiles ; which is to say, that you would find it easier
to put a grain of salt upon a sparrow's tail than to persuade
me, the Chevalier de Valois, to believe that I have had any
share in your affair.

"Go to Paris, my child, go at the expense of a bachelor's
vanity ; I am not going to hinder you, I will help you, for the
old bachelor, Suzanne, is the cash-box provided by nature for
a young girl. But do not thrust me into the affair. Now,
listen, my queen, understanding life so well as you do—you
see, you might do me a good deal of harm and give me
trouble ; harm, because you might spoil my marriage in a
place where people are so particular ; trouble on your account,
because you will get yourself in a scrape for nothing, a scrape
entirely of your own invention, sly girl ; and you know, my
pet, that I have no money left, I am as poor as a church
mouse. Ah ! if I were to marry Mademoiselle Cormon, if I
were rich again, I would certainly rather have you than
Césarine. You were always fine gold enough to gild lead, it
seemed to me ; you were made to be a great lord's love ; and
as I knew you were a clever girl, I am not at all surprised by
this trick of yours, I expected as much. For a girl, this
means that you burn your boats. It is no common mind,
my angel, that can do it ; and for that reason you have my
esteem," and he bestowed confirmation•upon her cheek after
the manner of a bishop, with two fingers.

"But, Monsieur le Chevalier, I do assure you that you are
mistaken, and——" she blushed, and dared not finish her
sentence, at a glance he had seen through her, and read her
plans from beginning to end.

"Yes, I understand, you wish me to believe you. Very
well, I believe. But take my advice and go to Monsieur du
Bousquier. You have taken Monsieur du Bousquier's linen
home from the wash for five or six months, have you not?
Very good. I do not ask to know what has happened between
you; but I know *him*, he is vain, he is an old bachelor, he is

very rich, he has an income of two thousand five hundred livres, and spends less than eight hundred. If you are the clever girl that I take you for, you will find your way to Paris at his expense. Go to him, my pet, twist him round your fingers, and of all things be supple as silk, and make a double twist and a knot at every word; he is just the man to be afraid of a scandal; and if he knows that you can make him sit on the stool of repentance—— In short, you understand, threaten to apply to the ladies of the charitable fund. He is ambitious beside. Well and good, with a wife to help him there should be nothing beyond a man's reach; and are you not handsome enough and clever enough to make your husband's fortune? Why, plague take it, you might hold your own with a court lady."

The chevalier's last words let the light into Suzanne's brain; she was burning with impatience to rush off to du Bousquier; but as she could not hurry away too abruptly, she helped the chevalier to dress, asking questions about Paris as she did so. As for the chevalier, he saw that his remarks had taken effect, and gave Suzanne an excuse to go, asking her to tell Césarine to bring up the chocolate that Mme. Lardot made for him every morning, and Suzanne forthwith slipped off in search of her prey.

And here follows du Bousquier's biography. He came of an old Alençon family in a middle rank between the burghers and the country squires. On the death of his father, a magistrate in the criminal court, he was left without resource, and, like most ruined provincials, betook himself to Paris to seek his fortune. When the Revolution broke out, du Bousquier was a man of affairs; and in those days (in spite of the Republicans, who are all up in arms for the honesty of their government) the word "affairs" was used very loosely. Political spies, jobbers, and contractors, the men who arranged with the syndics of communes for the sale of the property of *émigrés*, and then brought up land at low prices to sell again

—all these people, like ministers and generals, were men of affairs.

From 1793 to 1799 du Bousquier held contracts to supply the army with forage and provisions. During those years he lived in a splendid mansion; he was one of the great capitalists of the time; he went shares with Ouvrard; kept open house and led the scandalous life of the times. A Cincinnatus, reaping where he had not sowed, and rich with stolen rations and sacks of corn, he kept *petites maisons* and a bevy of mistresses, and gave fine entertainments to the directors of the Republic. Citizen du Bousquier was one of Barras' intimates; he was on the best of terms with Fouché, and hand and glove with Bernadotte. He thought to be a minister of State one day, and threw himself heart and soul into the party that secretly plotted against Bonaparte before the battle of Marengo. And but for Kellermann's charge and the death of Desaix, du Bousquier would have played a great part in the State. He was one of the upper members of the permanent staff of the promiscuous government which was driven by Napoleon's luck to vanish into the side-scenes of 1793.*

The victory unexpectedly won by stubborn fighting ended in the downfall of this party; they had placards ready printed, and were only waiting for the First Consul's defeat to proclaim a return to the principles of the Mountain.

Du Bousquier, feeling convinced that a victory was impossible, had two special messengers on the battlefield, and speculated with the larger part of his fortune for a fall in the Funds. The first courier came with the news that Mélas was victorious; but the second arriving four hours afterward, at night, brought the tidings of the Austrian defeat. Du Bousquier cursed Kellermann and Desaix; the First Consul owed him millions, he dared not curse him. But between the chance of making millions on the one hand, and stark ruin on the other, he lost his head. For several days he was half idiotic; he had under-

* See " A Historical Mystery."

mined his constitution with excesses to such an extent that the
thunderbolt left him helpless.   He had something to hope
from the settlement of his claims upon the Government; but
in spite of bribes, he was made to feel the weight of Napoleon's
displeasure against army contractors who speculated on his
defeat.   M. de Fermon, so pleasantly nicknamed *"Fermons
la caisse,"* left du Bousquier without a penny.   The First
Consul was even more incensed by the immorality of his private life and his connection with Barras and Bernadotte than
by his speculations on the Bourse; he erased M. du Bousquier's
name from the list of receivers-general, on which a last remnant
of credit had placed him for Alençon.

Of all his former wealth, nothing now remained to du
Bousquier save an income of twelve hundred francs from the
Funds, an investment entirely due to chance, which saved
him from actual want.   His creditors, knowing nothing of
the results of his liquidation, only left him enough in consols
to bring in a thousand francs per annum; but their claims
were paid in full after all, when the outstanding debts had
been collected, and the Hôtel de Beauséant, du Bousquier's
town house, sold beside.   So, after a close shave of bankruptcy, the sometime speculator emerged with his name intact.
Preceded by a tremendous reputation due to his relations with
former heads of government departments, his manner of life,
his brief day of authority, and final ruin through the First
Consul, the man interested the city Alençon, where Royalism
was secretly predominant.   Du Bousquier, exasperated against
Bonaparte, with his tales of the First Consul's pettiness, of
Josephine's lax morals, and a whole store of anecdotes of ten
years of revolution, seen from within, met with a good reception.

It was about this period of his life that du Bousquier, now
well over his fortieth year, came out as a bachelor of thirty-
six.   He was of medium height, fat as became a contractor,
and willing to display a pair of calves that would have done

credit to a gay and gallant attorney. He had strongly marked features; a flattened nose with tufts of hair in the equine nostrils; bushy black brows, and eyes beneath them that looked out shrewd as M. de Talleyrand's own, though they had lost something of their brightness. He wore his brown hair very long, and retained the side-whiskers (*nageoires*, as they were called) of the time of the Republic. You had only to look at his fingers, tufted at every joint, or at the blue knotted veins that stood out upon his hands, to see the unmistakable signs of a very remarkable muscular development; and, in truth, he had the chest of the Farnese Hercules, and shoulders fit to bear the burden of the national debt; you never see such shoulders nowadays. His was a luxuriant virility admirably described by an eighteenth-century phrase which is scarcely intelligible to-day; the gallantry of a bygone age would have summed up du Bousquier as a " payer of arrears "—*un vrai payeur d'arrèrages.*

Yet, as in the case of the Chevalier de Valois, there were sundry indications at variance with the ex-contractor's general appearance. His vocal powers, for instance, were not in keeping with his muscles; not that it was the mere thread of a voice which sometimes issues from the throats of such two-footed seals; on the contrary, it was loud but husky, something like the sound of a saw cutting through damp, soft wood; it was, in fact, the voice of a speculator brought to grief. For a long while du Bousquier wore the costume in vogue in the days of his glory: the boots with turned-down tops, the white silk stockings, the short cloth breeches, ribbed with cinnamon color, the blue coat, the Robespierre vest.

His hatred of the First Consul should have been a sort of passport into the best Royalist houses of Alençon; but the seven or eight families that made up the local Faubourg Saint-Germain, into which the Chevalier de Valois had the entrance, held aloof. Almost from the first, du Bousquier had aspired to marry one Mlle. Armande, whose brother was one of the most esteemed nobles of the town ; he thought to make this brother play a great part in his own schemes, for he was dreaming of a brilliant return match in politics. He met with a refusal, for which he consoled himself with such compensation as he might find among some half-score of retired manufacturers of Point d'Alençon lace, owners of grass lands or cattle, or wholesale linen merchants, thinking that among these chance might put a good match in his way. Indeed, the old bachelor had centred all his hopes on a prospective fortunate marriage, which a man, eligible in so many ways, might fairly expect to make. For he was not without a certain financial acumen, of which not a few availed themselves. He pointed out business speculations as a ruined gambler gives hints to new hands ; and he was expert at discovering the resources, chances, and management of a concern. People looked upon him as a good administrator. It was an often-discussed question whether he should not be mayor of Alençon, but the recollection of his Republican jobberies spoiled his chances, and he was never received at the prefecture.

Every successive government, even the government of the Hundred Days, declined to give him the coveted appointment, which would have assured his marriage with an elderly spinster whom he now had in his mind. It was his detestation of the Imperial Government that drove him into the Royalist camp, where he stayed in spite of insults there received ; but when the Bourbons returned, and still he was excluded from the prefecture, that final rebuff filled him with a hatred deep as the profound secrecy in which he wrapped it. Outwardly, he remained patiently faithful to his opinions; secretly, he became the leader of the Liberal party in Alençon, the invisible controller of elections ; and, by his cunningly devised manœuvres and underhand methods, he worked no little harm to the restored Monarchy.

When a man is reduced to live through his intellect alone,

his hatred is something as quiet as a little stream; insignificant to all appearance, but unfailing. This was the case with du Bousquier. His hatred was like a negro's, so placid, so patient, that it deceives the enemy. For fifteen years he brooded over a revenge which no victory, not even the Three Days of July, 1830, could sate.

When the chevalier sent Suzanne to du Bousquier, he had his own reasons for so doing. The Liberal and the Royalist divined each other, in spite of the skillful dissimulation which hid their common aim from the rest of the town.

The two old bachelors were rivals. Both of them had planned to marry the Demoiselle Cormon, whose name came up in the course of the chevalier's conversation with Suzanne. Both of them, engrossed by their idea and masquerading in indifference, were waiting for the moment when some chance should deliver the old maid to one or other of them. And the fact that they were rivals in this way would have been enough to make enemies of the pair even if each had not been the living embodiment of a political system.

Men take their color from their time. This pair of rivals is a case in point; the historic tinge of their characters stood out in strong contrast in their talk, their ideas, their costume. The one, blunt and energetic, with his burly abrupt ways, curt speech, dark looks, dark hair, and dark complexion, alarming in appearance, but impotent in reality as insurrection, was the Republic personified; the other, bland and polished, elegant and fastidious, gaining his ends slowly but surely by diplomacy, and never unmindful of good taste, was the typical old-world courtier. They met on the same ground almost every evening. It was a rivalry always courteous and urbane on the part of the chevalier, less ceremonious on du Bousquier's, though he kept within the limits prescribed by Alençon, for he had no wish to be driven ignominiously from the field. The two men understood each other well; but no one else saw what was going on. In spite of the minute and

curious interest which provincials take in the small details of
which their lives are made up, no one so much as suspected
that the two men were rivals.

M. le Chevalier's position was somewhat the stronger; he
had never proposed for Mlle. Cormon, whereas du Bousquier
had declared himself after a rebuff from one of the noblest families, and had met with a second refusal.   Still, the chevalier
thought so well of his rival's chances that he considered it
worth while to deal him a *coup de Jarnac*, a treacherous thrust
from a weapon as finely tempered as Suzanne.   He had fathomed du Bousquier; and, as will shortly be seen, he was not
mistaken in any of his conjectures.

Suzanne tripped away down the Rue du Cours, along the
Rue de la Porte de Séez and the Rue du Bercail to the Rue
du Cygne, where du Bousquier, five years ago, had bought a
small countrified house built of the gray stone of the district,
which is used like granite in Normandy, or Breton schist in
the West.   The sometime forage-contractor had established
himself there in more comfort than any other house in the
town could boast, for he had brought with him some relics of
past days of splendor; but provincial manners and customs
were slowly darkening the glory of the fallen Sardanapalus.
The vestiges of past luxury looked about as much out of place
in the house as a chandelier in a barn.   Harmony, which links
the works of man or of God together, was lacking in all
things large or small.   A ewer with a metal lid, such as you
only see on the outskirts of Brittany, stood on a handsome
nest of drawers; and while the bedroom floor was covered
with a fine carpet, the window-curtains displayed a flower pattern only known to cheap, printed cottons.   The stone mantelpiece, daubed over with paint, was out of all keeping with a
handsome clock disgraced by a shabby pair of candlesticks.
Local talent had made an unsuccessful attempt to paint the
doors in vivid contrasts of startling colors; while the stair-

case, ascended by all and sundry in muddy boots, had not been painted at all. In short, du Bousquier's house, like the time which he represented, was a confused mixture of grandeur and squalor.

Du Bousquier was regarded as well-to-do, but he led the parasitical life of the Chevalier de Valois, and he is always rich enough that spends less than his income. His one servant was a country bumpkin, a dull-witted youth enough; but he had been trained, by slow degrees, to suit du Bousquier's requirements, until he had learned, much as an ourang-outang might learn, to scour floors, black boots, brush clothes, and to come for his master of an evening with a lantern if it was dark, and a pair of sabots if it rained. On great occasions, du Bousquier made him discard the blue-checked cotton blouse with loose sagging pockets behind, which always bulged with a handkerchief, a clasp knife, apples, or "stickjaw taffy." Arrayed in a regulation suit of clothes, he accompanied his master to wait at table, and overate himself afterward with the other servants. Like many other mortals, René had only stuff enough in him for one vice, and his was gluttony. Du Bousquier made a reward of this service, and in return his Breton factotum was absolutely discreet.

"What, have you come our way, miss?" René asked when he saw Suzanne in the doorway. "It is not your day; we have not got any linen for Madame Lardot."

"Big stupid!" laughed the fair Suzanne, as she went up the stairs, leaving René to finish a porringer full of buckwheat bannocks boiled in milk.

Du Bousquier was still in bed, ruminating his plans for fortune. To him, as to all who have squeezed the orange of pleasure, there was nothing left but ambition. Ambition, like gambling, is inexhaustible. And, moreover, given a good constitution, the passions of the brain will always outlive the heart's passions.

"Here I am!" said Suzanne, sitting down on the bed; the

curtain-rings grated along the rods as she swept them sharply back with an imperious gesture.

"*Quésaco*, my charmer?" asked du Bousquier, sitting upright.

"Monsieur," Suzanne began, with much gravity, "you must be surprised to see me come in this way; but, under the circumstances, it is no use my minding what people will say."

"What is all this about?" asked du Bousquier, folding his arms.

"Why, do you not understand?" returned Suzanne. "I know" (with an engaging little pout), "I know how ridiculous it is when a poor girl comes to bother a man about things that you think mere trifles. But if you really knew me, monsieur, if you only knew all that I would do for a man, if he cared about me as I could care about you, you would never repent of marrying me. It is not that I could be of so much use to you *here*, by the way; but if we went to Paris, you should see how far I could bring a man of spirit with such brains as yours, and especially just now, when they are re-making the Government from top to bottom, and the foreigners are the masters. Between ourselves, does this thing in question really matter after all? Is it not a piece of good fortune for which you would be glad to pay a good deal one of these days? For whom are you going to think and work?"

"For myself, to be sure!" du Bousquier answered most brutally.

"Old monster! you shall never be a father!" said Suzanne, with a ring in her voice which turned the words to a prophecy and a curse.

"Come, Suzanne, no nonsense; I am dreaming still, I think."

"What more do you want in the way of reality?" cried Suzanne, rising to her feet. Du Bousquier scrubbed his head with his cotton nightcap, which he twisted round and round with a fidgety energy that told plainly of prodigious mental ferment.

"He actually believes it!" Suzanne said within herself. "And his vanity is tickled. Good Lord, how easy it is to take them in!"

"Suzanne! What the deuce do you want me to do? It is so extraordinary—— I that thought—— The fact is—— But no, no, it can't be——"

"Do you mean that you cannot marry me?"

"Oh, as to that, no. I am not free."

"Is it Mademoiselle Armande or Mademoiselle Cormon, who have both refused you already? Look here, Monsieur du Bousquier, it is not as if I was obliged to get gendarmes to drag you to the registrar's office to save my character. There are plenty that would marry me, but I have no intention whatever of taking a man that does not know my value. You may be sorry some of these days that you behaved like this; for if you will not take your chance to-day, not for gold, nor silver, nor anything in this world will I give it you again."

"But, Suzanne—are you sure——?"

"Sir, for what do you take me?" asked the girl, draping herself in her virtue. "I am not going to put you in mind of the promises you made, promises that have been the ruin of a poor girl, when all her fault was that she looked too high and loved too much."

But joy, suspicion, self-interest, and a host of contending emotions had taken possession of du Bousquier. For a long time past he had made up his mind that he would marry Mlle. Cormon; for, after long ruminations over the Charter, he saw that it opened up magnificent prospects to his ambition through the channels of a representative government. His marriage with that mature spinster would raise his social position very much; he would acquire a great influence in Alençon. And here this wily Suzanne had conjured up a storm, which put him in a most awkward dilemma. But for that private hope of his, he would have married Suzanne out of hand, and put himself openly at the head of the Liberal party in the town. Such a marriage meant the final renunciation of the best society, and a drop into the ranks of the wealthy trades-men, storekeepers, rich manufacturers, and graziers, who, beyond a doubt, would carry him as their candidate in triumph. Already du Bousquier caught a glimpse of the Opposition benches. He did not attempt to hide his solemn deliberations; he rubbed his hand over his head, made a wisp of the cotton nightcap, and a damaging confession of the nudity beneath it. As for Suzanne, after the wont of those who succeed beyond their utmost hopes, she sat dumfounded. To hide her amazement at his behavior, she drooped like a hapless victim before her seducer, while within herself she laughed like a grisette on a frolic.

"My dear child, I will have nothing to do with hanky-panky of this sort."

This brief formula was the result of his cogitations. The ex-contractor to the Government prided himself upon belong-ing to that particular school of cynic philosophers which declines to be "taken in" by women, and includes the whole sex in one category as suspicious characters. Strong-minded men of this stamp, weaklings are they for the most part, have a catechism of their own in the matter of woman-kind. Every woman, according to them, from the Queen of France to the milliner, is at heart a rake, a hussy, a dangerous creature, not to say a bit of a rascal, a liar in grain, a being incapable of a serious thought. For du Bousquier and his like, woman is a maleficent *bayadère** that must be left to dance, and sing, and laugh. They see nothing holy, nothing great in woman; for them she represents, not the poetry of the senses, but gross sensuality. They are like gluttons who mistake the kitchen for the dining-room. On this showing, a man must be a consistent tyrant, unless he means to be en-

* Indian dancing-girl.

slaved. And in this respect, again, du Bousquier and the Chevalier de Valois stood at opposite poles.

As he delivered himself of the above remark, he flung his nightcap to the foot of the bed, much as Gregory the Great might have flung down the candle while he launched the thunders of an excommunication; and Suzanne learned that the old bachelor wore a false front.

"Bear in mind, Monsieur du Bousquier, that by coming here I have done my duty," she remarked majestically. "Remember that I was bound to offer you my hand and to ask for yours; but, at the same time, remember that I have behaved with the dignity of a self-respecting woman; I did not lower myself so far as to cry like a fool; I did not insist; I have not worried you at all. Now you know my position. You know that I cannot stay in Alençon. If I do, my mother will beat me; and Madame Lardot is as high and mighty over principles as if she washed and ironed with them. She will turn me away. And where am I to go, poor workgirl that I am? To the hospital? Am I to beg for bread? Not I. I would sooner fling myself into the Brillante or the Sarthe. Now, would it not be simpler for me to go to Paris? Mother might find some excuse for sending me, an uncle wants me to come, or an aunt is going to die, or some lady takes an interest in me. It is just a question of money for the traveling expenses and—you know what——"

This news was immeasurably more important to du Bousquier than to the Chevalier de Valois, for reasons which no one knew as yet but the two rivals, though they will appear in the course of the story. At this point, suffice it to say that Suzanne's fib had thrown the sometime forage-contractor's ideas into such confusion that he was incapable of thinking seriously. But for that bewilderment, but for the secret joy in his heart (for a man's own vanity is a swindler that never lacks a dupe), it must have struck him that any honest girl, with a heart still unspoiled, would have died a hundred deaths rather than enter upon such a discussion, or make a demand for money. He must have seen the look in the girl's eyes, seen the gambler's ruthless meanness that would take a life to gain money for a stake.

"Would you really go to Paris?" he asked.

The words brought a twinkle to Suzanne's gray eyes, but it was lost upon du Bousquier's self-satisfaction.

"I would indeed, sir."

But at this du Bousquier broke out into a singular lament. He had just paid the balance of the purchase-money for his house; and there was the painter, and the glazier, and the bricklayer, and the carpenter. Suzanne let him talk; she was waiting for the figures. Du Bousquier at last proposed three hundred francs, and at this Suzanne, with an assumption of dignity, got up as if to go.

"Eh, what! Where are you going?" du Bousquier cried uneasily. "A fine thing to be a bachelor," he said to himself. "I'll be hanged if I remember doing more than rumple the girl's collar; and hey presto! on the strength of a joke she takes upon herself to draw a bill upon you, point-blank!"

Suzanne meanwhile began to cry. "Monsieur," she said, "I am going to Madame Granson, the treasurer of the Maternity Fund; she pulled one poor girl in the same strait out of the water (as you may say) to my knowledge."

"Madame Granson?"

"Yes. She is related to Mademoiselle Cormon, the lady patroness of the society. Asking your pardon, some ladies in the town have started a society that will keep many a poor creature from making away with her child, like that pretty Faustine of Argentan did; and paid for it with her life at Mortagne just three years ago."

"Here, Suzanne," returned du Bousquier, holding out a key, "open the desk yourself. There is a bag that has been opened, with six hundred francs still left in it. It is all I have."

Du Bousquier's chopfallen expression plainly showed how little good-will went with his compliance.

"An old thief!" said Suzanne to herself. "I will tell tales about his false hair!" Mentally she compared him with that delightful old Chevalier de Valois; he had given her nothing, but he understood her, he had advised her, he had the welfare of his grisettes at heart.

"If you are deceiving me, Suzanne," exclaimed the object of this unflattering comparison, as he watched her hand in the drawer, "you shall——"

"So, monsieur, you would not give me the money if I asked you for it?" interrupted she with queenly insolence.

Once recalled to the ground of gallantry, recollections of his prime came back to the ex-contractor. He grunted assent. Suzanne took the bag and departed, first submitting her forehead to a kiss which he gave, but in a manner which seemed to say, "This is an expensive privilege; but it is better than being brow-beaten by counsel in a court of law as the seducer of a young woman accused of child-murder."

Suzanne slipped the bag into a pouch-shaped basket on her arm, execrating du Bousquier's stinginess as she did so, for she wanted a thousand francs. If a girl is once possessed by a desire, and has taken the first step in trickery and deceit, she will go to great lengths. As the fair laundress took her way along the Rue de Bercail, it suddenly occurred to her that the Maternity Fund under Mlle. Cormon's presidency would probably make up the sum which she regarded as sufficient for a start, a very large amount in the eyes of an Alençon grisette. And beside, she hated du Bousquier, and du Bousquier seemed frightened when she talked of confessing her so-called strait to Mme. Granson. Wherefore Suzanne determined that whether or not she made a centime out of the Maternity Fund, she would entangle du Bousquier in the inextricable undergrowth of the gossip of a country town. There is something of a monkey's love of mischief in every grisette. Suzanne com-

3

posed her countenance dolorously and betook herself accordingly to Madame Granson.

Mme. Granson was the widow of a lieutenant-colonel of artillery who fell at Jena. Her whole yearly income consisted of a pension of nine hundred francs for her lifetime, and her one possession beside was a son whose education and maintenance had absorbed every penny of her savings. She lived in the Rue du Bercail, in one of the cheerless first-floor apartments through which you can see from back to front at a glance as you walk down the main street of any little town. Three steps, rising pyramid fashion, brought you to the level of the house-door, which opened upon a passageway and a little yard beyond, with a wooden-roofed staircase at the farther end. Mme. Granson's kitchen and dining-room occupied the space on one side of the passage, on the other side a single room did duty for a variety of purposes, for the widow's bedroom among others. Her son, a young man of three-and-twenty, slept upstairs in an attic above the second floor. Athanase Granson contributed six hundred francs to the poor mother's housekeeping. He was distantly related to Mlle. Cormon, whose influence had obtained him a little post in the registrar's office, where he was employed in making out certificates of births, marriages, and deaths.

After this, any one can see the little chilly, yellow-curtained parlor, the furniture covered with yellow Utrecht velvet, and Mme. Granson going round the room, after her visitors had left, to straighten the little straw mats put down in front of each chair, so as to save the waxed and polished red brick floor from contact with dirty boots; and, this being accomplished, returning to her place beside her work-table under the portrait of her lieutenant-colonel. The becushioned armchair, in which she sat at her sewing, was always drawn up between the two windows, so that she could look up and down the Rue du Bercail and see every one that passed. She was a good sort of woman, dressed with a homely simplicity in keep-

ing with a pale face, beaten thin, as it were, by many cares.
You felt the stern soberness of poverty in every little detail in
that house, just as you breathed a moral atmosphere of auster-
ity and upright provincial ways.

Mother and son at this moment were sitting together in the
dining-room over their breakfast—a cup of coffee, bread
and butter, and radishes. And here, if the reader is to understand how gladly Mme. Granson heard Suzanne, some explanation of the secret hopes of the household must be given.

Athanase Granson was a thin, hollow-cheeked young man
of medium height, with a white face in which a pair of dark
eyes, bright with thought, looked like two marks made with
charcoal. The somewhat worn contours of that face, the
curving line of the lips, a sharply turned-up chin, a regularly
cut marble forehead, a melancholy expression caused by the
consciousness of power on the one hand and of poverty on
the other—all these signs and characteristics told of impris-
oned genius. So much so, indeed, that anywhere but at Alençon his face would have won help for him from distinguished
men, or from the women that can discern genius incognito.
For if this was not genius, at least it was the outward form
that genius takes; and if the strength of a high heart was
wanting, it looked out surely from those eyes. And yet,
while Athanase could fine expression for the loftiest feeling,
an outer husk of shyness spoiled everything in him, down to
the very charm of youth, just as the frost of penury disheart-
ened every effort. Shut in by the narrow circle of provincial life, without approbation, encouragement, or any way of
escape, the thought within him was dying out before its dawn.
And Athanase, beside, had the fierce pride which poverty in-
tensifies in certain natures, the kind of pride by which a man
grows great in the stress of battle with men and circumstance,
while at the outset it only handicaps him.

Genius manifests itself in two ways—either by taking its
own as soon as it finds it, like a Napoleon or a Molière, or by

patiently revealing itself and waiting for recognition. Young
Granson belonged to the latter class. He was easily discouraged, ignorant of his value. His turn of mind was contem-
plative, he lived in thought rather than in action, and possibly,
to those who cannot imagine genius without the Frenchman's
spark of enthusiasm, he might have seemed incomplete. But
Athanase's power lay in the world of thought. He was to
pass through successive phases of emotion, hidden from
ordinary eyes, to one of those sudden resolves which bring
the chapter to a close and set fools declaring that "the man
is mad." The world's contempt for poverty was sapping the
life in Athanase. The bow, continually strung tighter and
tighter, was slackened by the enervating close air of a solitude with never a breath of fresh air in it. He was giving
way under the strain of a cruel and fruitless struggle. Athanase had that in him which might have placed his name
among the foremost names of France; he had known what it
was to gaze with glowing eyes over Alpine heights and fields
of air whither unfettered genius soars, and now he was pining
to death like some caged and starved eagle.

While he had worked on unnoticed in the town library, he
buried his dreams of fame in his own soul lest they should
injure his prospects; and he carried beside another secret
hidden even more deeply in his heart, the secret love which
hollowed his cheeks and sallowed his forehead.

Athanase loved his distant cousin, that Mlle. Cormon, for
whom his unconscious rivals du Bousquier and the Chevalier
de Valois were laying in ambush. It was a love born of self-
interest. Mlle. Cormon was supposed to be one of the
richest people in the town; and he, poor boy, had been drawn
to love her partly through the desire for material welfare,
partly through a wish formed times without number to gild
his mother's declining years, and partly also through cravings
for the physical comfort necessary to men who live an intellectual life. In his own eyes, his love was dishonored by its

very natural origin; and he was afraid of the ridicule which people pour on the love of a young man of three-and-twenty for a woman of forty. And yet his love was quite sincere. Much that happens in the provinces would be improbable upon the face of it anywhere else, especially in matters of this kind.

But in a country town there are no unforeseen contingencies; there is no coming and going, no mystery, no such thing as chance. Marriage is a necessity, and no family will accept a man of dissolute life. A connection between a young fellow like Athanase and a handsome girl might seem a natural thing enough in a great city; in a country town it would be enough to ruin a young man's chances of marriage, especially if he were poor; for when the prospective bridegroom is wealthy an awkward business of this sort may be smoothed over. Between the degradation of certain courses and a sincere love, a man that is not heartless can make but one choice if he happens to be poor; he will prefer the disadvantages of virtue to the disadvantages of vice. But in a country town the number of women with whom a young man can fall in love is strictly limited. A pretty girl with a fortune is beyond his reach in a place where every one's income is known to a farthing. A penniless beauty is equally out of the question. To take her for a wife would be "to marry hunger and thirst," as the provincial saying goes. Finally, celibacy has its dangers in youth. These reflections explain how it has come to pass that marriage is the very basis of provincial life.

Men in whom genius is hot and unquenchable, who are forced to take their stand on the independence of poverty, ought to leave these cold regions; in the provinces thought meets with the persecution of brutal indifference, and no woman cares, or dares, to play the part of a sister of charity to the worker, the lover of art or sciences.

Who can rightly understand Athanase's love for Mlle.

Cormon? Not the rich, the sultans of society, who can find seraglios at their pleasure; not respectability, keeping to the track beaten hard by prejudice; nor yet those women who shut their eyes to the cravings of the artist temperament, and, taking it for granted that both sexes are governed by the same laws, insist upon a system of reciprocity in their particular virtues. The appeal must, perhaps, be made to young men who suffer from the repression of young desires just as they are putting forth their full strength; to the artist whose genius is stifled within him by poverty till it becomes a disease; to power at first unsupported, persecuted, and too often unfriended till it emerges at length triumphant from the twofold agony of soul and body.

These will know the throbbing pangs of the cancer which was gnawing Athanase. Such as these have raised long, cruel debates within themselves, with the so high end in sight and no means of attaining it. They have passed through the experience of abortive effort; they have left the spawn of genius on the barren sands. They know that the strength of desire is as the scope of the imagination; the higher the leap, the lower the fall; and how many restraints are broken in such falls? These, like Athanase, catch glimpses of a glorious future in the distance; all that lies between seems but a transparent film of gauze to their piercing sight; but of that film which scarcely obscures the vision, society makes a wall of brass. Urged on by their vocation, by the artist's instinct within them, they too seek times without number to make a stepping-stone of sentiments which society turns in the same way to practical ends. What! when marriages in the provinces are calculated and arranged on every side with a view to securing material welfare, shall it be forbidden to a struggling artist or man of science to keep two ends in view, to try to insure his own subsistence that the thought within him may live?

Athanase Granson, with such ideas as these fermenting in

his head, thought at first of marriage with Mlle. Cormon as a
definite solution of the problem of existence.   He would be
free to work for fame, he could make his mother comfortable,
and he felt sure of himself—he knew that he could be faithful
to Mlle. Cormon.   But soon his purpose bred a real passion
in him.   It was an unconscious process.   He set himself to
study Mlle. Cormon ; then familiarity exercised its spell, and
at length Athanase saw nothing but beauties—the defects were
all forgotten.

The senses count for so much in the love of a young man
of three-and-twenty.   Through the heat of desire woman is
seen as through a prism.   From this point of view it was a
touch of genius in Beaumarchais to make the page Cherubino
in the play strain Marcellina to his heart.   If you recollect,
moreover, that poverty restricted Athanase to a life of great
loneliness, that there was no other woman to look at, that his
eyes were always fastened upon Mlle. Cormon, and that all
the light in the picture was concentrated upon her, it seems
natural, does it not, that he should love her ?   The feeling
hidden in the depths of his heart could but grow stronger day
by day.   Desire and pain and hope and meditation, in silence
and repose, were filling up Athanase's soul to the brim ; every
hour added its drop.   As his senses came to the aid of imagination and widened the inner horizon, Mlle. Cormon became
more and more awe-inspiring, and he grew more and more
timid.

The mother had guessed it all.   She was a provincial, and
she frankly calculated the advantages of the match.   Mlle.
Cormon might think herself very lucky to marry a young man
of twenty-three with plenty of brains, a likely man to do honor
to his name and country.   Still the obstacles, Athanase's
poverty and Mlle. Cormon's age, seemed to her to be insur-
mountable ; there was nothing for it that she could see but
patience.   She had a policy of her own, like du Bousquier
and the Chevalier de Valois ; she was on the lookout for her

opportunity, waiting, with wits sharpened by self-interest and a mother's love, for the propitious moment.

Of the Chevalier de Valois, Mme. Granson had no suspicion whatsoever ; du Bousquier she still credited with views upon the lady, albeit Mlle. Cormon had once refused him. An adroit and secret enemy, Mme. Granson did the ex-contractor untold harm to serve the son to whom she had not spoken a word. After this, who does not see the importance of Suzanne's lie once confided to Mme. Granson ? What a weapon put into the hands of the charitable treasurer of the Maternity Fund ! How demurely she would carry the tale from house to house when she asked for subscriptions for the chaste Suzanne !

At this particular moment Athanase was pensively sitting with his elbow on the table, balancing a spoon on the edge of the empty bowl before him. He looked with unseeing eyes round the poor room, over the walls covered with an old-fashioned paper only seen in wine-saloons, at the window-curtains with a chessboard pattern of pink-and-white squares, at the red-brick floor, the straw-bottomed chairs, the painted wooden sideboard, the glass door that opened into the kitchen. As he sat facing his mother and with his back to the fire, and as the fireplace was almost opposite the door, the first thing which caught Suzanne's eyes was his pale face, with the light from the street window falling full upon it, a face framed in dark hair, and eyes with the gleam of despair in them, and a fever kindled by the morning's thoughts.

The grisette surely knows by instinct the pain and sorrow of love ; at the sight of Athanase, she felt that sudden electric thrill which comes we know not whence. We cannot explain it ; some strong-minded persons deny that it exists, but many a woman and many a man has felt that shock of sympathy. It is a flash, lighting up the darkness of the future, and at the same time a presentiment of the pure joy of love shared by two souls, and a certainty that this other too understands. It is more like the strong, sure touch of a master hand upon the clavier of the senses than anything else. Eyes are riveted by an irresistible fascination, hearts are troubled, the music of joy rings in the ears and thrills the soul ; a voice cries, " It is he ! " And then—then very likely, reflection throws a douche of cold water over all this turbulent emotion, and there is an end of it.

In a moment, swift as a clap of thunder, a broadside of new thoughts poured in upon Suzanne. A lightning flash of love burned the weeds which had sprung up in dissipation and wantonness. She saw all that she was losing by blighting her name with a lie, the desecration, the degradation of it. Only last evening this idea had been a joke, now it was like a heavy sentence passed upon her. She recoiled before her success. But, after all, it was quite impossible that anything should come of this meeting ; and the thought of Athanase's poverty, and a vague hope of making money and coming back from Paris with both hands full, to say: " I loved you all along " —or fate, if you will have it so—dried up the beneficent dew. The ambitious damsel asked shyly to speak for a moment with Mme. Granson, who took her into her bedroom.

When Suzanne came out again she looked once more at Athanase. He was still sitting in the same attitude. She choked back her tears.

As for Mme. Granson, she was radiant. She had found a terrible weapon to use against du Bousquier at last ; she could deal him a deadly blow. So she promised the poor victim of seduction the support of all the ladies who subscribed to the Maternity Fund. She foresaw a dozen calls in prospect. In the course of the morning and afternoon she would conjure down a terrific storm upon the elderly bachelor's head. The Chevalier de Valois certainly foresaw the turn that matters were likely to take, but he had not expected anything like the amount of scandal that came of it.

" We are going to dine with Mademoiselle Cormon, you

know, dear boy," said Mme. Granson; "take rather more pains with your appearance. It is a mistake to neglect your dress as you do; you look so untidy. Put on your best frilled shirt and your green cloth coat. I have my reasons," she added, with a mysterious air. "And beside, there will be a great many people; Mademoiselle Cormon is going to the Prébaudet directly. If a young man is thinking of marrying, he ought to make himself agreeable in every possible way. If girls would only tell the truth, my boy, dear me! you would be surprised at the things that take their fancy. It is often quite enough if a young man rides by at the head of a company of artillery, or comes to a dance in a suit of clothes that fits him passably well. A certain way of carrying the head, a melancholy attitude, is enough to set a girl imagining a whole life; we invent a romance to suit the hero; often he is only a stupid young man, but the marriage is made. Take notice of Monsieur de Valois, study him, copy his manners; see how he looks at ease; he has not a constrained manner, as you have. And talk a little; any one might think that you knew nothing at all, *you* that know Hebrew by heart."

Athanase heard her submissively, but he looked surprised. He rose, took his cap, and went back to his work.

"Can mother have guessed my secret?" he thought, as he went round by the Rue de Val-Noble where Mademoiselle Cormon lived, a little pleasure in which he indulged of a morning. His head was swarming with romantic fancies.

"How little she thinks that going past her house at this moment is a young man who would love her dearly, and be true to her, and never cause her a single care, and leave her fortune entirely in her own hands! Oh me! what a strange fatality it is that we two should live as we do in the same town and within a few paces of each other, and yet nothing can bring us any nearer! How if I spoke to her to-night?"

Meanwhile Suzanne went home to her mother, thinking the while of poor Athanase, feeling that for him she could find it

in her heart to do what many a woman must have longed
to do for the one beloved with superhuman strength; she
could have made a stepping-stone of her beautiful body if so
he might come to his kingdom the sooner.

And now we must enter the house where all the actors in
this Scene (Suzanne excepted) were to meet that very evening,
the house belonging to the old maid, the converging point of
so many interests. As for Suzanne, that young woman with
her well-grown beauty, with courage sufficient to burn her
boats, like Alexander, and to begin the battle of life with an
uncalled-for sacrifice of her character, she now disappears
from the stage after bringing about a violently exciting situation. Her wishes, moreover, were more than fulfilled. A
few days afterward she left her native place with a stock of
money and fine clothes, including a superb green rep gown
and a green bonnet lined with rose color, M. de Valois' gifts,
which Suzanne liked better than anything else, better even
than the Maternity Society's money. If the chevalier had
gone to Paris while Suzanne was in her heyday, she would
assuredly have left all for him.

And so this chaste Susannah, of whom the elders scarcely
had more than a glimpse, settled herself comfortably and
hopefully in Paris, while all Alençon was deploring the misfortunes with which the ladies of the Charitable and Maternity
Societies had manifested so lively a sympathy.

While Suzanne might be taken as a type of the handsome
Norman virgins who furnish, on the showing of a learned physician, one-third of the supply devoured by the monster, Paris,
she entered herself, and remained in those higher branches of
her profession in which some regard is paid to appearances.
In an age in which, as M. de Valois said, "woman has ceased
to be woman," she was known merely as Mme. du Val-Noble;
in other times she would have rivaled an Imperia, a Rhodope,
a Ninon. One of the most distinguished writers of the Res-

toration took her under his protection, and very likely will marry her some day; he is a journalist, and above public opinion, seeing that he creates a new one every six years.

In almost every prefecture of the second magnitude there is some salon frequented not exactly by the cream of the local society, but by personages both considerable and well considered. The host and hostess probably will be among the foremost people in the town. To them all houses are open; no entertainment, no public dinner is given, but they are asked to it; but in their salon you will not meet the *gens à château*—lords of the manor, peers of France living on their broad acres, and persons of the highest quality in the department, though these are all on visiting terms with the family, and exchange invitations to dinners and evening parties. The mixed society to be found there usually consists of the lesser noblesse resident in the town, with the clergy and judicial authorities. It is an influential assemblage. All the wit and sense of the district is concentrated in its solid, unpretentious ranks. Everybody in the set knows the exact amount of his neighbor's income, and professes the utmost indifference to dress and luxury, trifles held to be mere childish vanity compared with the acquisition of a *mouchoir à bœufs*—a pocket-handkerchief of some ten or a dozen acres, purchased after as many years of pondering and intriguing and a prodigious deal of diplomacy.

Unshaken in its prejudices whether good or ill, the coterie goes on its way without a look before or behind. Nothing from Paris is allowed to pass without a prolonged scrutiny; innovations are ridiculous, and bonds and cashmere shawls alike objectionable. Provincials read nothing and wish to learn nothing; for them, science, literature, and mechanical invention are as the thing that is not. If a prefect does not suit their notions, they do their best to have him removed; if this cannot be done, they isolate him. So will you see the inmates of a beehive wall up an intruding snail with wax.

Finally, of the gossip of the salon, history is made. Young married women put in an appearance there occasionally (though the card-table is the one resource) that their conduct may be stamped with the approval of the coterie and their social status confirmed.

Native susceptibilities are sometimes wounded by the supremacy of a single house, but the rest comfort themselves with the thought that they save the expense entailed by the position. Sometimes it happens that no one can afford to keep open house, and then the big-wigs of the place look about them for some harmless person whose character, position, and social standing offer guarantees for the neutrality of the ground, and alarm nobody's vanity or self-interest. This had been the case at Alençon. For a long time past the best society of the town has been wont to assemble in the house of the old maid before mentioned, who little suspected Mme. Granson's designs on her fortune, or the secret hopes of the two elderly bachelors who have just been unmasked.

Mlle. Cormon was Mme. Granson's fourth cousin. She lived with her mother's brother, a sometime vicar-general of the bishopric of Séez; she had been her uncle's ward, and would one day inherit his fortune. Rose-Marie-Victoire Cormon was the last representative of a house which, plebeian though it was, had associated and often allied itself with the noblesse, and ranked among the oldest families in the province. In former times the Cormons had been intendants of the duchy of Alençon, and had given a goodly number of magistrates to the bench, and several bishops to the church. M. de Sponde, Mlle. Cormon's maternal grandfather, was elected by the noblesse to the States-General; and M. Cormon, her father, had been asked to represent the Third Estate, but neither of them accepted the responsibility. For the last century, the daughters of the house had married into the noble families of the province, in such sort that the Cormons were grafted into pretty nearly every genealogical tree in the duchy. No burgher family came so near being noble.

The house in which the present Mlle. Cormon lived had never passed out of the family since it was built by Pierre Cormon in the reign of Henri IV.; and of all the old maid's worldly possessions, this one appealed most to the greed of her elderly suitors; though, so far from bringing in money, the ancestral home of the Cormons was a positive expense to its owner. But it is such an unusual thing, in the very centre of a country town, to find a house handsome without, convenient within, and free from mean surroundings, that all Alençon shared the feeling of envy.

The old mansion stood exactly half-way down the Rue du Val-Noble, *The Val-Noble*, as it was called, probably because the Brillante, the little stream which flows through the town, has hollowed out a little valley for itself in a dip of the land thereabout. The most noticeable feature of the house was its massive architecture, of the style introduced from Italy by Marie de' Medici; all the corner-stones and facings were cut with diamoned-shaped bosses, in spite of the difficulty of working in the granite of which it is built. It was a two-storied house with a very high-pitched roof, and a row of dormer windows, each with its carved tympanum standing picturesquely enough above the lead-lined parapet with its ornamental balustrade. A grotesque gargoyle, the head of some fantastic bodyless beast, discharged the rain-water through its jaws into the street below, where great stone slabs, pierced with five holes, were placed to receive it. Each gable terminated in a leaden finial, a sign that this was a burgher's house, for none but nobles had a right to put up a weather-cock in olden times. To the right and left of the yard stood the stables and the coach-house; the kitchen, laundry, and wood-shed. One of the leaves of the great gate used to stand open; so that passers-by, looking in through the little low wicket with the bell attached, could see the parterre in the

middle of a spacious paved court, and the low-clipped privet
hedges which marked out miniature borders full of monthly
roses, clove gilliflowers, scabious, lilies, and Spanish broom;
as well as the laurel-bushes and pomegranates and myrtles
which grew in tubs put out of doors for the summer.

The scrupulous neatness and tidiness of the place must
have struck any stranger, and furnished him with a clue to
the old maid's character. The mistress' eyes must have been
unemployed, careful, and prying; less, perhaps, from any
natural bent, than for want of any occupation. Who but an
elderly spinster, at a loss how to fill an always empty day,
would have insisted that no blade of grass should show itself in
the paved courtyard, that the wall-copings should be scoured,
that the broom should always be busy, that the coach should
never be left with the leather curtains undrawn? Who else,
from sheer lack of other employment, could have introduced
something like Dutch cleanliness into a little province between
Perche, Normandy, and Brittany, where the natives make
boast of their crass indifference to comfort? The chevalier
never climbed the steps without reflecting inwardly that the
house was fit for a peer of France; and du Bousquier similarly
considered that the Mayor of Alençon ought to live there.

A glass door at the top of the flight of steps gave admittance
to an antechamber lighted by a second glass door opposite,
above a corresponding flight of steps leading into the garden.
This part of the house, a kind of gallery floored with square
red tiles, and wainscoted to elbow-height, was a hospital for
invalid family portraits; one here and there had lost an eye
or sustained injury to a shoulder, another stood with a hole in
the place where his hat should have been, yet another had
lost a leg by amputation. Here cloaks, clogs, overshoes, and
umbrellas were left; everybody deposited his belongings in
the antechamber on his arrival, and took them again on his
departure. A long bench was set against either wall for the
servants who came of an evening with their lanterns to fetch

home their masters and mistresses, and a big stove was set in the middle to mitigate the icy blasts which swept across from door to door.

This gallery, then, divided the first floor into two equal parts. The staircase rose to the left on the side nearest the courtyard, the rest of the space being taken up by the great dining-room, with its windows looking out upon the garden, and a pantry beyond, which communicated with the kitchen. To the right lay the salon, lighted by four windows, and a couple of smaller rooms beyond it, a boudoir which gave upon the garden, and a room which did duty as a study and looked into the courtyard. There was a complete suite of rooms on the second floor, beside the Abbé de Sponde's apartments; while the attic story, in all probability roomy enough, had long since been given over to the tenancy of rats and mice. Mlle. Cormon used to report their nocturnal exploits to the Chevalier de Valois, and marvel at the futility of all measures taken against them.

The garden, about half an acre in extent, was bounded by the Brillante, so called from the mica spangles which glitter in its bed ; not, however, in the Val-Noble, for the manufacturers and dyers of Alençon pour all their refuse into the shallow stream before it reaches this point ; and the opposite bank, as always happens wherever a stream passes through a town, was lined with houses where various thirsty industries were carried on. Luckily, Mlle. Cormon's neighbors were all of them quiet tradesmen—a baker, a fuller, and one or two cabinet-makers. Her garden, full of old-fashioned flowers, naturally ended in a terrace, by way of a quay, with a short flight of steps down to the water's edge. Try to picture the wallflowers growing in blue-and-white glazed jars along the balustrade by the river, behold a shady walk to right and left beneath the square-clipped lime-trees, and you will have some idea of a scene full of unpretending cheerfulness and sober tranquillity ; you can see the views of homely humble life along the opposite bank, the quaint houses, the trickling stream of the Brillante, the garden itself, the linden walks under the garden walls, and the venerable home built by the Cormons.   How peaceful, how quiet it was !   If there was no ostentation, there was nothing transitory, everything seemed to last forever there.

The first-floor rooms, therefore, were given over to social uses.   You breathed the atmosphere of the Province, ancient, unalterable Province.   The great square-shaped salon, with its four doors and four windows, was modestly wainscoted with carved panels, and painted gray.   On the wall, above the single oblong mirror on the mantel, the Hours, in mono-chrome, were ushering in the Day.   For this particular style of decoration, which used to infest the spaces above doors, the artist's invention devised the eternal Seasons which meet your eyes almost anywhere in central France, till you loathe the detestable Cupids engaged in reaping, skating, sowing seeds, or flinging flowers about.   Every window was over-arched with a sort of baldachin with green damask curtains drawn back with cords and huge tassels.   The tapestry-covered furniture, with a darn here and there at the edges of the chairs, belonged distinctly to that period of the eighteenth century when curves and contortions were in the very height of fashion ; the frames were painted and varnished, the sub-jects in the medallions on the backs were taken from La Fon-taine.   Four card-tables, a table for piquet, and another for backgammon filled up the immense space.   A rock crystal chandelier, shrouded in green gauze, hung suspended from the prominent cross-beam which divided the ceiling, the only plastered ceiling in the house.   Two branched candle-sconces were fixed into the wall above the mantel, where a couple of blue Sèvres vases· stood on either side of a copper-gilt clock which represented a scene taken from ''Le Déserteur ''—a proof of the prodigious popularity of Sedaine's work.   It was a group of no less than eleven figures, four inches high ; the deserter

4

emerging from jail escorted by a guard of soldiers, while a young person, swooning in the foreground, held out his reprieve. The hearth and fire-irons were of the same date and style. The more recent family portraits—one or two Rigauds and three pastels by Latour—adorned the handsome wainscot panels.

The study, paneled entirely in old lacquer work, red and black and gold, would have fetched fabulous sums a few years later; Mlle. Cormon was as far as possible from suspecting its value; but if she had been offered a thousand crowns for every panel, she would not have parted with a single one. It was a part of her system to alter nothing, and everywhere in the provinces the belief in ancestral hoards is very strong. The boudoir, never used, was hung with the old-fashioned chintz so much run after nowadays by amateurs of the "Pompadour style," as it is called.

The dining-room was paved with black-and-white stone; it had not been ceiled, but the joists and beams were painted. Ranged round the walls, beneath a flowered trellis, painted in fresco, stood the portentous, marble-topped sideboards, indispensable in the warfare waged in the provinces against the powers of digestion. The chairs were cane-seated and varnished, the doors of unpolished walnut-wood. Everything combined admirably to complete the general effect, the old-world air of the house within and without. The provincial spirit had preserved all as it had always been; nothing was new or old, young or decrepit. You felt a sense of chilly precision everywhere.

Any tourist in Brittany, Normandy, Maine, or Anjou must have seen some house more or less like this in one or other provincial town; for the Hôtel de Cormon was in its way a very pattern and model of burgher houses over a large part of France, and the better deserves a place in this chronicle because it is at once a commentary on the manners of the place and the expression of its ideas. Who does not feel, even now, how much the life within the old walls was one of peaceful routine?

For such library as the house possessed you must have descended rather below the level of the Brillante. There stood a solidly clasped oak-bound collection, none the worse, nay, rather the better, for a thick coating of dust; a collection kept as carefully as a cider-growing district is wont to keep the products of the presses of Burgundy, Touraine, Gascony, and the South. Here were works full of native force, and exquisite qualities, with an added perfume of antiquity. No one will import poor wines when the cost of carriage is so heavy.

Mlle. Cormon's whole circle consisted of about a hundred and fifty persons. Of these, some went into the country, some were ill, others from home on business in the department, but there was a faithful band which always came, unless Mlle. Cormon gave an evening party in form; so also did those persons who were bound either by their duties or old habit to live in Alençon itself. All these people were of ripe age. A few among them had traveled, but scarcely any of them had gone beyond the province, and one or two had been implicated in Chouannerie. People could begin to speak freely of the war, now that rewards had come to the heroic defenders of the good cause. M. de Valois had been concerned in the last rising, when the Marquis de Montauran lost his life, betrayed by his mistress; and Marche-à-Terre, now peacefully driving a grazier's trade by the banks of the Mayenne, had made a famous name for himself. M. de Valois, during the past six months, had supplied the key to several shrewd tricks played off upon Hulot the old Republican, commander of a demi-brigade stationed at Alençon from 1798 till 1800. There was talk of Hulot yet in the countryside.*

The women made little pretense of dress, except on Wednes-

* See "The Chouans."

days, when Mlle. Cormon gave a dinner party, and last week's
guests came to pay their "visit of digestion." On Wednesday evening the rooms were filled.   Guests and visitors came
in gala dress ; here and there a woman brought her knitting
or her tapestry work, and some young ladies unblushingly
drew patterns for point d'Alençon, by which they supported
themselves.   Men brought their wives, because there were so
few young fellows there ; no whisper could pass unnoticed,
and therefore there was no danger of love-making for maid or
matron.   Every evening at six o'clock the lobby was filled
with articles of dress, with sticks, cloaks, and lanterns.   Every
one was so well acquainted, the customs of the house were so
primitive, that if by any chance the Abbé de Sponde was in
the lime-tree walk, and Mlle. Cormon in her room, neither
Josette the maid nor Jacquelin the man thought it necessary
to inform them of the arrival of visitors.   The first comer
waited till some one else arrived ; and when they mustered
players sufficient for whist or boston, the game was begun
without waiting for the Abbé de Sponde or mademoiselle.
When it grew dark, Josette or Jacquelin brought lights as
soon as the bell rang, and the old abbé out in the garden,
seeing the drawing-room windows illuminated, hastened slowly
toward the house.   Every evening the piquet, boston, and
whist tables were full, giving an average of twenty-five or
thirty persons, including those who came to chat ; but often
there were as many as thirty or forty, and then Jacquelin took
candles into the study and the boudoir.   Between eight and
nine at night the servants began to fill the antechamber ; and
nothing short of a revolution would have found any one in the
salon at ten o'clock.   At that hour the frequenters of the
house were walking home through the streets, discussing the
points made, or keeping up a conversation begun in the salon.
Sometimes the talk turned on a pocket-handkerchief of land on
which somebody had an eye, sometimes it was the division of
an inheritance and disputes among the legatees, or the pre-

tensions of the aristocratic set. You see exactly the same thing at Paris when the theatres disgorge.

Some people who talk a great deal about poetry and understand nothing about it are wont to rail at provincial towns and provincial ways ; but lean your forehead on your left hand, as you sit with your feet on the fire-dogs, and rest your elbow on your knee, and then—if you have fully realized for yourself the level, pleasant landscape, the house, the interior, the folk within it and their interests, interests that seem all the larger because the mental horizon is so limited (as a grain of gold is beaten thin between two sheets of parchment)—then ask yourself what human life is. Try to decide between the engraver of the hieroglyphic birds on an Egyptian obelisk, and one of these folk in Alençon playing boston through a score of years with du Bousquier, M. de Valois, Mlle. Cormon, the president of the Tribunal, the public prosecutor, the Abbé de Sponde, Mme. Granson, and all.the rest. If the daily round, the daily pacing of the same track in the footsteps of many yesterdays, is not exactly happiness, it is so much like it that others, driven by dint of storm-tossed days to reflect on the blessings of calm, will say that it is happiness indeed.

To give the exact measure of the importance of Mlle. Cormon's salon, it will suffice to add that du Bousquier, a born statistician, computed that its frequenters mustered among them a hundred and thirty-one votes in the electoral college, and eighteen hundred thousand livres of income derived from lands in the province. The town of Alençon was not, it is true, completely represented there. The aristocratic section, for instance, had a salon of their own, and the receiver-general's house was a sort of official inn kept, as in duty bound, by the Government, where everybody who was anybody danced, flirted, fluttered, fell in love, and supped. One or two unclassified persons kept up the communications between Mlle. Cormon's salon and the other two, but the Cormon salon criticised all that passed in the opposed camps very severely.

Sumptuous dinners gave rise to unfavorable comment; ices at
a dance caused searchings of heart; the women's behavior
and dress and any innovations were much discussed.

Mlle. Cormon being, as it were, the style of the firm and
figure-head of an imposing coterie, was inevitably the object
of any ambition as profound as that of the du Bousquier or
the Chevalier de Valois. To both gentlemen she meant a
seat in the Chamber of Deputies, with a peerage for the chevalier, a receiver-general's post for du Bousquier. A salon ad-
mittedly of the first rank is every whit as hard to build up in
a country town as in Paris. And here was the salon ready
made. To marry Mlle. Cormon was to be lord of Alençon.
Finally, Athanase, the only one of the three suitors that had
ceased to calculate, cared as much for the woman as for her
money.

Is there not a whole strange drama (to use the modern cant
phrase) in the relative positions of these four human beings?
There is something grotesque, is there not, in the idea of
three rival suitors eagerly pressing about an old maid who
never so much as suspected their intentions, in spite of her
intense and very natural desire to be married? Yet, although
things being so, it may seem an extraordinary thing that she
should not have married before, it is not difficult to explain
how and why, in spite of her fortune and her three suitors,
Mlle. Cormon was still unwed.

From the first, following the family tradition, Mlle. Cormon
had always wished to marry a noble, but between the years
1789 and 1799 circumstances were very much against her.
While she would have wished to be the wife of a person of condition, she was horribly afraid of the Revolutionary Tribunal;
and these two motives weighing about equally, she remained
stationary, according to a law which holds equally good in
æsthetics or statics. At the same time, the condition of suspended judgment is not unpleasant for a girl, so long as she
feels young and thinks that she can choose where she pleases.

But, as all France knows, the system of government immediately preceding the wars of Napoleon produced a vast number of widows; and the number of heiresses was altogether out of proportion to the number of eligible men. When order was restored in the country, in the time of the Consulate, external difficulties made marriage as much of a problem as ever for Rose-Marie-Victoire. On the one hand, she declined to marry an elderly man; and, on the other, dread of ridicule and circumstances put quite young men out of the question. In those days heads of families married their sons as mere boys, because in this way they escaped the conscription. With the obstinacy of a landed proprietor, mademoiselle would not hear of marrying a military man; she had no wish to take a husband only to give him back to the Emperor, she wished to keep him for herself. And so, between 1804 and 1815, it was impossible to compete with a younger generation of girls, too numerous already in times when cannon-shot had thinned the ranks of marriageable men.

Again, apart from Mlle. Cormon's predilection for birth, she had a very pardonable craze for being loved for her own sake. You would scarcely believe the lengths to which she carried this fancy. She set her wits to work to lay snares for her admirers, to try their sentiments; and that with such success, that the unfortunates one and all fell into them, and succumbed in the whimsical ordeals through which they passed at unawares. Mlle. Cormon did not study her suitors, she played the spy upon them. A careless word or a joke, and the lady did not understand jokes very well, was excuse enough to dismiss an aspirant as found wanting. This had neither spirit nor delicacy; that was untruthful and not a Christian; one wanted to cut down tall timber and coin money under the marriage canopy; another was not the man to make her happy; or, again, she had her suspicions of gout in the family, or took fright at her wooer's antecedents. Like mother church, she would fain see a priest without blemish at her altar. And then Rose-Marie-Victoire made the worst of herself, and was as anxious to be loved, with all her factitious plainness and imaginary faults, as other women are to be married for virtues which they have not and for borrowed beauty. Mlle. Cormon's ambition had its source in the finest instincts of womanhood. She would reward her lover by discovering to him a thousand virtues after marriage, as other women reveal the many little faults kept hitherto strenuously out of sight. But no one understood. The noble girl came in contact with none but commonplace natures, with whom practical interests came first; the finer calculations of feeling were beyond their comprehension.

She grew more and more suspicious as the critical period so ingenuously called "second youth" drew nearer. Her fancy for making the worst of herself with increasing success frightened away the latest recruits; they hesitated to unite their lot with hers. The strategy of her game of blind-man's bluff (the virtues to be revealed when the finder's eyes were opened) was a complex study for which few men have inclination; they prefer perfection ready-made. An ever-present dread of being married for her money made her unreasonably distrustful and uneasy. She fell foul of the rich, and the rich could look higher; she was afraid of poor men, she would not believe them capable of that disinterestedness on which she set such store; till at length her rejections and other circumstances let in an unexpected light upon the minds of suitors thus presented for her selection like dried peas on a seedman's sieve. Every time a marriage project came to nothing, the unfortunate girl, being gradually led to despise mankind, saw the other sex at last in a false light. Inevitably, in her inmost soul, she grew misanthropic, a tinge of bitterness was infused into her conversation, a certain harshness into her expression. And her manners became more and more rigid under the stress of enforced celibacy; in her despair she sought to perfect herself. It was a characteristic and a noble vengeance.

She would polish and cut for God the rough diamond rejected by men.

Before long public opinion was against Mlle. Cormon. People accept the verdict which a woman passes upon herself if, being free to marry, she fails to fulfill expectations, or is known to have refused eligible suitors.   Every one decides that she has her own reasons for declining marriage, and those reasons are always misinterpreted.   There was some hidden physical defect or deformity, they said; but she, poor girl, was pure as an angel, healthy as a child, and overflowing with kindness.   Nature had meant her to know all the joys, all the happiness, all the burdens of motherhood.

Yet in her person Mlle. Cormon did not find a natural auxiliary to gain her heart's desire.   She had no beauty, save of the kind so improperly called "the devil's;" that full-blown freshness of youth which, theologically speaking, the devil never could have possessed; unless, indeed, we are to look for an explanation of the expression in the devil's continual desire of refreshing himself.   The heiress' feet were large and flat; when, on rainy days, she crossed the wet streets between her house and St. Leonard's, her raised skirt displayed (without malice, be it said) a leg which scarcely seemed to belong to a woman, so muscular was it, with a small, firm, prominent calf like a sailor's.   She had a figure for a wet nurse.   Her thick, honest waist, her strong, plump arms, her red hands; everything about her, in short, was in keeping with the round, expansive contours and portly fairness of the Norman style of beauty.   Wide-open, prominent eyes of no particular color, gave to a face, by no means distinguished in its round outlines, a sheepish, astonished expression not altogether inappropriate, however, in an old maid: even if Rose had not been innocent, she must still have seemed so.   An aquiline nose was oddly assorted with a low forehead, for a feature of that type is almost invariably found in company with a lofty brow.   In spite of thick, red lips, the sign of great kindliness of nature, there were evidently so few ideas behind that forehead, that Rose's heart could scarcely have been directed by her brain. Kind she must certainly be, but not gracious. And we are apt to judge the defects of goodness very harshly, while we make the most of the redeeming qualities of vice.

An extraordinary length of chestnut hair lent Rose Cormon such beauty as belongs to vigor and luxuriance, her chief personal characteristics. In the time of her pretensions she had a trick of turning her face in three-quarters profile to display a very pretty ear, gracefully set between the azure-streaked white throat and the temple, and thrown into relief by thick masses of her hair. Dressed in a ball gown, with her head poised at this angle, Rose might almost seem beautiful. With her protuberant bust, her waist, her high health, she used to draw exclamations of admiration from Imperial officers. "What a fine girl!" they used to say.

But, as years went on, the stoutness induced by a quiet, regular life distributed itself so unfortunately over her person, that its original porportions were destroyed. No known variety of corset could have discovered the poor spinster's hips at this period of her existence; she might have been cast in one uniform piece. The youthful proportions of her figure were completely lost; her dimensions had grown so excessive that no one could see her stoop without fearing that, being so top-heavy, she would certainly overbalance herself; but nature had provided a sufficient natural counterpoise, which enabled her to dispense with all adventitious aid from "dress improvers." Everything about Rose was very genuine.

Her chin developed a triple fold, which reduced the apparent length of her throat, and made it no easy matter to turn her head. She had no wrinkles, she had creases. Wags used to assert that she powdered herself, as nurses powder babies, to prevent chafing of the skin. To a young man, consumed, like Athanase, with suppressed desires, this excessive corpulence offered just the kind of physical charm which could not fail to attract youth. Youthful imaginations, essentially intrepid, stimulated by appetite, are prone to dilate upon the beauties of that living expanse. So does the plump partridge allure the epicure's knife. And, indeed, any debt-burdened young man of fashion in Paris would have resigned himself readily enough to fulfilling his part of the contract and making Mademoiselle Cormon happy. Still the unfortunate spinster had already passed her fortieth year!

At this period of enforced loneliness, after the long, vain struggle to fill her life with those interests that are all in all to woman, she was fortifying herself in virtue by the most strict observance of religious duties; she had turned to the great consolation of well-preserved virginity. A confessor, endowed with no great wisdom, had directed Mademoiselle Cormon in the paths of asceticism for some three years past, recommending a system of self-scourging calculated, according to modern doctors, to produce an effect the exact opposite of that expected by the poor priest, whose knowledge of hygiene was but limited. These absurd practices were beginning to bring a certain monastic tinge to Rose Cormon's face; with frequent pangs of despair, she watched the sallow hues of middle age creeping across its natural white and red; while the trace of down about the corners of her upper lip showed a distinct tendency to darken and increase like smoke. Her temples grew shiny. She had passed the turning-point, in fact. It was known for certain in Alençon that Mademoiselle Cormon suffered from heated blood. She inflicted her confidence upon the Chevalier de Valois, reckoning up the number of foot-baths that she took, and devising cooling treatment with him. And that shrewd observer would end by taking out his snuff-box, and gazing at the portrait of the Princess Goritza as he remarked: "But the real sedative, my dear young lady, would be a good and handsome husband."

"But whom could one trust?" returned she.

But the chevalier only flicked away the powdered snuff from the creases of his paduasoy vest. To anybody else the proceeding would have seemed perfectly natural, but it always made the poor old maid feel uncomfortable.

The violence of her objectless longings grew to such a height that she shrank from looking a man in the face, so afraid was she that the thoughts which pierced her heart might be read in her eyes. It was one of her whims, possibly a later development of her former tactics, to behave almost ungraciously to the possible suitors toward whom she still felt herself attracted, so afraid was she of being accused of folly. Most people in her circle were utterly incapable of appreciating her motives, so noble throughout; they explained her manner to her coevals in single blessedness by a theory of revenge for some past slight.

With the beginning of the year 1815 Rose Cormon had reached the fatal age, to which she did not confess. She was forty-two. By this time her desire to be married had reached a degree of intensity bordering on monomania. She saw her chances of motherhood fast slipping away forever; and, in her divine ignorance, she longed above all things for children of her own. There was not a soul found in Alençon to impute a single unchaste desire to the virtuous girl. She loved love, taking all for granted, without realizing for herself what love would be—a devout Agnès, incapable of inventing one of the little shifts of Molière's heroine.

She had been counting upon chance of late. The disbanding of the Imperial troops and the reconstruction of the King's army was sending a tide of military men back to their native places, some of them on half-pay, some with pensions, some without, and all of them anxious to find some way of amending their bad fortune, and of finishing their days in a fashion which would mean the beginning of happiness for Mlle. Cormon. It would be hard indeed if she could not find a single brave and honorable man among all those who were coming back to the neighborhood. He must have a sound constitution in the first place, he must be of suitable age, and a man whose personal character would serve as a passport to his Bonapartist opinions; perhaps he might even be willing to turn Royalist for the sake of gaining a lost social position.

Supported by these mental calculations, Mlle. Cormon maintained the severity of her attitude for the first few months of the year; but the men that came back to the town were all either too old or too young, or their characters were too bad, or their opinions too Bonapartist, or their station in life was incompatible with her position, fortune, and habits. The case grew more and more desperate every day. Officers high in the service had used their advantages under Napoleon to marry, and these gentlemen now became Royalists for the sake of their families. In vain had she put up prayers to heaven to send her a husband that she might be happy in Christian fashion; it was written, no doubt, that she should die virgin and martyr, for not a single likely-looking man presented himself.

In the course of conversation in her drawing-room of an evening, the frequenters of the house kept the police register under tolerably strict supervision; no one could arrive at Alençon but they informed themselves at once as to the newcomer's mode of life, quality, and fortune. But, at the same time, Alençon is not a town to attract many strangers; it is not on the high road to any large city; there are no chance arrivals; naval officers on their way to Brest do not so much as stop in the place.

Poor Mlle. Cormon at last comprehended that her choice was reduced to the natives. At times her eyes took an almost fierce expression, to which the chevalier would respond with a keen glance at her as he drew out his snuff-box to gaze at the Princess Goritza. M. de Valois knew that, in feminine jurisprudence, fidelity to an old love is a guarantee for the new.

But Mlle. Cormon, it cannot be denied, was not very intelligent. His snuff-box strategy was wasted upon her.

She redoubled her watchfulness, the better to combat the
"evil one," and with devout rigidness and the sternest principles she consigned her cruel sufferings to the secret places of
her life.

At night, when she was alone, she thought of her lost
youth, of her faded bloom, of the thwarted instincts of her
nature ; and while she laid her passionate longings at the foot
of the cross, together with all the poetry doomed to remain
pent within her, she vowed inwardly to take the first man that
was willing to marry her, just as he was, without putting him
to any proof whatsoever. Sounding her own dispositions,
after a series of vigils, each more trying than the last, in her
own mind she went so far as to espouse a sub-lieutenant, a
tobacco-smoker to boot ; nay, he was even head over ears in
debt. Him she proposed to transform with care, submission,
and gentleness into a pattern for mankind. But only in the
silence of night could she plan these imaginary marriages, in
which she amused herself with playing the sublime part of
guardian angel ; with morning, if Josette found her mistress'
bed-clothes turned topsy-turvy, mademoiselle had recovered
her dignity ; with morning, after breakfast, she would have
nothing less than a solid landowner, a well-preserved man of
forty—a young man—as you may say.

The Abbé de Sponde was incapable of giving his niece
assistance of any sort in schemes for marriage. The good
man, aged seventy or thereabout, referred all the calamities
of the Revolution to the design of a providence prompt to
punish a dissolute church. For which reasons M. de Sponde
had long since entered upon a deserted path to heaven, the
way trodden by the hermits of old. He led an ascetic life,
simply, unobtrusively ; hiding his deeds of charity, his constant prayer and fasting from all other eyes. Necessity was
laid upon all priests, he thought, to do as he did ; he preached

by example, turning a serene and smiling face upon the world, while he completely cut himself off from worldly interests. All his thoughts were given to the afflicted, to the needs of the church, and the saving of his own soul. He left the management of his property to his niece. She paid over his yearly income to him, and, after a slight deduction for his maintenance, the whole of it went in private almsgiving or in donations to the church.

All the abbé's affections were centred upon his niece, and she looked upon him as a father. He was a somewhat absent-minded father, however, without the remotest conception of the rebellion of the flesh; a father who gave thanks to God for maintaining his beloved daughter in a state of virginity; for from his youth up he had held, with St. John Chrysostom, "that virginity is as much above the estate of marriage as the angels are above man."

Mlle. Cormon was accustomed to look up to her uncle; she did not venture to confide her wishes for a change of condition to him; and he, good man, on his side was accustomed to the ways of the house, and perhaps might not have relished the introduction of a master into it. Absorbed in thoughts of the distress which he relieved, or lost in fathomless inner depths of prayer, he was often unconscious of what was going on about him; frequenters of the house set this down to absent-mindedness; but while he said little, his silence was neither unsociable nor ungenial. A tall, spare, grave, and solemn man, his face told of kindly feeling and a great inward peace. His presence in the house seemed, as it were, to consecrate it. The abbé entertained a strong liking for that elderly skeptic the Chevalier de Valois. Far apart as their lives were, the two grand wrecks of the eighteenth-century clergy and noblesse recognized each other by generic signs and tokens; and the chevalier, for that matter, could converse with unction with the abbé, just as he talked like a father with his grisettes.

Some may think that Mlle. Cormon would leave no means

untried to gain her end; that among other permissible feminine artifices, for instance, she would turn to her toilettes, wear low-cut bodices, use the passive coquetry of a display of the splendid equipment with which she might take the field. On the contrary, she was as heroic and steadfast in her high-necked gown as a sentry in his sentry-box. All her dresses, bonnets, and finery were made in Alençon by two hunch-backed sisters, not wanting in taste. But in spite of the entreaties of the two artists, Mlle. Cormon utterly declined the adventitious aid of elegance; she must be substantial throughout, body and plumage, and possibly her heavy-look-ing dresses became her not amiss. Laugh who will at her, poor thing. Generous natures, those who never trouble them-selves about the form in which good feeling shows itself, but admire it wherever they find it, will see something sublime in this trait. Perhaps some slight-natured feminine critic may begin to carp, and say that there is no woman in France so simple but that she can angle for a husband, that Mlle. Cormon is one of those abnormal creatures which commonsense forbids us to take for a type; that the best or the most babyish un-married woman that has a mind to hook a gudgeon can put forward some physical charm wherewith to bait her line. But when you begin to think that the sublime Apostolic Roman Catholic is still a power in Brittany and the ancient duchy of Alençon, these criticisms fall to the ground. Faith and piety admit no such subtleties. Mlle. Cormon kept to the straight path, preferring the misfortune of a maidenhood infinitely prolonged to the misery of untruthfulness, to the sin of small deceit. Armed with self-discipline, such a girl cannot make a sacrifice of a principle; and therefore love (or self-interest) must make a very determined effort to find her out and win her.

Let us have the courage to make a confession, painful in these days when religion is nothing but a means of advance-ment for some, a dream for others; the devout are subject to a kind of moral ophthalmia, which, by the especial grace of providence, removes a host of small earthly concerns out of the sight of the pilgrim of eternity. In a word, the devout are apt to be dense in a good many ways. Their stupidity, at the same time, is a measure of the force with which their spirits turn heavenward; albeit the skeptical M. de Valois maintained that it is a moot point whether stupid women take naturally to piety or whether piety, on the other hand, has a stupefying effect upon an intelligent girl.

It must be borne in mind that it is the purest orthodox goodness, ready to drink rapturously of every cup set before it, to submit devoutly to the will of God, to see the print of the divine finger everywhere in the clay of life—that it is catholic virtue stealing like hidden light into the innermost recesses of this history that alone can bring everything into right relief, and widen its significance for those who yet have faith. And, again, if the stupidity is admitted, why should the misfortunes of stupidity be less interesting than the woes of genius in a world where fools so overwhelmingly preponderate?

To resume: Mlle. Cormon's divine girlish ignorance of life was an offense in the eyes of the world. She was anything but observant, as her treatment of her suitors sufficiently showed. At this very moment, a girl of sixteen who had never opened a novel in her life might have read a hundred chapters of romance in Athanase's eyes. But Mlle. Cormon saw nothing all the while; she never knew that the young man's voice was unsteady with emotion which he dared not express, and the woman who could invent refinements of high sentiment to her own undoing could not discern the same feelings in Athanase.

Those who know that qualities of heart and brain are as independent of each other as genius and greatness of soul will see nothing extraordinary in this psychological phenomenon. A complete human being is so rare a prodigy that Socrates, that pearl among mankind, agreed with a contemporary phre-

5

nologist that he himself was born to be a very scurvy knave. A great general may save his country at Zurich, and yet take a commission from contractors; a banker's doubtful honesty does not prevent him from being a statesman; a great composer may give the world divine music, and yet forge another man's signature; and a woman of refined feeling may be excessively weak-minded. In short, a devout woman may have a very lofty soul, and yet have no ears to hear the voice of another noble soul at her side.

The unaccountable freaks of physical infirmity find a parallel in the moral world. Here was a good creature making her preserves and breaking her heart till she grew almost ridiculous, because, forsooth, there was no one to eat them but her uncle and herself. Those who sympathized with her for the sake of her good qualities, or, in some cases, on account of her defects, used to laugh over her disappointments. People began to wonder what would become of so fine a property with all Mlle. Cormon's savings, and her uncle's to boot.

It was long since they began to suspect that at bottom, and in spite of appearances, Mlle. Cormon was "an original." Originality is not allowed in the provinces; originality means that you have ideas which nobody else can understand, and in a country town people's intellects, like their manner of life, must all be on a level. Even in 1804 Rose's matrimonial prospects were considered so problematical, that "to marry like Mlle. Cormon" was a current saying in Alençon, and the most ironical way of suggesting Such-an-one would never marry at all.

The necessity to laugh at some one must indeed be imperious in France, if any one could be found to raise a smile at the expense of that excellent creature. Not merely did she entertain the whole town, she was charitable, she was good; she was incapable of saying a spiteful word; and more than that, she was so much in unison with the whole spirit of the place, its manners and its customs, that she was generally be-

loved as the very incarnation of the life of the province; she
had imbibed all its prejudices and made its interests hers; she
had never gone beyond its limits, she adored it; she was im-
bedded in provincial tradition. In spite of her eighteen thousand livres per annum, a tolerably large income for the neighborhood, she accommodated herself to the ways of her less
wealthy neighbors. When she went to her country house,
the Prébaudet, for instance, she drove over in an old-fashioned
wicker cariole hung with white leather straps, and fitted
with a couple of rusty weather-beaten leather curtains, which
scarcely closed it in. The equipage, drawn by a fat, broken-
winded mare, was known all over the town. Jacquelin, the
manservant, cleaned it as carefully as if it had been the finest
carriage from Paris. Mademoiselle was fond of it; it had
lasted her a dozen years, a fact which she was wont to point
out with the triumphant joy of contented parsimony. Most
people were grateful to her for forbearing to humiliate them
by splendor which she might have flaunted before their eyes;
it is even credible that if she had sent for a calèche from
Paris, it would have caused more talk than any of her "disappointments." After all, the finest carriage in the world,
like the old-fashioned cariole, could only have taken her to
the Prébaudet; and in the provinces they always keep the end
in view, and trouble themselves very little about the elegance
of the means, provided that they are sufficient.

To complete the picture of Mlle. Cormon's household and
domestic life, several figures must be grouped round Mlle.
Cormon and the Abbé de Sponde. Jacquelin, and Josette,
and Mariette, the cook, ministered to the comfort of uncle
and niece.

Jacquelin, a man of forty, short and stout, dark-haired and
ruddy, with a countenance of the Breton sailor type, had been
in service in the house for twenty-two years. He waited at
table, groomed the mare, worked in the garden, cleaned the
abbé's shoes, ran errands, chopped firewood, drove the cariole,

went to the Prébaudet for corn, hay, and straw, and slept like
a dormouse in the antechamber of an evening. He was supposed to be fond of Josette, and Josette was six-and-thirty.
But if she had married him, Mlle. Cormon would have dismissed her, and so the poor lovers were fain to save up their
wages in silence, and to wait and hope for mademoiselle's
marriage, much as the Jews look for the advent of the Mes-
siah.

Josette came from the district between Alençon and Mortagne ; she was a fat little woman. Her face, which reminded
you of a mud-bespattered apricot, was not wanting either in
character or intelligence. She was supposed to rule her mistress. Josette and Jacquelin, feeling sure of the event, found
consolation, presumably, by discounting the future. Mariette,
the cook, had likewise been in the family for fifteen years ;
she was skilled in the cookery of the country and the preparation of the most esteemed provincial dishes.

Perhaps the fat, old bay mare, of the Normandy breed,
which Mlle. Cormon used to drive to the Prébaudet, ought
to count for a good deal, for the affection which the five
inmates of the house bore the animal amounted to mania.
Penelope, for that was her name, had been with them for
eighteen years ; and so well was she cared for, so regularly
tended, that Jacquelin and mademoiselle hoped to get quite
another ten years of work out of her. Penelope was a stock
subject and source of interest in their lives. It seemed as if
poor Mlle. Cormon, with no child of her own, lavished all her
maternal affection upon the lucky beast. Almost every human
being leading a solitary life in a crowded world will surround
himself with a make-believe family of some sort, and Penelope
took the place of dogs, cats, or canaries.

These four faithful servants—for Penelope's intelligence had
been trained till it was very nearly on a par with the wits of the
other three, while they had sunk pretty much into the dumb,
submissive jog-trot life of the animal—these four retainers

came and went and did the same things day after day, with the unfailing regularity of clockwork. But, to use their own expression, "they had first eaten their white bread." Mlle. Cormon suffered from a fixed idea upon the nerves; and, after the wont of such sufferers, she grew fidgety and hard to please, not by force of nature, but because she had no outlet for her energies. She had neither husband nor children to fill her thoughts, so they fastened upon trifles. She would talk for hours at a stretch of some inconceivably small matter, of a dozen serviettes, for instance, lettered Z, which somehow or other had been put before O.

"Why, what can Josette be thinking about?" she cried. "Has she no notion what she is doing?"

Jacquelin chanced to be late in feeding Penelope one afternoon, so every day for a whole week afterward mademoiselle inquired whether the horse had been fed at two o'clock. Her narrow imagination spent itself on small matters. A layer of dust forgotten by the feather-duster, a slice of scorched toast, an omission to close the blinds on Jacquelin's part when the sun shone in upon furniture and carpets—all these important trifles produced serious trouble, mademoiselle lost her temper over them. "Nothing was the same as it used to be. The servants of old days were so changed that she did not know them. They were spoilt. She was too good to them," and so forth and so forth. One day Josette gave her mistress the "Journée du Chrétien"* instead of the "Quinzaine de Pâques."† The whole town heard of the mistake before night. Mademoiselle had been obliged to get up and come out of church, disturbing whole rows of chairs and raising the wildest conjectures, so that she was obliged afterward to give all her friends a full account of the mishap.

"Josette," she said mildly, when she had come the whole way home from St. Leonard's, "this must never happen again."

* The Christian's Journey.   † Fifteen Easters.

Mlle. Cormon was far from suspecting that it was a very fortunate thing for her that she could vent her spleen in petty squabbles. The mind, like the body, requires exercise; these quarrels were a sort of mental gymnastics. Josette and Jacquelin took such unevennesses of temper as the agricultural laborer takes the changes of the weather. The three good souls could say among themselves that "It is a fine day," or "It rains," without murmuring against the powers above. Sometimes in the kitchen of a morning they would wonder in what humor mademoiselle would wake, much as a farmer studies the morning mists. And of necessity Mlle. Cormon ended by seeing herself in all the infinitely small details which made up her life. Herself and God, her confessor and her washing-days, the preserves to be made, the services of the church to attend, and the uncle to take care of—all these things absorbed faculties that were none of the strongest. For her the atoms of life were magnified by virtue of an optical process peculiar to the selfish or the self-absorbed. To so perfectly healthy a woman, the slightest symptom of indigestion was a positively alarming portent. She lived, moreover, under the ferule of the system of medicine practiced by our grandsires; a drastic purgative dose fit to kill Penelope, taken four times a year, merely gave Mlle. Cormon a fillip.

What tremendous ransackings of the week's dietary if Josette, assisting her mistress to dress, discovered a scarcely visible pimple on shoulders that still boasted a satin skin! What triumph if the maid could bring a certain hare to her mistress' recollection, and trace the accursed pimple to its origin in that too heating article of food! With what joy the two women would cry: "It is the hare beyond a doubt!"

"Mariette over-seasoned it," mademoiselle would add; "I always tell her not to overdo it for my uncle and me, but Mariette has no more memory than——"

"Than the hare," suggested Josette.

"It is the truth," returned mademoiselle; "she has no more memory than the hare; you have just hit it."

Four times in a year, at the beginning of each season, Mlle. Cormon went to spend a certain number of days at the Prébaudet. It was now the middle of May, when she liked to see how her apple trees had "snowed," as they say in the cider country, an allusion to the white blossoms strewn in the orchards in the spring. When the circles of fallen petals look like snowdrifts under the trees, the proprietor may hope to have abundance of cider in the autumn. Mlle. Cormon estimated her barrels, and at the same time superintended any necessary after-winter repairs, planning out work in the garden and orchard, from which she drew no inconsiderable supplies. Each time of year had its special business.

Mademoiselle used to give a farewell dinner to her faithful inner circle before leaving, albeit she would see them again at the end of three weeks. All Alençon knew when the journey was to be undertaken. Any one that had fallen behindhand immediately paid a call, her drawing-room was filled; everybody wished her a prosperous journey, as if she had been starting for Calcutta. Then, in the morning, all the tradespeople were standing in their doorways; every one, great and small, watched the cariole go past, and it seemed as if everybody learned a piece of fresh news when one repeated after another, "So Mademoiselle Cormon is going to the Prébaudet."

One would remark: "She has bread ready baked, she has!"

And his neighbor would return: "Eh! my lad, she is a good woman; if property always fell into such hands as hers, there would not be a beggar to be seen in the countryside."

Or another would exclaim: "Halloo! I should not wonder if our oldest vines are in flower, for there is Mademoiselle Cormon setting out for the Prébaudet. How comes it that she is so little given to marrying?"

"I should be quite ready to marry her, all the same," a

wag would answer. "The marriage is half made—one side is willing, but the other isn't. Pooh! the oven is heating for Monsieur du Bousquier."

"*Monsieur du Bousquier?* She has refused him."

At every house that evening people remarked solemnly: "Mademoiselle Cormon has gone."

Or perhaps: "So you have let Mademoiselle Cormon go!"

The Wednesday selected by Suzanne for making a scandal chanced to be this very day of leave-taking, when Mlle. Cormon nearly drove Josette to distraction over the packing of the parcels which she meant to take with her. A good deal that was done and said in the town that morning was like to lend additional interest to the farewell gathering at night. While the old maid was busily making preparations for her journey; while the astute chevalier was playing his game of piquet in the house of Mlle. Armande de Gordes, sister of the aged Marquis de Gordes and queen of the aristocratic salon, Mme. Granson had sounded the alarm bell in half a score of houses. There was not a soul but felt some curiosity to see what sort of figure the seducer would cut that evening; and to Mme. Granson and the Chevalier de Valois it was an important matter to know how Mlle. Cormon would take the news, in her double quality of marriageable spinster and lady president of the Maternity Fund. As for the unsuspected du Bousquier, he was taking the air on the parade. He was just beginning to think that Suzanne had made a fool of him; and this suspicion only confirmed the rules which he had laid down with regard to womankind.

On these high days the cloth was laid about half-past three in the Cormon house. Four o'clock was the state dinner hour in Alençon, on ordinary days they dined at two, as in the time of the Empire; but then, they supped!

Mlle. Cormon always felt an inexpressible sense of satisfaction when she was dressed to receive her guests as mistress of her house. It was one of the pleasures which she most relished, be it said without malice, though egoism certainly lay beneath the feeling. When thus arrayed for conquest, a ray of hope slid across the darkness of her soul; a voice within her cried that nature had not endowed her so abundantly in vain, that surely some enterprising man was about to appear for her. She felt the younger for the wish and the fresher for her toilet; she looked at her stout figure with a certain elation; and afterward, when she went downstairs to submit salon, study, and boudoir to an awful scrutiny, this sense of satisfaction still remained with her. To and fro she went, with the naïve contentment of the rich man who feels conscious at every moment that he is rich and will lack for nothing all his life long. She looked round upon her furniture, the eternal furniture, the antiquities, the lacquered panels, and told herself that such fine things ought to have a master.

After admiring the dining-room, where the space was filled by the long table with its snowy cloth, its score of covers symmetrically laid; after going through the roll-call of a squadron of bottles ordered up from the cellar, and making sure that each bore an honorable label; and finally, after a most minute verification of a score of little slips of paper on which the abbé had written the names of the guests with a trembling hand—it was the sole occasion on which he took an active part in the household, and the place of every guest always gave rise to grave discussion—after this review, Mlle. Cormon in her fine array went into the garden to join her uncle; for at this pleasantest hour of the day he used to walk up and down the terrace beside the Brillante, listening to the twittering of the birds, which, hidden closely among the leaves in the lime-tree walk, knew no fear of boys or sportsmen.

Mlle. Cormon never came out to the abbé during these intervals of waiting without asking some hopelessly absurd question, in the hope of drawing the good man into a discussion which might interest him.   Her reasons for so doing must be given, for this very characteristic trait adds the finishing touch to her portrait.

Mlle. Cormon considered it a duty to talk ; not that she was naturally loquacious, for, unfortunately, with her dearth of ideas and very limited stock of phrases, it was difficult to hold forth at any length ; but she thought that in this way she was fulfilling the social duties prescribed by religion, which bids us be agreeable to our neighbor.   It was a duty which weighed so much upon her mind that she had submitted this case of conscience out of the " Child's Guide to Manners " to her director, the Abbé Couturier.   Whereupon, so far from being disarmed by the penitent's humble admission of the violence of her mental struggles to find something to say, the old ecclesiastic, being firm in matters of discipline, read her a whole chapter out of St. François de Sales on the " Duties of a Woman in the World ; " on the decent gayety of the pious Christian female, and the duty of confining her austerities to herself ; a woman, according to this authority, ought to be amiable in her home and to act in such sort that her neighbor never feels dull in her company.   After this, Mlle. Cormon, with a deep sense of duty, was anxious to obey her director at any cost.   He had bidden her to discourse agreeably, so every time the conversation languished she felt the perspiration breaking out over her with the violence of her exertions to find something to say which should stimulate the flagging interest.   She would come out with odd remarks at such times.   Once she revived, with some success, a discussion on the ubiquity of the apostles (of which she understood not a syllable) by the unexpected observation that " You cannot be in two places at once unless you are a bird."   With such conversational cues as these, the lady had earned the title of " dear, good Mademoiselle Cormon " in her set, which phrase, in the mouth of local wits, might be taken to mean that she was as ignorant as a carp, and a bit of a " natural ; " but there were plenty of people of her own calibre to take the remark literally, and reply: "Oh, yes, Mademoiselle Cormon is very good."

Sometimes (always in her desire to be agreeable to her guests and fulfill her duties as a hostess) she asked such absurd questions that everybody burst out laughing. She wanted to know, for example, what the Government did with the taxes which it had been receiving all these years; or how it was that the Bible had not been printed in the time of Christ, seeing that it had been written by Moses. Altogether she was on a par with the English country gentleman, a member of the House of Commons, who made the famous speech in which he said: "I am always hearing of Posterity; I should very much like to know what Posterity has done for the country."

On such occasions, the heroic Chevalier de Valois came to the rescue, bringing up all the resources of his wit and tact at the sight of the smiles exchanged by pitiless smatterers. He loved to give to woman, did this elderly noble; he lent his wit to Mlle. Cormon by coming to her assistance with a paradox, and covered her retreat so well, that sometimes it seemed as if she had said nothing foolish. She once owned seriously that she did not know the difference between an ox* and a bull. The enchanting chevalier stopped the roars of laughter by saying that oxen could never be more than uncles to the bullocks. Another time, hearing much talk of cattle-breeding and its difficulties—a topic which often comes up in conversation in the neighborhood of the superb du Pin stud—she so far grasped the technicalities of horse-breeding as to ask: "Why, if they wanted colts, they did not serve a mare twice a year?" The chevalier drew down the laughter upon himself.

"It is quite possible," said he. The company pricked up its ears.

"The fault lies with the naturalists," he continued; "they

* Draught oxen are emasculated.

have not found out how to breed mares that are less than eleven months in foal.''

Poor Mlle. Cormon no more understood the meaning of the words than the difference between the ox and the bull. The chevalier met with no gratitude for his pains; his chivalrous services were beyond the reach of the lady's comprehension. She saw that the conversation grew livelier; she was relieved to find that she was not so stupid as she imagined. A day came at last when she settled down in her ignorance, like the Duc de Brancas; and the hero of "Le Distrait," it may be remembered, made himself so comfortable in the ditch after his fall that, when the people came to pull him out, he asked what they wanted with him. Since a somewhat recent period Mlle. Cormon had lost her fears. She brought out her conversational cues with a self-possession akin to that solemn manner—the very coxcombry of stupidity—which accompanies the fatuous utterances of British patriotism.

As she went with stately steps toward the terrace, therefore, she was chewing the cud of reflection, seeking for some question which should draw her uncle out of a silence which always hurt her feelings; she thought that he felt dull.

"Uncle," she began, hanging on his arm, and nestling joyously close to him (for this was another of her make-believes, "If I had a husband, I should do just so!" she thought); "uncle, if everything on earth happens by the will of God, there must be a reason for everything.''

"Assuredly," the Abbé de Sponde answered gravely. He loved his niece, and submitted with angelic patience to be torn from his meditations.

" Then if I never marry at all, it will be because it is the will of God ? ''

" Yes, my child.''

" But still, as there is nothing to prevent me from marrying to-morrow, my will perhaps might thwart the will of God ? ''

" That might be so, if we really knew God's will,'' returned the sub-prior of the Sorbonne. "Remark, my dear, that you insert an *if.*"

Poor Rose was bewildered. She had hoped to lead her uncle to the subject of marriage by way of an argument *ad omnipotentem.* But the naturally obtuse are wont to adopt the remorseless logic of childhood, which is to say, they proceed from the answer to another question, a method frequently found embarrassing.

"But, uncle," she persisted, "God cannot mean women never to marry; for if He did, all of them ought to be either unmarried or married. Their lots are distributed unjustly."

"My child," said the good abbé, "you are finding fault with the church, which teaches that celibacy is a more excellent way to God."

"But if the church was right, and everybody was a good Catholic, there would soon be no more people, uncle."

"You are too ingenious, Rose; there is no need to be so ingenious to be happy."

Such words brought a smile of satisfaction to poor Rose's lips and confirmed her in the good opinion which she began to conceive of herself. Behold how the world, like our friends and enemies, contributes to strengthen our faults. At this moment guests began to arrive, and the conversation was interrupted. On these high festival occasions, the disposition of the rooms brought about little familiarities between the servants and invited guests. Mariette saw the president of the Tribunal, a triple expansion glutton, as he passed by her kitchen.

"Oh, Monsieur du Ronceret, I have been making cauliflower *au gratin* on purpose for you, for mademoiselle knows how fond you are of it. 'Mind you do not fail with it, Mariette,' she said; 'Monsieur le Président is coming.'"

"Good Mademoiselle Cormon," returned the man of law. "Mariette, did you baste the cauliflowers with gravy instead of stock? It is more savory." And the president did not disdain to enter the council-chamber where Mariette ruled the roast, nor to cast an epicure's eye over her preparations, and give his opinion as a master of the craft.

"Good-day, madame," said Josette, addressing Mme. Granson, who sedulously cultivated the waiting-woman. "Mademoiselle has not forgotten you; you are to have a dish of fish."

As for the Chevalier de Valois, he spoke to Mariette with the jocularity of a great noble unbending to an inferior—

"Well, dear cordon bleu, I would give you the cross of the Legion of Honor if I could; tell me, is there any dainty morsel for which one ought to save one's self?"

"Yes, yes, Monsieur de Valois, a hare from the Prébaudet; it weighed fourteen pounds!"

"That's a good girl," said the chevalier, patting Josette on the cheek with two fingers. "Ah! weighs fourteen pounds, does it?"

Du Bousquier was not of the party. Mlle. Cormon treated him hardly, faithful to her system before described. In the very bottom of her heart she felt an inexplicable drawing toward this man of fifty, whom she had once refused. Sometimes she repented of that refusal, and yet she had a presentiment that she should marry him after all, and a dread of him which forbade her to wish for the marriage. These ideas stimulated her interest in du Bousquier. The Republican's herculean proportions produced an effect upon her which she would not admit to herself; and the Chevalier de Valois and Mme. Granson, while they could not explain Mlle. Cormon's inconsistencies, had detected naïve, furtive glances, sufficiently clear in their significance to set them both on the watch to ruin the hopes which du Bousquier clearly entertained in spite of a first check.

Two guests kept the others waiting, but their official duties excused them both. One was M. du Coudrai, registrar of mortgages; the other, M. Choisnel, had once acted as land-steward to the Marquis de Gordes. Choisnel was the notary of the old noblesse, and received everywhere among them with the distinction which his merits deserved; he had beside a not inconsiderable private fortune. When the two late-comers arrived, Jacquelin, the manservant, seeing them turn to go into the drawing-room, came forward with: "'They' are all in the garden."

The registrar of mortgages was one of the most amiable men in the town. There were but two things against him— he had married an old woman for her money in the first place, and in the second it was his habit to perpetrate outrageous puns, at which he was the first to laugh. But, doubtless, the stomachs of the guests were growing impatient, for at first sight he was hailed with that faint sigh which usually welcomes last-comers under such circumstances. Pending the official announcement of dinner, the company strolled up and down the terrace by the Brillante, looking out over the stream with its bed of mosaic and its water-plants, at the so picturesque details of the row of houses huddled together on the opposite bank; the old-fashioned wooden balconies, the tumble-down window-sills, the balks of timber that shored up a story projecting over the river, the cabinet-maker's workshop, the tiny gardens where odds and ends of clothing were hanging out to dry. It was, in short, the poor quarter of a country town, to which the near neighborhood of the water, a weeping willow drooping over the bank, a rosebush or so, and a few flowers had lent an indescribable charm, worthy of a landscape painter's brush.

The chevalier meanwhile was narrowly watching the faces of the guests. He knew that his firebrand had very successfully taken hold of the best coteries in the town; but no one spoke openly of Suzanne and du Bousquier and the great news as yet. The art of distilling scandal is possessed by provincials in a supreme degree. It was felt that the time was not yet ripe for open discussion of the strange event. Every one was bound to go through a private rehearsal first.   So it was whispered—

"Have you heard?"

"Yes."

"Du Bousquier?"

"And the fair Suzanne."

"Does Mademoiselle Cormon know anything?"

"No."

"Ah!"

This was gossip *piano*, presently destined to swell into a *crescendo* when they were ready to discuss the first dish of scandal.

All of a sudden the chevalier confronted Mme. Granson. That lady had sported her green bonnet, trimmed with auriculas; her face was beaming.   Was she simply longing to begin the concert?   Such news is as good as a gold-mine to be worked in the monotonous lives of these people; but the observant and uneasy chevalier fancied that he read something more in the good lady's expression—to wit, the exultation of self-interest!   At once he turned to look at Athanase, and detected in his silence the signs of profound concentration of some kind.   In another moment the young man's glance at Mlle. Cormon's figure, which sufficiently resembled a pair of regimental kettledrums, shot a sudden light across the chevalier's brain.   By that gleam he could read the whole past.

"Egad!" he said to himself, "what a slap in the face I have laid myself out to get!"

He went across to offer his arm to Mlle. Cormon, so that he might afterward take her in to dinner.   She regarded the chevalier with respectful esteem; for, in truth, with his name and position in the aristocratic constellations of the province, he was one of the most brilliant ornaments of her salon.   In her heart of hearts, she had longed to be Mme. de Valois at any time during the past twelve years.   The name was like a branch for the swarming thoughts of her brain to cling about

IT ONCE HE TU

—he fulfilled all her ideals as to the birth, quality, and externals of an eligible man. But while the Chevalier de Valois was the choice of heart and brain and social ambition, the elderly ruin, curled though he was like a St. John of a procession-day, filled Mlle. Cormon with dismay; the heiress saw nothing but the noble; the woman could not think of him as a husband. The chevalier's affectation of indifference to marriage, and still more his unimpeachable character in a houseful of workgirls, had seriously injured him, contrary to his own expectations. The man of quality, so clear-sighted in the matter of the annuity, miscalculated on this subject; and Mlle. Cormon herself was not aware that her private reflections upon the too well-conducted chevalier might have been translated by the remark: "What a pity that he is not a little bit of a rake!"

Students of human nature have remarked these leanings of the saint toward the sinner, and wondered at a taste so little in accordance, as they imagine, with Christian virtue. But, to go no further, what nobler destiny for a virtuous woman than the task of cleansing, after the manner of charcoal, the turbid waters of vice? How is it that nobody has seen that these generous creatures, confined by their principles to strict conjugal fidelity, must naturally desire a mate of great practical experience? A reformed rake makes the best husband. And so it came to pass that the poor spinster must sigh over the chosen vessel, offered her as it were in two pieces. Heaven alone could weld the Chevalier du Valois and du Bousquier in one.

If the significance of the few words exchanged between the chevalier and Mlle. Cormon is to be properly understood, it is necessary to put other matters before the reader. Two very serious questions were dividing Alençon into two camps, and, moreover, du Bousquier was mixed up in both affairs in some mysterious way. The first of these debates concerned the curé. He had taken the oath of allegiance in the time of the

6

Revolution, and now was living down orthodox prejudices by setting an example of the loftiest goodness. He was a Cheverus on a smaller scale, and so much was he appreciated, that when he died the whole town wept for him. Mlle. Cormon and the Abbé de Sponde belonged, however, to the minority, to the church sublime in its orthodoxy, a section which was to the Court of Rome as the Ultras were shortly to be to the Court of Louis XVIII. The abbé, in particular, declined to recognize the church that had submitted to force and made terms with the Constitutionnels. So the curé was never seen in the salon of the Maison Cormon, and the sympathies of its frequenters were with the officiating priest of St. Leonard's, the aristocratic church in Alençon. Du Bousquier, that rabid Liberal under a Royalist's skin, knew how necessary it is to find standards to rally the discontented, who form, as it were, the back-shop of every opposition, and therefore he had already enlisted the sympathies of the trading classes for the curé.

Now for the second affair. The same blunt diplomatist was the secret instigator of a scheme for building a theatre, an idea which had only lately sprouted in Alençon. Du Bousquier's zealots knew not their Mahomet, but they were the more ardent in their defense of what they believed to be their own plan. Athanase was one of the very hottest of the partisans in favor of the theatre; in the mayor's office for several days past he had been pleading for the cause which all the younger men had taken up.

To return to the chevalier. He offered his arm to Mlle. Cormon, who thanked him with a radiant glance for this attention. For all answer, the chevalier indicated Athanase by a meaning look.

"Mademoiselle," he began, "as you have such well-balanced judgment in matters of social convention, and as that young man is related to you in some way——"

"Very distantly," she broke in.

"Ought you not to use the influence which you possess with him and his mother to prevent him from going utterly to the bad? He is not very religious as it is; he defends that perjured priest; but that is nothing. It is a much more serious matter; is he not plunging thoughtlessly into opposition without realizing how his conduct may affect his prospects? He is scheming to build this theatre; he is the dupe of that Republican in disguise, du Bousquier——"

"Dear me, Monsieur de Valois, his mother tells me that he is so clever, and he has not a word to say for himself; he always stands planted before you like a 'statute'——"

"Of limitations," cried the registrar. "I caught that flying. I present my *devoars* to the Chevalier de Valois," he added, saluting the latter with the exaggeration of Henri Monnier as "Joseph Prudhomme," an admirable type of the class to which M. du Coudrai belonged.

M. de Valois, in return, gave him the abbreviated patronizing nod of a noble standing on his dignity; then he drew Mlle. Cormon farther along the terrace by the distance of several flower-pots, to make the registrar understand that he did not wish to be overheard.

Then, lowering his voice, he bent to say in Mlle. Cormon's ear: "How can you expect that lads educated in these detestable Imperial Lyceums should have any ideas? Great ideas and a lofty love can only come of right courses and nobleness of life. It is not difficult to foresee, from the look of the poor fellow, that he will be weak in his intellect and come to a miserable end. See how pale and haggard he looks!"

"His mother says that he works far too hard," she replied innocently. "He spends his nights, think of it! in reading books and writing. What good can it possibly do a young man's prospects to sit up writing at night?"

"Why, it exhausts him," said the chevalier, trying to bring the lady's thoughts back to the point, which was to disgust her with Athanase. "The things that went on in those Imperial Lyceums were something really shocking."

"Oh yes," said the simple lady. "Did they not make them walk out with drums in front? The masters had no more religion than heathens; and they put them in uniform, poor boys, exactly as if they had been soldiers. What notions!"

"And see what comes of it," continued the chevalier, indicating Athanase. "In my time, where was the young man that could not look a pretty woman in the face? Now, *he* lowers his eyes as soon as he sees you. That young man alarms me, because I am interested in him. Tell him not to intrigue with Bonapartists, as he is doing, to build this theatre; if these little youngsters do not raise an insurrection and demand it (for insurrection and constitution, to my mind, are two words for the same thing), the authorities will build it. And tell his mother to look after him."

"Oh, she will not allow him to see these half-pay people or to keep low company, I am sure. I will speak to him about it," said Mlle. Cormon; "he might lose his situation at the mayor's office. And then what would they do, he and his mother? It makes one shudder."

As M. de Talleyrand said of his wife, so said the chevalier within himself at that moment, as he looked at the lady—

"If there is a stupider woman, I should like to see her. On the honor of a gentleman, if virtue makes a woman so stupid as this, is it not a vice? And yet, what an adorable wife she would make for a man of my age! What principle! What ignorance of life"

Please to bear in mind that these remarks were addressed to the Princess Goritza during the manipulation of a pinch of snuff.

Mme. Granson felt instinctively that the chevalier was talking of Athanase. In her eagerness to know what he had been saying, she followed Mlle. Cormon, who walked up to the young man in question, putting out six feet of dignity in front; but at that very moment Jacquelin announced that "Mademoiselle was served," and the mistress of the house shot an appealing glance at the chevalier. But the gallant registrar of mortgages was beginning to see a something in M. de Valois' manner, a glimpse of the barrier which the noblesse were about to raise between themselves and the bourgeoisie; so, delighted with a chance to cut out the chevalier, he crooked his arm, and Mlle. Cormon was obliged to take it. M. de Valois, from motives of policy, fastened upon Mme. Granson.

"Mademoiselle Cormon takes the liveliest interest in your dear Athanase, my dear lady," he said, as they slowly followed in the wake of the other guests, "but that interest is falling off through your son's fault. He is lax and Liberal in his opinions; he is agitating for this theatre; he is mixed up with the Bonapartists; he takes the part of the Constitutionnel curé. This line of conduct may cost him his situation. You know how carefully his majesty's government is weeding the service. If your dear Athanase is once cashiered, where will he find employment? He must not get into bad odor with the authorities."

"Oh, Monsieur le Chevalier," cried the poor startled mother, "what do I not owe you for telling me this! You are right; my boy is a tool in the hands of a bad set; I will open his eyes to his position."

It was long since the chevalier had sounded Athanase's character at a glance. He saw in the depths of the young man's nature the scarcely malleable material of Republican convictions; a lad at that age will sacrifice everything for such ideas if he is smitten with the word Liberty, that so vague, so little comprehended word which is like a standard of revolt for those at the bottom of the wheel for whom revolt means revenge. Athanase was sure to stick to his opinions, for he had woven them, with his artist's sorrows and his embittered views of the social framework, into his political creed. He was ready to sacrifice his future at the outset for these opinions, not knowing that he, like all men of real ability, would have seen reason to modify them by the time he reached the age of six-and-thirty, when a man has formed his own conclusions of life, with its intricate relations and interdependences. If Athanase was faithful to the opposition in Alençon, he would fall into disgrace with Mlle. Cormon. Thus far the chevalier saw clearly.

And so this little town, so peaceful in appearance, was to the full as much agitated internally as any congress of diplomates, when craft and guile and passion and self-interest are met to discuss the weightiest questions between empire and empire.

Meanwhile the guests gathered about the table were eating their way through the first course as people eat in the provinces, without a blush for an honest appetite; whereas, in Paris, it would appear that our jaws are controlled by sumptuary edicts which deliberately set the laws of anatomy at defiance. We eat with the tips of our teeth in Paris, we filch the pleasures of the table, but in the provinces things are taken more naturally; possibly existence centres a little too much about the great and universal method of maintenance to which God condemns all His creatures. It was at the end of the first course that Mlle. Cormon brought out the most celebrated of all her conversational cues; it was talked of for two years afterward; it is quoted even now, indeed, in the lower bourgeois strata of Alençon whenever her marriage is under discussion. Over the last entrée but one, the conversation waxed lively and wordy, turning, as might have been expected, upon the affair of the theatre and the curé. In the first enthusiasm of royalism in 1816, those extremists, who were afterward called *les jésuites du pays*, or country jesuits, were for expelling the Abbé François from his cure. M. de Valois suspected du Bousquier of supporting the priest

and instigating the intrigues; at any rate, the noble chevalier
piled the burdens on du Bousquier's back with his wonted
skill; and du Bousquier, being unrepresented by counsel, was
condemned and put in the pillory.   Among those present,
Athanase was the only person sufficiently frank to stand up for
the absent, and he felt that he was not in a position to bring out
his ideas before these Alençon magnates, of whose intellects
he had the meanest opinion.   Only in the provinces nowadays will you find young men keeping a respectful countenance before people of a certain age without daring to have a
a fling at their elders or to contradict them too flatly.   To
resume: On the advent of some delicious *canards aux olives*,
the conversation first decidedly flagged, and then suddenly
dropped dead.   Mlle. Cormon, emulous of her own poultry,
invented another *canard* in her anxiety to defend du Bousquier, who had been represented as an arch-concoctor of
intrigue, and a man to set mountains fighting.

"For my own part," said she, "I thought that Monsieur
du Bousquier gave his whole attention to childish matters."

Under the circumstances, the epigram produced a tremendous effect.   Mlle. Cormon had a great success; she brought
the Princess Goritza face downward on the table.   The chevalier, by no means expecting his Dulcinea to say anything so
much to the purpose, could find no words to express his admiration; he applauded after the Italian fashion, noiselessly,
with the tips of his fingers.

"She is adorably witty," he said, turning to Mme. Granson.
"I have always said that she would unmask her batteries some
day."

"But when you know her very well, she is charming,"
said the widow.

"All women, madame, have *esprit* when you know them
well."

When the Homeric laughter subsided, Mlle. Cormon asked
for an explanation of her success.   Then the chorus of scandal

grew to a height. Du Bousquier was transformed into a bachelor Father Gigogne ; it was he who filled the Foundling Hospital ; the immorality of his life was laid bare at last ; it was all of a piece with his Paris orgies, and so forth and so forth. Led by the Chevalier de Valois, the cleverest of conductors of this kind of orchestra, the overture was something magnificent.

"I do not know," said he, with much indulgence, "what there could possibly be to prevent a du Bousquier from marrying Mademoiselle Suzanne whatever-it-is, what do you call her ? Suzette ! I only know the children by sight, though I lodge with Mme. Lardot. If this Suzon is a tall, fine-looking forward sort of girl with gray eyes, a slender figure, and little feet—I have not paid much attention to these things, but she seemed to me to be very insolent and very much du Bousquier's superior in the matter of manners. Beside, Suzanne has the nobility of beauty ; from that point of view, she would certainly make a marriage beneath her. The Emperor Joseph, you know, had the curiosity to go to see the du Barry at Luciennes. He offered her his arm ; and when the poor courtesan, overcome by such an honor, hesitated to take it : ' Beauty is always a queen,' said the Emperor. Remark that the Emperor Joseph was an Austrian German," added the chevalier ; "but, believe me, that Germany, which we think of as a very boorish country, is really a land of noble chivalry and fine manners, especially toward Poland and Hungary, where there are——" Here the chevalier broke off, fearing to make an allusion to his own happy fortune in the past ; he only took up his snuff-box and confided the rest to the princess who had smiled on him for thirty-six years.

"The speech was delicately considerate for Louis XV.," said du Ronceret.

"But we are talking of the Emperor Joseph, I believe," returned Mlle. Cormon, with a knowing little air.

"Mademoiselle," said the chevalier, seeing the wicked

glances exchanged by the president, the registrar, and the notary, "Madame du Barry was Louis Quinze's Suzanne, a fact known well enough to us scapegraces, but which young ladies are not expected to know. Your ignorance shows that the diamond is flawless. The corruptions of history have not so much as touched you."

At this the Abbé de Sponde looked graciously upon M. de Valois and bent his head in laudatory approval.

"Do you not know history, mademoiselle?" asked the registrar.

"If you muddle up Louis XV. and Suzanne, how can you expect me to know your history?" was Mlle. Cormon's angelic reply. She was so pleased! The dish was empty and the conversation revived to such purpose that everybody was laughing with their mouths full at her last simple but ingenuous observation.

"Poor young thing!" said the Abbé de Sponde. "When once trouble comes, that love divine called charity is as blind as the pagan love, and should see nothing of the causes of the trouble. You are president of the Maternity Society, Rose; this child will need help; it will not be easy for her to find a husband."

"Poor child!" said Mlle. Cormon.

"Is du Bousquier going to marry her, do you suppose?" asked the president of the Tribunal.

"It would be his duty to do so if he were a decent man," said Mme. Granson; "but, really, my dog has better notions of decency——"

"And yet Azor is a great forager," put in the registrar, trying a joke this time as a change from a pun.

They were still talking of du Bousquier over the dessert. He was the butt of uncounted playful jests, which grew more and more thunder-charged under the influence of wine. Led off by the registrar, they followed up one pun with another. Du Bousquier's character was now ap-parent; he was not a

father of the church, nor a reverend father, nor yet a con-
script father, and so on and so on, till the Abbé de Sponde
said: "In any case, he is not a foster-father," with a gravity
that checked the laughter.

"Nor a heavy father," added the chevalier.

The church and the aristocracy had descended into the
arena of word-play without loss of dignity.

"Hush!" said the registrar, "I can hear du Bousquier's
boots creaking; he is in over shoes over boots, and no mistake."

It nearly always happens that when a man's name is in
every one's mouth, he is the last to hear what is said of him;
the whole town may be talking of him, slandering him or
crying him down, and if he has no friends to repeat what
other people say of him, he is not likely to hear it. So the
blameless du Bousquier, du Bousquier who would fain have
been guilty, who wished that Suzanne had not lied to him,
was supremely unconscious of all that was taking place. Nobody had spoken to him of Suzanne's revelations; for that
matter, everybody thought it indiscreet to ask questions about
the affair, when the man most concerned sometimes possesses
secrets which compel him to keep silence. So when the people
adjourned for coffee to the drawing-room, where several evening visitors were already assembled, du Bousquier wore an
irresistible and slightly fatuous air.

Mlle. Cormon, counseled by confusion, dared not look
toward the terrible seducer. She took possession of Athanase
and administered a lecture, bringing out the oddest assort-
ment of the commonplaces of Royalist doctrines and edifying
truisms. As the unlucky poet had no snuff-box with a portrait
of a princess on the lid to sustain him under the shower-bath
of foolish utterances, it was with a vacant expression that he
heard his adored lady. His eyes were fixed on that enormous
bust, which maintained the absolute repose characteristic of
great masses. Desire wrought a kind of intoxication in him.

The old maid's thin, shrill voice became low music for his ears; her platitudes were fraught with ideas.

Love is an utterer of false coin; he is always at work transforming common copper into gold louis; sometimes, also, he makes his seeming douzains* of fine gold.

"Well, Athanase, will you promise me?"

The final phrase struck on the young man's ear; he woke with a start from a blissful dream.

"What, mademoiselle?" returned he.

Mlle. Cormon rose abruptly and glanced across at du Bousquier. At that moment he looked like the brawny fabulous deity, whose likeness you behold upon Republican three-franc pieces. She went over to Mme. Granson and said in a confidential tone:

"Your son is weak in his intellect, my poor friend. That lyceum has been the ruin of him," she added, recollecting how the Chevalier de Valois had insisted on the bad education given in those institutions.

Here was a thunderbolt! Poor Athanase had had his chance of flinging fire upon the dried stems heaped up in the old maid's heart, and he had not known it! If he had but listened to her, he might have made her understand; for in Mlle. Cormon's present highly wrought mood a word would have been enough, but the very force of the stupefying cravings of love-sick youth had spoiled his chances; so sometimes a child full of life kills himself through ignorance.

"What can you have been saying to Mademoiselle Cormon?" asked his mother.

"Nothing."

"Nothing? I will have this cleared up," she said, and put off serious business to the morrow; du Bousquier was hopelessly lost, she thought, and the speech troubled her very little.

Soon the four card-tables received their complement of

* Old French sou.

players.   Four persons sat down to piquet, the most expensive amusement of the evening, over which a good deal of money changed hands.   M. Choisnel, the attorney for the crown, and a couple of ladies went to the red-lacquered cabinet for a game of tric-trac.   The candles in the wall-sconces were lighted, and then the flower of Mlle. Cormon's set blossomed out about the fire, on the settees, and about the tables.   Each new couple, on entering the room, made the same remark to Mlle. Cormon: "So you are going to the Prébaudet to-morrow?"

"Yes, I really must," she said, in answer to each.

All through the evening the hostess wore a preoccupied air. Mme. Granson was the first to see that she was not at all like herself.   Mlle. Cormon was thinking.

"What are you thinking about, cousin?" Mme. Granson asked at last, finding her sitting in the boudoir.

"I am thinking of that poor girl.   Am I not patroness of the Maternity Society?   I will go now to find ten crowns for you."

"*Ten crowns!*" exclaimed Mme. Granson.   "Why, you have never given so much to any one before!"

"But, my dear, it is so natural to have a child."

This improper cry from the heart struck the treasurer of the Maternity Society dumb from sheer astonishment.   Du Bousquier had actually gone up in Mlle. Cormon's opinion!

"Really," began Mme. Granson, "du Bousquier is not merely a monster—he is a villain into the bargain.   When a man has spoiled somebody else's life, it is his duty surely to make amends.   It should be his part rather than ours to rescue this young person; and when all comes to all, she is a bad girl, it seems to me, for there are better men in Alençon than that cynic of a du Bousquier.   A girl must be shameless indeed to have anything to do with him."

"Cynic?   Your son, dear, teaches you Latin words that are quite beyond me.   Certainly I do not want to make excuses for Monsieur du Bousquier ; but explain to me why it is immoral for a woman to prefer one man to another ?''

"Dear cousin, suppose now that you were to marry my Athanase ; there would be nothing but what was very natural in that. He is young and good-looking ; he has a future before him ; Alençon will be proud of him some day. But—every one would think that you took such a young man as your husband for the sake of greater conjugal felicity. Slanderous tongues would say that you were making a sufficient provision of bliss for yourself. There would be jealous women to bring charges of depravity against you. But what would it matter to you? You would be dearly loved—loved sincerely. If Athanase seemed to you to be weak of intellect, my dear, it is because he has too many ideas. Extremes meet. He is as clean in his life as a girl of fifteen ; *he* has not wallowed in the pollutions of Paris. Well, now, change the terms, as my poor husband used to say. It is relatively just the same situation as du Bousquier's and Suzanne's. But what would be slander in your case is true in every way of du Bousquier. Now do you understand ?''

"No more than if you were talking Greek," said Rose Cormon, opening wide eyes and exerting all the powers of her understanding.

"Well, then, cousin, since one must put dots on all the *i*'s, it is quite out of the question that Suzanne should love du Bousquier. And when the heart counts for nothing in such an affair——''

"Why, really, cousin, how should people love if not with their hearts?''

At this Mme. Granson thought within herself, as the chevalier had thought—

"The poor cousin is too innocent by far. This goes beyond the permissible——'' Aloud she said : "Dear girl, it seems to me that a child is not conceived of spirit alone.''

"Why, yes, dear, for the Holy Virgin——''

"But, my dear, good girl, du Bousquier is not the Holy Ghost."

"That is true," returned the spinster; "he is a man—a man dangerous enough for his friends to recommend him strongly to marry."

"You, cousin, might bring that about——"

"Oh, how?" cried the spinster, with a glow of Christian charity.

"Decline to receive him until he takes a wife. For the sake of religion and morality, you ought to make an example of him under the circumstances."

"We will talk of this again, dear Madame Granson, when I come back from the Prébaudet. I will ask advice of my uncle and the Abbé Couturier," and Mlle. Cormon went back to the large drawing-room. The liveliest hour of the evening had begun.

The lights, the groups of well-dressed women, the serious and magisterial air of the assembly, filled Mlle. Cormon with pride in the aristocratic appearance of the rooms, a pride in which her guests all shared. There were plenty of people who thought that the finest company of Paris itself was no finer. At that moment du Bousquier, playing a rubber with M. de Valois and two elderly ladies, Mme. du Coudrai and Mme. du Ronceret, was the object of suppressed curiosity. Several women came up on the pretext of watching the game, and gave him such odd, albeit furtive, glances that the old bachelor at last began to think that there must be something amiss with his appearance.

"Can it be that my toupet is askew?" he asked himself. And he felt that all-absorbing uneasiness to which the elderly bachelor is peculiarly subject. A blunder gave him an excuse for leaving the table at the end of the seventh rubber.

"I cannot touch a card but I lose," he said; "I am decidedly too unlucky at cards."

"You are lucky in other respects," said the chevalier, with

a knowing look. Naturally, the joke made the round of the room, and every one exclaimed over the exquisite breeding shown by the Prince Talleyrand of Alençon.

"There is no one like Monsieur de Valois' for saying such things," said the niece of the curé of St. Leonard's.

Du Bousquier went up to the narrow mirror above The Deserter, but he could detect nothing unusual.

Toward ten o'clock, after innumerable repetitions of the same phrase with every possible variation, the long ante-chamber began to fill with visitors preparing to embark; Mlle. Cormon convoying a few favored guests as far as the steps for a farewell embrace. Knots of guests took their departure, some in the direction of the Brittany road and the château, and others turning toward the quarter by the Sarthe. And then began the exchange of remarks with which the streets had echoed at the same hour for a score of years. There was the inevitable : "Mademoiselle Cormon looked very well this evening."

"Mademoiselle Cormon? She looked strange, I thought."

"How the abbé stoops, poor man! And how he goes to sleep—did you see? He never knows where the cards are now; his mind wanders."

"We shall be very sorry to lose him."

"It is a fine night. We shall have a fine day to-morrow."

"Fine weather for the apples to set."

"You beat us to-night; you always do when Monsieur de Valois is your partner."

"Then how much did he win?"

"To-night? Why, he won three or four francs. He never loses."

"Faith, no. There are three hundred and sixty-five days in the year, you know; at that rate, whist is as good as a farm for him."

"Oh! what bad luck we had to-night!"

"You are very fortunate, monsieur and madame, here you

are at your own doorstep, while we have half the town to cross."

"I do not pity you; you could keep a gig if you liked, you need not go afoot."

"Ah! monsieur, we have a daughter to marry (that means one wheel), and a son to keep in Paris, and that takes the other."

"Are you still determined to make a magistrate of him?"

"What can one do? You must do something with a boy, and beside, it is no disgrace to serve the King."

Sometimes a discussion on cider or flax was continued on the way, the very same things being said at the same season year after year. If any observer of human nature had lived in that particular street, their conversation would have supplied him with an almanac. At this moment, however, the talk was of a decidedly Rabelaisian turn; for du Bousquier, walking on ahead by himself, was humming the well-known tune *"Femme sensible, écouter-tu le ramage ?"* without a suspicion of its appropriateness. Some of the party held that du Bousquier was uncommonly long-headed, and that people judged him unjustly. President du Ronceret inclined toward this view since he had been confirmed in his post by a new royal decree. The rest regarded the forage-contractor as a dangerous man of lax morals, of whom anything might be expected. In the provinces, as in Paris, public men are very much in the position of the statue in Addison's ingenious fable. The statue was erected at a place where four roads met; two cavaliers coming up on opposite sides declared, the one that it was white, the other that it was black, until they came to blows, and both of them lying on the ground discovered that it was black on one side and white on the other, while a third cavalier coming up to their assistance affirmed that it was red.

When the Chevalier de Valois reached home, he said to himself: "It is time to spread a report that I am going to

marry Mademoiselle Cormon. The news shall come from the
d'Esgrignon's salon; it shall go straight to the bishop's palace
at Séez and come back through one of the vicars-general to
the curé of St. Leonard's. He will not fail to tell the Abbé
Couturier, and in this way Mademoiselle Cormon will receive
the shot well under the water-line. The old Marquis d'Esgrignon is sure to ask the Abbé de Sponde to dinner to put a
stop to gossip which might injure Mademoiselle Cormon if I
fail to come forward; or me, if she refuses me. The abbé
shall be well and duly entangled; and after a call from Mademoiselle de Gordes, in the course of which the grandeur and
the prospects of the alliance will be put before Mademoiselle
Cormon, she is not likely to hold out. The abbé will leave
her more than a hundred thousand crowns; and as for her,
she must have put by more than a hundred thousand livres by
this time; she has her house, the Prébaudet, and some fifteen
thousand livres per annum. One word to my friend the
Comte de Fontaine, and I am Mayor of Alençon, and deputy;
then, once seated on the right-hand benches, the way to a
peerage is cleared by a well-timed cry of ' Clôture,' or
' Order.' ''

When Mme. Granson reached home, she had a warm explanation with her son. He could not be made to understand the connection between his political opinions and his
love. It was the first quarrel which had troubled the peace
of the poor little household.

Next morning, at nine o'clock, Mlle. Cormon, packed into
the cariole with Josette by her side, drove up the Rue Saint-
Blaise on her way to the Prébaudet, looking like a pyramid
above an ocean of packages. And the event which was to
surprise her there and hasten on her marriage was unseen as
yet by Mme. Granson, or du Bousquier, or M. de Valois, or
by Mlle. Cormon herself. Chance is the greatest artist of
all.

7

On the morrow of mademoiselle's arrival at the Prébaudet, she was very harmlessly engaged in taking her eight-o'clock breakfast, while she listened to the reports of her bailiff and gardener, when Jacquelin, in a great flurry, burst into the dining-room.

"Mademoiselle," cried he, "Monsieur l'Abbé has sent an express messenger to you; that boy of Mother Grosmort's has come with a letter. The lad left Alençon before daybreak, and yet here he is! He came almost as fast as Penelope. Ought he to have a glass of wine?"

"What can have happened, Josette? Can uncle be——"

"He would not have written if he was," said the woman, guessing her mistress' fears.

Mlle. Cormon glanced over the first few lines.

"Quick! quick!" she cried. "Tell Jacquelin to put Penelope in. Get ready, child, have everything packed in half an hour, we are going back to town," she added, turning to Josette.

"Jacquelin!" called Josette, excited by the expression of Mlle. Cormon's face. Jacquelin on receiving his orders came back to the house to expostulate.

"But, mademoiselle, Penelope has only just been fed."

"Eh! what does that matter to me? I want to start this moment."

"But, mademoiselle, it is going to rain."

"Very well. We shall be wet through."

"The house is on fire," muttered Josette, vexed because her mistress said nothing, but read her letter through to the end, and then began again at the beginning.

"Just finish your coffee at any rate. Don't upset yourself! See how red you are in the face."

"Red in the face, Josette!" exclaimed Mlle. Cormon, going up to the mirror; and as the quick-silvered sheet had come away from the glass, she beheld her countenance doubly distorted. "Oh, dear!" she thought, "I shall look ugly!

Come, come, Josette, child, help me to dress. I want to be
ready before Jacquelin puts Penelope in. If you cannot put
all the things into the chaise, I would rather leave them here
than lose a minute."

If you have fully comprehended the degree of monomania
to which Mlle. Cormon had been driven by her desire to
marry, you will share her excitement. Her worthy uncle informed her that M. de Troisville, a retired soldier from the
Russian service, the grandson of one of his best friends, wishing to settle down in Alençon, had asked for his hospitality
for the sake of the abbé's old friendship with the mayor, his
grandfather, the Vicomte de Troisville of the reign of Louis
XV. M. de Sponde, in alarm, begged his niece to come home
at once to help him to entertain the guest and to do the
honors of the house; for as there had been some delay in
forwarding the letter, M. de Troisville might be expected to
drop in upon him that very evening.

How was it possible after reading that letter to give any
attention to affairs at the Prébaudet? The tenant and the
bailiff, beholding their mistress' dismay, lay low and waited
for orders. When they stopped her passage to ask for instructions, Mlle. Cormon, the despotic old maid, who saw to everything herself at the Prébaudet, answered them with an "As
you please," which struck them dumb with amazement. This
was the mistress who carried administrative zeal to such
lengths that she counted the fruit and entered it under headings, so that she could regulate the consumption by the quantity of each sort!

"I must be dreaming, I think," said Josette, when she saw
her mistress flying upstairs like some elephant on which God
should have bestowed wings.

In a little while, in spite of the pelting rain, mademoiselle
was driving away from the Prébaudet, leaving her people to
have things all their own way. Jacquelin dared not take it
upon himself to drive the placid Penelope any faster than her

usual jog-trot pace ; and the old mare, something like the fair queen after whom she was named, seemed to take a step back for every step forward. Beholding this, mademoiselle bade Jacquelin, in a vinegar voice, to urge the poor astonished beast to a gallop, and to use the whip if necessary, so appalling was the thought that M. de Troisville might arrive before the house was ready for him. A grandson of an old friend of her uncle's could not be much over forty, she thought ; a military man must infallibly be a bachelor. She vowed inwardly that, with her uncle's help, M. de Troisville should not depart in the estate in which he entered the Maison Cormon. Penelope galloped ; but mademoiselle, absorbed in dresses and dreams of a wedding-night, told Jacquelin again and again that he was standing still. She fidgeted in her seat, without vouchsafing any answer to Josette's questions, and talked to herself as if she was revolving mighty matters in her mind.

At last the cariole turned into the long street of Alençon, known as the Rue Saint-Blaise if you come in on the side of Mortagne, the Rue de la Porte de Séez by the time you reach the sign of the Three Moors, and lastly as the Rue du Bercail, when it finally debouches into the highway into Brittany. If Mlle. Cormon's departure for the Prébaudet made a great noise in Alençon, anybody can imagine the hubbub caused by her return on the following day, with the driving rain lashing her face. Everybody remarked Penelope's furious pace, Jacquelin's sly looks, the earliness of the hour, the bundles piled up topsy-turvy, the lively conversation between mistress and maid, and, more than all things, the impatience of the party.

The Troisville estates lay between Alençon and Mortagne. Josette, therefore, knew about the different branches of the family. A word let fall by her mistress just as they reached the paved street of Alençon put Josette in possession of the facts, and a discussion sprang up, in the course of which the two women settled between themselves that the expected guest must be a man of forty or forty-two, a bachelor, neither rich nor poor. Mademoiselle saw herself Vicomtesse de Trois-ville.

"And here is uncle telling me nothing, knowing nothing, and wanting to know nothing! Oh, so like uncle! He would forget his nose if it was not fastened to his face."

Have you not noticed how mature spinsters, under these circumstances, grow as intelligent, fierce, bold, and full of promises as a Richard III.? To them, as to clerics in liquor, nothing is sacred.

In one moment, from the upper end of the Rue Saint-Blaise to the Porte de Séez, the town of Alençon heard of Mlle. Cormon's return with aggravating circumstances, heard with a mighty perturbation of its vitals and trouble of the organs of life public and domestic. Cook-maids, storekeepers, and passers-by carried the news from door to door, then, without delay, it circulated in the upper spheres, and almost simultaneously the words: "Mademoiselle Cormon has come back," exploded like a bomb in every house.

Meanwhile Jacquelin climbed down from his wooden bench in front, polished by some process unknown to cabinet-makers, and with his own hands opened the great gates with the rounded tops. They were closed in Mlle. Cormon's absence as a sign of mourning; for when she went away her house was shut up, and the faithful took it in turn to show hospitality to the Abbé de Sponde. (M. de Valois used to pay his debt by an invitation to dine at the Marquis d'Esgrignon's.) Jacquelin gave the familiar call to Penelope standing in the middle of the road; and the animal, accustomed to this manœuvre, turned into the courtyard, steering clear of the flower-bed, till Jacquelin took the bridle and walked round with the chaise to the steps before the door.

"Mariette!" called Mlle. Cormon.

"Mademoiselle?" returned Mariette, engaged in shutting the gates.

"Has the gentleman come?"

" No, mademoiselle."

" And is my uncle here ? "

" He is at the church, mademoiselle."

Jacquelin and Josette were standing on the lowest step of the flight, holding out their hands to steady their mistress' descent from the cariole ; she, meanwhile, had hoisted herself upon the shaft, and was clutching at the curtains, before springing down into their arms. It was two years since she had dared to trust herself upon the iron step of double strength, secured to the shaft by a fearfully made contrivance with huge bolts.

From the height of the steps, mademoiselle surveyed her courtyard with an air of satisfaction.

" There, there, Mariette, let the great gate alone and come here."

" There is something up," Jacquelin said to Mariette as she came past the chaise.

" Let us see now, child, what is there in the house ? " said Mlle. Cormon, collapsing on the bench in the long antechamber as if she were exhausted.

" Just nothing at all," replied Mariette, hands on hips. " Mademoiselle knows quite well that Monsieur l'Abbé always dines out when she is not at home ; yesterday I went to bring him back from Mademoiselle Armande's."

" Then where is he ? "

" Monsieur l'Abbé ? He is gone to church ; he will not be back till three o'clock."

" Uncle thinks of nothing ! Why couldn't he have sent you to market ? Go down now, Mariette, and, without throwing money away, spare for nothing, get the best, finest, and daintiest of everything. Go to the coach office and ask where people send orders for pâtés. And I want cray-fish from the brooks along the Brillante. What time is it ? "

" Nine o'clock all but a quarter."

" Oh dear, oh dear ; don't lose any time in chattering,

Mariette.   The visitor my uncle is expecting may come at any moment ; pretty figures we should cut if he comes to breakfast.''

Mariette, turning round, saw Penelope in a lather, and gave Jacquelin a glance which said: '' Mademoiselle means to put her hand on a husband this time.''

Mlle. Cormon turned to her housemaid.   '' Now, it is our turn, Josette ; we must make arrangements for Monsieur de Troisville to sleep here to-night.''

How gladly those words were uttered !   '' We must arrange for Monsieur de Troisville '' (pronounced Tréville) '' to sleep here to-night ! ''   How much lay in those few words !   Hope poured like a flood through the old maid's soul.

'' Will you put him in the green chamber ? ''

'' The bishop's room ?   No,'' said mademoiselle, ''it is too near mine.   It is very well for his lordship, a holy man.''

'' Give him your uncle's room.''

'' It looks so bare ; it would not do.''

'' Lord, mademoiselle, you could have a bed put up in the boudoir in a brace of shakes ; there is a fireplace there. Moreau will be sure to find a bedstead in his warehouse that will match the hangings as nearly as possible.''

'' You are right, Josette.   Very well ; run round to Moreau's and ask his advice about everything necessary ; I give you authority.   If the bed, Monsieur de Troisville's bed, can be set up by this evening, so that Monsieur de Troisville shall notice nothing, supposing that Monsieur de Troisville should happen to come in while Moreau is here, I am quite willing. If Moreau cannot promise that, Monsieur de Troisville shall sleep in the green chamber, although Monsieur de Troisville will be very near me.''

Josette departed ; her mistress called her back.

'' Tell Jacquelin all about it,'' she exclaimed in a stern and awful voice ; '' let *him* go to Moreau.   How about my dress ? Suppose Monsieur de Troisville came and caught me like

this, without uncle here to receive him!   Oh, uncle! uncle!
Come, Josette, you shall help me to dress."

"But how about Penelope?" the woman began imprudently.   Mlle. Cormon's eyes shot sparks for the first and
last time in her life.

"It is always Penelope!   Penelope this, Penelope that!   Is
Penelope mistress here?"

"She is all of a lather, and she has not been fed."

"Eh! and if she dies, let her die——" cried Mlle. Cormon—"so long as I am married," she added in her own
mind.

Josette stood stockstill a moment in amazement, such a
remark was tantamount to murder; then, at a sign from
her mistress, she dashed headlong down the steps into the
yard.

"Mademoiselle is possessed, Jacquelin!" were Josette's
first words.

And in this way, everything that occurred throughout the
day led up to the great climax which was to change the whole
course of Mlle. Cormon's life.   The town was already turned
upside down by five aggravating circumstances which attended
the lady's sudden return, to wit—the pouring rain; Penelope's panting pace and sunk flanks covered with foam; the
earliness of the hour; the untidy bundles; and the spinster's
strange, scared looks.   But when Mariette invaded the market
to carry off everything that she could lay her hands on; when
Jacquelin went to inquire for a bedstead of the principal up-
holsterer in the Rue Porte de Séez, close by the church; here,
indeed, was material on which to build the gravest conjecture!
The strange event was discussed on the parade and the promenade; every one was full of it, not excepting Mlle. Armande,
on whom the Chevalier de Valois happened to be calling at
the time.

Only two days ago Alençon had been stirred to its depths
by occurrences of such capital importance that worthy matrons

were still exclaiming that it was like the end of the world! And now, this last news was summed up in all houses by the inquiry:

" What can be happening at the Cormons'? "

The Abbé de Sponde, skillfully questioned when he emerged from St. Leonard's to take a walk with the Abbé Couturier along the parade, made reply in the simplicity of his heart, to the effect that he expected a visit from the Vicomte de Troisville, who had been in the Russian service during the Emigration, and now was coming back to settle in Alençon. A kind of labial telegraph, at work that afternoon between two and five o'clock, informed all the inhabitants of Alençon that Mlle. Cormon at last had found herself a husband by advertisement. She was going to marry the Vicomte de Troisville. Some said that "Moreau was at work on a bed-stead already." In some places the bed was six feet long. It was only four feet at Mme. Granson's house in the Rue du Bercail. At President du Ronceret's, where du Bousquier was dining, it dwindled into a sofa. The tradespeople said that it cost eleven hundred francs. It was generally thought that this was like counting your chickens before they were hatched.

Farther away, it was said that the price of carp had gone up. Mariette had swooped down upon the market and created a general scarcity. Penelope had dropped down at the upper end of the Rue Saint-Blaise; the death was called in question at the receiver-general's; nevertheless, at the prefecture it was known for a fact that the animal fell dead just as she turned in at the gate of the Hôtel Cormon, so swiftly had the old maid come down upon her prey. The saddler at the corner of the Rue de Séez, in his anxiety to know the truth about Penelope, was hardy enough to call in to ask if anything had happened to Mlle. Cormon's chaise. Then from the utmost end of the Rue Saint-Blaise to the furthermost parts of the Rue du Bercail, it was known that, thanks to Jacquelin's care,

Penelope, dumb victim of her mistress' intemperate haste, was still alive, but she seemed to be in a bad way.

All along the Brittany road the Vicomte de Troisville was a penniless younger son, for the domains of Perche belonged to the marquis of that ilk, a peer of France with two children. The match was a lucky thing for an impoverished *émigré;* as for the vicomte himself, that was Mlle. Cormon's affair. Altogether the match received the approval of the aristocratic section on the Brittany road; Mlle. Cormon could not have put her fortune to a better use.

Among the bourgeoisie, on the other hand, the Vicomte de Troisville was a Russian general that had borne arms against France. He was bringing back a large fortune made at the court of St. Petersburg. He was a "foreigner," one of the "Allies" detested by the Liberals. The Abbé de Sponde had manœuvred the match on the sly. Every person who had any shadow of a right of entrance to Mlle. Cormon's drawing-room vowed to be there that night.

While the excitement went through the town, and all but put Suzanne out of people's heads, Mlle. Cormon herself was not less excited; she felt as she had never felt before. She looked round the drawing-room, the boudoir, the cabinet, the dining-room, and a dreadful apprehension seized upon her. Some mocking demon seemed to show her the old-fashioned splendor in a new light; the beautiful furniture, admired ever since she was a child, was suspected, nay, convicted, of being out of date. She was shaken, in fact, by the dread that catches almost every author by the throat when he begins to read his own work aloud to some exigent or jaded critic. Before he began, it was perfect in his eyes; now the novel situations are stale; the finest periods turned with such secret relish are turgid or halting; the metaphors are mixed or grotesque; his sins stare him in the face. Even so, poor Mlle. Cormon shivered to think of the smile on M. de Troisville's lips when he looked round that salon, which looked

like a bishop's drawing-room, unchanged for one possessor
after another. She dreaded his cool survey of the ancient
dining-room; in short, she was afraid that the picture might
look the older for the ancient frame. How if all these old
things should tinge her with their age? The bare thought
of it made her flesh creep. At that moment she would have
given one-fourth of her savings for the power of renovating
her house at a stroke of a magic wand. Where is the general
so conceited that he will not shudder on the eve of an
action? She, poor thing, was between an Austerlitz and a
Waterloo.

"Madame la Vicomtesse de Troisville," she said to herself,
"what a fine name! Our estates will pass to a good house,
at any rate."

Her excitement fretted her. It sent a thrill through every
fibre of every nerve to the least of the ramifications and the
papillæ so well wadded with flesh. Hope tingling in her
veins set all the blood in her body in circulation. She felt
capable, if need was, of conversing with M. de Troisville.

Of the activity with which Josette, Mariette, Jacquelin,
Moreau, and his assistants set about their work, it is needless
to speak. Ants rescuing their eggs could not have been
busier than they. Everything, kept so neat and clean with
daily care, was starched and ironed, scrubbed, washed, and
polished. The best china saw the light. Linen damask cloths
and serviettes docketed A B C D emerged from the depths
where they lay shrouded in triple wrappings and defended by
bristling rows of pins. The rarest shelves of that oak-bound
library were made to give account of their contents; and
finally, mademoiselle offered up three bottles of liqueurs to
the coming guest, three bottles bearing the label of the most
famous distiller of over-sea—Mme. Amphoux, name dear to
connoisseurs.

Mlle. Cormon was ready for battle, thanks to the devotion
of her lieutenants. The munitions of war, the heavy artillery

of the kitchen, the batteries of the pantry, the victuals, provisions for the attack, and body of (p)reserves, had all been brought up in array. Orders were issued to Jacquelin, Mariette, and Josette to wear their best clothes. The garden was raked over. Mademoiselle only regretted that she could not come to an understanding with the nightingales in the trees, that they might warble their sweetest songs for the occasion. At length, at four o'clock, just as the abbé came in, and mademoiselle was beginning to think that she had brought out her daintiest linen and china and made ready the most exquisite of dinners in vain, the crack of a postillion's whip sounded outside in the Val-Noble.

"It is *he!*" she thought, and the lash of the whip struck her in the heart.

And indeed, heralded by all this tittle-tattle, a certain postchaise, with a single gentleman inside it, had made such a prodigious sensation as it drove down the Rue Saint-Blaise and turned into the Rue du Cours, that several small urchins and older persons gave chase to the vehicle, and now were standing in a group about the gateway of the Hôtel Cormon to watch the postillion drive in. Jacquelin, feeling that his own marriage was in the wind, had also heard the crack of the whip, and was out in the yard to throw open the gates. The postillion (an acquaintance) was on his mettle, he turned the corner to admiration, and came to a stand before the flight of steps. And, as you can understand, he did not go until Jacquelin had duly and properly made him tipsy.

The abbé came out to meet his guest, and in a trice the chaise was despoiled of its occupant, robbers in a hurry could not have done their work more nimbly; then the chaise was put into the coach-house, the great door was closed, and in a few minutes there was not a sign of M. de Troisville's arrival. Never did two chemicals combine with a greater alacrity than that displayed by the house of Cormon to absorb the Vicomte de Troisville. As for mademoiselle, if she had been a lizard caught by a shepherd, her heart could not have beat faster. She sat heroically in her low chair by the fireside ; Josette threw open the door, and the Vicomte de Troisville, followed by the Abbé de Sponde, appeared before her.

" This is Monsieur le Vicomte de Troisville, niece, a grand-son of an old schoolfellow of mine. Monsieur de Troisville, my niece, Mademoiselle Cormon."

" Dear uncle, how nicely he puts it," thought Rose-Marie-Victoire.

The Vicomte de Troisville, to describe him in a few words, was a du Bousquier of noble family. Between the two men there was just that difference which separates the gentleman from the ordinary man. If they had been standing side by side, even the most furious Radical could not have denied the signs of race about the vicomte. There was all the distinc-tion of refinement about his strength, his figure had lost nothing of its magnificent dignity. Blue-eyed, dark-haired, and olive-skinned, he could not have been more than six-and-forty. You might have thought him a handsome Spaniard preserved in Russian ice. His manner, gait, and bearing, and everything about him, suggested a diplomatist, and one that has seen Europe. He looked like a gentleman in his traveling dress.

M. de Troisville seemed to be tired. The abbé rose to conduct him to his room, and was overcome with astonish-ment when Rose opened the door of the boudoir, now trans-formed into a bedroom. Then uncle and niece left the noble visitor leisure to attend to his toilet with the help of Jacquelin, who brought him all the luggage which he needed. While M. de Troisville was dressing, they walked on the terrace by the Brillante. The abbé, by a strange chance, was more absent-minded than usual, and Mlle. Cormon no less preoccu-pied, so they paced to and fro in silence. Never in her life had Mlle. Cormon seen so attractive a man as this Olympian vicomte. She could not say to herself, like a German girl,

"I have found my Ideal!" but she felt that she was in love from head to foot. "The very thing for me," she thought. On a sudden she fled to Mariette, to know whether dinner could be put back a little without serious injury.

"Uncle, this Monsieur de Troisville is very pleasant," she said when she came back again.

"Why, my girl, he has not said a word as yet," returned the abbé, laughing.

"But one can tell by his general appearance. Is he a bachelor?"

"I know nothing about it," replied her uncle, his thoughts full of that afternoon's discussion with the Abbé Couturier on Divine Grace. "Monsieur de Troisville said in his letter that he wanted to buy a house here. If he were married, he would not have come alone," he added carelessly. It never entered his head that his niece could think of marriage for herself.

"Is he rich?"

"He is the younger son of a younger branch. His grandfather held a major's commission, but this young man's father made a foolish marriage."

"Young man!" repeated his niece. "Why, he is quite five-and-forty, uncle, it seems to me." She felt an uncontrollable desire to compare his age with hers.

"Yes," said the abbé. "But to a poor priest at seventy, a man of forty seems young, Rose."

By this time all Alençon knew that M. le Vicomte de Troisvilla had arrived at the Cormon house.

The visitor very soon rejoined his host and hostess, and began to admire the Brillante, the garden, the house, and surroundings.

"Monsieur l'Abbé," he said, "to find such a place as this would be the height of my ambition."

The old maid wished to read a declaration in the speech. She lowered her eyes.

"You must be very fond of it, mademoiselle," continued the vicomte.

"How could I help being fond of it ? It has been in our family since 1574, when one of our ancestors, an Intendant of the Duchy of Alençon, bought the ground and built the house. It is laid on piles."

Jacquelin having announced that dinner was ready, M. de Troisville offered his arm. The radiant spinster tried not to lean too heavily upon him ; she was still afraid that he might think her forward.

"Everything is quite in harmony here," remarked the vicomte as they sat down to table.

"Yes, the trees in our garden are full of birds that give us music for nothing. Nobody molests them ; the nightingales sing there every night," said Mlle. Cormon.

"I am speaking of the inside of the house," remarked the vicomte ; he had not troubled himself to study his hostess particularly, and was quite unaware of her vacuity. "Yes, everything contributes to the general effect ; the tones of color, the furniture, the character of the house," added he, addressing Mlle. Cormon.

"It costs a great deal, though," replied that excellent spinster, "the taxes are something enormous." The word "contribute" had impressed itself on her mind.

"Ah ! then are the taxes high here ?" asked Monsieur de Troisville, too full of his own ideas to notice the absurd *non sequitur.*

"I do not know," said the abbé. "My niece manages her own property and mine."

"The taxes are a mere trifle if people are well to do," struck in Mlle. Cormon, anxious not to appear stingy. "As to the furniture, I leave things as they are. I shall never make any changes here ; at least I shall not, unless I marry, and in that case everything in the house must be arranged to suit the master's taste."

"You are for great principles, mademoiselle," smiled the vicomte; "somebody will be a lucky man."

"Nobody ever made me such a pretty speech before," thought Mlle. Cormon.

The vicomte complimented his hostess upon the appointments of the table and the housekeeping, admitting that he had thought that the provinces were behind the times, and found himself in most delectable quarters.

"*Delectable*, good Lord! what does it mean?" thought she. "Where is the Chevalier de Valois to reply to him? De-lect-able? Is it made up of several words? There! courage; perhaps it is Russian, and if so I am not obliged to say anything." Then she added aloud, her tongue loosed by an eloquence which almost every human creature can find in a great crisis, "We have the most brilliant society here, Monsieur le Vicomte. You will be able to judge for yourself, for it assembles in this very house; on some of our acquaintances we can always count; they will have heard of my return no doubt, and will be sure to come to see me. There is the Chevalier de Valois, a gentleman of the old court, a man of infinite wit and taste; then there is Monsieur le Marquis d'Esgrignon and Mademoiselle Armande, his sister"—she bit her lip and changed her mind—"a—a remarkable woman in her way. She refused all offers of marriage so as to leave her fortune to her brother and his son."

"Ah! yes; the d'Esgrignons, I remember them," said the vicomte.

"Alençon is very gay," pursued mademoiselle, now that she had fairly started off. "There is so much going on; the receiver-general gives dances; the prefect is a very pleasant man; his lordship the bishop occasionally honors us with a visit——"   .

"Come!" said the vicomte, smiling as he spoke, "I have done well, it seems, to come creeping back like a hare (*un lièvre*) to die in my form."

"It is the same with me," replied mademoiselle; "I am like a creeper (*le lierre*), I must cling to something or die."

The vicomte took the saying thus twisted for a joke, and smiled.

"Ah!" thought his hostess, "that is all right, *he* understands me."

The conversation was kept up upon generalities. Under pressure of a strong desire to please, the strange, mysterious, indefinable workings of consciousness brought all the Chevalier de Valois' tricks of speech uppermost in Mlle. Cormon's brain. It fell out, as it sometimes does in a duel, when the devil himself seems to take aim; and never did duelist hit his man more fairly and squarely than the old maid. The Vicomte de Troisville was too well mannered to praise the excellent dinner, but his silence was panegyric in itself! As he drank the delicious wines with which Jacquelin plied him, he seemed to be meeting old friends with the liveliest pleasure; for your true amateur does not applaud, he enjoys. He informed himself curiously of the prices of land, houses, and sites; he drew from mademoiselle a long description of the property between the Brillante and the Sarthe. He was amazed that the town and the river lay so far apart, and showed the greatest interest in local topography. The abbé sat silent, leaving all the conversation to his niece. And, in truth, mademoiselle considered that she interested M. de Troisville; he smiled graciously at her, he made far more progress with her in the course of a single dinner than the most ardent of her former wooers in a whole fortnight. For which reasons, you may be certain that never was guest so cosseted, so lapped about with small attentions and observances. He might have been a much-loved lover, newly come home to the house of which he was the delight.

Mademoiselle forestalled his wants. She saw when he needed bread, her eyes brooded over him; if he turned his head, she adroitly supplemented his portion of any dish which

8

he seemed to like; if he had been a glutton, she would have
killed him.   What a delicious earnest of all that she counted
upon doing for her lover!   She made no silly blunders of
self-depreciation this time!   She went gallantly forward, full
sail, and all flags flying; posed as the queen of Alençon, and
vaunted her preserves.   Indeed, she fished for compliments,
talking about herself as if her trumpeter were dead.   And she
saw that she pleased the vicomte, for her wish to please had so
transformed her that she grew almost feminine.   It was not
without inward exultation that she heard footsteps while they
sat at dessert; sounds of going and coming in the antechamber and noises in the salon; and knew that the usual company
was arriving.   She called the attention of her uncle and M.
de Troisville to this fact as a proof of the affection in which
she was held, whereas it really was a symptom of the paroxysm
of curiosity which convulsed the whole town.   Impatient to
show herself in her glory, she ordered coffee and the liqueurs
to be taken to the salon, whither Jacquelin went to display to
the élite of Alençon the splendors of a Dresden china service,
which only left the cupboard twice in a twelvemonth.   All
these circumstances were noted by people disposed to criticise
under their breath.

"Egad!" cried du Bousquier, "nothing but Madame
Amphoux's liqueurs, which only come out on the four great
festival days!"

"Decidedly, this match must have been arranged by correspondence for a year past," said M. le Président du Ronceret.   "The postmaster here has been receiving letters with
an Odessa postmark for the last twelve months."

Mme. Granson shuddered.   M. le Chevalier de Valois had
eaten a heavy dinner, but he felt the pallor spreading over his
left cheek; felt, too, that he was betraying his secret, and
said: "It is cold to-day, do you not think?   I am freez-
ing."

"It is the neighborhood of Russia," suggested du Bousquier.

And the chevalier looked at his rival as who should say: "Well put in!"

Mlle. Cormon was so radiant, so triumphant, that she looked positively handsome, it was thought. Nor was this unwonted brilliancy wholly due to sentiment; ever since the morning the blood had been surging through her veins; the presentiments of a great crisis at hand affected her nerves. It needed a combination of circumstances to make her so little like herself. With what joy did she not solemnly introduce the vicomte to the chevalier, and the chevalier to the vicomte; all Alençon was presented to M. de Troisville, and M. de Troisville made the acquaintance of all Alençon. It fell out, naturally enough, that the vicomte and the chevalier, two born aristocrats, were in sympathy at once; they recognized each other for inhabitants of the same social sphere. They began to chat as they stood by the fire. A circle formed about them listening devoutly to their conversation, though it was carried on *sotto voce*. Fully to realize the scene, imagine Mlle. Cormon standing with her back to the chimney-piece, busy preparing coffee for her supposed suitor.

M. DE VALOIS. "So Monsieur le Vicomte is coming to settle here, people say."

M. DE TROISVILLE. "Yes, monsieur. I have come to look for a house." (*Mlle. Cormon turns, cup in hand.*) "And I must have a large one"—(*Mlle. Cormon offers the cup of coffee*)—"to hold my family." (*The room grows dark before the old maid's eyes.*)

M. DE VALOIS. "Are you married?"

M. DE TROISVILLE. "Yes, I have been married for sixteen years. My wife is the daughter of the Princess Scherbelloff."

Mlle. Cormon dropped like one thunderstruck. Du Bousquier, seeing her reel, sprang forward, and caught her in his arms. Somebody opened the door to let him pass out with his enormous burden. The melted Republican, counseled by Josette, summoned up his strength, bore the old maid to her room, and deposited her upon the bed. Josette, armed with a pair of scissors, cut the stay-laces, drawn outrageously tight. Du Bousquier, rough and ready, dashed cold water over Mlle. Cormon's face and bust, which broke from its bounds like the Loire in flood. The patient opened her eyes, saw du Bousquier, and gave a cry of alarmed modesty. Du Bousquier withdrew, leaving half-a-dozen women in possession, with Mme. Granson at their head, Mme. Granson beaming with joy.

What had the Chevalier de Valois done? True to his system, he had been covering the retreat.

"Poor Mademoiselle Cormon!" he said, addressing M. de Troisville, but looking round the room, quelling the beginnings of an outbreak of laughter with his haughty eyes. "She is dreadfully troubled with heated blood. She would not be bled before going to the Prébaudet (her country house), and this is the result of the spring weather."

"She drove over in the rain this morning," said the Abbé de Sponde. "She may have taken a little cold, and so caused the slight derangement of the system to which she is subject. But she will soon get over it."

"She was telling me the day before yesterday that she had not had a recurrence of it for three months; she added at the time that it was sure to play her a bad turn," added the chevalier.

"Ah! so you are married!" thought Jacquelin, watching M. de Troisville, who was sipping his coffee.

The faithful manservant made his mistress' disappointment his own. He guessed her feelings. He took away the liqueurs brought out for a bachelor, and not for a Russian woman's husband. All these little things were noticed with amusement.

The Abbé de Sponde had known all along why M. de Troisville had come to Alençon, but in his absent-mindedness he had said nothing about it; it had never entered his mind that his niece could take the slightest interest in that gentleman.

As for the vicomte, he was engrossed by the object of his journey; like many other married men, he was in no great hurry to introduce his wife into the conversation; he had had no opportunity of saying that he was married; and beside, he thought that Mlle. Cormon knew his history. Du Bousquier reappeared, and was questioned without mercy. One of the six women came down, and reported that Mlle. Cormon was feeling much better, and that her doctor had come; but she was to stay in bed, and it appeared that she ought to be bled at once. The salon soon filled. In Mlle. Cormon's absence, the ladies were free to discuss the tragic-comic scene which had just taken place; and duly they enlarged, annotated, embellished, colored, adorned, embroidered, and bedizened the tale which was to set all Alençon thinking of the disappointed old maid on the morrow.

Meanwhile, Josette upstairs was saying to her mistress, "That good Monsieur du Bousquier! How he carried you upstairs! What a fist! Really, your illness made him quite pale. He loves you still."

And with this final phrase, the solemn and terrible day came to a close.

Next day, all morning long, the news of the comedy, with full details, circulated over Alençon, raising laughter everywhere, to the shame of the town be it said. Next day, Mlle. Cormon, very much the better for the blood-letting, would have seemed sublime to the most hardened of those who jeered at her, if they could but have seen her noble dignity and the Christian resignation in her soul, as she gave her hand to the unconscious perpetrator of the hoax, and went in to breakfast. Ah! heartless wags, who were laughing at her expense, why could you not hear her say to the vicomte—

"Madame de Troisville will have some difficulty in finding a house to suit her. Do me the favor of using my house, monsieur, until you have made all your arrangements."

"But I have two girls and two boys, mademoiselle. We should put you to a great deal of inconvenience."

"Do not refuse me," said she, her eyes full of apprehension and regret.

"I made the offer, however you might decide, in my letter; but you did not take it," remarked the abbé.

"What, uncle! did you know?——"

Poor thing, she broke off. Josette heaved a sigh, and neither M. de Troisville nor the uncle noticed anything.

After breakfast, the Abbé de Sponde, carrying out the plan agreed upon over night, took the vicomte to see houses for sale and suitable sites for building. Mlle. Cormon was left alone in the salon.

"I am the talk of the town, child, by this time," she said, looking piteously at Josette.

"Well, mademoiselle, get married."

"But, my girl, I am not at all prepared to make a choice."

"Bah! I should take Monsieur du Bousquier if I were you."

"Monsieur de Valois says that he is such a Republican, Josette."

"Your gentlemen don't know what they are talking about; they say that he robbed the Republic, so he can't have been at all fond of it," said Josette, and with that she went.

"That girl is amazingly shrewd," thought Mlle. Cormon, left alone to her gnawing perplexity.

She saw that the only way of silencing talk was to marry at once. This last so patently humiliating check was enough to drive her to extreme measures; and it takes a great deal to force a feeble-minded human being out of a groove, be it good or bad. Both the old bachelors understood the position of affairs, both made up their minds to call in the morning to make inquiries, and (in their own language) to press the point.

M. de Valois considered that the occasion demanded a

scrupulous toilet; he took a bath, he groomed himself with unusual care, and for the first time and the last Césarine saw him applying "a suspicion of rouge" with incredible skill.

Du Bousquier, rough and ready Republican that he was, inspired by dogged purpose, paid no attention to his appearance, he hurried round, and came in first. The fate of men, like the destinies of empires, hangs on small things. History records all such principal causes of great failure or success—a Kellermann's charge at Marengo, a Blücher coming up at the battle of Waterloo, a Prince Eugène slighted by Louis XIV., a curé on the battlefield of Denain; but nobody profits by the lesson to be diligently attentive to the little trifles of his own life. Behold the results. The Duchesse de Langeais in "The Thirteen" entering a convent for want of ten minutes' patience; Judge Popinot in "The Commission in Lunacy" putting off his inquiries as to the Marquis d'Espard till to-morrow; Charles Grandet coming home by way of Bordeaux instead of Nantes—and these things are said to happen by accident and mere chance! The few moments spent in putting on that suspicion of rouge wrecked M. de Valois' hopes. Only in such a way could the chevalier have succumbed. He had lived for the Graces, he was foredoomed to die through them. Even as he gave a last look in the mirror, the burly du Bousquier was entering the disconsolate old maid's drawing-room. His entrance coincided with a gleam of favor in the lady's mind, though in the course of her deliberations the chevalier had decidedly had the advantage.

"It is God's will," she said to herself when du Bousquier appeared.

"Mademoiselle, I trust you will not take my importunity in bad part; I did not like to trust that great stupid of a René to make inquiries, and came myself."

"I am perfectly well," she said nervously; then, after a

pause, and in a very emphatic tone, "Thank you, Monsieur du Bousquier, for the trouble that you took and that I gave you yesterday——"

She recollected how she had lain in du Bousquier's arms, and the accident seemed to her to be a direct order from heaven. For the first time in her life a man had seen her with her belt wrenched apart, her stay-laces cut, the jewel shaken violently out of its case.

"I was so heartily glad to carry you that I thought you a light weight," said he.

At this Mlle. Cormon looked at du Bousquier as she never looked at any man in the world before ; and thus encouraged, the ex-contractor for forage flung a side-glance that went straight to the old maid's heart.

"It is a pity," added he, "that this has not given me the right to keep you always." (She was listening with rapture in her face.) "You looked dazzling as you lay swooning there on the bed ; I never saw such a fine woman in my life, and I have seen a good many. There is this about a stout woman, she is superb to look at, she has only to show herself, she triumphs."

"You mean to laugh at me," said the old maid ; "that is not kind of you, when the whole town is perhaps putting a malicious and bad construction on things that happened here yesterday."

"It is as true as that my name is du Bousquier, mademoiselle. My feelings toward you have never changed ; your first rejection did not discourage me."

The old maid lowered her eyes. There was a pause, a painful ordeal for du Bousquier. Then Mlle. Cormon made up her mind and raised her eyelids ; she looked up tenderly at du Bousquier through her tears.

"If this is so, monsieur," she said, in a tremulous voice, " I only ask you to allow me to lead a Christian life, do not ask me to change any of my habits as to religion, leave me free to

choose my spiritual directors, and I will give you my hand,"
holding it out to him as she spoke.

Du Bousquier caught the plump, honest hand that held so
many francs, and kissed it respectfully.

"But I have one thing more to ask," added Mlle. Cormon,
suffering him to kiss her hand.

"It is granted, and if it is impossible, it shall be done"
(a reminiscence of Beaujon).

"Alas!" began the old maid, "for love of me you must
burden your soul with a sin which I know is heinous; falsehood is one of the seven deadly sins; but still you can make
confession, can you not? We will both of us do penance."
They looked tenderly at each other at those words.

"Perhaps," continued Mlle. Cormon, "after all, it is one
of those deceptions which the church calls venial——"

"Is she going to tell me that she is in Suzanne's plight?"
thought du Bousquier. "What luck!——" Aloud he said,
"Well, mademoiselle?"

"And you must take it upon you——"

"What?"

"To say that this marriage was agreed upon between us six
months ago."

"Charming woman!" exclaimed the forage-contractor,
and by his manner he implied that he was prepared to make
even this sacrifice; "a man only does thus for the woman
he has worshiped for ten years."

"In spite of my severity?" asked she.

"Yes, in spite of your severity."

"Monsieur du Bousquier, I have misjudged you." Again
she held out her big, red hand, and again du Bousquier
kissed it.

At that very moment the door opened, and the betrothed
couple, turning their heads, perceived the charming but too
tardy chevalier.

"Ah! fair queen," said he, "so you have risen?"

Mlle. Cormon smiled at him, and something clutched at her heart. M. de Valois, grown remarkably young and irresistible, looked like Lauzun entering La Grande Mademoiselle's apartments.

"Ah! my dear du Bousquier!" he continued, half laughingly, so sure was he of success. "Monsieur de Troisville and the Abbé de Sponde are in front of your house, looking it over like a pair of surveyors."

"On my word," said du Bousquier, "if the Vicomte de Troisville wants it, he can have it for forty thousand francs. It is of no use whatever to me. Always, if mademoiselle has no objection, that must be ascertained first. Mademoiselle, may I tell? Yes? Very well, *my dear chevalier*, you shall be the first to hear"—Mlle. Cormon dropped her eyes—"of the honor and the favor that mademoiselle is doing me; I have kept it a secret for more than six months. We are going to be married in a very few days, the contract is drawn up, we shall sign it to-morrow. So, you see, that I have no further use for my house in the Rue du Cygne. I am quietly on the lookout for a purchaser; and the Abbé de Sponde, *who knew this*, naturally took Monsieur du Troisville to see it."

There was such a color of truth about this monstrous fib that the chevalier was quite taken in by it. *My dear chevalier* was a return for all preceding defeats; it was like the victory won at Pultowa by Peter the Great over Charles XII. And thus du Bousquier enjoyed a delicious revenge for hundreds of pin-pricks endured in silence; but in his triumph he forgot that he was not a young man, he passed his fingers through the false toupet, and—it came off in his hand!

"I congratulate you both," said the chevalier, with an agreeable smile; "I wish that you may end like the fairy stories, 'They lived very happily and had a fine—*family of children*!'" Here he shaped a cone of snuff in his palm before adding mockingly, "But, monsieur, you forgot that—er—you wear borrowed plumes."

Du Bousquier reddened. The false toupet was ten inches awry. Mlle. Cormon raised her eyes to the face of her betrothed, saw the bare cranium, and bashfully looked down again. Never toad looked more venomously at a victim than du Bousquier at the chevalier.

"A pack of aristocrats that look down on me!" he thought. "I will crush you all some of these days."

The Chevalier de Valois imagined that he had regained all the lost ground. But Mlle. Cormon was not the woman to understand the connection between the chevalier's congratulation and the allusion to the false toupet; and, for that matter, even if she had understood, her hand had been given. M. de Valois saw too clearly that all was lost. Meantime, as the two men stood without speaking, Mlle. Cormon innocently studied how to amuse them.

"Play a game of reversis," suggested she, without any malicious intention.

Du Bousquier smiled, and went as future master of the house for the card-table. Whether the Chevalier de Valois had lost his head, or whether he chose to remain to study the causes of his defeat and to remedy it, certain it is that he allowed himself to be led like a sheep to the slaughter. But he had just received the heaviest of all bludgeon blows; and a noble might have been excused if he had been at any rate stunned by it. Very soon the worthy Abbé de Sponde and M. de Troisville returned, and at once Mlle. Cormon hurried into the antechamber, took her uncle aside, and told him in a whisper of her decision. Then, hearing that the house in the Rue du Cygne suited M. de Troisville, she begged her betrothed to do her the service of saying that her uncle knew that the place was for sale. She dared not confide the fib to the abbé, for fear that he should forget. The falsehood was destined to prosper better than if it had been a virtuous action. All Alençon heard the great news that night. For four days the town had found as much to say as in the ominous days of

1814 and 1815. Some laughed at the idea, others thought it true; some condemned, others approved the marriage. The bourgeoisie of Alençon regarded it as a conquest, and they were the best pleased.

The Chevalier de Valois, next day, among his own circle, brought out this cruel epigram : "The Cormons are ending as they began; stewards and contractors are all on a footing."

The news of Mlle. Cormon's choice went to poor Athanase's heart; but he showed not a sign of the dreadful tumult surging within. He had heard of the marriage at President du Ronceret's while his mother was playing a game of boston. Mme. Granson, looking up, saw her son's face in the glass; he looked white, she thought, but then he had been pale ever since vague rumors had reached him in the morning. Mlle. Cormon was the card on which Athanase staked his life, and chill presentiments of impending catastrophe already wrapped him about. When intellect and imagination have exaggerated a calamity till it becomes a burden too heavy for shoulders and brow to bear, when some long-cherished hope fails utterly, and with it the visions which enable a man to forget the fierce vulture-cares gnawing at his heart; then, if that man has no belief in himself, in spite of his powers; no belief in the future, in spite of the Power Divine—he is broken in pieces. Athanase was a product of education under the Empire. Fatalism, the Emperor's creed, spread downward to the lowest ranks of the army, to the very schoolboys at their desks. Athanase followed Mme. du Ronceret's play with a stolidity which might so easily have been taken for indifference, that Mme. Granson fancied she had been mistaken as to her son's feelings.

Athanase's apparent carelessness explained his refusal to sacrifice his so-called "Liberal" opinions. This word, then recently coined for the Emperor Alexander, proceeded into the language, I believe, by way of Mme. de Staël through Benjamin Constant.

After that fatal evening the unhappy young man took to haunting one of the most picturesque walks along the Sarthe; every artist who comes to Alençon sketches it from that point of view, for the sake of the water-mills, and the river gleaming brightly out among the fields, between the shapely well-grown trees on either side. Flat though the land may be, it lacks none of the subdued peculiar charm of French landscape; for in France your eyes are never wearied by glaring Eastern sunlight, nor saddened by too continual mist. It is a lonely spot. Dwellers in the provinces care nothing for beautiful scenery, perhaps because it is always about them, perhaps because there is a sense lacking in them. If there is such a thing as a promenade, a mall, or any spot from which you see a beautiful view, it is sure to be the one unfrequented part of the town. Athanase liked the loneliness, with the water like a living presence in it, and the fields just turning green in the warmth of the early spring sunlight. Occasionally some one who had seen him sitting at a poplar foot, and received an intent gaze from his eyes, would speak to Mme. Granson about him.

"There is something the matter with your son."

"I know what he is about," the mother would say with a satisfied air, hinting that he was meditating some great work.

Athanase meddled no more in politics; he had no opinions; and yet, now and again, he was merry enough, merry at the expense of others, after the wont of those who stand alone and apart in contempt of public opinion. The young fellow lived so entirely outside the horizon of provincial ideas and amusements that he was interesting to few people; he did not so much as rouse curiosity. Those who spoke of him to his mother did so for her sake, not for his. Not a creature in Alençon sympathized with Athanase; the Sarthe received the tears which no friend, no loving woman dried. If the magnificent Suzanne had chanced to pass that way, how much misery might have been prevented—the two young creatures would have fallen in love.

And yet Suzanne certainly passed that way.   Her ambition
had been first awakened by a sufficiently marvelous tale of
things which happened in 1799; an old story of adventures
begun at the sign of the Three Moors had turned her childish
brain.   They used to tell how an adventuress, beautiful as an
angel, had come from Paris with a commission from Fouché
to ensnare the Marquis de Montauran, the Chouan leader sent
over by the Bourbons; how she met him at that very inn of
the Three Moors as he came back from his Mortagne expedition; and how she won his love, and gave him up to his
enemies.   The romantic figure of this woman, the power of
beauty, the whole story of Marie de Verneuil and the Marquis
de Montauran, dazzled Suzanne, till, as she grew older, she
too longed to play with men's lives.   A few months after her
flight, she could not resist the desire to see her native place
again, on her way to Brittany with an artist.   She wanted to
see Fougères, where the Marquis de Montauran met his death;
and thought of making a pilgrimage to the scenes of stories
told to her in childhood of that war in the West, so little
known even yet.   She wished, beside, to revisit Alençon with
such splendor in her surroundings, and so completely meta-
morphosed, that nobody should know her again.   She intended
to put her mother beyond the reach of want in one moment,
and, in some tactful way, to send a sum of money to poor
Athanase—a sum which for genius in modern days is the
equivalent of a Rebecca's gift of horse and armor to an
Ivanhoe of the Middle Ages.

    A month went by.   Opinions as to Mlle. Cormon's mar-
riage fluctuated in the strangest way.   There was an incredulous
section which strenuously denied the truth of the report, and
a party of believers who persistently affirmed it.   At the end
of fourteen days, the doubters received a severe check.   Du
Bousquier's house was sold to M. de Troisville for forty-three-
thousand francs.   M. de Troisville meant to live quite quietly
in Alençon; he intended to return to Paris after the death of

the Princess Scherbelloff, but until the inheritance fell in he would spend his time in looking after his estates. This much appeared to be fact. But the doubting faction declined to be crushed. Their assertion was that, married or not, du Bousquier had done a capital stroke of business, for his house only stood him in a matter of twenty-seven thousand francs. The believers were taken aback by this peremptory decision on the part of their opponents. "Choisnel, Mademoiselle Cormon's notary, had not heard a word of marriage settlements," added the incredulous.

But on the twentieth day the unshaken believers enjoyed a signal victory over the doubters. M. Lepresseur, the Liberal notary, went to Mlle. Cormon's house, and the contract was signed. This was the first of many sacrifices which Rose made to her husband. The fact was that du Bousquier detested Choisnel; he blamed the notary for Mlle. Armande's refusal in the first place, as well as for his previous rejection by Mlle. Cormon, who, as he believed, had followed Mlle. Armande's example. He managed Mlle. Cormon so well, that she, noble-hearted woman, believing that she had misjudged her future husband, wished to make reparation for her doubts, and sacrifice her notary to her love. Still she submitted the contract to Choisnel, and he—a man worthy of Plutarch—defended Mlle. Cormon's interests by letter. This was the one cause of delay.

Mlle. Cormon received a good many anonymous letters. She was informed, to her no small astonishment, that Suzanne was as honest a woman as she was herself; and that the seducer in the false toupet could not possibly have played the part assigned to him in such an adventure. Mlle. Cormon scorned anonymous letters; she wrote, however, to Suzanne with a view to gaining light on the creeds of the Maternity Society. Suzanne probably had heard of du Bousquier's approaching marriage; she confessed to her stratagem, sent a thousand francs to the Fund, and damaged the forage-contractor's character very considerably. Mlle. Cormon called an extraordinary meeting of the Maternity Charity, and the assembled matrons passed a resolution that hencefoward the Fund should give help after and not before misfortunes befell.

In spite of these proceedings, which supplied the town with titbits of gossip to discuss, the banns were published at the church and the mayor's office. It was Athanase's duty to make out the needful documents. The betrothed bride had gone to the Prébaudet, a measure taken partly by way of conventional modesty, partly for general security. Thither du Bousquier went every morning, fortified by atrocious and sumptuous bouquets, returning in the evening to dinner.

At last, one gray rainy day in June, the wedding took place ; and Mlle. Cormon and the Sieur du Bousquier, as the incredulous faction called him, were married at the parish church in the sight of all Alençon. Bride and bridegroom drove to the mayor's office, and afterward to the church, in a calèche—a splendid equipage for Alençon. Du Bousquier had it sent privately from Paris. The loss of the old cariole was a kind of calamity for the whole town. The saddler of the Porte de Séez lost an income of fifty francs per annum for repairs ; he lifted up his voice and wept. With dismay the town of Alençon beheld the luxury introduced by the Maison Cormon ; every one feared a rise of prices all round, an increase of house rent, an invasion of Paris furniture. There were some whose curiosity pricked them to the point of giving Jacquelin ten sous for a nearer sight of so startling an innovation in a thrifty province. A pair of Normandy horses likewise caused much concern.

"If we buy horses for ourselves in this way, we shall not sell them long to those that come to buy of us,", said du Ronceret's set.

The reasoning seemed profound, stupid though it was, in so far as it prevented the district from securing a monopoly of

money from outside. In the political economy of the provinces the wealth of nations consists not so much in a brisk
circulation of money as in hoards of unproductive coin.

At length the old maid's fatal wish was fulfilled. Penelope
sank under the attack of pleurisy contracted forty days before
the wedding. Nothing could save her. Mme. Granson,
Mariette, Mme. du Coudrai, Mme. du Ronceret—the whole
town, in fact—noticed that the bride came into church with
the left foot foremost, an omen all the more alarming because
the word Left even than had acquired a political significance.

The officiating priest chanced to open the mass-book at the
De profundis. And so the wedding passed off, amid presages
so ominous, so gloomy, so overwhelming, that nobody was
found to augur well of it. Things went from bad to worse.
There was no attempt at a wedding-party; the bride and
bridegroom started out for the Prébaudet. Paris fashions
were to supplant old customs! In the evening Alençon said
its say as to all these absurdities; some persons had reckoned
upon one of the usual provincial jollifications, which they considered they had a right to expect, and these spoke their
minds pretty freely. But Mariette and Jacquelin had a merry
wedding, and they alone in all Alençon gainsaid the dismal
prophecies.

Du Bousquier wished to spend the profit made by the sale
of his house on restoring and modernizing the Cormon place.
He had quite made up his mind to stay for some months at the
Prébaudet, whither he brought his Uncle de Sponde. The
news spead dismay through Alençon; every one felt that du
Bousquier was about to draw the country into the downward
path of domestic comfort. The foreboding grew to a fear
one morning when du Bousquier drove over from the Prébaudet to superintend his workmen at the Val-Noble; and the
townspeople beheld a tilbury, harnessed to a new horse, and
René in livery by his master's side. Du Bousquier had invested his wife's savings in the Funds which stood at sixty-

9

seven francs fifty centimes.   This was the first act of the new
administration.   In the space of one year, by constantly
speculating for a rise, he made for himself a fortune almost as
considerable as his wife's.   But something else happened in
connection with this marriage to make it seem yet more inaus-
picious, and put all previous overwhelming portents and alarming innovations into the background.

It was the evening of the wedding-day.   Athanase and his
mother were sitting in the salon by the little fire of brush-
wood (or *régalades*, as they say in the patois), which the servant had lighted after dinner.

"Well," said Mme. Granson, "we will go to President
du Ronceret's to-night, now that we have no Mademoiselle
Cormon.   Goodness me ! I shall never get used to calling her
Madame du Bousquier; that name makes my lips sore."

Athanase looked at his mother with a sad constraint; he could
not smile, and he wanted to acknowledge, as it were, the artless thoughtfulness which soothed the wound it could not
heal.

"Mamma," he began—it was several years since he had
used that word, and his tones were so gentle that they sounded
like his child's voice—"mamma, dear, do not let us go out
just yet; it is so nice here by the fire ! "

It was a supreme cry of mortal anguish ; the mother heard
it but did not understand.

"Let us stay, child," she said.   "I would certaintly
rather talk with you and listen to your plans than play at
boston and perhaps lose my money."

"You are beautiful to-night; I like to look at you.   And
beside, the current of my thoughts is in harmony with this
poor little room, where we have been through so much trouble
—you and I."

"And there is still more in store for us, poor Athanase,
until your work succeeds.   For my own part, I am used to
poverty ; but, oh, my treasure, to look on and see your youth

go by while you have no joy of it! Nothing but work in
your life! That thought is like a disease for a mother. It
tortures me night and morning. I wake up to it. Ah, God
in heaven! what have I done? What sin of mine is punished
with this?"

She left her seat, took a little chair, and sat down beside
Athanase, nestling close up to his side, till she could lay her
head on her child's breast. Where a mother is truly a mother,
the grace of love never dies. Athanase kissed her on the eyes,
on the gray hair, on the forehead, with the reverent love that
fain would lay the soul where the lips are laid.

"I shall never succeed," he said, trying to hide the fatal
purpose which he was revolving in his mind.

"Pooh! you are not going to be discouraged? Mind can
do all things, as you say. With ten bottles of ink, ten reams
of paper, and a strong will, Luther turned Europe upside
down. Well, and you are going to make a great name for
yourself; you are going to use to good ends the powers which
he used for evil. Did you not say so? Now *I* remember
what you say, you see; I understand much more than you
think; for you still lie so close under my heart, that your least
little thought thrills through it, as your slightest movement
did once."

"I shall not succeed *here*, you see, mamma, and I will not
have you looking on while I am struggling and heartsore and
in anguish. Mother, let me leave Alençon; I want to go
through it all away from you."

"*I* want to be at your side always," she said proudly.
"Suffering alone! *you* without your mother! your poor
mother that would be your servant if need were, and keep
out of sight for fear of injuring you, if you wished it, and
never accuse you of pride! No, no, Athanase, we will never
be parted!"

Athanase put his arms about her and held her with a passionate, tight clasp, as a dying man might cling to life.

"And yet I wish it," he said.   "If we do not part, it is all over with me.   The double pain—yours and mine—would kill me.   It is better that I should live, is it not?"

Mme. Granson looked with haggard eyes into her son's face.

"So this is what you have been brooding over!   They said truth.   Then are you going away?"

"Yes."

"But you are not going until you have told me all about it, and without giving me any warning?   You must have some things to take with you, and money.   There are some louis d'ors sewed into my petticoat; you must have them."

Athanase burst into tears.

"That was all that I wanted to tell you," he said after a while.   "Now, I will see you to the president's house."

Mother and son went out together.   Athanase left Mme. Granson at the door of the house where she was to spend the evening.   He looked long at the shafts of light that escaped through chinks in the shutters.   He stood there glued to the spot, while a quarter of an hour went by, and it was with almost delirious joy that he heard his mother say: "Grand independence of hearts."

"Poor mother, I have deceived her!" he exclaimed to himself as he reached the river.

He came down to the tall poplar on the bank where he had been wont to sit and meditate during the last six weeks.   Two big stones lay there; he had brought them himself for a seat. And now, looking out over the fair landscape lying in the moonlight, he passed in review all the so glorious future that should have been his.   He went through cities stirred to enthusiasm by his name; he heard the cheers of crowded streets, breathed the incense of banquets, looked with a great yearning over that life of his dreams, rose uplifted and radiant in glorious triumph, raised a statue to himself, summoned up all his illusions to bid them farewell in a last Olympian carouse.

The magic could only last for a little while; it fled, it had vanished forever.   In that supreme moment he clung to his beautiful tree as if it had been a friend; then he put the stones, one in either pocket, and buttoned his overcoat.   His hat he had purposely left at home.   He went down the bank to look for a deep spot which he had had in view for some time; and slid in resolutely, trying to make as little noise as possible. There was scarcely a sound.

When Mme. Granson came home about half-past nine that night, the maid-of-all-work said nothing of Athanase, but handed her a letter.   Mme. Granson opened it and read—

" I have gone away, my kind mother; do not think hardly of me."   That was all.

"A pretty thing he has done!" cried she.   "And how about his linen and the money?   But he will write, and I shall find him.   The poor children always think themselves wiser than their fathers and mothers."   And she went to bed with a quiet mind.

The Sarthe had risen with yesterday's rain.   Fishers and anglers were prepared for this, for the swollen river washes down the eels from the little streams on its course.   It so happened that an eel-catcher had set his lines over the very spot where poor Athanase had chosen to drown himself, thinking that he should never be heard of again; and next morning, about six o'clock, the man drew out the newly dead body.

One or two women among Mme. Granson's few friends went to prepare the poor widow with all possible care to receive the dreadful yield of the river.   The news of the suicide, as might be expected, produced a tremendous sensation.   Only last evening the poverty-stricken man of genius had not a single friend; the morning after his death scores of voices cried: " I would so willingly have helped him!"   So easy is it to play a charitable part when no outlay is involved. The Chevalier de Valois, in the spirit of revenge, explained the suicide.   It was a boyish, sincere, and noble passion for Mlle. Cormon that drove Athanase to take his own life.   And when the chevalier had opened Mme. Granson's eyes, she saw a multitude of little things to confirm this view.   The story grew touching; women cried over it.

Even before Mme. du Bousquier came back to town, her obliging friend, Mme. du Ronceret, went to fling a dead body down among the roses of her new-wedded happiness, to let her know what a love she had refused.   Ever so gently Mme. President squeezed a shower of drops of wormwood over the honey of the first month of married life.   And as Mme. du Bousquier returned, it so happened that she met Mme. Granson at the corner of the Val-Noble, and the look in the heartbroken mother's eyes cut her to the quick.   It was a look from a woman dying of grief, a thousand curses gathered up into one glance of malediction, a thousand sparks in one gleam of hate.   It frightened Mme. du Bousquier; it boded ill and invoked ill upon her.

Mme. Granson had belonged to the party most opposed to the curé; she was a bitter partisan of the priest of St. Leonard's; but on the very evening of the tragedy she thought of the rigid orthodoxy of her own party, and she shuddered. She herself laid her son in his shroud, thinking all the while of the Mother of the Saviour; then, with a soul quivering with agony, she betook herself to the house of the perjured priest. She found him busy, the humble good man, storing the hemp and flax which he gave to poor women and girls to spin, so that no worker should ever want work, a piece of wise charity which had saved more than one family that could not endure to beg.   He left his hemp at once and brought his visitor into the dining-room, where the stricken mother saw the frugality of her own housekeeping in the supper that stood waiting for the curé.

"Monsieur l'Abbé," she began. "I have come to entreat you——"

She burst into tears, and could not finish the sentence.

"I know why you have come," answered the holy man, "and I trust to you, madame, and to your relative Madame du Bousquier to make it right with his lordship at Séez. Yes, I will pray for your unhappy boy; yes, I will say masses; but we must avoid all scandal, we must give no occasion to ill-disposed people to gather together in the church. I myself, alone, and at night——"

"Yes, yes, as you wish, if only he is laid in consecrated ground!" she said, poor mother; and taking the priest's hand in hers, she kissed it.

And so, just before midnight, a bier was smuggled into the parish church. Four young men, Athanase's friends, carried it. There were a few little groups of veiled and black-clad women, Mme. Granson's friends, and some seven or eight lads that had been intimate with the dead. The bier was covered with a pall, torches were lit at the corners, and the curé read the office for the dead, with the help of one little choir boy whom he could trust. Then the suicide was buried, noiselessly, in a corner of the churchyard, and a dark wooden cross with no name upon it marked the grave for the mother. Athanase lived and died in the shadow.

Not a voice was raised against the curé; his lordship at Séez was silent; the mother's piety redeemed her son's impious deed.

Mme. Granson, by the river-side, whither she had gone to see the place where her son had drowned himself, saw a woman at some distance—a woman who came nearer, till she reached the fatal spot, and exclaimed—

"Then this is the place!"

One other woman in the world wept there as the mother was weeping, and that woman was Suzanne. She had heard of the tragedy on her arrival that morning at the Three Moors. If poor Athanase had been alive, she might have done what poor and generous people dream of doing, and the rich never think of putting in practice; she would have inclosed a thousand francs with the words: "Money lent by your father to a comrade who now repays you." During her journey Suzanne had thought of this angelic way of giving. She looked up and saw Mme. Granson.

"I loved him," she said; then she hurried away.

Susanne, true to her nature, did not leave Alençon till she had changed the bride's wreath of orange flowers to water-lilies. She was the first to assert that Mme. du Bousquier would be Mlle. Cormon as long as she lived. And with that one jibe she avenged both Athanase and the dear Chevalier de Valois.

Alençon beheld another and more piteous suicide. Athanase was promptly forgotten by a world that willingly, and indeed of necessity, forgets its dead as soon as possible; but the poor chevalier's existence became a kind of death-in-life, a suicide continued morning after morning during fourteen years. Three months after du Bousquier's marriage, people remarked, not without astonishment, that the chevalier's linen was turning yellow, and his hair irregularly combed. M. de Valois was no more, for a disheveled M. de Valois could not be said to be himself. An ivory tooth here and there deserted from the ranks, and no student of human nature could discover to what corps they belonged, whether they were native or foreign, animal or vegetable; nor whether, finally, they had been extracted by old age, or were merely lying out of sight and out of mind in the chevalier's dressing-table drawer. His cravat was wisped, careless of elegance, into a cord. The negroes' heads grew pale for lack of soap and water. The lines on the chevalier's face deepened into wrinkles and darkened as his complexion grew more and more like parchment; his neglected nails were sometimes adorned with an edge of black velvet. Grains of snuff lay scattered like autumn leaves in the furrows of his vest.

Hitherto the chevalier's nose had made a peculiarly elegant

appearance in public; never had it been seen to distill a drop of amber, to let fall a dark wafer of moist rappee; but now, with a snuff-bedabbled border about the nostrils, and an unsightly stream taking advantage of the channel hollowed above the upper lip, that nose, which no longer took pains to please, revealed the immense trouble that the chevalier must have formerly taken with himself.

Latterly the chevalier's witticisms had been few and far between; the anecdotes went the way of the teeth, but his appetite continued as good as ever; out of the great shipwreck of his hopes he saved nothing but his digestion; and while he took his snuff feebly, he dispatched his dinner with an avidity alarming to behold. You may mark the extent of the havoc wrought in his ideas in the fact that his colloquies with the Princess Goritza grew less and less frequent. He came to Mlle. Armande's one day with a false calf in front of his shins. The bankruptcy of elegance was something painful, I protest; all Alençon was shocked by it. It scared society to see an elderly young man drop suddenly into his dotage, and from sheer depression of spirits pass from fifty to ninety years. And beside, he had betrayed his secret. He had been waiting and lying in wait for Mlle. Cormon. For ten long years, persevering sportsman that he was, he had been stalking the game, and then he had missed his shot.

He became a man of the worst character. The Liberal party laid all du Bousquier's foundlings on the chevalier's doorstep, while the Faubourg Saint-Germain of Alençon boastingly accepted them; laughed and cried: "The dear chevalier! What else could he do?" Saint-Germain pitied the chevalier, took him to its bosom, and smiled more than ever upon him; while an appalling amount of unpopularity was drawn down upon du Bousquier's head.

But the especial result of the marriage was a more sharply marked division of parties in Alençon. The Maison d'Esgrignon represented undiluted aristocracy; for the Troisvilles

on their return joined the clique.   The Maison Cormon, skillfully influenced by du Bousquier, was not exactly Liberal, nor
yet resolutely Royalist, but of that unlucky shade of opinion
which produced the 221 members, so soon as the political
struggle took a definite shape, and the greatest, most august,
and only real power of kingship came into collision with that
most false, fickle, and tyrannical power which, when wielded
by an elective body, is known as the power of Parliament.

The third salon, the salon du Ronceret, out-and-out Radical
in its politics, was firmly but secretly allied with the Maison
Cormon.

With the return from the Prébaudet, a life of continual
suffering began for the Abbé de Sponde.   He kept all that he
endured locked within his soul, uttering not a word of complaint to his niece ; but to Mlle. Armande he opened his heart,
admitting that, taking one folly with another, he should have
preferred the chevalier.

"Mademoiselle," the old abbé said as the thin tears fell
from his faded old eyes, "the lime-tree walk, where I have
been used to meditate these fifty years, is gone.   My dear
lime-trees have all been cut down !   Just as I am nearing the
end of my days the Republic has come back again in the
shape of a horrible revolution in the house."

"Your niece must be forgiven," said the Chevalier de
Valois.   "Republicanism is a youthful error ; youth goes out
to seek for liberty, and finds tyranny in its worst form—the
tyranny of the impotent rabble.   Your niece, poor thing, has
not been punished by the thing wherein she sinned."

"What is to become of me in a house with naked women
dancing all over the walls ?   Where shall I find the lime-tree
walks where I used to read my breviary ? "

Like Kant, who lost the thread of his ideas when somebody
cut down the fir-tree on which he fixed his eyes as he meditated, the good abbé pacing up and down the shadowless

alleys could not say his prayers with the same uplifting of soul. Du Bousquier had laid out an English garden!

"It looked nicer," Mme. du Bousquier said. Not that she really thought so, but the Abbé Couturier had authorized her to say and do a good many things that she might please her husband.

The Abbé de Sponde was the first to see the unhappiness which lay beneath the surface of his dear child's married life. The old dignified simplicity which ruled their way of living was gone; du Bousquier gave two balls every month in the course of the first winter. The venerable house—oh, to think of it !—echoed with the sound of violins and worldly gayety. The abbé, on his knees, prayed while the merriment lasted.

The politics of the sober salon underwent a gradual change for the worse. The Abbé de Sponde, divined du Bousquier; he shuddered at his nephew's dictatorial tone. He saw tears in his niece's eyes when the disposal of her fortune was taken out of her hands; her husband left her only the control of the linen, the table, and such things as fall to a woman's lot.

Does any one know how much it costs to give up the delicious exercise of authority? If the triumph of will is one of the most intoxicating of the great man's joys, to have one's own way is the whole life of narrow natures. No one but a cabinet minister fallen into disgrace can sympathize with Mme. du Bousquier's bitter pain when she saw herself reduced to a cipher in her own house.

But these beginnings were the roses of life. Every concession was counseled by poor Rose's love for her husband, and at first du Bousquier behaved admirably to his wife. He was very good to her; he brought forward sufficient reasons for every encroachment. The room, so long left empty, echoed with the voices of husband and wife in fireside talk. And so, for the first few years of married life, Mme. du Bousquier wore a face of content, and that little air of emancipation and mystery often seen in a young wife after a marriage of love.

She had no more trouble with "heated blood." This countenance of hers routed scoffers, gave the lie to gossip concerning du Bousquier's impotence, and put observers of human
nature at fault.

Rose-Marie-Victoire was so afraid lest she should lose her
husband's affection or drive him from her side by setting her
will against his, that she would have made any sacrifice, even
of her uncle if need be. And the Abbé de Sponde, deceived
by Mme. du Bousquier's poor foolish little joys, bore his own
discomforts the more easily for the thought that his niece was
happy.

At first Alençon shared this impression. But there was one
man less easy to deceive than all the rest of Alençon put
together. The Chevalier de Valois had taken refuge on the
sacred mount of the most aristocratic section, and spent his
time with the d'Esgrignons. The perpetrator of puns had
been already brought low, and he meant to stab du Bousquier
to the heart.

The poor abbé, knowing as he did the cowardliness of his
niece's first and last love, shuddered as he guessed his nephew's
hypocritical nature and the man's intrigues. Du Bousquier,
be it said, put some constraint upon himself; he had an eye
to the abbé's property, and had no wish to annoy his wife's
uncle in any way, yet he dealt the old man his death-blow.

If you can translate the word Intolerance by Firmness of
Principle; if you can forbear to condemn in the old Roman
Catholic vicar-general that stoicism which Scott has taught us
to revere in Jeanie Deans' puritan father; if, finally, you can
recognize in the Roman church the nobility of a *Potius mori
quam fœdari* which you admire in a Republican—then you
can understand the anguish that rent the great Abbé de Sponde
when he saw the apostate in his nephew's drawing-room;
when he was compelled to meet the renegade, the backslider,
the enemy of the church, the aider and abettor of the Oath to
the Constitution. It was du Bousquier's private ambition to

lord it over the countryside ; and as a first proof of his power, he determined to reconcile the officiating priest of St. Leonard's with the curé of Alençon. He gained his object. His wife imagined that peace had been made where the stern abbé saw no peace, but surrender of principle. M. de Sponde was left alone in the faith. The bishop came to du Bousquier's house, and appeared satisfied with the cessation of hostilities. The Abbé François' goodness had conquered every one—every one except the old Roman of the Roman church, who might have cried with Cornélie : " Ah, God ! what virtues you make me hate ! " The Abbé de Sponde died when orthodoxy expired in the diocese.

In 1819 the Abbé de Sponde's property raised Mme. du Bousquier's income from land to twenty-five thousand livres without counting the Prébaudet or the house in the Val-Noble. About the same time du Bousquier returned the amount of his wife's savings (which she had made over to him) and instructed her to invest the money in purchases of land near the Pré-baudet, so that the estate, including the Abbé de Sponde's adjoining property, was one of the largest in the department. As for du Bousquier, he invested his money with the Kellers, and made a journey to Paris four times a year. Nobody knew the exact amount of his private fortune, but at this time he was supposed to be one of the wealthiest men in the department of the Orne. A dexterous man, and the permanent candidate of the Liberal party, he always lost his election by seven or eight votes under the Restoration. Ostensibly he repudiated his connection with the Liberals, offering himself as a Ministerial-Royalist candidate ; but although he succeeded in gaining the support of the Congrégation and of the magistrature, the repugnance of the administration was too strong to be overcome.

Then the rabid Republican, frantic with ambition, conceived the idea of beginning a struggle with the royalism and aristocracy of the country, just as they were carrying all before

them.   He gained the support of the clergy by an appearance
of piety very skillfully kept up; always going with his wife to
mass, giving money to the convents, and supporting the con-
fraternity of the Sacred Heart ; and whenever a dispute arose
between the clergy and the town, or the department, or the
State, he was very careful to take the clerical side.   And so,
while secretly supported by the Liberals, he gained the influence of the church; and as a Constitutional-Royalist kept
close beside the aristocratic section, the better to ruin it.
And ruin it he did.   He brought about an industrial revolution ; and his detestation of certain families on the high road
to Brittany rapidly increased the material prosperity of the
province.

   And so he paved the way for his revenge upon the *gens à
châteaux* in general, and the d'Esgrignons in particular ; some
day, not so very far distant, he would plunge a poisoned
blade into the very heart of the clique.   He found capital to
revive the manufacture of point d'Alençon and to increase
the linen trade.   Alençon began to spin its own flax by
machinery.   And while his name was associated with all these
interests, and written in the hearts of the masses, while he did
all that Royalty left undone, du Bousquier risked not a centime of his own.   With his means, he could afford to wait
while enterprising men with little capital were obliged to give
up and leave the results of their labors to luckier successors.
He posed as a banker.   A Laffitte on a small scale, he became a sleeping partner in all new inventions, taking security
for his money.   And as a public benefactor he did remarkably
well for himself.   He was a promoter of insurance companies,
a patron of new public conveyances ; he got up memorials for
necessary roads and bridges.   The authorities, being left
behind in this way, regarded this activity in the light of an
encroachment ; they blundered, and put themselves into the
wrong, for the prefecture was obliged to give way for the good
of the country.

Du Bousquier embittered the provincial noblesse against the court nobles and the peerage. He helped, in short, to bring it to pass that a very large body of Constitutional-Royalists supported the "Journal des Débats" and M. de Chateaubriand in a contest with the throne. It was an ungrateful opposition based on ignoble motives which contributed to bring about the triumph of the bourgeoisie and the press in 1830. Wherefore du Bousquier, like those whom he represented, had the pleasure of watching a funeral procession of Royalty* pass through their district without a single demonstration of sympathy for a population alienated from them in ways so numerous that they cannot be indicated here.

Then the old Republican, with all that weight of masses on his conscience, hauled down the white flag above the townhall amid the applause of the people. For fifteen years he had acted a part to satisfy his vendetta, and no man in France beholding the new throne raised in August, 1830, could feel more intoxicated than he with the joy of revenge. For him, the succession of the younger branch meant the triumph of the Revolution; for him, the hoisting of the tricolor flag was the resurrection of the Mountain; and *this* time the nobles should be brought low by a surer method than the guillotine, in that its action should be less violent. A peerage for life only; a National Guard which stretches the marquis and the grocer from the corner-store on the same camp-bed; the abolition of entail demanded by a bourgeois barrister; a Catholic church deprived of its supremacy; in short, all the legislative inventions of August, 1830, simply meant for du Bousquier the principles of 1793 carried out in a more ingenious manner.

Du Bousquier has been receiver-general of taxes since 1830. He relied for success upon his old connections with Égalité Orléans (father of Louis Philippe) and M. de Folmon, steward of the dowager duchess. He is supposed to have an income

* Charles X. on his way to England.

of eighty thousand livres.   In the eyes of his fellow-country-men, *Monsieur* du Bousquier is a man of substance, honorable, upright, obliging, unswerving in his principles.   To him, Alençon owes her participation in the industrial movement which makes her, as it were, the first link in a chain which some day perhaps may bind Brittany to the state of things which we nickname "modern civilization."   In 1816 Alençon boasted but two carriages, properly speaking ; ten years after-ward, calèches, coupés, landaus, cabriolets, and tilburies were rolling about the streets without causing any astonishment. At first the townsmen and landowners were alarmed by the rise of prices, afterward they discovered that the increased expenditure produced a corresponding increase in their in-comes.

Du Ronceret's prophetic words : " Du Bousquier is a very strong man," were now taken up by the country.   But, un-fortunately for du Bousquier's wife, the remark is a shocking misnomer.   Du Bousquier, the husband, is a very different person from du Bousquier the public man and politician. The great citizen, so liberal in his opinions, so easy humored, so full of love for his country, is a despot at home, and has not a particle of love for his wife.   The Cromwell of the Val-Noble is profoundly astute, hypocritical, and crafty ; he be-haves to those of his own household as he behaved to the aristocrats on whom he fawned, until he could cut their throats. Like his friend Bernadotte, he has an iron hand in a velvet glove.   His wife gave him no children.   Suzanne's epigram and the Chevalier de Valois' insinuations were justified ; but the Liberals and Constitutional-Royalists among the towns-people, the little squires, the magistrature, and the "clericals" (as the "Constitutionnel" used to say), all threw the blame upon Mme. du Bousquier.   M. du Bousquier had married such an elderly wife, they said ; and beside, how lucky it was for her, poor thing, for at her age bearing a child meant such a risk.   If, in periodically recurrent despair, Mme. du Bous-

quier confided her troubles with tears to Mme. du Coudrai or
Mme. du Ronceret:

"Why you must be mad, dear!" those ladies would reply.
"You do not know what you want; a child would be the
death of you."

Men like M. du Coudrai, who followed du Bousquier's lead
because they fastened their hopes to his success, would prompt
their wives to sing du Bousquier's praises; and Rose must
listen to speeches that wounded like a stab.

"You are very fortunate, dear, to have such a capable husband; some men have no energy, and can neither manage
their own property nor bring up their children; you are
spared these troubles."

Or, "Your husband is making you queen of the district,
fair lady. *He* will never leave you at a loss; he does everything in Alençon."

"But I should like him to take less trouble for the public
and rather——"

"My dear Mme. du Bousquier, you are very hard to please;
all the women envy you your husband."

Unjustly treated by a world which condemned her without
a hearing, she found ample scope for the exercise of Christian
virtues in her inner life. She who lived in tears always turned
a serene face upon the world. For her, pious soul, was there
not sin in the thought which was always pecking at her heart
—"I loved the Chevalier de Valois, and I am du Bousquier's
wife?" Athanase's love rose up like a remorse to haunt her
dreams.

The Chevalier de Valois was the malignant artificer of her
misfortune. He had it on his mind to snatch his opportunity
and undeceive Mme. du Bousquier as to one of her articles of
faith; for the chevalier, a man of experience, saw through du
Bousquier the married man, as he had seen through du Bousquier the bachelor. But it was not easy to take the astute
Republican by surprise. His salon, naturally, was closed to

10

the Chevalier de Valois, as to all others who discontinued
their visits to the Maison Cormon at the time of his marriage.
And beside, du Bousquier was above the reach of ridicule ; he
possessed an immense fortune, he was king of Alençon ; and
as for his wife, he cared about her much as Richard III. might
have cared for the loss of the horse with which he thought to
win the battle.   To please her husband, Mme. du Bousquier
had broken with the Maison d'Esgrignon, but sometimes,
when he was away at Paris for a few days, she paid Mlle.
Armande a visit.

Two years after Mme. du Bousquier's marriage, just at the
time of the abbe's death, Mlle. Armande went up to her as
she came out of church.   Both women had been to St. Leonard's to hear a *messe noire* (lit., black mass) said for M. de
Sponde ; and Mlle. Armande, a generous natured woman,
thinking that she ought to try to comfort the weeping heiress,
walked with her as far as the parade.   Prom the parade, still
talking of the beloved and lost, they came to the forbidden
Hôtel d'Esgrignon, and Mlle. Armande drew Mme. du Bousquier into the house by the charm of her talk.   Perhaps the
poor broken-hearted woman loved to speak of her uncle with
some one whom her uncle had loved so well.   And beside,
she wished to receive the old marquis' greetings after an interval of nearly three years.   It was half-past one o'clock ;
the Chevalier de Valois had come to dinner, and with a bow
he held out both hands.

"Ah ! well, dear, good, and well-beloved lady," he said
tremulously, " *we* have lost our sainted friend.   Your mourning is ours.   Yes ; your loss is felt as deeply here as under
your own roof—more deeply," he added, alluding to du Bousquier.

A funeral oration followed, to which every one contributed
his phrase ; then the chevalier, gallantly taking the lady's
hand, drew it under his arm, pressed it in the most adorable
way, and led her aside into the embrasure of a window.

"You are happy, at any rate?" he asked with a fatherly tone in his voice.

"Yes," she said, lowering her eyes.

Hearing that "Yes," Mme. de Troisville (daughter of the Princess Scherbelloff) and the old Marquise de Castéran came up; Mlle. Armande also joined them, and the group took a turn in the garden till dinner should be ready. Mme. du Bousquier was so stupid with grief that she did not notice that a little conspiracy of curiosity was on foot among the ladies.

"We have her here, let us find out the answer to the riddle," the glances exchanged among them seemed to say.

"You should have children to make your happiness complete," began Mlle. Armande, "a fine boy like my nephew now——"

Tears came to Mme. du Bousquier's eyes.

"I have heard it said that it was entirely your own fault if you had none," said the chevalier, "that you were afraid of the risk."

"*I!*" she cried, innocently; "I would endure a hundred years in hell to have a child."

The subject thus broached, Mme. la Vicomtesse de Troisville and the dowager Marquise de Castéran steered the conversation with such exceeding tact that they entangled poor Rose until, all unsuspectingly, she revealed the secrets of her married life. Mlle. Armande laid her hand on the chevalier's arm, and they left the three matrons to talk confidentially. Then Mme. du Bousquier's mind was disabused with regard to the deception of her marriage; and as she was still "a natural," she amused her confidantes with her irresistible naïveté. Before long the whole town was in the secret of du Bousquier's manœuvres, and knew that Mlle. Cormon's marriage was a mockery; but after the first burst of laughter, Mme. du Bousquier gained the esteem and sympathy of every woman in it. While Mlle. Cormon rushed unsuccessfully at opportunities of establishing herself, every one had laughed; but people admired her when they knew the position in which she was placed by the severity of her religious principles. "Poor, dear Mademoiselle Cormon!" was replaced by "poor Madame du Bousquier!"

In this way the chevalier made du Bousquier both ridiculous and very unpopular for a while, but the ridicule died down with time; the slander languished when everybody had cut his joke; and beside, it seemed to many persons that the mute Republican had a right to retire at the age of fifty-seven. But if du Bousquier previously hated the Maison d'Esgrignon, this incident so increased his rancor that he was pitiless afterward in the day of vengeance. Mme. du Bousquier received orders never to set foot in that house again; and by way of reprisals, he inserted the following paragraph in the "Orne Courier," his own new paper:

"A REWARD of Funds to bring in a thousand francs will be paid to any person who shall prove that one M. de Pombreton existed either before or after the Emigration."

Though Mme. du Bousquier's happiness was essentially negative, she saw that her marriage had its advantages. Was it not better to take an interest in the most remarkable man in the place than to live alone? After all, du Bousquier was better than the dogs, cats, and canaries on which old maids centre their affections; and his feeling for his wife was something more genuine and disinterested than the attachment of servants, confessors, and legacy-hunters. At a still later period she looked upon her husband as an instrument in God's hands to punish her for the innumerable sins which she discovered in her desires for marriage; she regarded herself as justly rewarded for the misery which she had brought on Mme. Granson, and for hastening her own uncle's end. She felt the strongest aversion for the conduct and opinions of the man she had married, and yet it was her duty to take a tender interest in him; and if, as often happened, du Bousquier ate her preserves, or thought that the dinner was good, she was in the seventh heaven. She saw that his comfort was secured even in the smallest details.

Did du Bousquier go on a journey, she fidgeted over his traveling cloak and his linen; she took the most minute precautions for his material comfort. If he was going over to the Prébaudet, she began to consult the weather-glass twenty-four hours beforehand. A sleeping dog has eyes and ears for his master, and so it was with Mme. du Bousquier; she used to watch the expression of her husband's face to read his wishes. And if that burly personage, vanquished by duty-prescribed love, caught her by the waist and kissed her on the forehead, exclaiming: "You are a good woman!" tears of joy filled the poor creature's eyes. It is probable that du Bousquier felt it incumbent upon him to make compensations which won Rose-Marie-Victoire's respect; for the church does not require that an assumption of wifely devotion should be carried quite so far as Mme. du Bousquier thought necessary. And yet when she listened to the rancorous talk of men who took Constitutional-Royalism as a cloak for their real opinions, the woman of saintly life uttered not a word. She foresaw the downfall of the church, and shuddered. Very occasionally she would hazard some foolish remark, promptly cut in two by a look from du Bousquier. The timid sheep walked in the way marked out by the shepherd; never leaving the bosom of the church, practicing austerities, without a thought of the devil, his pomps and works. And so, within herself, she united the purest Christian virtues, and du Bousquier truly was one of the luckiest men in the kingdom of France and Navarre.

"She will be a simpleton till her last sigh," said the cruel ex-registrar (now cashiered). But, all the same, he dined at her table twice a week.

The story would be singularly incomplete if it omitted to mention a last coincidence : the Chevalier de Valois and Suzanne's mother died at the same time.

The chevalier died with the Monarchy in August, 1830. He went to Nonancourt to join the funeral procession ; piously making one of the King's escort to Cherbourg, with the Troisvilles, Castérans, d'Esgrignons, Verneuil's, and the rest.   He had brought with him his little hoard of savings and the principal which brought him in his annual income, some fifty thousand francs in all, which he offered to a faithful friend of the elder branch to convey to his majesty.   His own death was very near, he said ; the money had come to him through the King's bounty ; and, after all, the property of the last of the Valois belonged to the Crown.   History does not say whether the chevalier's fervent zeal overcame the repugnance of the Bourbon who left his fair kingdom of France without taking one centime into exile ; but the King surely must have been touched by the old noble's devotion ; and this much is at least certain—Césarine, M. de Valois' universal legatee, inherited scarcely six hundred livres of income at his death. The chevalier came back to Alençon, broken-hearted and spent with the fatigue of the journey, to die just as Charles X. set foot on foreign soil.

Mme. du Val-Noble and her journalist protector, fearing reprisals from the Liberals, were glad of an excuse to return *incognito* to the village where the old mother died.   Suzanne attended the sale of the chevalier's furniture to buy some relic of her first good friend, and ran up the price of the snuffbox to the enormous amount of a thousand francs.   The Princess Goritza's portrait alone was worth that sum.   Two years afterward, a young man of fashion, struck with its marvelous workmanship, obtained it of Suzanne for his collection of fine eighteenth-century snuff-boxes ; and so the delicate toy which had been the confidante of the most courtly of love affairs, and the delight of an old age till its very end, is now brought into the semi-publicity of a collection. If the dead could know what is done after they are gone, there would be a flush at this moment on the chevalier's left cheek.

If this history should inspire owners of sacred relics with a holy fear, and set them drafting codicils to provide for the fate of such precious souvenirs of a happiness now no more, by giving them into sympathetic hands ; even so an enormous service would have been rendered to the chivalrous and sentimental section of the public ; but it contains another and a much more exalted moral. Does it not show that a new branch of education is needed ? Is it not an appeal to the so enlightened solicitude of Ministers of Public Instruction to create chairs of anthropology, a science in which Germany is outstripping us?

Modern myths are even less understood of the people than ancient myths, eaten up with myths though we may be. Fables crowd in upon us on every side, allegory is pressed into service on all occasions to explain everything. If fables are the torches of history, as the humanist school maintains, they may be a means of securing empires from revolution, if only professors of history will undertake that their interpretations thereof shall permeate the masses in the departments. If Mlle. Cormon had had some knowledge of literature ; if there had been a professor of anthropology in the department of the Orne ; if (a final if) she had read her Ariosto, would the appalling misfortune of her marriage have befallen her ? She would, perhaps, have found out for herself why the Italian poet makes his heroine Angelica prefer Medoro (a suave Chevalier de Valois) to Orlando, who had lost his mare, and could do nothing but work himself into a fury.* Might not Medoro be taken as an allegorical figure as the courtier of woman's sovereignty, whereas Orlando is revolution personified, an undisciplined, furious, purely destructive force, incapable of producing anything ? This is the opinion

* Ariosto's " Orlando Furioso."

of one of M. Ballanche's pupils ; we publish it, declining all responsibility.

As for the tiny negroes' heads, no information of any kind concerning them is forthcoming.   Mme. du Val-Noble you may see any day at the opera.   Thanks to the primary education given to her by the Chevalier de Valois, she looks almost like a woman who makes a necessity of virtue, while in truth she only exists by virtue of necessity.

Mme. du Bousquier is still living, which is to say, is it not, that her troubles are not yet over ?   At sixty, when women can permit themselves to make admissions, talking confidentially to Mme. du Courdrai, whose husband was reinstated in August, 1830, she said that the thought that she must die without knowing what it was to be a wife and mother was more then she could bear.

PARIS, *October,* 1836.

THE COLLECTION OF ANTIQUITIES
(*Le Cabinet des antiques*).

TO BARON VON HAMMER-PURGSTALL,

*Member of the Aulic Council, Author of the History of the
Ottoman Empire.*

*Dear Baron :— You have taken so warm an interest
in my long, vast* History of French Manners in the
Nineteenth Century, *you have given me so much encouragement to persevere with my work, that you have
given me a right to associate your name with some
portion of it. Are you not one of the most important
representatives of conscientious, studious Germany ?
Will not your approval win for me the approval of
others, and protect this attempt of mine ? So proud
am I to have gained your good opinion, that I have
striven to deserve it by continuing my labors with the
unflagging courage characteristic of your methods of
study, and of that exhaustive research among documents without which you could never have given your
monumental work to the world of letters. Your sympathy with such labor as you yourself have bestowed
upon the most brilliant civilization of the East, has
often sustained my ardor through nights of toil given
to the details of our modern civilization. And will
not you, whose naïve kindliness can only be compared
with that of our own La Fontaine, be glad to know
of this ?*

*May this token of my respect for you and your work
find you at Dobling, dear baron, and put you and
yours in mind of one of your most sincere admirers
and friends.* DE BALZAC.

(153)

THERE stands a house at a corner of a street, in the middle of a town, in one of the least important prefectures in France, but the name of the street and the name of the town must be suppressed here. Every one will appreciate the motives of this sage reticence demanded by convention ; for if a writer takes upon himself the office of annalist of his own time, he is bound to touch on many sore subjects. The house was called the Hôtel d'Esgrignon ; but let d'Esgrignon be considered a mere fancy name, neither more nor less connected with real people than the conventional Belval, Floricour, or Derville of the stage, or the Adalberts and Monbreuses of romance. After all, the names of the principal characters will be quite as much disguised ; for though in this history the chronicler would prefer to conceal the facts under a mass of contradictions, anachronisms, improbabilities, and absurdities ; the truth will out in spite of him. You uproot a vine-stock, as you imagine, and the stem will send up lusty shoots after you have ploughed your vineyard over.

The " Hôtel d'Esgrignon " was nothing more nor less than the house in which the old marquis lived ; or, in the style of ancient documents, Charles-Marie-Victor-Ange-Carol, Marquis d'Esgrignon. It was only an ordinary house, but the townspeople and tradesmen had begun by calling it the Hôtel d'Esgrignon in jest, and ended after a score of years by giving it that name in earnest.

The name of Carol, or Karawl, as the Thierrys would have spelt it, was glorious among the names of the most powerful chieftains of the Northmen who conquered Gaul and established the feudal system there. Never had Carol bent his head before King or communes, the church or finance. Intrusted in the days of yore with the keeping of a French March, the title of marquis in their family meant no shadow of imaginary office ; it had been a post of honor with duties to discharge. Their fief had always been their domain. Provincial nobles were they in every sense of the word ; they might boast of an unbroken line of great descent; they had been neglected by the court for two hundred years; they were lords paramount in the estates of a province where the people looked up to them with superstitious awe, as to the image of the Holy Virgin that cures the toothache. The house of d'Esgrignon, buried in its remote border country, was preserved as the charred piles of one of Cæsar's bridges are maintained intact in a river-bed. For thirteen hundred years the daughters of the house had been married without a dowry or taken the veil; the younger sons of every generation had been content with their share of their mother's dower and gone forth to be captains or bishops; some had made a marriage at Court; one cadet of the house became an admiral, a duke, and a peer of France, and died without issue. Never would the Marquis d'Esgrignon of the elder branch accept the title of duke.

"I hold my marquisate as his majesty holds the realm of France, and on the same conditions," he told the Constable de Luynes, a very paltry fellow in his eyes, at that time.

You may be sure that d'Esgrignons lost their heads on the scaffold during the troubles. The old blood showed itself proud and high even in 1789. The marquis on that day would not emigrate; he was answerable for his March. The reverence in which he was held by the countryside saved his head; but the hatred of the genuine *sans-culottes*, the old Jacobins, was strong enough to compel him to pretend to fly, and for a while he lived in hiding. Then, in the name of the Sovereign People, the d'Esgrignon lands were dishonored by the District, and the woods sold by the Nation in spite of the personal protest made by the marquis, then turned of forty. Mlle. d'Esgrignon, his half-sister, saved some portions of the fief, thanks to the young steward of the family, who claimed on her behalf the *partage de présuccession*, which is to say, the right of a relative to a portion of an *émigré's* lands. To Mlle. d'Esgrignon, therefore, the Republic made over the castle itself and a few farms. Chesnel, the faithful steward, was obliged to buy in his own name the church, the parsonage house, the castle gardens, and other places to which his patron was attached—the marquis advancing the money.

The slow, swift years of the Terror went by, and the marquis, whose character had won the respect of the whole country, decided that he and his sister ought to return to the castle and improve the property which Maître Chesnel—for he was now a notary—had contrived to save for them out of the wreck.

It was in the month of October, 1800, that Chesnel brought the marquis back to the old feudal castle, and saw with deep emotion, almost beyond control, his patron standing in the midst of the empty courtyard, gazing round upon the moat, now filled up with rubbish, and the castle towers razed to the level of the roof. The descendant of the Franks looked for the missing Gothic turrets and the picturesque weather-vanes which used to rise above them ; and his eyes turned to the sky, as if asking of heaven the reason of this social upheaval. No one but Chesnel could understand the profound anguish of the great d'Esgrignon, now known as Citizen Carol. For a long while the marquis stood in silence, drinking in the influences of the place, the ancient home of his forefathers, with the air that he breathed ; then he flung out a most melancholy exclamation :

"Chesnel," he said, "we will come back again some day when the troubles are over ; I could not bring myself to live here until the edict of pacification has been published ; *they* will not allow me to set my escutcheon on the wall."

He waved his hand toward the castle, mounted his horse, and rode back beside his sister, who had driven over in the notary's shabby basket chaise.

The Hôtel d'Esgrignon in the town had been demolished ; a couple of factories now stood on the site of the aristocrat's house. So Maître Chesnel spent the marquis' last bag of louis on the purchase of the old-fashioned building in the square,

HE SAW WITH DEEP EMOTION, ALMOST BEYOND CONTROL,
HIS PATRON STANDING IN THE MIDST OF
THE EMPTY COURTYARD.

with its gables, weather-vane, turret, and dovecot. Once it had been the court-house of the bailiwick, and subsequently the *présidial;* it had belonged to the d'Esgrignons from generation to generation ; and now, in consideration of five hundred louis d'or, the present owner made it over with the title given by the Nation to its rightful lord. And so, half in jest, half in earnest, the old house was christened the Hôtel d'Esgrignon.

In 1800 little or no difficulty was made over erasing names from the fatal list, and some few *émigrés* began to return. Among the very first nobles to come back to the old town were the Baron de Nouastre and his daughter. They were completely ruined. M. d'Esgrignon generously offered them the shelter of his roof; and in his house, two months later, the baron died, worn out with grief. The Nouastres came of the best blood of the province ; Mlle. de Nouastre was a girl of two-and-twenty ; the Marquis d'Esgrignon married her to continue his line. But she died in childbirth, a victim to the unskillfulness of her physician, leaving, most fortunately, a son to bear the name of the d'Esgrignons. The old marquis—he was but fifty-three, but adversity and sharp distress had added months to every year—the poor old marquis saw the death of the loveliest of human creatures, a noble woman in whom the charm of the feminine figures of the sixteenth century lived again, a charm now lost save to men's imaginations. With her death the joy died out of his old age. It was one of those terrible shocks which reverberate through every moment of the years that follow. For a few moments he stood beside the bed where his wife lay, with her hands folded like a saint, then he kissed her on the forehead, turned away, drew out his watch, broke the mainspring, and hung it up beside the hearth. It was eleven o'clock in the morning.

"Mademoiselle d'Esgrignon," he said, "let us pray God that this hour may not prove fatal yet again to our house. My uncle the archbishop was murdered at this hour ; at this hour also my father died——"

He knelt down beside the bed and buried his face in the coverlet; his sister did the same. In another moment they both rose to their feet. Mlle. d'Esgrignon burst into tears; but the old marquis looked with dry eyes at the child, round the room, and again on his dead wife. To the stubbornness of the Frank he united the fortitude of a Christian.

These things came to pass in the second year of the nineteenth century. Mlle. d'Esgrignon was then twenty-seven years of age. She was a beautiful woman. An ex-contractor for forage to the armies of the Republic, a man of the district, with an income of six thousand francs, persuaded Chesnel to carry a proposal of marriage to the lady. The marquis and his sister were alike indignant with such presumption in their man of business, and Chesnel was almost heart-broken; he could not forgive himself for yielding to the Sieur du Croisier's blandishments. The marquis' manner with his old servant changed somewhat; never again was there quite the old affectionate kindliness, which might almost have been taken for friendship. From that time forth the marquis was grateful, and his magnanimous and sincere gratitude continually wounded the poor notary's feelings. To some sublime natures gratitude seems an excessive payment; they would rather have that sweet equality of feeling which springs from similar ways of thought, and the blending of two spirits by their own choice and will. And Maître Chesnel had known the delights of such high friendship; the marquis had raised him to his own level. The old noble looked on the good notary as something more than a servant, something less than a child; he was the voluntary liege man of the house, a serf bound to his lord by all the ties of affection. There was no balancing of obligations; the sincere affection on either side put that out of the question.

In the eyes of the marquis, Chesnel's official dignity was as nothing; his old servitor was merely disguised as a notary. As for Chesnel, the marquis was now, as always, a being of a divine race; he believed in nobility; he did not blush to remember that his father had thrown open the doors of the salon to announce that "My Lord Marquis is served." His devotion to the fallen house was due not so much to his creed as to egoism; he looked on himself as one of the family. So his vexation was intense. Once he had ventured to allude to his mistake in spite of the marquis' prohibition, and the old noble answered gravely—"Chesnel, before the troubles you would not have permitted yourself to entertain such injurious suppositions. What can these new doctrines be if they have spoiled *you* ?"

Maître Chesnel had gained the confidence of the whole town; people looked up to him; his high integrity and considerable fortune contributed to make him a person of importance. From that time forth he felt a very decided aversion for the Sieur du Croisier; and though there was little rancor in his composition, he set others against the sometime forage-contractor. Du Croisier, on the other hand, was a man to bear a grudge and nurse a vengeance for a score of years. He hated Chesnel and the d'Esgrignon family with the smothered, all-absorbing hate only to be found in a country town. His rebuff had simply ruined him with the malicious provincials among whom he had come to live, thinking to rule over them. It was so real a disaster that he was not long in feeling the consequences of it. He betook himself in desperation to a wealthy old maid, and met with a second refusal. Thus failed the ambitious schemes with which he had started. He had lost his hope of a marriage with Mlle. d'Esgrignon, which would have opened the Faubourg Saint-Germain of the province to him; and after the second rejection, his credit fell away to such an extent that it was almost as much as he could do to keep his position in the second rank.

In 1805, M. de la Roche-Guyon, the oldest son of an ancient family which had previously intermarried with the d'Esgrignons, made proposals in form through Maître Chesnel

for Mlle. Marie-Armande-Claire d'Esgrignon. She declined
to hear the notary.

"You must have guessed before now that I am a mother,
dear Chesnel," she said ; she had just put her nephew, a fine
little boy of five, to bed.

The old marquis rose and went up to his sister, but just
returned from the cradle ; he kissed her hand reverently, and
as he sat down again, found words to say—

"My sister, you are a d'Esgrignon."

A quiver ran through the noble girl ; the tears stood in her
eyes.   M. d'Esgrignon, the father of the present marquis, had
married a second wife, the daughter of a farmer-general* ennobled by Louis XIV.   It was a shocking *mésalliance* in the
eyes of his family, but fortunately of no importance, since a
daughter was the one child of the marriage.   Armande knew
this.   Kind as her brother had always been, he looked on her
as a stranger in blood.   And this speech of his had just recognized her as one of the family.

And was not her answer the worthy crown of eleven years
of her noble life?   Her every action since she came of age
had borne the stamp of the purest devotion ; love for her
brother was a sort of religion with her.

"I shall die Mademoiselle d'Esgrignon," she said simply,
turning to the notary.

"For you there could be no fairer title," returned Chesnel,
meaning to convey a compliment.   Poor Mlle. d'Esgrignon
reddened.

"You have blundered, Chesnel," said the marquis, flattered
by the steward's words, but vexed that his sister had been hurt.
"A d'Esgrignon may marry a Montmorency ; their descent is
not so pure as ours.   The d'Esgrignons bear *or, two bends,
gules,*" he continued, "and nothing during nine hundred
years has changed their escutcheon ; as it was at first, so it is
to-day.   Hence our device, *Cil est nostre*, taken at a tourna-

---

* Private contractors who rented the tax collecting.

ment in the reign of Philip Augustus, with the supporters, a knight in armor *or* on the right, and a lion *gules* on the left."

"I do not remember that any woman I have ever met has struck my imagination as Mademoiselle d'Esgrignon did," said Émile Blondet, to whom contemporary literature is indebted for this history among other things. "Truth to tell, I was a boy, a mere child at the time, and perhaps my memory-pictures of her owe something of their vivid color to a boy's natural turn for the marvelous.

"If I was playing with other children on the parade, and she came to walk there with her nephew Victurnien, the sight of her in the distance thrilled me with very much the effect of galvanism on a dead body. Child as I was, I felt as though new life had been given me.

"Mlle. Armande had hair of tawny gold; there was a delicate fine down on her cheek, with a silver gleam upon it which I loved to catch, putting myself so that I could see the outlines of her face lit up by the daylight, and feel the fascination of those dreamy emerald eyes, which sent a flash of fire through me whenever they fell upon my face. I used to pretend to roll on the grass before her in our games, only to try to reach her little feet, and 'admire them on a closer view. The soft whiteness of her skin, her delicate features, the clearly cut lines of her forehead, the grace of her slender figure, took me with a sense of surprise, while as yet I did not know that her shape was graceful, nor her brows beautiful, nor the outline of her face a perfect oval. I admired as children pray at that age, without too clearly understanding why they pray. When my piercing gaze attracted her notice, when she asked me (in that musical voice of hers, with more volume in it, as it seemed to me, than all other voices), 'What are you doing, little one? Why do you look at me?' I used to come nearer and wriggle and bite my finger-nails, and redden and say: 'I do not know.' And if she chanced

11

to stroke my hair with her white hand, and ask me how old I was, I would run away and call from a distance: 'Eleven!'

"Every princess and fairy of my visions, as I read the 'Arabian Nights,' looked and walked like Mlle. d'Esgrignon; and afterward, when my drawing-master gave me heads from the antique to copy, I noticed that their hair was braided like Mlle. d'Esgrignon's. Still later, when the foolish fancies had vanished one by one, Mlle. Armande remained vaguely in my memory as a type; that Mlle. Armande for whom men made way respectfully, following the tall brown-robed figure with their eyes along the parade and out of sight. Her exquisitely graceful form, the rounded curves sometimes revealed by a chance gust of wind, and always visible to my eyes in spite of the ample folds of stuff, revisited my young man's dreams. Later yet, when I came to think seriously over certain mysteries of human thought, it seemed to me that the feeling of reverence was first inspired in me by something expressed in Mlle. d'Esgrignon's face and bearing. The wonderful calm of her face, the surpressed passion in it, the dignity of her movements, the saintly life of duties fulfilled—all this touched and awed me. Children are more susceptible than people imagine to the subtle influences of ideas; they never make game of real dignity; they feel the charm of real graciousness, and beauty attracts them, for childhood itself is beautiful, and there are mysterious ties between things of the same nature.

"Mlle. d'Esgrignon was one of my religions. To this day I can never climb the staircase of some old manor-house but my foolish imagination must needs picture Mlle. Armande standing there, like the spirit of feudalism. I can never read old chronicles but she appears before my eyes in the shape of some famous woman of old time; she is Agnes Sorel, Marie Touchet, Gabrielle; and I lend her all the love that was lost in her heart, all the love that she never expressed. The angel shape seen in glimpses through the haze of childish fancies visits me now sometimes across the mists of dreams.''

Keep this portrait in mind, it is a faithful picture and sketch of character. Mlle. d'Esgrignon is one of the most instructive figures in this story; she affords an example of the mischief that may be done by the purest goodness for lack of intelligence.

Two-thirds of the *émigrés* returned to France during 1804 and 1805, and almost every exile from the Marquis d'Esgrignon's province came back to the land of his fathers. There were certainly defections. Men of good birth entered the service of Napoleon, and went into the army or held places at the Imperial court, and others made alliances with the upstart families. All those who cast in their lots with the Empire retrieved their fortunes and recovered their estates, thanks to the Emperor's munificence; and these for the most part went to Paris and stayed there. But some eight or nine families still remained true to the proscribed noblesse and loyal to the fallen monarchy. The La Roche-Guyons, Nouastres, Verneuils, Castérans, Troisvilles, and the rest were some of them rich, some of them poor; but money, more or less, scarcely counted anything among them. They took an antiquarian view of themselves; for them the age and preservation of the pedigree was the one all-important matter; precisely as, for an amateur, the weight of metal in a coin is a small matter in comparison with clean lettering, a flawless stamp, and high antiquity. Of these families, the Marquis d'Esgrignon was the acknowledged head. His house became their inner chamber. There his majesty, Emperor and King, was never anything but ''Monsieur de Buonaparte;'' there ''the King'' meant Louis XVIII., then at Mittau; there the Department was still the Province, and the prefecture the *intendance.*

The marquis was honored among them for his admirable behavior, his loyalty as a noble, his undaunted courage; even as he was respected throughout the town for his misfortunes, his fortitude, his steadfast adherence to his political convictions.   All gently bred Imperialists and the authorities themselves showed as much indulgence for his prejudices as respect for his personal character ; but there was another and a large section of the new society which was destined to be known after the Restoration as the Liberal party ; and these, with du Croisier as their unacknowledged head, laughed at an aristocratic oasis which nobody might enter without proof of irreproachable descent.   Their animosity was all the more bitter because honest country squires and the higher officials, with a good many worthy folk in the town, were of the opinion that all the best society thereof was to be found in the Marquis d'Esgrignon's salon.   The prefect himself, the Emperor's chamberlain, made overtures to the d'Esgrignons, humbly sending his wife (a Grandlieu) as ambassadress.

Wherefore, those excluded from the miniature provincial Faubourg Saint-Germain nicknamed .the salon " The Collection of Antiquities," and called the marquis himself " Mons Carol."   The receiver of taxes, for instance, addressed his applications to " M. Carol (*ci-devant* des Grignons)," maliciously adopting the obsolete way of spelling.

" For my own part," said Émile Blondet, " if I try to call up childish memories, I remember that the nickname of ' Collection of Antiquities ' always made me laugh, in spite of my respect—my love, I ought to say—for Mlle. d'Esgrignon. The Hôtel d'Esgrignon stood at the angle of two of the busiest thoroughfares in the town, and not five hundred paces away from the market-place.   Two of the drawing-room windows looked upon the street and two upon the square ; the room was like a glass cage, every one who came past could look through it from side to side.   I was only a boy of twelve at the time, but I thought, even then, that the salon was one of those rare curiosities which seem, when you come to think of them afterward, to lie just on the borderland between reality and dreams, so that you can scarcely tell to which side they most belong.

"The room, the ancient Hall of Audience, stood above a row of cellars with grated air-holes, once the prison-cells of the old court-house, now converted into a kitchen. I do not know that the magnificent lofty chimney-piece of the Louvre, with its marvelous carving, seemed more wondeiful to me than the vast open hearth of the salon d'Esgrignon when I saw it for the first time. It was covered like a melon with a network of tracery. Over it stood an equestrian portrait of Henry III., under whom the ancient duchy of appanage reverted to the crown; it was a great picture executed in low relief, and set in a carved and gilded frame. The ceiling spaces between the chestnut cross-beams in the fine old roof were decorated with scroll-work patterns; there was a little faded gilding still left along the angles. The walls were covered with Flemish tapestry, six scenes from the Judgment of Solomon, framed in golden garlands, with satyrs and cupids playing among the leaves. The parquet floor had been laid down by the present marquis, and Chesnel had picked up the furniture at sales of the wreckage of old châteaux between 1793 and 1795; so that there were Louis XIV. consoles, tables, clock-cases, andirons, candle-sconces and tapestry-covered chairs, which marvelously completed a stately room, large out of all proportion to the house. Luckily, however, there was an equally lofty antechamber, the ancient Salle des Pas Perdus of the présidial, which communicated likewise with the magistrate's deliberating chamber, used by the d'Esgrignons as a dining-room.

"Beneath the old paneling, amid the threadbare braveries of a bygone day, some eight or ten dowagers were drawn up in state in a quavering line; some with palsied heads, others dark and shriveled like mummies; some erect and stiff, others bowed and bent, but all of them tricked out in more or less fantastic costumes as far as possible removed from the fashion of the day, with be-ribboned caps above their curled and powdered 'heads,' and old discolored lace. No painter however earnest, no caricature however wild, ever caught the haunting fascination of those aged women; they come back to me in dreams; their puckered faces shape themselves in my memory whenever I meet an old woman who puts me in mind of them by some faint resemblance of dress or feature. And whether it is that misfortune has initiated me into the secrets of irremediable and overwhelming disaster; whether that I have come to understand the whole range of human feelings, and, best of all, the thoughts of Old Age and Regret; whatever the reason, nowhere and never again have I seen among the living or in the faces of the dying the wan look of certain gray eyes that I remember, nor the dreadful brightness of others that were black.

"Neither Hoffmann nor Maturin, the two weirdest imaginations of our time, ever gave me such a thrill of terror as I used to feel when I watched the automaton movements of those bodies sheathed in whalebone. The paint on actors' faces never caused me a shock; I could see below it the rouge in grain, the *rouge de naissance*, to quote a comrade at least as malicious as I can be. Years had leveled those women's faces, and at the same time furrowed them with wrinkles, till they looked like the heads on wooden nutcrackers carved in Germany. Peeping in through the window-panes, I gazed at the battered bodies, and ill-jointed limbs (how they were fastened together, and, indeed, their whole anatomy was a mystery I never attempted to explain); I saw the lantern jaws, the protuberant bones, the abnormal development of the hips; and the movements of these figures as they came and went seemed to me no whit less extraordinary than their sepulchral immobility as they sat round the card-tables.

"The men looked gray and faded like the ancient tapestries on the wall; in dress they were much more like the men of

the day, but even they were not altogether convincingly alive.
Their white hair, their withered waxen-hued faces, their de-
vastated foreheads and pale eyes, revealed their kinship to the
women, and neutralized any effects of reality borrowed from
their costume.

" The very certainty of finding all these people seated at or
among the tables every day at the same hours invested them
at length in my eyes with a sort of spectacular interest as it
were; there was something theatrical, something unearthly
about them.

" Whenever, in after times, I have gone through museums
of old furniture in Paris, London, Munich, or Vienna, with
the gray-headed custodian who shows you the splendors of
time past, I have peopled the rooms with figures from the
Collection of Antiquities.   Often, as little schoolboys of eight
or ten we used to propose to go and take a look at the curiosities in their glass cage, for the fun of the thing.   But as soon
as I caught sight of Mlle. Armande's sweet face, I used to
tremble; and there was a trace of jealousy in my admiration
for the lovely child Victurnien, who belonged, as we all instinctively felt, to a different and higher order of being from
our own.   It struck me as something indescribably strange that
the young fresh creature should be there in that cemetery
awakened before the time.   We could not have explained
our thoughts to ourselves, yet we felt that we were bourgeois,
utterly insignificant, and of no account in the presence of that
proud court."

The disasters of 1813 and 1814, which brought about the
downfall of Napoleon, gave new life to the Collection of
Antiquities, and what was more than life, the hope of recovering their past importance; but the events of 1815, the
troubles of the foreign occupation, and the vacillating policy
of the Government until the fall of M. Decazes, all contributed to defer the fulfillment of the expectations of the

personages so vividly described by Blondet.   This story, therefore, only begins to shape itself in 1822.

In 1822 the Marquis d'Esgrignon's fortunes had not improved in spite of the changes worked by the Restoration in the condition of *émigrés*.   Of all nobles hardly hit by Revolutionary legislation, his case was the hardest.   Like other great families, the d'Esgrignons before 1789 derived the greater part of their income from their rights as lords of the manor in the shape of dues paid by those who held of them; and, naturally, the old *seigneurs* had reduced the size of the holdings in order to swell the amounts paid in quit-rents and heriots.   Families in this position were hopelessly ruined. They were not affected by the ordinance by which Louis XVIII. put the *émigrés* into possession of such of their lands as had not been sold; and at a later date it was impossible that the law of indemnity should indemnify them.   Their suppressed rights, as everybody knows, were revived in the shape of a land tax known by the very name of *domaines*, but the money went into the coffers of the State.

The marquis by his position belonged to that small section of the Royalist party which would hear of no kind of compromise with those whom they styled, not Revolutionaries, but revolted subjects, or, in more parliamentary language, they had no dealings with Liberals or Constitutionnels.   Such Royalists, nicknamed Ultras by the opposition, took for leaders and heroes those courageous orators of the Right, who from the very beginning attempted, with M. de Polignac, to protest against the charter granted by Louis XVIII.   This they regarded as an ill-advised edict extorted from the Crown by the necessity of the moment, only to be annulled later on. And, therefore, so far from coöperating with the King to bring about a new condition of things, the Marquis d'Esgrignon stood aloof, an upholder of the straitest sect of the Right in politics, until such time as his vast fortune should be restored to him.

The miracles of the Restoration of 1814, the still greater miracle of Napoleon's return in 1815, the portents of a second flight of the Bourbons, and a second reinstatement (that almost fabulous phase of contemporary history), all these things took the marquis by surprise at the age of sixty-seven. At that time of life, the most high-spirited men of their age were not so much vanquished as worn out in the struggle with the Revolution; their activity, in their remote provincial retreats, had turned into a passionately held and immovable conviction; and almost all of them were shut in by the enervating, easy round of daily life in the country. Could worse luck befall a political party than this—to be represented by old men at a time when its ideas are already stigmatized as old-fashioned?

When the legitimate sovereign appeared to be firmly seated on the throne again in 1818, the marquis asked himself what a man of seventy should do at court; and what duties, what office, he could discharge there? The noble and high-minded d'Esgrignon was fain to be content with the triumph of the Monarchy and religion, while he waited for the results of that unhoped-for, indecisive victory, which proved to be simply an armistice. He continued as before, lord-paramount of his salon, so felicitously named the Collection of Antiquities.

But when the victors of 1793 became the vanquished in their turn, the nickname given at first in jest began to be used in bitter earnest. The town was no more free than other country towns from the hatreds and jealousies bred of party spirit. Du Croisier, contrary to all expectation, married the rich old maid who had refused him at first; carrying her off from his rival, the darling of the aristocratic quarter, a certain chevalier whose illustrious name will be sufficiently hidden by suppressing it altogether, in accordance with the usage formerly adopted in the place itself, where he was known by his title only. He was "the chevalier" in the town, as the Comte d'Artois was "monsieur" at court. Now, not only had that marriage produced a war after the provincial manner, in which all weapons are fair; it had hastened the separation of the great and little noblesse, of the aristocratic and bourgeois social elements, which had been united for a little space by the heavy weight of Napoleonic rule. After the pressure was removed, there followed that sudden revival of class divisions which did so much harm to the country.

The most national of all sentiments in France is vanity. The wounded vanity of the many induced a thirst for Equality; though, as the most ardent innovator will some day discover, Equality is an impossibility. The Royalists pricked the Liberals in the most sensitive spots, and this happened especially in the provinces, where either party accused the other of unspeakable atrocities. In those days the blackest deeds were done in politics, to secure public opinion on one side or another, to catch the votes of that public of fools which holds up hands for those that are clever enough to serve out weapons to them. It is very difficult in a country town to avoid a man-to-man conflict of this kind over interests or questions which in Paris appear in a more general and theoretical form, with the result that political combatants also rise to a higher level; M. Laffitte, for example, or M. Casimir Périer can respect M. de Villèle or M. de Peyronnet as a man. M. Laffitte, who drew the fire on the ministry, would have given them an asylum in his house if they had fled thither on the 29th of July, 1830. Benjamin Constant sent a copy of his work on Religion to the Vicomte de Chateaubriand, with a flattering letter acknowledging benefits received from the former minister.

In such warfare as this, waged ceremoniously and without rancor on the side of the Antiquities, while du Croisier's faction went so far as to use the poisoned weapons of savages —in this warfare the advantages of wit and delicate irony lay on the side of the nobles. But it should never be forgotten.

that the wounds made by the tongue and the eyes, by gibe or slight, are the last of all to heal. When the chevalier turned his back on mixed society and intrenched himself on the Mons Sacer of aristocracy, his witticisms thenceforward were directed at du Croisier's salon; he stirred up the fires of war, not knowing how far the spirit of revenge was to urge the rival faction. None but purists and loyal gentlemen and women sure one of another entered the Hôtel d'Esgrignon; they committed no indiscretions of any kind; they had their ideas, true or false, good or bad, noble or trivial, but there was nothing to laugh at in all this. If the Liberals meant to make the nobles ridiculous, they were obliged to fasten on the political actions of their opponents; while the intermediate party, composed of officials and others who paid court to the higher powers, kept the nobles informed of all that was done and said in the Liberal camp, and much of it was abundantly laughable. Du Croisier's adherents smarted under a sense of inferiority, which increased their thirst for revenge.

In 1822, du Croisier put himself at the head of the manufacturing interest of the province, as the Marquis d'Esgrignon headed the noblesse. Each represented his party. But du Croisier, instead of giving himself out frankly for a man of the extreme Left, ostensibly adopted the opinions formulated at a later day by the 221 deputies.

By taking up this position, he could keep in touch with the magistrates and local officials and the capitalists of the department. Du Croisier's salon, a power at least equal to the salon d'Esgrignon, larger numerically, as well as younger and more energetic, made itself felt all over the countryside; the Collection of Antiquities, on the other hand, remained inert, a passive appendage, as it were, of a central authority which was often embarrassed by its own partisans; for not merely did they encourage the Government in a mistaken policy, but some of its most absurd and fatal blunders were made in consequence of the pressure brought to bear upon it by the Conservative party.

The Liberals, so far, had never contrived to carry their candidate. The department declined to obey their command, knowing that du Croisier, if elected, would take his place on the Left Centre benches, and as far as possible to the Left. Du Croisier was in correspondence with the Brothers Keller, the bankers, the oldest of whom shone conspicuous among "the nineteen deputies of the Left," that phalanx made famous by the efforts of the entire Liberal press. This same M. Keller, moreover, was related by marriage to the Comte de Gondreville, a Constitutional peer who remained in favor with Louis XVIII. For these reasons, the Constitutional Opposition (as distinct from the liberal party) was always prepared to vote at the last moment, not for the candidate whom they professed to support, but for du Croisier, if that worthy could succeed in gaining a sufficient number of Royalist votes; but at every election du Croisier was regularly thrown out by the Royalists. The leaders of that party, taking their tone from the Marquis d'Esgrignon, had pretty thoroughly fathomed and gauged their man; and with each defeat, du Croisier and his party waxed more bitter. Nothing so effectually stirs up strife as the failure of some snare set with elaborate pains.

In 1822 there seemed to be a lull in hostilities which had been kept up with great spirit during the first four years of the Restoration. The salon du Croisier and the salon d'Esgrignon, having measured their strength and weakness, were in all probability waiting for opportunity, that Providence of party strife. Ordinary persons were content with the surface quiet which deceived the Government; but those who knew du Croisier better were well aware that the passion of revenge in him, as in all men whose whole life consists in mental activity, is implacable, especially when political ambitions are involved. About this time du Croisier, who used to turn white and red at the bare mention of d'Esgrignon or the chevalier, and shuddered at the name of the Collection of Antiquities, chose to wear the impassive countenance of a savage. He smiled upon his enemies, hating them but the more deeply, watching them the more narrowly from hour to hour. One of his own party, who seconded him in these calculations of cold wrath, was the president of the Tribunal, M. du Ronceret, a little country squire, who had vainly endeavored to gain admittance among the Antiquities.

The d'Esgrignons' little fortune, carefully administered by Maître Chesnel, was barely sufficient for the worthy marquis' needs; for though he lived without the slightest ostentation, he also lived like a noble. The governor found by his lordship the bishop for the hope of the house, the young Comte Victurnien d'Esgrignon, was an elderly Oratorian who must be paid a certain salary, although he lived with the family. The wages of a cook, a waiting-woman for Mlle. Armande, an old valet for M. le Marquis, and a couple of other servants, together with the daily expenses of the household, and the cost of an education for which nothing was spared, absorbed the whole family income, in spite of Mlle. Armande's economies, in spite of Chesnel's careful management, and the servants' affection. As yet, Chesnel had not been able to set about repairs at the ruined castle; he was waiting till the leases fell in to raise the rent of the farms, for rents had been rising lately, partly on account of improved methods of agriculture, partly by the fall in the value of money, of which the landlord would get the benefit at the expiration of leases granted in 1809.

The marquis himself knew nothing of the details of the management of the house or of his property. He would have been thunderstruck if he had been told of the excessive precautions needed "to make both ends of the year meet in December," to use the housewife's saying, and he was so near the end of his life that every one shrank from opening his eyes. The marquis and his adherents believed that a House, to which no one at Court or in the Government gave a thought, a House that was never heard of beyond the gates of the town, save here and there in the same department, was about to revive its ancient greatness, to shine forth in all its glory. The d'Esgrignons' line should reappear with renewed lustre in the person of Victurnien, just as the despoiled nobles came into their own again, and the handsome heir to a great estate would be in a position to go to Court, enter the King's service, and marry (as other d'Esgrignons had done before him) a Navarreins, a Cadignan, a d'Uxelles, a Beauséant, a Blamont-Chauvry; a wife, in short, who should unite all the distinctions of birth and beauty, wit and health, and character.

The intimates who came to play their game of cards of an evening—the Troisvilles (pronounced Tréville), the La Roche-Guyons, the Castérans (pronounced Catéran), and the Duc de Verneuil—had all so long been accustomed to look up to the marquis as a person of immense consequence, that they encouraged him in such notions as these. They were perfectly sincere in their belief; and, indeed, it would have been well founded if they could have wiped out the history of the last forty years. But the most honorable and undoubted sanctions of right, such as Louis XVIII. had tried to set on record when he dated the Charter from the one-and-twentieth year of his reign, only exist when ratified by the general consent. The d'Esgrignons not only lacked the very rudiments of the language of latter-day politics, to wit, money, the great modern *relief*, or sufficient rehabilitation of nobility; but, in their case, too, "historical continuity" was lacking, and that is a kind of renown which tells quite as much at Court as on the battlefield, in diplomatic circles as in Parliament, with a book, or in connection with an adventure; it is, as it were, a sacred *ampulla* poured upon the heads of each successive generation. Whereas a noble family, inactive and forgotten, is very much in the position of a hard-featured, poverty-stricken, simpleminded, and virtuous maid, these qualifications being the four cardinal points of misfortune. The marriage of a daughter of the Troisvilles with General Montcornet, so far from opening the eyes of the Antiquities, very nearly brought about a rupture between the Troisvilles and the salon d'Esgrignon, the latter declaring that the Troisvilles were mixing themselves up with all sorts of people.

There was one, and one only, among all these people who did not share their illusions. And that one, needless to say, was Chesnel the notary. Although his devotion, sufficiently proved already, was simply unbounded for the great house now reduced to three persons; although he accepted all their ideas, and thought them nothing less than right, he had too much commonsense, he was too good a man of business to more than half the families in the department, to miss the significance of the great changes that were taking place in people's minds, or to be blind to the different conditions brought about by industrial development and modern manners. He had watched the Revolution pass through the violent phase of 1793, when men, women, and children wore arms, and heads fell on the scaffold, and victories were won in pitched battles with Europe; and now he saw the same forces quietly at work in men's minds, in the shape of ideas which sanctioned the issues. The soil had been cleared, the seed sown, and now came the harvest. To his thinking, the Revolution had formed the mind of the younger generation; he touched the hard facts, and knew that although there were countless unhealed wounds, what had been done was done past recall. The death of a king on the scaffold, the protracted agony of a queen, the division of the nobles' lands, in his eyes were so many binding contracts; and where so many vested interests were involved, it was not likely that those concerned would allow them to be attacked. Chesnel saw clearly. His fanatical attachment to the d'Esgrignons was whole-hearted, but it was not blind, and it was all the fairer for this. The young monk's faith that sees heaven laid open and beholds the angels is something far below the power of the old monk who points them out to him.   The ex-steward was like the old monk ; he would have given his life to defend a worm-eaten shrine.

He tried to explain the "innovations" to his old master, using a thousand tactful precautions ; sometimes speaking jestingly, sometimes affecting surprise or sorrow over this or that ; but he always met the same prophetic smile on the marquis' lips, the same fixed conviction in the marquis' mind, that these follies would go by like others.   Events contributed in a way which has escaped attention to assist such noble champions of forlorn hopes to cling to their superstitions. What could Chesnel do when the old marquis said, with a lordly gesture: "God swept away Bonaparte with his armies, his new great vassals, his crowned kings, and his vast conceptions !   God will deliver us from the rest."   And Chesnel hung his head sadly, and did not dare to answer: "It cannot be God's will to sweep away France."   Yet both of them were grand figures ; the one, standing out against the torrent of facts like an ancient block of lichen-covered granite, still upright in the depths of an Alpine gorge ; the other, watching the course of the flood to turn it to account.   Then the good gray-headed notary would groan over the irreparable havoc which these superstitions were sure to work in the mind, the habits, and ideas of the Comte Victurnien d'Esgrignon.

Idolized by his father, idolized by his aunt, the young heir was a spoilt child in every sense of the word ; but still a spoilt child who justified paternal and maternal illusions.   Maternal, be it said, for Victurnien's aunt was truly a mother to him ; and yet, however careful and tender she may be that never bore a child, there is a something lacking in her motherhood.   A mother's second-sight cannot be acquired.   An aunt, bound to her nursing by ties of such a pure affection as united Mlle. Armande to Victurnien, may love as much as a mother might ; may be as careful, as kind, as tender, as indulgent, but she lacks the mother's instinctive knowledge when and how to be

severe; she has no sudden warnings, none of the uneasy presentiments of the mother's heart; for a mother, bound to her
child from the beginnings of life by all the fibres of her being,
is still conscious of the communication, still vibrates with the
shock of every trouble, and thrills with every joy in the child's
life as if it were her own. If Nature has made of woman,
physically speaking, a neutral ground, it has not been forbidden to her, under certain conditions, to identify herself
completely with her offspring. When she has not merely
given life, but given of her whole life, you behold that wonderful, unexplained, and inexplicable thing—the love of a woman
for one of her children above the others. The outcome of
this story is one more proof of a proven truth—a mother's
place cannot be filled. A mother foresees danger long before
a Mlle. Armande can admit the possibility of it, even if the
mischief is done. The one prevents the evil, the other
remedies it. And beside, in the maiden's motherhood there
is an element of blind adoration, she cannot bring herself to
scold a beautiful boy.

A practical knowledge of life and the experience of business had taught the old notary a habit of distrustful, clear-
sighted observation something akin to the mother's instinct.
But Chesnel counted for so little in the house (especially since
he had fallen into something like disgrace over that unlucky
project of a marriage between a d'Esgrignon and a du Croisier),
that he had made up his mind to adhere blindly in future to
the family doctrines. He was a common soldier; faithful to
his post, and ready to give his life; it was never likely that
they would take his advice, even in the height of the storm;
unless chance should bring him, like the King's bedesman in
"The Antiquary," to the edge of the sea, when the old
baronet and his daughter were caught by the high tide.

Du Croisier caught a glimpse of his revenge in the anomalous
education given to the lad. He hoped, to quote the expressive words of the author quoted above, "to drown the lamb

12

in its mother's milk." *This* was the hope which had produced his taciturn resignation and brought that savage smile on his lips.

The young Comte Victurnien was taught to believe in his own supremacy so soon as an idea could enter his head. All the great nobles of the realm were his peers, his one superior was the King, and the rest of mankind were his inferiors, people with whom he had nothing in common, toward whom he had no duties. They were defeated and conquered enemies, whom he need not take into account for a moment; their opinions could not affect a noble, and they all owed him respect. Unluckily, with the rigorous logic of youth, which leads children and young people to proceed to extremes whether good or bad, Victurnien pushed these conclusions to their utmost consequences. His own external advantages, moreover, confirmed him in his beliefs. He had been extraordinarily beautiful as a child; he became as accomplished a young man as any father could wish.

Personal beauty has this in common with noble birth, it cannot be acquired afterward; it is everywhere recognized, and often is more valued than either money or brains; beauty has only to appear and triumph; nobody asks more of beauty than that it should simply exist.

Fate had endowed Victurnien, over and above the privileges of good looks and noble birth, with a high spirit, a wonderful aptitude of comprehension, and a good memory. His education, therefore, had been complete. He knew a good deal more than is usually known by young provincial nobles, who develop into highly distinguished sportsmen, owners of land, and consumers of tobacco; and are put to treat art, sciences, letters, poetry, or anything offensively above their intellects cavalierly enough. Such gifts of nature and education surely would one day realize the Marquis d'Esgrignon's ambitions; he already saw his son a Marshal of France if Victurnien's tastes were for the army; an ambassador if diplomacy held any attractions for him ; a cabinet minister if that career seemed good in his eyes; every place in the State belonged to Victurnien. And, most gratifying thought of all for a father, the young count would have made his way in the world by his own merits even if he had not been a d'Esgrignon.

All through his happy childhood and golden youth, Victurnien had never met with opposition to his wishes. He had been the king of the house ; no one curbed the little prince's will ; and naturally he grew up insolent and audacious, selfish as a prince, self-willed as the most high-spirited cardinal of the Middle Ages—defects of character which any one might guess from his qualities, essentially those of the noble.

The chevalier was a man of the good old times when the Gray Musketeers were the terror of the Paris theatres, when they horsewhipped the watch and drubbed servers of writs, and played a host of page's pranks, at which majesty was wont to smile so long as they were amusing. This charming deceiver and hero of the *ruelles* had no small share in bringing about the disasters which afterward befell. The amiable old gentleman, with nobody to understand him, was not a little pleased to find a budding Faublas, who looked the part to admiration, and put him in mind of his own young days. So, making no allowance for the difference of the times, he sowed the maxims of a *roué* of the Encyclopædic period broadcast in the boy's mind. He told wicked anecdotes of the reign of his majesty Louis XV.; he glorified the manners and customs of the year 1750; he told of the orgies in *petites maisons* (little houses—abodes of mistresses), the follies of courtesans, the capital tricks played on creditors, the manners, in short, which furnished forth Dancourt's comedies and Beaumarchais' epigrams. And unfortunately, the corruption lurking beneath the utmost polish tricked itself out in Voltairean wit. If the chevalier went rather too far at times, he always added as a corrective that a man must always behave himself like a gentleman.

Of all this discourse, Victurnien comprehended just so much

as flattered his passions.   From the first he saw his old father laughing with the chevalier.   The two elderly men considered that the pride of a d'Esgrignon was a sufficient safeguard against anything unbefitting ; as for a dishonorable action, no one in the house imagined that a d'Esgrignon could be guilty of it.   HONOR, the great principle of Monarchy, was planted firm like a beacon in the hearts of the family ; it lighted up the least action, it kindled the least thought of a d'Esgrignon. "A d'Esgrignon ought not to permit himself to do such and such a thing, he bears a name, which pledges him to make the future worthy of the past "—a noble teaching which should have been sufficient in itself to keep alive the tradition of noblesse—had been, as it were, the burden of Victurnien's cradle song.   He heard them from the old marquis, from Mlle. Armande, from Chesnel, from the intimates of the house. And so it came to pass that good and evil met, and in equal forces, in the boy's soul.

At the age of eighteen, Victurnien went into society.   He noticed some slight discrepancies between the outer world of the town and the inner world of the Hôtel d'Esgrignon, but he in no wise tried to seek the causes of them.   And, indeed, the causes were to be found in Paris.   He had yet to learn that the men who spoke their minds out so boldly in evening talk with his father were extremely careful of what they said in the presence of the hostile persons with whom their interests compelled them to mingle.   His own father had won the right of freedom of speech.   Nobody dreamed of contradicting an old man of seventy, and beside, every one was willing to overlook fidelity to the old order of things in a man who had been violently despoiled.

Victurnien was deceived by appearances, and his behavior set up the backs of the townspeople.   In his impetuous way he tried to carry matters with too high a hand over some difficulties in the way of sport, which ended in formidable lawsuits, hushed up by Chesnel for money paid down.   Nobody dared to tell the marquis of these things. You may judge of his astonishment if he had heard that his son had been prosecuted for shooting over his lands, his domains, his covers, under the reign of a son of St. Louis! People were too much afraid of the possible consequences to tell him about such trifles, Chesnel said.

The young count indulged in other escapades in the town. These the chevalier regarded as "*amourettes*," but they cost Chesnel something considerable in portions for forsaken damsels seduced under imprudent promises of marriage: yet other cases there were which came under an article of the Code as to the abduction of minors; and but for Chesnel's timely intervention, the new law would have been allowed to take its brutal course, and it is hard to say where the count might have ended. Victurnien grew the bolder for these victories over bourgeois justice. He was so accustomed to be pulled out of scrapes, that he never thought twice before any prank. Courts of law, in his opinion, were bugbears to frighten people, but had no hold on him. Things which he would have blamed in common people were for him only pardonable amusements. His disposition to treat the new laws cavalierly while obeying the maxims of a Code for aristocrats, his behavior and character, were all pondered, analyzed, and tested by a few adroit persons in du Croisier's interests. These people supported each other in the effort to make the people believe that Liberal slanders were revelations, and that the Ministerial policy at bottom meant a return to the old order of things.

What a bit of luck to find something by way of proof of their assertions! President du Ronceret, and the public prosecutor likewise, lent themselves admirably, so far as was compatible with their duty as magistrates, to the design of letting off the offender as easily as possible; indeed, they went deliberately out of their way to do this, well pleased to raise a Liberal clamor against their overlarge concessions.

And so, while seeming to serve the interests of the d'Esgrig-nons, they stirred up ill feeling against them.   The treacher-ous du Ronceret had it in his mind to pose as incorruptible at the right moment over some serious charge, with public opinion to back him up.   The young count's worst tendencies, moreover, were insidiously encouraged by two or three young men who followed in his train, paid court to him, won his favor, and flattered and obeyed him, with a view to confirm-ing his belief in a noble's supremacy; and all this at a time when a noble's one chance of preserving his power lay in using it with the utmost discretion for half a century to come.

Du Croisier hoped to reduce the d'Esgrignons to the last extremity of poverty; he hoped to see their castle demolished, and their lands sold piecemeal by auction, through the follies which this hare-brained boy was pretty certain to commit. This was as far as he went; he did not think, with President du Ronceret, that Victurnien was likely to give justice another kind of hold upon him.   Both men found an ally for their schemes of revenge in Victurnien's overweening vanity and love of pleasure.   President du Ronceret's son, a lad of seventeen, was admirably fitted for the part of instigator. He was one of the count's companions, a new kind of spy in du Croisier's pay; du Croisier taught him his lesson, set him to track down the noble and beautiful boy through his better qualities, and sardonically prompted him to encourage his victim in his worst faults.   Fabien du Ronceret was a sophis-ticated youth, to whom such a mystification was attractive; he had precisely the keen brain and envious nature which finds in such a pursuit as this the absorbing amusement which a man of an ingenious turn lacks in the provinces.

In three years, between the ages of eighteen and one-and-twenty, Victurnien cost poor Chesnel nearly eighty thousand francs!   And this without the knowledge of Mlle. Armande or the marquis.   More than half of the money had been spent in buying off lawsuits; the lad's extravagance had squandered the rest. Of the marquis' income of ten thousand livres, five thousand were necessary for the housekeeping; two thousand more represented Mlle. Armande's allowance (parsimonious though she was) and the marquis' expenses. The handsome young heir-presumptive, therefore, had not a hundred louis to spend. And what sort of figure can a man make on two thousand livres? Victurnien's tailor's bills alone absorbed his whole allowance. He had his linen, his clothes, gloves, and perfumery from Paris. He wanted a good English saddle-horse, a tilbury, and a second horse. M. du Croisier had a tilbury and a thoroughbred. Was the bourgeoisie to cut out the noblesse? Then, the young count must have a man in the d'Esgrignon livery. He prided himself on setting the fashion among young men in the town and the department; he entered that world of luxuries and fancies which suit youth and good looks and wit so well. Chesnel paid for it all, not without using, like ancient parliaments, the right of protest, albeit he spoke with angelic kindness.

"What a pity it is that so good a man should be so tire-some!" Victurnien would say to himself every time that the notary stanched some wound in his purse.

Chesnel had been left a widower, and childless; he had taken his old master's son to fill the void in his heart. It was a pleasure to him to watch the lad driving up the High Street, perched aloft on the box-seat of the tilbury, whip in hand, and a rose in his button-hole, handsome, well turned out, envied by every one.

Pressing need would bring Victurnien with uneasy eyes and coaxing manner, but steady voice, to the modest house in the Rue du Bercail; there had been losses at cards at the Trois-villes, or the Duc de Verneuil's, or the prefecture, or the receiver-general's, and the count had come to his providence, the notary. He had only to show himself to carry the day.

"Well, what is it, Monsieur le Comte? What has happened?" the old man would ask, with a tremor in his voice.

On great occasions Victurnien would sit down, assume a melancholy, pensive expression, and submit with little coquetries of voice and gesture to be questioned. Then when he had thoroughly roused the old man's fears (for Chesnel was beginning to fear how such a course of extravagance would end), he would own up to a peccadillo which a bill for a thousand francs would absolve. Chesnel possessed a private income of some twelve thousand livres, but the fund was not inexhaustible. The eighty thousand francs thus squandered represented his savings, accumulated for the day when the marquis should send his son to Paris, or open negotiations for a wealthy marriage.

Chesnel was clear-sighted so long as Victurnien was not there before him. One by one he lost the illusions which the marquis and his sister still fondly cherished. He saw that the young fellow could not be depended upon in the least, and wished to see him married to some modest, sensible girl of good birth, wondering within himself how a young man could mean so well and do so ill, for he made promises one day only to break them all on the next.

But there is never any good to be expected of young men who confess their sins and repent, and straightway fall into them again. A man of strong character only confesses his faults to himself, and punishes himself for them; as for the weak, they drop back into the old ruts when they find that the bank is too steep to climb. The springs of pride which lie in a great man's secret soul had been slackened in Victurnien. With such guardians as he had, such company as he kept, such a life as he had led, he had suddenly become an enervated voluptuary at that turning-point in his life when a man most stands in need of the harsh discipline of misfortune and poverty to bring out the strength that is in him, the pinch of adversity which formed a Prince Eugène, a Frederick II., a Napoleon. Chesnel saw that Victurnien possessed that uncontrollable appetite for enjoyments which should be the prerogative of men endowed with giant powers; the men who feel the need of counterbalancing their gigantic labors by pleasures which bring one-sided mortals to the pit.

At times the good man stood aghast; then, again, some profound sally, some sign of the lad's remarkable range of intellect, would reassure him. He would say, as the marquis said at the rumor of some escapade: "Boys will be boys." Chesnel had spoken to the chevalier, lamenting the young lord's propensity for getting into debt; but the chevalier manipulated his pinch of snuff, and listened with a smile of amusement.

"My dear Chesnel, just explain to me what a national debt is," he answered. "If France has debts, egad! why should not Victurnien have debts? At this time and at all times princes have debts, every gentleman has debts. Perhaps you would rather that Victurnien should bring you his savings? Do you know what our great Richelieu (not the cardinal, a pitiful fellow that put nobles to death, but the maréchal), do you know what he did once when his grandson the Prince de Chinon, the last of the line, let him see that he had not spent his pocket-money at the University?"

"No, Monsieur le Chevalier."

"Oh, well; he flung the purse out of the window to a sweeper in the courtyard, and said to his grandson: 'Then they do not teach you to be a prince here?'"

Chesnel bent his head and made no answer. But that night, as he lay awake, he thought that such doctrines as these were fatal in times when there was one law for everybody, and foresaw the first beginnings of the ruin of the d'Esgrignons.

But for these explanations which depict one side of provincial life in the time of the Empire and the Restoration, it would not be easy to understand the opening scene of this history, an incident which took place in the great salon one evening toward the end of October, 1822.   The card-tables were forsaken, the Collection of Antiquities—elderly nobles, elderly countesses, young marquises, and simple baronesses—had settled their losses and winnings.   The master of the house was pacing up and down the room, while Mlle. Armande was putting out the candles on the card-tables.   He was not taking exercise alone, the chevalier was with him, and the two wrecks of the eighteenth century were talking of Victurnien.   The chevalier had undertaken to broach the subject with the marquis.

"Yes, marquis," he was saying, "your son is wasting his time and his youth; you ought to send him to Court."

"I have always thought," said the marquis, "that if my great age prevents me from going to Court—where, between ourselves, I do not know what I should do among all these new people whom his majesty receives, and all that is going on there—that if I could not go myself, I could at least send my son to present our homage to his majesty.   The King surely would do something for the count—give him a company, for instance, or a place in the Household, a chance, in short, for the boy to win his spurs.   My uncle the archbishop suffered a cruel martyrdom; I have fought for the cause without deserting the camp with those who thought it their duty to follow the princes.   I held that while the King was in France his nobles should rally round him.   Ah! well, no one gives us a thought; a Henri IV. would have written before now to the d'Esgrignons, 'Come to me, my friends; we have won the day!'   After all, we are something better than the Troisvilles, yet here are two Troisvilles made peers of France; and another, I hear, represents the nobles in the Chamber." (He took the upper electoral colleges for assemblies of his own order.)   "Really, they think no more of us than if we did not exist.   I was waiting for the princes to make their journey through this part of the world; but as the princes do not come to us, we must go to the princes."

"I am enchanted to learn that you think of introducing our

dear Victurnien into society," the chevalier put in adroitly. "He ought not to bury his talents in a hole like this town. The best fortune that he can look for here is to come across some Norman girl" (mimicking the accent), "country-bred, stupid, and rich. What could he make of her?—his wife? Oh! good Lord!"

"I sincerly hope that he will defer his marriage until he has obtained some great office or appointment under the Crown," returned the gray-haired marquis. "Still, there are serious difficulties in the way."

And these were the only difficulties which the marquis saw at the outset of his son's career.

"My son, the Comte d'Esgrignon, cannot make his appearance at court like a tatterdemalion," he continued after a pause, marked by a sigh; "he must be equipped. Alas! for these two hundred years we have had no retainers. Ah! chevalier, this demolition from top to bottom always brings me back to the first hammer-stroke delivered by Monsieur de Mirabeau. The one thing needful nowadays is money; that is all that the Revolution has done that I can see. The King does not ask you whether you are a descendant of the Valois or a conqueror of Gaul; he asks whether you pay a thousand francs in *tailles* which nobles never used to pay. So I cannot well send the count to Court without a matter of twenty thousand crowns——"

"Yes," assented the chevalier, "with that trifling sum he could cut a brave figure."

"Well," said Mlle. Armande, "I have asked Chesnel to come to-night. Would you believe it, chevalier, ever since the day when Chesnel proposed that I should marry that miserable du Croisier——"

"Ah! that was truly unworthy, mademoiselle!" cried the chevalier.

"Unpardonable!" said the marquis.

"Well, since then my brother has never brought himself

to ask anything whatsoever of Monsieur Chesnel," continued
Mlle. Armande.

"Of your old household servant? Why, marquis, you
would do Chesnel honor—an honor which he would grate-
fully remember till his latest breath."

" No," said the marquis, " the thing is beneath one's dignity, it seems to me."

"There is not much question of dignity; it is a matter of
necessity," said the chevalier, with the trace of a shrug.

"Never," said the marquis, riposting with a gesture which
decided the chevalier to risk a great stroke to open his old
friend's eyes.

"Very well," he said, "since you do not know it, I will
tell you myself that Chesnel has let your son have something
already, something like——"

" My son is incapable of accepting anything whatever from
Chesnel," the marquis broke in, drawing himself up as he
spoke.   " He might have asked *you* for twenty-five louis——"

"Something like a hundred thousand livres," said the
chevalier, finishing his sentence.

"The Comte d'Esgrignon owes a hundred thousand livres
to a Chesnel!" cried the marquis, with every sign of deep
pain. "Oh! if he were not an only son, he should set out
to-night for Mexico with a captain's commission. A man
may be in debt to money-lenders, they charge a heavy interest,
and you are quits; that is right enough; but *Chesnel!* a man
to whom one is attached !——"

" Yes, our adorable Victurnien has run through a hundred
thousand livres, dear marquis," resumed the chevalier, flick-
ing a trace of snuff from his vest; "it is not much, I know.
I myself at his age—— But, after all, let us leave old memories, marquis. The count is living in the provinces; all
things taken into consideration, it is not so much amiss. He
will go far; these irregularities are common in men who do
great things afterward——"

"And he is sleeping upstairs, without a word of this to his father," exclaimed the marquis.

"Sleeping innocently as a child who has merely got five or six little bourgeoises into trouble, and now must have duchesses," returned the chevalier.

"Why, he deserves a *lettre de cachet!*"

"'They' have done away with *lettres de cachet,*"* said the chevalier. "You know what a hubbub there was when they tried to institute a law for special cases. We could not keep the provost's courts, which Monsieur *de* Bonaparte used to call *commissions militaires.*"

"Well, well; what are we to do if our boys are wild or turn out scapegraces? Is there no locking them up in these days?" asked the marquis.

The chevalier looked at the heart-broken father and lacked courage to answer: "We shall be obliged to bring them up properly."

"And you have never said a word of this to me, Mademoiselle d'Esgrignon," added the marquis, turning suddenly round upon Mlle. Armande. He never addressed her as Mlle. d'Esgrignon except when he was vexed; usually she was called "my sister."

"Why, monsieur, when a young man is full of life and spirits, and leads an idle life in a town like this, what else can you expect?" asked Mlle. d'Esgrignon. She could not understand her brother's anger.

"Debts! eh! why, hang it all!" added the chevalier. "He plays cards, he has little adventures, he shoots—all these things are horribly expensive nowadays."

"Come," said the marquis, "it is time to send him to the King. I will spend to-morrow morning in writing to our kinsmen."

"I have some acquaintance with the Ducs de Navarreins, de Lenoncourt, de Maufrigneuse, and de Chaulieu," said the

* An arbitrary warrant of imprisonment sealed with the king's *cachet*—seal.

chevalier, though he knew, as he spoke, that he was pretty thoroughly forgotten.

"My dear chevalier, there is no need of such formalities to present a d'Esgrignon at Court," the marquis broke in. "A hundred thousand livres," he muttered; "this Chesnel makes very free. This is what comes of these accursed troubles. Mons. Chesnel protects my son. And now I must ask him—— No, sister, you must undertake this business. Chesnel shall secure himself for the whole amount by a mortgage on our lands. And just give this hare-brained boy a good scolding; he will end by ruining himself if he goes on like this."

The chevalier and Mlle. d'Esgrignon thought these words perfectly simple and natural, absurd as they would have sounded to any other listener. So far from seeing anything ridiculous in the speech, they were both very much touched by a look of something like anguish in the old noble's face.

Just then the Marquis d'Esgrignon looked exactly as any imagination with a touch of romance could wish. He was almost bald, but a fringe of silken, white locks, curled at the tips, covered the back of his head. All the pride of race might be seen in a noble forehead, such as you may admire in a Louis XV., a Beaumarchais, a Maréchal de Richelieu; it was not the square, broad brow of the portraits of the Maréchal de Saxe; nor yet the small, hard circle of Voltaire, compact to overfulness; it was graciously rounded and finely moulded, the temples were ivory-tinted and soft; and mettle and spirit, unquenched by age, flashed from the brilliant eyes. The marquis had the Condé nose and the lovable Bourbon mouth, from which, as they used to say of the Comte d'Artois, only witty and urbane words proceed. His cheeks, sloping rather than foolishly rounded to the chin, were in keeping with his spare frame, thin legs, and plump hands. The strangulation cravat at his throat was of the kind which every marquis wears in all the portraits which adorn eighteenth-century literature; it is common alike to Saint-Preux and to Lovelace, to the elegant Montesquieu's heroes and to Diderot's homespun characters (see the first editions of those writers' works).

The marquis always wore a white, gold-embroidered, high vest, with the red ribbon of a commander of the Order of St. Louis blazing upon his breast; and a blue coat with wide skirts, and fleurs-de-lys on the flaps, which were turned back —an odd costume which the King had adopted. But the marquis could not bring himself to give up the Frenchman's knee-breeches nor yet the white silk stockings or the buckles at the knees. After six o'clock in the evening he appeared in full dress.

He read no newspapers but the "Quotidienne" and the "Gazette de France," two journals accused by the Constitutional press of obscurantist views and uncounted "monarchical and religious" enormities; while the Marquis d'Esgrignon, on the other hand, found heresies and revolutionary doctrines in every issue.

The Marquis d'Esgrignon rested his elbows on his knees and leaned his head on his hands. During his meditations Mlle. Armande and the chevalier looked at one another without uttering the thoughts in their minds. Was he pained by the discovery that his son's future must depend upon his sometime land-steward? Was he doubtful of the reception awaiting the young count? Did he regret that he had made no preparation for launching his heir into that brilliant world of court? Poverty had kept him in the depths of his province; how should he have appeared at Court? He sighed heavily as he raised his head.

That sigh, in those days, came from the real aristocracy all over France; from the loyal provincial noblesse, consigned to neglect with most of those who had drawn sword and braved the storm for the cause.

"What have the princes done for the du Guénics, or the Fontaines, or the Bauvans, who never submitted?" he muttered to himself. "They fling miserable pensions to the

men who fought most bravely, and give them a royal lieu-
tenancy in a fortress somewhere on the outskirts of the
kingdom.''

Evidently the marquis doubted the reigning dynasty.
Mlle. d'Esgrignon was trying to reassure her brother as to
the prospects of the journey, when a step outside on the dry,
narrow footway gave them notice of Chesnel's coming. In
another moment Chesnel appeared ; Joséphin, the count's
gray-haired valet, admitted the notary without announcing
him.

"Chesnel, my boy——" (Chesnel was a white-haired man
of sixty-nine, with a square-jawed, venerable countenance ;
he wore knee-breeches, ample enough to fill several chapters
of dissertation in the manner of Sterne, ribbed stockings,
shoes with silver clasps, an ecclesiastical-looking coat and a
high vest of scholastic cut.

"Chesnel, my boy, it was very presumptuous of you to lend
money to the Comte d'Esgrignon ! If I repaid you at once
and we never saw each other again, it would be no more than
you deserve for giving wings to his vices.''

There was a pause, a silence such as there falls at Court when
the King publicly reprimands a courtier. The old notary
looked humble and contrite.

"I am anxious about that boy, Chesnel,'' continued the
marquis in a kindly tone ; "I should like to send him to
Paris to serve his majesty. Make arrangements with my
sister for his suitable appearance at Court. And we will settle
accounts——''

The marquis looked grave as he left the room with a friendly
gesture of farewell to Chesnel.

"I thank Monsieur le Marquis for all his goodness,''
returned the old man, who still remained standing.

Mlle. Armande rose to go to the door with her brother ;
she had rung the bell, old Joséphin was in readiness to light
his master to his room.

"Take a seat, Chesnel," said the lady, as she returned, and with womanly tact she explained away and softened the marquis' harshness. And yet beneath that harshness Chesnel saw a great affection. The marquis' attachment for his old servant was something of the same order as a man's affection for his dog; he will fight any one who kicks the animal, the dog is like a part of his existence, a something which, if not exactly himself, represents him in that which is nearest and dearest—his sensibilities.

"It is quite time that Monsieur le Comte should be sent away from the town, mademoiselle," he said sententiously.

"Yes," returned she. "Has he been indulging in some new escapade?"

"No, mademoiselle."

"Well, why do you blame him?"

"I am not blaming him, mademoiselle. No, I am not blaming him. I am very far from blaming him. I will even say that I shall never blame him, whatever he may do."

There was a pause. The chevalier, nothing if not quick to take in a situation, began to yawn like a sleep-ridden mortal. Gracefully he made his excuses and went, with as little mind to sleep as to go and drown himself. The imp Curiosity kept the chevalier wide awake, and with airy fingers plucked away the cotton-batting from his ears.

"Well, Chesnel, is it something new?" Mlle. Armande began anxiously.

"Yes, things that cannot be told to Monsieur le Marquis; he would drop down in an apoplectic fit."

"Speak out," she said. With her beautiful head leant on the back of her low chair and her arms extended listlessly by her side, she looked as if she were waiting passively for her death-blow.

"Mademoiselle, Monsieur le Comte, with all his cleverness, is a plaything in the hands of mean creatures, petty natures on the lookout for a crushing revenge. They want to ruin us

13

and bring us low! There is the president of the Tribunal, Monsieur du Ronceret; he has, as you know, a very great notion of his descent——"

"His grandfather was an attorney," interposed Mlle. Armande.

"I know he was. And for that reason you have not received him; nor does he go to Monsieur de Troisville's, nor to le Duc de Verneuil's, nor to the Marquis de Castéran's; but he is one of the pillars of du Croisier's salon. Your nephew may rub shoulders with young Fabien du Ronceret without condescending too far, for he must have companions of his own age. Well and good. That young fellow is at the bottom of all Monsieur le Comte's follies; he and two or three of the rest of them belong to the other side, the side of Monsieur le Chevalier's enemy, who does nothing but breathe threats of vengeance against you and all the nobles together. They all hope to ruin you through your nephew. The ringleader of the conspiracy is this sycophant of a du Croisier, the pretended Royalist. Du Croisier's wife, poor thing, knows nothing about it; you know her, I should have heard of it before this if she had ears to hear evil. For some time these wild young fellows were not in the secret, nor was anybody else; but the ringleaders let something drop in jest, and then the fools got to know about it, and after the count's recent escapades they let fall some words while they were drunk. And those words were carried to me by others who are sorry to see such a fine, handsome, noble, charming lad ruining himself with pleasure. So far people feel sorry for him; before many days are over they will—I am afraid to say what, but——"

"They will despise him; say it out, Chesnel!" Mlle. Armande cried piteously.

"Ah! How can you keep the best people in the town from finding out faults in their neighbors? They do not know what to do with themselves from morning to night. And so

Monsieur le Comte's losses at play are all reckoned up. Thirty thousand francs have taken flight during these two months, and everybody wonders where he gets the money. If they mention it when I am present, I just call them to order. Ah! but—— 'Do you suppose' (I told them this morning), 'do you suppose that if the d'Esgrignon family have lost their manorial rights, that therefore they have been robbed of their hoard of treasure? The young count has a right to do as he pleases; and so long as he does not owe you a sol, you have no right to say a word.' "

Mlle. Armande held out her hand, and the notary kissed it respectfully.

"Good Chesnel! But, my friend, how shall we find the money for this journey? Victurnien must appear as befits his rank at Court."

"Oh! I have borrowed money on Le Jard, mademoiselle."

"What? You had nothing left! Ah, heaven! what can we do to reward you?"

"You can take the hundred thousand francs which I hold at your disposal. You can understand that the loan was negotiated in confidence, so that it might not reflect on you; for it is known in the town that I am closely connected with the d'Esgrignon family."

Tears came into Mlle. Armande's eyes. Chesnel saw them, took a fold of the noble woman's dress in his hands, and kissed it.

"Never mind," he said, "a lad must sow his wild oats. In great salons in Paris his boyish ideas will take a new turn. And, really, though our old friends here are the worthiest people in the world, and no one could have nobler hearts than they, they are not amusing. If Monsieur le Comte wants amusement, he is obliged to look below his rank, and he will end by getting into low company."

Next day the old traveling coach saw the light, and was sent to be put in repair. In a solemn interview after breakfast, the hope of the house was duly informed of his father's intentions regarding him—he was to go to Court and ask to serve his majesty. He would have time during the journey to make up his mind about his career. The navy or the army, the privy council, an embassy, or the royal household—all were open to a d'Esgrignon, a d'Esgrignon had only to choose. The King would certainly look favorably upon the d'Esgrignons, because they had asked nothing of him, and had sent the youngest representative of their house to receive the recognition of majesty.

But young d'Esgrignon, with all his wild pranks, had guessed instinctively what society in Paris meant, and formed his own opinions of life. So, when they talked of his leaving the country and the paternal roof, he listened with a grave countenance to his revered parent's lecture, and refrained from giving him a good deal of information in reply. As, for instance, that young men no longer went into the army or the navy as they used to do; that if a man had a mind to be a second lieutenant in a cavalry regiment without passing through a special training in the Écoles, he must first serve in the Cadets; that sons of the greatest houses went exactly like commoners to Saint-Cyr and the Polytechnic, and took their chances of being beaten by base blood. If he had enlightened his relatives on these points, funds might not have been forthcoming for a stay in Paris; so he allowed his father and Aunt Armande to believe that he would be permitted a seat in the King's carriages, that he must support his dignity at Court as the d'Esgrignons of the time, and rub shoulders with great lords of the realm.

It grieved the marquis that he could send but one servant with his son; but he gave him his own old valet Joséphin, a man who could be trusted to take care of his young master, and to watch faithfully over his interests. The poor father must do without Joséphin, and hope to replace him with a young lad.

"Remember that you are a Carol, my boy," he said; "remember that you come of an unalloyed descent, and that your escutcheon bears the motto *Cil est nostre ;* with such arms you may hold your head high everywhere, and aspire to queens. Render grace to your father, as I to mine. We owe it to the honor of our ancestors, kept stainless until now, that we can look all men in the face, and need bend the knee to none save a mistress, the King, and God. This is the greatest of your privileges.''

Chesnel, good man, was breakfasting with the family. He took no part in counsels based on heraldry, nor in the inditing of letters addressed to divers mighty personages of the day ; but he had spent the night in writing to an old friend of his, one of the oldest established notaries of Paris. Without this letter it is not possible to understand Chesnel's real and assumed fatherhood. It almost recalls Dædalus' address to Icarus ; for where, save in old mythology, can you look for comparisons worthy of this man of antique mould ?

"My Dear and Estimable Sorbier :—I remember with no little pleasure that I made my first campaign in our honorable profession under your father, and that you had a liking for me, poor little clerk that I was. And now I appeal to old memories of the days when we worked in the same office, old pleasant memories for our hearts, to ask you to do me the one service that I have ever asked of you in the course of our long lives, crossed as they have been by political catastrophes, to which, perhaps, I owe it that I have the honor to be your colleague. And now I ask this service of you, my friend, and my white hairs will be brought with sorrow to the grave if you should refuse my entreaty. It is no question of myself or of mine, Sorbier, for I lost poor Mme. Chesnel, and I have no child of my own. Something more to me than my own family (if I had had one) is involved—it is the Marquis d'Esgrignon's only son. I have had the honor to be the marquis' land-steward ever since I left the office to which his father sent me at his own expense, with the idea of providing for me.   The house which nurtured me has passed through all the troubles of the Revolution.   I have managed to save some of their property; but what is it, after all, in comparison with the wealth that they have lost?   I cannot tell you, Sorbier, how deeply I am attached to the great house, which has been all but swallowed up under my eyes by the abyss of time. M. le Marquis was proscribed, and his lands confiscated, he was getting on in years, he had no child.   Misfortunes upon misfortunes!   Then M. le Marquis married, and his wife died when the young count was born, and to-day this noble, dear, and precious child is all the life of the d'Esgrignon family; the fate of the house hangs upon him.   He has got into debt here with amusing himself.   What else should he do in the provinces with an allowance of a miserable hundred louis? Yes, my friend, a hundred louis, the great house had come to this.

"In this extremity his father thinks it necessary to send the count to Paris to ask for the King's favor at Court.   Paris is a very dangerous place for a lad; if he is to keep steady there he must have the grain of sense which makes notaries of us. Beside, I should be heart-broken to think of the poor boy living amid such hardships as we have known.   Do you remember the pleasure with which you shared my roll in the pit of the Théâtre-Français when we spent a day and a night there waiting to see 'The Marriage of Figaro?'   Oh, blind that we were!   We were happy and poor, but a noble cannot be happy in poverty.   A noble in want—it is a thing against nature!   Ah! Sorbier, when one has known the satisfaction of propping one of the grandest genealogical trees in the kingdom in its fall, it is so natural to interest one's self in it and to grow fond of it, and love it and water it and look to see it blossom. So you will not be surprised at so many precautions on my part; you will not wonder when I beg the help of your lights, so that all may go well with our young man.

" The family has allowed a hundred thousand francs for the expenses of M. le Comte's journey. There is not a young man in Paris fit to compare with him, as you will see ! You will take an interest in him as if he were your only son ; and, lastly, I am quite sure that Mme. Sorbier will not hesitate to second you in the office of guardian. M. le Comte Victurnien's monthly allowance is fixed at two thousand francs, but give him ten thousand for his preliminary expenses. The family has provided in this way for a stay of two years, unless he takes a journey abroad, in which case we will see about making other arrangements. Join me in this work, my old friend, and keep the purse-strings fairly tight. Represent things to M. le Comte without reproving him ; hold him in as far as you can, and do not let him anticipate his monthly allowance without sufficient reason, for he must not be driven to desperation if honor is involved.

" Keep yourself informed of his movements and doings, of the company which he keeps, and watch over his connections with women. M. le Chevalier says that an opera-dancer often costs less than a court lady. Obtain information on that point and let me know. If you are too busy, perhaps Mme. Sorbier might know what becomes of the young man, and where he goes. The idea of playing the part of guardian angel to such a noble and charming boy might have attractions for her. God will remember her for accepting the sacred trust. Perhaps when you see M. le Comte Victurnien, her heart may tremble at the thought of all the dangers awaiting him in Paris ; he is very young and very handsome, clever, and at the same time disposed to trust others. If he forms a connec· tion with some designing woman, Mme. Sorbier could counsel him better than you yourself could do. The old manservant who is with him can tell you many things ; sound Joséphin, I have told him to go to you in delicate matters.

" But why should I say more ? We once were clerks together, and a pair of scamps ; remember our escapades, and be a little bit young again, my old friend, in your dealings with him. The sixty thousand francs will be remitted to you in the shape of a bill on the Treasury by a gentleman who is going to Paris,'' and so forth.

If the old couple to whom this epistle was addressed had followed out Chesnel's instructions, they would have been compelled to take three private detectives into their pay. And yet there was ample wisdom shown in Chesnel's choice of a depository. A banker pays money to any one accredited to him so long as the money lasts; whereas, Victurnien was obliged, every time that he was in want of money, to make a personal visit to the notary, who was quite sure to use the right of remonstrance.

Victurnien heard that he was to be allowed two thousand francs every month, and thought that he betrayed his joy. He knew nothing of Paris. He fancied that he could keep up princely state on such a sum.

Next day he started on his journey. The sudden departure supplied material for conversation for several evenings; and what was more, it stirred the rancorous minds of the salon du Croisier to the depths. The forage-contractor, the president, and others who had vowed to ruin the d'Esgrignons, saw their prey escaping out of their hands. They had based their schemes of revenge on a young man's follies, and now he was beyond their reach.

The tendency in human nature, which often gives a bigot a rake for a daughter, and makes a frivolous woman the mother of a narrow pietist; that rule of contraries, which, in all probability, is the "resultant" of the law of similarities, drew Victurnien to Paris by a desire to which he must sooner or later have yielded. Brought up as he had been in the old-fashioned provincial house, among the quiet, gentle faces that smiled upon him, among sober servants attached to the family, and surroundings tinged with a general color of age, the boy had only seen friends worthy of respect. All of those about him, with the exception of the chevalier, that example of venerable age, were elderly men and women, sedate of manner, decorous and sententious of speech. He had been petted by those women in the gray gowns and embroidered mittens described by Blondet. The antiquated splendors of his father's house were as little calculated as possible to suggest frivolous thoughts; and, lastly, he had been educated by a sincerely religious abbé, possessed of all the charm of an old age, which has dwelt in two centuries, and brings to the Present its gifts of the dried roses of experience, the faded flowers of the old customs of its youth.

For him, his noble birth was a stepping-stone which raised him above other men. He felt that the idol of Noblesse, before which they burned incense at home, was hollow; he had come to be one of the commonest as well as one of the worst types from a social point of view—a consistent egoist. The aristocratic cult of the *Ego* simply taught him to follow his own fancies; he had been idolized by those who had the care of him in childhood, and adored by the companions who shared in his boyish escapades, and so he had formed a habit of looking and judging everything as it affected his own pleasure; he took it as a matter of course when good souls saved him from the consequences of his follies, a piece of mistaken kindness which could only lead to his ruin.

Victurnien was quick-sighted, he saw clearly and without illusion, but he acted on impulse, and unwisely. An indefinable flaw of character, often seen in young men, but impossible to explain, led him to will one thing and do another. In spite of an active mind, which showed itself in unexpected ways, the senses had but to assert themselves, and the darkened brain seemed to exist no longer. He might have astonished wise men; he was capable of setting fools agape. His desires, like a sudden squall of bad weather, overclouded all the clear and lucid spaces of his brain in a moment; and then, after the dissipations which he could not resist, he sank, utterly exhausted in body, heart, and mind, into a collapsed condition bordering upon imbecility. Such a character will drag a man down into the mire if he is left to himself, or bring him to the highest heights of political power if he has some stern friend to keep him in hand. Neither Chesnel, nor the lad's father, nor Aunt Armande had fathomed the depths of a nature so nearly akin on many sides to the poetic temperament, yet smitten with a terrible weakness at its core.

By the time the old town lay several miles away, Victurnien felt not the slightest regret ; he thought no more about the father, who had loved ten generations in his son ; nor of the aunt, and her almost insane devotion. He was looking forward to Paris with vehement ill-starred longings, in thought he had lived in that fairyland, it had been the background of his brightest dreams. He imagined that he would be first in Paris, as he had been in the town and the department where his father's name was potent ; but it was vanity, not pride, that filled his soul, and in his dreams his pleasures were to be magnified by all the greatness of Paris ; he hastened to take possession of it as a famished horse rushes into a meadow.

He was not long in finding out the difference between country and town, and was rather surprised than abashed by the change. His mental quickness soon discovered how small an entity he was in the midst of this all-comprehending Babylon ; how insane it would be to attempt to stem the torrent of new ideas and new ways. A single incident was enough. He delivered his father's letter of introduction to the Duc de Lenoncourt, a noble who stood high in favor with the King. He saw the duke in his splendid mansion, among surroundings befitting his rank. Next day he met him again. This time the Peer of France was lounging on foot along the boulevard, just like any ordinary mortal, with an umbrella in his hand ; he did not even wear the Blue Ribbon, without which no knight of the order could have appeared in public in other times. And, duke and peer and first gentleman of the bedchamber though he was, M. de Lenoncourt, spite of his high courtesy, could not repress a smile as he read his relative's letter; and that smile told Victurnien that the Collection of Antiquities and the Tuileries were separated by more than sixty leagues of road—the distance of several centuries lay between them.

The names of the families grouped about the throne are quite different in each successive reign, and the characters change with the names. It would seem that, in the sphere of Court, the same thing happens over and over again in each generation; but each time there is a quite different set of personages. If history did not prove that this is so, it would seem incredible. The prominent men at the Court of Louis XVIII., for instance, had scarcely any connection with the Rivières, Blacas, d'Avarays, Vitrolles, d'Autichamps, Pasquiers, Larochejaqueleins, Decazes, Dambrays, Lainés, de Villèles, La Bourdonnayes, and others who shone at the Court of Louis XV. Compare the courtiers of Henri IV. with those of Louis XIV.; you will hardly find five great families of the former time still in existence. The nephew of the great Richelieu was a very insignificant person at the Court of Louis XIV.; while his majesty's favorite, Villeroi, was the grandson of a secretary ennobled by Charles IX. And so it befell that the d'Esgrignons, all but princes under the Valois, and all-powerful in the time of Henri IV., had no fortune whatever at the Court of Louis XVIII., which gave them not so much as a thought. At this day there are names as famous as those of royal houses—the Foix-Graillys, for instance, or the d'Hérouvilles—left to obscurity tantamount to extinction for want of money, the one power of the time.

All which things Victurnien beheld entirely from his own point of view; he felt the equality that he saw in Paris as a personal wrong. The monster Equality was swallowing down the last fragments of social distinction in the Restoration. Having made up his mind on this head, he immediately proceeded to try to win back his place with such dangerous, if blunted, weapons as the age left to the noblesse. It is an expensive matter to gain the attention of Paris. To this end, Victurnien adopted some of the ways then in vogue. He felt that it was a necessity to have horses and fine carriages, and all the accessories of modern luxury; he felt, in short, "that a man must keep abreast of the times," as de Marsay said—de Marsay, the first dandy that he came across in the first drawing-room to which he was introduced. For his misfortune, he fell in with a set of roues, with de Marsay, de Ronquerolles, Maxime de Trailles, des Lupeaulx, Rastignac, Ajuda-Pinto, Beaudenord, de la Roche-Hugon, de Manerville, and the Vandenesses, whom he met wherever he went, and a great many houses were open to a young man with his ancient name and reputation for wealth. He went to the Marquise d'Espard's, to the Duchesses de Grandlieu, de Carigliano, and de Chaulieu, to the Marquises d'Aiglemont and de Listomère, to Mme. de Sérizy's, to the opera, to the embassies and elsewhere. The Faubourg Saint-Germain has its provincial genealogies at its fingers' ends; a great name once recognized and adopted therein is a passport which opens many a door that will scarcely turn on its hinges for unknown names or the lions of a lower rank.

Victurnien found his relatives both amiable and ready to welcome him so long as he did not appear as a suppliant; he saw at once that the surest way of obtaining nothing was to ask for something. At Paris, if the first impulse moves people to protect, second thoughts (which last a good deal longer) impel them to despise the protege. Independence, vanity, and pride, all the young count's better and worse feelings combined, led him, on the contrary, to assume an aggressive attitude. And therefore the Ducs de Verneuil, de Lenoncourt, de Chaulieu, de Navarreins, d'Hérouville, de Grandlieu, and de Maufrigneuse, the Princes de Cadignan and de Blamont-Chauvry, were delighted to present the charming survivor of the wreck of an ancient family at Court.

Victurnien went to the Tuileries in a splendid carriage with his armorial bearings on the panels; but his presentation to his majesty made it abundantly clear to him that the people occupied the royal mind so much that his nobility was like to be forgotten. The restored dynasty, moreover, was surrounded by triple ranks of eligible old men and gray-headed courtiers; the young noblesse was reduced to a cipher, and this Victurnien guessed at once. He saw that there was no suitable place for him at Court, nor in the government, nor the army, nor, indeed, anywhere else. So he launched out into the world of pleasure. Introduced at the Élysée-Bourbon, at the Duchesse d'Angoulême's, at the Pavillon Marsan, he met on all sides with the surface civilities due to the heir of an old family, not so old but it could be called to mind by the sight of a living member. And, after all, it was not a small thing to be remembered. In the distinction with which Victurnien was honored lay the way to the peerage and a splendid marriage; he had taken the field with a false appearance of wealth, and his vanity would not allow him to declare his real position. Beside, he had been so much complimented on the figure that he made, he was so pleased with his first success, that, like many other young men, he felt ashamed to draw back. He took a suite of rooms in the Rue du Bac, with stables and a complete equipment for the fashionable life to which he had committed himself. These preliminaries cost him fifty thousand francs, which money, moreover, the young gentleman managed to draw in spite of all Chesnel's wise precautions, thanks to a series of unforeseen events.

Chesnel's letter certainly reached his friend's office, but Maître Sorbier was dead; and Mme. Sorbier, a matter-of-fact person, seeing that it was a business letter, handed it on to her husband's successor. Maître Cardot, the new notary, informed the young count that a draft on the Treasury made payable to the deceased would be useless; and by way of reply to the letter, which had cost the old provincial notary so much thought, Cardot dispatched four lines intended not to reach Chesnel's heart, but to produce the money. Chesnel made the draft payable to Sorbier's young successor; and the latter, feeling but little inclination to adopt his correspondent's sentimentality, was delighted to put himself at the count's orders, and gave Victurnien as much money as he wanted.

Now those who know what life in Paris means, know that fifty thousand francs will not go very far in furniture, horses, carriages, and elegance generally; but it must be borne in mind that Victurnien immediately contracted some twenty thousand francs' worth of debts beside, and his tradespeople at first were not at all anxious to be paid, for our young gentleman's fortune had been prodigiously increased, partly by rumor, partly by Joséphin, that Chesnel in livery.

Victurnien had not been in town a month before he was obliged to repair to his man of business for ten thousand francs; he had only been playing whist with the Ducs de Navarreins, de Chaulieu, and de Lenoncourt, and now and again at his club. He had begun by winning some thousands of francs, but pretty soon lost five or six thousand, which brought home to him the necessity of a purse for play. A man ought to renew his wealth perpetually, and as Nature does—below the surface and out of sight. People talk if somebody comes to grief; they joke about a new-comer's fortune till their minds are set at rest, and at this they draw the line. Victurnien d'Esgrignon, with all the Faubourg Saint-Germain to back him, with all his protectors exaggerating the amount of his fortune (were it only to rid themselves of responsibility), and magnifying his possessions in the most refined and well-bred way, with a hint or a word; with all these advantages—to repeat—Victurnien was, in fact, an eligible count. He was handsome, witty, sound in politics; his father still possessed the ancestral castle and the lands of the marquisate. Such a young fellow is sure of an admirable reception in houses where there are marriageable daughters, fair but portionless partners at dances, and young married women who find that time hangs heavy on their hands. So the world, smiling, beckoned him to the foremost benches in its booth ; the seats reserved for marquises are still in the same place in Paris ; and if the names are changed, the things are the same as ever.

In the must exclusive circle of society in the Faubourg Saint-Germain, Victurnien found the chevalier's double in the person of the Vidame de Pamiers. The vidame was a Chevalier de Valois raised to the tenth power, invested with all the prestige of wealth, enjoying all the advantages of high position. The dear vidame was a repository for everybody's secrets, and the gazette of the Faubourg beside ; nevertheless, he was discreet, and, like other gazettes, only said things that might safely be published. Again Victurnien listened to the chevalier's esoteric doctrines. The vidame told young d'Esgrignon, without mincing matters, to make conquests among women of quality, supplementing the advice with anecdotes from his own experience. The Vicomte de Pamiers, it seemed, had permitted himself much that it would serve no purpose to relate here ; so remote was it from all our modern manners, in which soul and passion play so large a part, that nobody would believe it. But the excellent vidame did more than this.

" Dine with me at a café to-morrow,'' said he, by way of conclusion. "We will digest our dinner at the opera, and afterward I will take you to a house where several people have the greatest wish to meet you.''

The vidame gave a delightful little dinner at the Rocher de Cancale ; three guests only were asked to meet Victurnien— de Marsay, Rastignac, and Blondet. Émile Blondet, the young count's fellow-townsman, was a man of letters on the outskirts of society to which he had been introduced by a charming woman from the same province. This was one of the Vicomte de Troisville's daughters, now married to the Comte de Montcornet, one of those of Napoleon's generals who went over to the Bourbons. The vidame held that a dinner-party of more than six persons was beneath contempt. In that case, according to him, there was an end alike of cookery and conversation, and a man could not sip his wine in a proper frame of mind.

"I have not yet told you, my dear boy, where I mean to take you to-night," he said, taking Victurnien's hands, and tapping on them. " You are going to see Mademoiselle des Touches; all the pretty women with any pretensions to wit will be at her house *en petit comité.** Literature, art, poetry, any sort of genius, in short, is held in great esteem there. It is one of our old-world *bureaux d'esprit*, with a veneer of monarchical doctrine, the livery of this present age."

"It is sometimes as tiresome and tedious there as a pair of new boots, but there are women with whom you cannot meet anywhere else," said de Marsay.

"If all the poets who went there to rub up their muse were like our friend here," said Rastignac, tapping Blondet famil-iarly on the shoulder, "we should have some fun. But a plague of odes, and ballads, and driveling meditations, and novels with wide margins, pervades the sofas and the atmos-phere."

"I don't dislike them," said de Marsay, "so long as they corrupt girls' minds and don't spoil women."

"Gentlemen," smiled Blondet, "you are encroaching on my field of literature."

"You need not talk. You have robbed us of the most charming woman in the world, you lucky rogue; we may be allowed to steal your less brilliant ideas," cried Rastignac.

"Yes, he is a lucky rascal," said the vidame, and he

* Having a little meeting.

twitched Blondet's ear. "But perhaps Victurnien here will be luckier still this evening——"

"*Already!*" exclaimed de Marsay. "Why, he only came here a month ago; he has scarcely had time to shake the dust of his old manor-house off his feet, to wipe off the brine in which his aunt kept him preserved; he has only just set up a decent horse, a tilbury in the latest style, a groom——"

"No, no, not a groom," interrupted Rastignac; "he has some sort of an agricultural laborer that he brought with him 'from his place.' Buisson, who understands a livery as well as most, declared that the man was physically incapable of wearing a jacket."

"I will tell you what, you ought to have modeled yourself on Beaudenord," the vidame said seriously. "He has this advantage over all of you, my young friends, he has a genuine specimen of the English tiger——"

"Just see, gentlemen, what the noblesse have come to in France!" cried Victurnien. "For them the one important thing is to have a tiger, a thoroughbred, and baubles——"

"Bless me!" said Blondet. "'This gentleman's good sense at times appalls me.' Well, yes, young moralist, you nobles have come to that. You have not even left to you that lustre of lavish expenditure for which the dear vidame was famous fifty years ago. We revel on a second floor in the Rue Montorgueil. There are no more wars with the cardinal, no Field of the Cloth of Gold. You, Comte d'Esgrignon, in short, are supping in the company of one Blondet, younger son of a miserable provincial magistrate, with whom you would not shake hands down yonder; and in ten years' time you may sit beside him among peers of the realm. Believe in yourself after that, if you can."

"Ah, well," said Rastignac, "we have passed from action to thought, from brute force to force of intellect—we are talking——"

"Let us not talk of our reverses," protested the vidame;

14

" I have made up my mind to die merrily.   If our friend here has not a tiger as yet, he comes of a race of lions, and can dispense with one."

" He cannot do without a tiger," said Blondet ; " he is too newly come to town."

" His elegance may be new as yet," returned de Marsay, " but we are adopting it.   He is worthy of us, he understands his age, he has brains, he is nobly born and gently bred ; we are going to like him, and serve him, and push him——"

" Whither ? " inquired Blondet.

" Inquisitive soul ! " said Rastignac.

" With whom will he take up to-night ? " de Marsay asked.

" With a whole seraglio," said the vidame.

" Plague take it !   What can we have done that the dear vidame is punishing us by keeping his word to the infanta ? I should be pitiable indeed if I did not know her——"

" And I was once a coxcomb even as he," said the vidame, indicating de Marsay.

The conversation continued pitched in the same key, charmingly scandalous and agreeably corrupt.   The dinner went off very pleasantly.   Rastignac and de Marsay went to the opera with the vidame and Victurnien, with a view to following them afterward to Mlle. des Touches' salon.   And thither, accordingly, this pair of rakes betook themselves, calculating that by that time the tragedy would have been read ; for of all things to be taken between eleven and twelve o'clock at night, a tragedy in their opinion was the most unwholesome. They went to keep a watch on Victurnien and to embarrass him, a piece of schoolboy's mischief embittered by a jealous dandy's spite.   But Victurnien was gifted with that page's effrontery which is a great help to ease of manner ; and Rastignac, watching him as he made his entrance, was surprised to see how quickly he caught the tone of the moment.

" That young d'Esgrignon will go far, will he not ? " he said, addressing his companion.

"That is as may be," returned de Marsay, "but he is in a fair way."

The vidame introduced his young friend to one of the most amiable and frivolous duchesses of the day, a lady whose adventures caused an explosion five years later. Just then, however, she was in the full blaze of her glory; she had been suspected, it is true, of equivocal conduct; but suspicion, while it is still suspicion and not proof, marks a woman out with the kind of distinction which slander gives to a man. Nonentities are never slandered; they chafe because they are left in peace. This woman was, in fact, the Duchesse de . Maufrigneuse, a daughter of the d'Uxelles; her father-in-law was still alive; she was not to be the Princesse de Cadignan for some years to come. A friend of the Duchesse de Langeais and the Vicomtesse de Beauséant, two glories departed, she was likewise intimate with the Marquise d'Espard, with whom she disputed her fragile sovereignty as queen of fashion. Great relations lent her countenance for a long while, but the Duchesse de Maufrigneuse was one of those women who, in some way, nobody knows how, or why, or where, will spend the rents of all the lands of earth, and of the moon likewise, if they were not out of reach. The general outline of her character was scarcely known as yet; de Marsay, and de Marsay only, really had read her. That redoubtable dandy now watched the Vidame de Pamier's introduction of his young friend to that lovely woman, and bent over to say in Rastignac's ear—

"My dear fellow, he will go up *whizz!* like a rocket, and come down like a stick," an atrociously vulgar saying which was remarkably fulfilled.

The Duchesse de Maufrigneuse had lost her heart to Victurnien after first giving her mind to a serious study of him. Any lover who should have caught the glance by which she expressed her gratitude to the vidame might well have been

jealous of such friendship. Women are like horses let loose
on a prairie when they feel, as the duchess felt with the Vidame de Pamiers, that the ground is safe; at such moments
they are themselves; perhaps it pleases them to give, as it were,
samples of their tenderness in intimacy in this way. It was a
guarded glance, nothing was lost between eye and eye; there
was no possibility of reflection in any mirror. Nobody inter-
cepted it.

"See how she has prepared herself," Rastignac said, turning
to de Marsay. "What a virginal toilette; what swan's grace
in that snow-white throat of hers! How white her gown is,
and she is wearing a sash like a little girl; she looks round
like a madonna inviolate. Who would think that you had
passed that way?"

"The very reason why she looks as she does," returned de
Marsay, with a triumphant air.

The two young men exchanged a smile. Mme. de Maufrigneuse saw the smile and guessed at their conversation, and
gave the pair a broadside of her eyes, an art acquired by
Frenchwomen since the Peace, when Englishwomen imported
it into this country, together with the shape of their silver,
their horses and harness, and the piles of insular ice which
impart a refreshing coolness to the atmosphere of any room in
which a certain number of British females are gathered together. The young men grew serious as a couple of clerks at
the end of a homily from headquarters before the receipt of
an unexpected bonus.

The duchess, when she lost her heart to Victurnien, had
made up her mind to play the part of romantic Innocence, a
role much understudied subsequently by other women, for the
misfortune of modern youth. Her grace of Maufrigneuse had
just come out as an angel at a moment's notice, precisely as
she meant to turn to literature and science somewhere about
her fortieth year instead of taking to devotion. She made a
point of being like nobody else. Her parts, her dresses, her

caps, opinions, toilettes, and manner of acting were all entirely
new and original.   Soon after her marriage, when she was
scarcely more than a girl, she had played the part of a knowing
and almost depraved woman ; she ventured on risky repartees
with shallow people, and betrayed her ignorance to those who
knew better.   As the date of that marriage made it impossible
to abstract one little year from her age without the knowledge
of Time, and as her grace had reached her twenty-sixth year,
she had taken it into her head to be immaculate.   She scarcely
seemed to belong to earth ; she shook out her wide sleeves as
if they had been wings.   Her eyes fled to heaven at too warm
a glance, or word, or thought.

There is a madonna painted by Piola, the great Genoese
painter, who bade fair to bring out a second edition of Raphael till his career was cut short by jealousy and murder ; his
madonna, however, you may dimly discern through a pane of
glass in a little street in Genoa.

A more chaste-eyed madonna than Piola's does not exist ;
but, compared with Mme. de Maufrigneuse, that heavenly
creature was a Messalina.   Women wondered among themselves how such a giddy young thing had been transformed by
a change of dress into the fair-veiled seraph who seemed (to
use an expression now in vogue) to have a soul as white as
new-fallen snow on the highest Alpine crests ?   How had she
solved in such short space the jesuitical problem how to
display a bosom whiter than her soul by hiding it in gauze ?
How could she look so ethereal while her eyes drooped so
murderously ?   Those almost wanton glances seemed to give
promise of untold languorous delight, while by an ascetic's
sigh of aspiration after a better life the mouth appeared to
add that none of those promises would be fulfilled.   Ingenuous
youths (for there were a few to be found in the Guards of that
day) privately wondered whether, in the most intimate moments,
it were possible to speak familiarly to this White Lady, this
starry vapor slidden down from the Milky Way.   This

system, which answered completely for some years at a stretch, was turned to good account by women of fashion, whose breasts were lined with a stout philosophy, for they could cloak no inconsiderable exactions with these little airs from the sacristy. Not one of the celestial creatures but was quite well aware of the possibilities of less ethereal love which lay in the longing of every well-conditioned male to recall such beings to earth. It was a fashion which permitted them to abide in a semi-religious, semi-Ossianic empyrean ; they could, and did, ignore all the practical details of daily life, a short and easy method of disposing of many questions. De Marsay, foreseeing the future developments of the system, added a last word, for he saw that Rastignac was jealous of Victurnien.

"My boy," said he, "stay as you are. Our Nucingen will make your fortune, whereas the duchess would ruin you. She is too expensive."

Rastignac allowed de Marsay to go without asking further questions. He knew Paris. He knew that the most refined and noble and disinterested of women—a woman who cannot be induced to accept anything but a bouquet—can be as dangerous an acquaintance for a young man as any opera girl of former days. As a matter of fact, the opera girl is an almost mythical being. As things are now at the theatres, dancers and actresses are about as amusing as a declaration of the rights of woman, they are puppets that go abroad in the morning in the character of respected and respectable mothers of families, and act men's parts in tight-fitting garments at night.

Worthy M. Chesnel, in his country notary's office, was right; he had foreseen one of the reefs on which the count might make shipwreck. Victurnien was dazzled by the poetic aureola which Mme. de Maufrigneuse chose to assume ; he was chained and padlocked from the first hour in her company, bound captive by that girlish sash, and caught by the curls twined round fairy fingers. Far corrupted the boy was already, but he really believed in that farrago of maidenliness and muslin, in sweet looks as much studied as an Act of Parliament. And if the one man, who is in duty bound to believe in feminine fibs, is deceived by them, is not that enough?

The converse which Victurnien held with the duchess can be kept up at his age without too great a strain. He was young enough and ignorant enough of life in Paris to feel no necessity to be upon his guard, no need to keep a watch over his lightest words and glances. The religious sentimentalism, which finds a broadly humorous commentary in the after-thoughts of either speaker, puts the old-world French chat of men and women, with its pleasant familiarity, its lively ease, quite out of the question; they make love in a mist nowadays.

Victurnien was just sufficient of an unsophisticated provincial to remain suspended in a highly appropriate and unfeigned rapture which pleased the duchess; for women are no more to be deceived by the comedies which men play than by their own. Mme. de Maufrigneuse calculated, not without dismay, that the young count's infatuation was likely to hold good for six whole months of disinterested love. She looked so lovely in this dove's mood, quenching the light in her eyes by the golden fringe of their lashes, that when the Marquise d'Espard bade her friend good-night, she whispered: " Good! very good, dear! " And with these farewell words, the fair marquise left her rival to make the tour of the modern *pays du Tendre;* which, by the way, is not so absurd a conception as some appear to think. New maps of the country are engraved for each generation; and if the names of the routes are different, they still lead to the same capital city.

In the course of an hour's *tête-à-tête,* on a corner sofa, under the eyes of the world, the duchess brought young d'Esgrignon as far as Scipio's Generosity, the Devotion of Amadis, and Chivalrous Self-abnegation (for the Middle Ages were just coming into fashion, with their daggers, machicolations, hau-

berks, chain-mail, peaked shoes, and romantic, painted card-
board properties). She had an admirable turn, moreover, for
leaving things unsaid, for leaving ideas in a discreet, seemingly careless way, to work their way down, one by one, into
Victurnien's heart, like needles into a cushion. She possessed
a marvelous skill in reticence ; she was charming in hypocrisy,
lavish of subtle promises, which revived hope and then melted
away like ice in the sun if you looked at them closely, and
most treacherous in the desire which she felt and inspired.
At the close of this charming encounter she produced the running noose of an invitation to call, and flung it over him with
a dainty demureness which the printed page can never set
forth.

"You will forget me," she said. "You will find so many
women eager to pay court to you instead of enlightening
you—— But you will come back to me undeceived. Are
you coming to me first?—— No. As you will. For my
own part, I tell you frankly that your visits will be a great
pleasure to me. People of soul are so rare, and I think that
you are one of them. Come, farewell ; people will begin to
talk about us if we talk together any longer."

She made good her words and took flight. Victurnien
went soon afterward, but not before others had guessed his
ecstatic condition ; his face wore the expression peculiar to
happy men, something between an Inquisitor's calm discretion and the self-contained beatitude of a devotee, fresh from
the confessional and absolution.

"Madame de Maufrigneuse went pretty briskly to the point
this evening," said the Duchesse de Grandlieu, when only
half-a-dozen persons were left in Mlle. des Touches' little
drawing-room—to wit, des Lupeaulx, a master of requests,
who at that time stood very well at Court, Vandenesse, the
Vicomtesse de Grandlieu, Monsieur Canalis, and Madame de
Sérizy.

"D'Esgrignon and Maufrigneuse are two names that are

sure to cling together," said Mme. de Sérizy, who aspired to epigram.

"For some days past she has been out at grass on Platonism," said des Lupeaulx.

"She will ruin that poor innocent," added Charles de Vandenesse.

"What do you mean?" asked Mlle. des Touches.

"Oh, morally and financially, beyond all doubt," said the vicomtesse, rising.

The cruel words were cruelly true for young d'Esgrignon.

Next morning he wrote to his aunt describing his introduction into the high world of the Faubourg Saint-Germain in bright colors flung by the prism of love, explaining the reception which met him everywhere in a way which gratified his father's family pride. The marquis would have the whole long letter read to him twice; he rubbed his hands when he heard of the Vidame des Pamiers' dinner—the vidame was an old acquaintance—and of the subsequent introduction to the duchess; but at Blondet's name he lost himself in conjectures. What could the younger son of a judge, a public prosecutor during the Revolution, have been doing there?

There was joy that evening among the Collection of Antiquities. They talked over the young count's success. So discreet were they with regard to Mme. de Maufrigneuse, that the one man who heard the secret was the chevalier. There was no financial postscript at the end of the letter, no unpleasant concluding reference to the sinews of war, which every young man makes in such a case. Mlle. Armande showed it to Chesnel. Chesnel was pleased and raised not a single objection. It was clear, as the marquis and the chevalier agreed, that a young man in favor with the Duchesse de Maufrigneuse would shortly be a hero at Court, where in the old days women were all-powerful. The count had not made a bad choice. The dowagers told over all the gallant adventures of the Maufrigneuses from Louis XIII. to Louis XVI.—

they spared to inquire into preceding reigns—and when all was done they were enchanted. Mme. de Maufrigneuse was much praised for interesting herself in Victurnien. Any writer of plays in search of a piece of pure comedy would have found it well worth his while to listen to the Antiquities in conclave.

Victurnien received charming letters from his father and aunt, and also from the chevalier. That gentleman recalled himself to the vidame's memory. He had been at Spa with M. de Pamiers in 1778, after a certain journey made by a celebrated Hungarian princess. And Chesnel also wrote. The fond flattery to which the unhappy boy was only too well accustomed shone out of every page; and Mlle. Armande seemed to share half of Mme. de Maufrigneuse's happiness.

Thus happy in the approval of his family, the young count made a spirited beginning in the perilous and costly ways of dandyism. He had five horses—he was moderate—de Marsay had fourteen! He returned the vidame's hospitality, even including Blondet in the invitation, as well as de Marsay and Rastignac. The dinner cost five hundred francs, and the noble provincial was fêted on the same scale. Victurnien played a good deal, and, for his misfortune, at the fashionable game of whist.

He laid out his days in busy idleness. Every day between twelve and three o'clock he was with the duchess; afterward he went to meet her in the Bois de Boulogne and ride beside her carriage. Sometimes the charming couple rode together, but this was early on fine summer mornings. Society, balls, the theatre, and gayety filled the count's evening hours. Everywhere Victurnien made a brilliant figure; everywhere he flung the pearls of his wit broadcast.

The duchess, so white and fragile and angel-like, felt attracted to the dissipations of bachelor life; she enjoyed first nights; she liked anything amusing, anything improvised.

Bohemian restaurants lay outside her experience; so d'Esgrignon got up a charming little party at the Rocher de Cancale for her benefit, asked all the amiable scamps whom she cultivated and sermonized, and there was a vast amount of merriment, wit, and gayety, and a corresponding bill to pay. That supper party led to others. And through it all Victurnien worshiped her as an angel. Mme. de Maufrigneuse for him was still an angel, untouched by any taint of earth; an angel at the Variétés, where she sat out the half-obscene, vulgar farces, which made her laugh; an angel through the cross-fire of highly flavored jests and scandalous anecdotes, which enlivened a stolen frolic; a languishing angel in the latticed box at the Vaudeville; an angel while she criticised the postures of opera-dancers with the experience of an elderly habitué of *le coin de la reine;* an angel at the Porte Saint-Martin, at the little boulevard theatres, at the masked balls, which she enjoyed like any schoolboy. She was an angel who asked him for the love that lives by self-abnegation and heroism and self-sacrifice; an angel who would have her lover live like an English lord, with an income of a million francs. D'Esgrignon once exchanged a horse because the animal's coat did not satisfy her notions. At play she was an angel, and certainly no bourgeoise that ever lived could have bidden d'Esgrignon "Stake for me!" in such an angelic way. She was so divinely reckless in her folly that a man might well have sold his soul to the devil lest this angel should lose her taste for earthly pleasures.

The first winter went by. The count had drawn on M. Cardot for the trifling sum of thirty thousand francs over and above Chesnel's remittance. As Cardot very carefully refrained from using his right of remonstrance, Victurnien now learned for the first time that he had overdrawn his account. He was the more offended by an extremely polite refusal to make any further advance, since it so happened that he had just lost six thousand francs at play at the club, and he could not very well show himself there until they were paid.

After growing indignant with Maître Cardot, who had trusted him with thirty thousand francs (Cardot had written to Chesnel, but to the fair duchess' favorite he made the most of his so-called confidence in him), after all this, d'Esgrignon was obliged to ask the lawyer to tell him how to set about raising the money, since debts of honor were in question.

"Draw bills on your father's banker, and take them to his correspondent; he, no doubt, will discount them for you. Then write to your family, and tell them to remit the amount to the banker."

An inner voice seemed to suggest du Croisier's name in this predicament. He had seen du Croisier on his knees to the aristocracy, and of the man's real disposition he was entirely ignorant. So to du Croisier he wrote a very off-hand letter, informing him that he had drawn a bill of exchange on him for ten thousand francs, adding that the amount would be repaid on receipt of the letter either by M. Chesnel or by Mlle. Armande d'Esgrignon. Then he indited two touching epistles—one to Chesnel, another to his aunt. In the matter of going headlong to ruin, a young man often shows singular ingenuity and ability, and fortune favors him. In the morning Victurnien happened on the name of the Paris bankers in correspondence with du Croisier, and de Marsay furnished him with the Kellers' address. De Marsay knew everything in Paris. The Kellers took the bill and gave him the sum without a word, after deducting the discount. The balance of the account was in du Croisier's favor.

But the gaming debt was as nothing in comparison with the state of things at home. Invoices and accounts showered in upon Victurnien.

"I say! Do you trouble yourself about that sort of thing?" Rastignac said, laughing. "Are you putting them in order, my dear boy? I did not think you were so business-like."

" My dear fellow, it is quite time I thought about it ; there are twenty-odd thousand francs there."

De Marsay, coming in to look up d'Esgrignon for a steeple-chase, produced a dainty little pocket-book, took out twenty thousand francs, and handed them to him.

" It is the best way of keeping the money safe," said he ; " I am twice enchanted to have won it yesterday from my honored father, Milord Dudley."

Such French grace completely fascinated d'Esgrignon ; he took it for friendship ; and as to the money, punctually forgot to pay his debts with it, and spent it on his pleasures. The fact was that de Marsay was looking on with an unspeakable pleasure while young d'Esgrignon " got out of his depth," in dandy's idiom ; it pleased de Marsay in all sorts of fondling ways to lay an arm on the lad's shoulder ; by-and-by he should feel its weight, and disappear the sooner. For de Marsay was jealous ; the duchess flaunted her love affair ; she was not at home to other visitors when d'Esgrignon was with her. And beside, de Marsay was one of those savage humor-ists who delight in mischief, as Turkish women in the bath. So, when he had carried off the prize, and bets were settled at the tavern where they breakfasted, and a bottle or two of good wine had appeared, de Marsay turned to d'Esgrignon with a laugh—

" Those bills that you are worrying over are not yours, I am sure."

" Eh ! if they weren't, why should he worry himself?" asked Rastignac.

" And whose should they be?" d'Esgrignon inquired.

" Then you do not know the duchess' position?" queried de Marsay, as he sprang into the saddle.

" No," said d'Esgrignon, his curiosity aroused.

" Well, dear fellow, it is like this," returned de Marsay— " thirty thousand francs to Victorine, eighteen thousand francs to Houbigaut, lesser amounts to Herbault, Nattier, Nourtier, and those Latour people—altogether a hundred thousand francs.''

"An angel ! '' cried d'Esgrignon, with eyes uplifted to heaven.

"This is the *bill* for her *wings*,'' Rastignac cried facetiously.

"She owes all that, my dear boy,'' continued de Marsay, "precisely because she is an angel. But we have all seen angels in this position,'' he added, glancing at Rastignac ; "there is this about women that is sublime, they understand nothing of money ; they do not meddle with it, it is no affair of theirs ; they are invited·guests at the 'banquet of life,' as some poet or other said that came to an end in the workhouse.''

"How do you know this when I do not ? '' d'Esgrignon artlessly returned.

"You are sure to be the last to know it, just as she is sure to be the last to hear that you are in debt.''

"I thought she had a hundred thousand livres a year,'' said d'Esgrignon.

"Her husband,'' replied de Marsay, "lives apart from her. He stays with his regiment and practices economy, for he has one or two little debts of his own as well, has our dear duke. Where do you come from ? Just learn to do as we do and keep our friends' accounts for them. Mademoiselle Diane (I fell in love with her for the name's sake), Mademoiselle Diane d'Uxelles brought her husband sixty thousand livres of income ; for the last eight years she has lived as if she had two hundred thousand. It is perfectly plain that at this moment her lands are mortgaged up to their full value ; some fine morning the crash must come, and the angel will be put to flight by—must it be said ?—by sheriff's officers that have the effrontery to lay hands on an angel just as they might take hold of one of us.''

"Poor angel ! ''

"Lord! it costs a great deal to dwell in a Parisian heaven; you must whiten your wings and your complexion every morning," said Rastignac.

Now as the thought of confessing his debts to his beloved Diane had passed through d'Esgrignon's mind, something like a shudder ran through him when he remembered that he still owed sixty thousand francs, to say nothing of bills to come for another ten thousand. He went back melancholy enough. His friends remarked his ill-disguised preoccupation, and spoke of it among themselves at dinner.

"Young d'Esgrignon is getting out of his depth. He is not up to Paris. He will blow his brains out. A little fool!" and so on and so on.

D'Esgrignon, however, promptly took comfort. His servant brought him two letters. The first was from Chesnel. A letter from Chesnel smacked of the stale grumbling faithfulness of honesty and its consecrated formulas. With all respect he put it aside till the evening. But the second letter he read with unspeakable pleasure. In Ciceronian phrases, du Croisier groveled before him, like a Sganarelle before a Géronte, begging the young count in future to spare him the affront of first depositing the amount of the bills which he should condescend to draw. The concluding phrase seemed meant to convey the idea that here was an open cash-box full of coin at the service of the noble d'Esgrignon family. So strong was the impression that Victurnien, like Sganarelle or Mascarille in the play, like everybody else who feels a twinge of conscience at his finger-tips, made an involuntary gesture.

Now that he was sure of unlimited credit with the Kellers, he opened Chesnel's letter gaily. He had expected four full pages, full of expostulation to the brim; he glanced down the sheet for the familiar words "prudence," "honor," "determination to do right," and the like, and saw something else instead which made his head swim.

" MONSIEUR LE COMTE :—Of all my fortune I have now but two hundred thousand francs left. I beg of you not to exceed that amount, if you should do one of the most devoted servants of your family the honor of taking it. I present my respects to you.   CHESNEL."

" He is one of Plutarch's men," Victurnien said to himself, as he tossed the letter on the table. He felt chagrined ; such magnanimity made him feel very small.

"There ! one must reform," he thought ; and instead of going to a restaurant and spending fifty or sixty francs over his dinner, he retrenched by dining with the Duchesse de Maufrigneuse, and told her about the letter.

"I should like to see that man," she said, letting her eyes shine like two fixed stars.

"What would you do?"

"Why, he should manage my affairs for me."

Diane de Maufrigneuse was divinely dressed ; she meant her toilet to do honor to Victurnien. The levity with which she treated his affairs, or, more properly speaking, his debts, fascinated him.

The charming pair went to the Italiens. Never had that beautiful and enchanting woman looked more seraphic, more ethereal. Nobody in the house could have believed that she had debts which reached the sum-total mentioned by de Marsay that very morning. No single one of the cares of earth had touched that sublime forehead of hers, full of woman's pride of the highest kind. In her, a pensive air seemed to be some gleam of an earthly love, nobly extinguished. The men for the most part were wagering that Victurnien, with his handsome figure, laid her under contribution ; while the women, sure of their rival's subterfuge, admired her as Michael Angelo admired Raphael, *in petto.* Victurnien loved Diane, according to one of these ladies, for the sake of her hair—she had the most beautiful fair hair in

France; another maintained that Diane's pallor was her principal merit, for she was not really well shaped, her dress made
the most of her figure; yet others thought that Victurnien
loved her for her foot, her one good point, for she had a flat
figure. But (and this brings the present-day manner of Paris
before you in an astonishing manner) whereas all the men
said that the duchess was subsidizing Victurnien's splendor,
the women, on the other hand, gave people to understand
that it was Victurnien who paid for the angel's wing-bills,
as Rastignac said.

As they drove back again, Victurnien had it on the tip of
his tongue a score of times to open this chapter, for the
duchess' debts weighed more heavily upon his mind than his
own; and a score of times his purpose died away before the
attitude of the divine creature beside him. He could see her
by the light of the carriage lamps; she was bewitching in the
love-languor which always seemed to be extorted by the
violence of passion from her madonna's purity. The duchess
did not fall into the mistake of talking of her virtue, of her
angel's estate, as provincial women, her imitators, do. She
was far too clever. She made him, for whom she made such
great sacrifices, think these things for himself. At the end
of six months she could make him feel that a harmless kiss on
her hand was a deadly sin; she contrived that every grace
should be extorted from her, and this with such consummate
art that it was impossible not to feel that she was more an
angel than ever when she yielded.

None but Parisian women are clever enough always to give
a new charm to the moon, to romanticize the stars, to roll
in the same sack of charcoal and emerge each time whiter than
ever. This is the highest refinement of intellectual and
Parisian civilization. Women beyond the Rhine or the
English Channel believe nonsense of this sort when they utter
it; while your Parisienne makes her lover believe that she is
an angel, the better to add to his bliss by flattering his vanity

15

on both sides—temporal and spiritual. Certain persons, detractors of the duchess, maintain that she was the first dupe of her own white magic. A wicked slander. The duchess believed in nothing but herself.

By the end of the year 1823, the Kellers had supplied Victurnien with two hundred thousand francs, and neither Chesnel nor Mlle. Armande knew anything about it. He had had, beside, two thousand crowns from Chesnel at one time and another, the better to hide the sources on which he was drawing. He wrote lying letters to his poor father and aunt, who lived on, happy and deceived, like most happy people under the sun. The insidious current of life in Paris was bringing a dreadful catastrophe upon the great and noble house; and only one person was in the secret of it. This was du Croisier. He rubbed his hands gleefully as he went past in the dark and looked in at the Antiquities. He had good hope of attaining his ends; and his ends were not, as heretofore, the simple ruin of the d'Esgrignons, but the dishonor of their house. He felt instinctively at such times that his revenge was at hand; he scented it in the wind! He had been sure of it, indeed, from the day when he discovered that the young count's burden of debt was growing too heavy for the boy to bear.

Du Croisier's first step was to rid himself of his most hated enemy, the venerable Chesnel. The good old man lived in the Rue du Bercail, in a house with a steep-pitched roof. There was a little paved courtyard in front, where the rose-bushes grew and clambered up to the windows of the upper story. Behind lay a little country garden, with its box-edged borders, shut in by damp, gloomy-looking walls. The prim, gray-painted street door, with its wicket opening and bell attached, announced quite as plainly as the official escutcheon that "a notary lives here."

It was half-past five o'clock in the afternoon, at which hour the old man usually sat digesting his dinner. He had drawn his black leather-covered armchair before the fire, and put on his armor, a painted pasteboard contrivance shaped like a top boot, which protected his stockinged legs from the heat of the fire; for it was one of the good man's habits to sit for a while after dinner with his feet on the dogs and to stir up the glowing coals. He always ate too much; he was fond of good living. Alas! if it had not been for that little failing, would he not have been more perfect than it is permitted to mortal man to be? Chesnel had finished his cup of coffee. His old housekeeper had just taken away the tray which had been used for this purpose for the last twenty years. He was waiting for his clerks to go before he himself went out for his game at cards, and meanwhile he was thinking—no need to ask of whom or what. A day seldom passed but he asked himself: "Where is *he?* What is *he* doing?" He thought that the count was in Italy with the fair Duchesse de Maufrigneuse.

When every franc of a man's fortune has come to him, not by inheritance, but through his own earning and saving, it is one of his sweetest pleasures to look back upon the pains that have gone to the making of it, and then to plan out a future for his crowns. This it is to conjugate the verb "to enjoy" in every tense. And the old lawyer, whose affections were all bound up in a single attachment, was thinking that all the carefully chosen, well-tilled land which he had pinched and scraped to buy would one day go to round out the d'Esgrignon estates, and the thought doubled his pleasure. His pride swelled as he sat at his ease in the old armchair; and the building of glowing coals, which he raised with the tongs, sometimes seemed to him to be the old noble house built up again, thanks to his care. He pictured the young count's prosperity, and told himself that he had done well to live for such an aim. Chesnel was not lacking in intelligence; sheer goodness was not the sole source of his great devotion; he had a pride of his own; he was like the nobles who used to rebuild a pillar in a cathedral to inscribe their name upon it;

he meant his name to be remembered by the great house which
he had restored.   Future generations of d'Esgrignons should
speak of old Chesnel.   Just at this point his old housekeeper
came in with signs of extreme alarm in her countenance.

"Is the house on fire, Brigitte?"

"Something of the sort," said she.   "Here is Monsieur du
Croisier wanting to speak to you——"

"Monsieur du Croisier," repeated the old lawyer.   A stab
of cold misgiving gave him so sharp a pang at the heart that
he dropped the tongs.   "Monsieur du Croisier here!"
thought he, "our chief enemy!"

Du Croisier came in at that moment, like a cat that scents
milk in a dairy.   He made a bow, seated himself quietly in
the easy-chair which the lawyer brought forward, and produced
a bill for two hundred and twenty-seven thousand francs, principal and interest, the total amount of sums advanced to M.
Victurnien in bills of exchange drawn upon du Croisier, and
duly honored by him.   Of these, he now demanded imme-
diate repayment, with a threat of proceeding to extremities with
the heir-presumptive of the house.   Chesnel turned the unlucky letters over one by one, and asked the enemy to keep
the secret.   This he engaged to do if he were paid within
forty-eight hours.   He was pressed for money; he had obliged
various manufacturers; and there followed a series of the
financial fictions by which neither notaries nor borrowers are
deceived.   Chesnel's eyes were dim; he could scarcely keep
back the tears.   There was but one way of raising the money;
he must mortgage his own lands up to their full value.   But
when du Croisier learned the difficulty in the way of repayment, he forgot that he was hard pressed; he no longer wanted
ready money, and suddenly came out with a proposal to buy
the old lawyer's property.   The sale was completed within
two days.   Poor Chesnel could not bear the thought of the
son of the house undergoing a five years' imprisonment for
debt.   So in a few days' time nothing remained to him but

his practice, the sums that were due to him, and the house in which he lived. Chesnel, stripped of all his lands, paced to and fro in his private office, paneled with dark oak, his eyes fixed on the beveled edges of the chestnut cross-beams of the ceiling, or on the trellised vines in the garden outside. He was not thinking of his farms now, nor of Le Jard, his dear house in the country ; not he.

"What will become of him? He ought to come back ; they must marry him to some rich heiress," he said to himself; and his eyes were dim, his head heavy.

How to approach Mlle. Armande, and in what words to break the news to her, he did not know. The man who had just paid the debts of the family quaked at the thought of confessing these things. He went from the Rue du Bercail to the Hôtel d'Esgrignon with pulses throbbing like some girl's heart when she leaves her father's roof by stealth, not to return again till she is a mother and her heart is broken.

Mlle. Armande had just received a charming letter, charming in its hypocrisy. Her nephew was the happiest man under the sun. He had been to the baths, he had been traveling in Italy with Mme. de Maufrigneuse, and now sent his journal to his aunt. Every sentence was instinct with love. There were enchanting descriptions of Venice and fascinating appreciations of the great works of Venetian art ; there were most wonderful pages full of the Duomo at Milan, and again of Florence ; he described the Apennines, and how they differed from the Alps, and how in some village like Chiavari happiness lay all around you, ready made.

The poor aunt was under the spell. She saw the far-off country of love ; she saw, hovering above the land, the angel whose tenderness gave to all that beauty a burning glow. She was drinking in the letter at long draughts ; how should it have been otherwise ! The girl who had put love from her was now a woman ripened by repressed and pent-up passion, by all the longings continually and gladly offered up as a sacrifice on

the altar of the hearth.   Mlle. Armande was not like the
duchess.   She did not look like an angel.   She was rather
like the little, straight, slim and slender, ivory-tinted statues,
which those wonderful sculptors, the builders of cathedrals,
placed here and there about the buildings.   Wild plants sometimes find a hold in the damp niches, and weave a crown of
beautiful bluebell flowers about the carved stone.   At this
moment the blue buds were unfolding in the fair saint's eyes.
Mlle. Armande loved the charming couple as if they stood
apart from real life ; she saw nothing wrong in the married
woman's love for Victurnien ; any other woman she would
have judged harshly ; but, in this case, not to have loved her
nephew would have been the unpardonable sin.   Aunts,
mothers, and sisters have a code of their own for nephews and
sons and brothers.

Mlle. Armande was in Venice ; she saw the lines of fairy
palaces that stand on either side of the Grand Canal; she was
sitting in Victurnien's gondola ; he was telling her what happiness it had been to feel that the duchess' beautiful hand lay
in his own, to know that she loved him as they floated together
on the breast of the amorous Queen of Italian seas.   But even
in that moment of bliss, such as angels know, some one appeared on the garden walk.   It was Chesnel !   Alas ! the
sound of his tread on the gravel might have been the sound of
the sands running from Death's hour-glass to be trodden under
his unshod feet.   The sound, the sight of a dreadful hopeless-
ness in Chesnel's face, gave her that painful shock which follows a sudden recall of the senses when the soul has sent them
forth into the world of dreams.

"What is it ?" she cried, as if some stab had pierced to
her heart.

"All is lost !" said Chesnel.   "Monsieur le Comte will
bring dishonor upon the house if we do not set it in order."
He held out the bills, and described the agony of the last few
days in a few simple but vigorous and touching words.

"He is deceiving us! The miserable boy!" cried Mlle. Armande, her heart swelling as the blood surged back to it in heavy throbs.

"Let us each say *mea culpa*,* mademoiselle," the old lawyer said stoutly; "we have always allowed him to have his own way; he needed stern guidance; he could not have it from you with your inexperience of life; nor from me, for he would not listen to me. He has had no mother."

"Fate sometimes deals terribly with a noble house in decay," said Mlle. Armande, with tears in her eyes.

The marquis came up as she spoke. He had been walking up and down the garden while he read the letter sent by his son after his return. Victurnien gave his itinerary from an aristocrat's point of view; telling how he had been welcomed by the greatest Italian families of Genoa, Turin, Milan, Florence, Venice, Rome, and Naples. This flattering reception he owed to his name, he said, and partly, perhaps, to the duchess as well. In short, he had made his appearance magnificently and as befitted a d'Esgrignon.

"Have you been at your old tricks, Chesnel?" asked the marquis.

Mlle. Armande made Chesnel an eager sign, dreadful to see. They understood each other. The poor father, the flower of feudal honor, must die with all his illusions. A compact of silence and devotion was ratified between the two noble hearts by a simple inclination of the head.

"Ah! Chesnel, it was not exactly in this way that the d'Esgrignons went into Italy at the end of the fourteenth century, when Marshal Trivulzio, in the service of the King of France, served under a d'Esgrignon, who had a Bayard too under his orders. Other times, other pleasures. And, for that matter, the Duchesse de Maufrigneuse is at least the equal of a Marchesa di Spinola."

And, on the strength of his genealogical tree, the old man

* I am the culprit.

swung himself off with a coxcomb's air, as if he himself had once made a conquest of the Marchesa di Spinola, and still possessed the duchess of to-day.

The two companions in unhappiness were left together on the garden bench, with the same thought for a bond of union. They sat for a long time, saying little save vague, unmeaning words, watching the father walk away in his happiness, gesticulating as if he were talking to himself.

" What will become of him now ? " Mlle. Armande asked after a while.

" Du Croisier has sent instructions to the Kellers ; he is not to be allowed to draw any more without authorization."

" And there are debts ? " continued Mlle. Armande.

" I am afraid so."

" If he is left without resources, what will he do ? "

" I dare not answer that question to myself."

" But he must be drawn out of that life, he must come back to us, or he will have nothing left."

" And nothing else left to him," Chesnel said gloomily. But Mlle. Armande as yet did not and could not understand the full force of those words.

" Is there any hope of getting him away from that woman, that duchess ? Perhaps she leads him on."

" He would not stick at a crime to be with her," said Chesnel, trying to pave the way to an intolerable thought by others less intolerable.

" Crime," repeated Mlle. Armande. " Oh, Chesnel, no one but you would think of such a thing ! " she added, with a withering look ; before such a look from a woman's eyes no mortal can stand. " There is but one crime that a noble can commit—the crime of high treason ; and when he is beheaded, the block is covered with a black cloth, as it is for kings."

" The times have changed very much," said Chesnel, shaking his head. Victurnien had thinned his last thin, white hairs. "Our Martyr-King did not die like the English King Charles."

That thought soothed Mlle. Armande's splendid indignation; a shudder ran through her; but still she did not realize what Chesnel meant.

"To-morrow we will decide what we must do," she said; "it needs thought. At the worst, we have our lands."

"Yes," said Chesnel. "You and Monsieur le Marquis own the estate conjointly; but the larger part of it is yours. You can raise money upon it without saying a word to him."

The players at whist, reversis, boston, and backgammon noticed that evening that Mlle. Armande's features, usually so serene and pure, showed signs of agitation.

"That poor heroic child!" said the old Marquise de Castéran, "she must be suffering still. A woman never knows what her sacrifices to her family may cost her."

Next day it was arranged with Chesnel that Mlle. Armande should go to Paris to snatch her nephew from perdition. If any one could carry off Victurnien, was it not the woman whose mother's heart yearned over him? Mlle. Armande made up her mind that she would go to the Duchesse de Maufrigneuse and tell her all. Still, some sort of pretext was necessary to explain the journey to the marquis and the whole town. At some cost to her maidenly delicacy, Mlle. Armande allowed it to be thought that she was suffering from a complaint which called for a consultation of skilled and celebrated physicians. Goodness knows whether the town talked of this or not! But Mlle. Armande saw that something far more to her than her own reputation was at stake. She set out. Chesnel brought her his last bag of louis; she took it, without paying any attention to it, as she took her white capuchine and thread mittens.

"Generous girl! What grace!" he said, as he put her into the carriage with her maid, a woman who looked like a gray sister.

Du Croisier had thought out his revenge, as provincials think out everything. For studying out a question in all its bearings, there are no people in this world like savages, peasants, and provincials; and this is how, when they proceed from thought to action, you find every contingency provided for from beginning to end. Diplomatists are children compared with these classes of mammals; they have time before them, an element which is lacking to those people who are obliged to think about a great many things, to superintend the progress of all kinds of schemes, to look forward for all sorts of contingencies in the wider interests of human affairs. Had du Croisier sounded poor Victurnien's nature so well that he foresaw how easily the young count would lend himself to his schemes of revenge? Or was he merely profiting by an opportunity for which he had been on the watch for years? One circumstance there was, to be sure, in his manner of preparing his stroke, which shows a certain skill. Who was it that gave du Croisier warning of the moment? Was it the Kellers? Or could it have been President du Ronceret's son, then finishing his law studies in Paris?

Du Croisier wrote to Victurnien, telling him that the Kellers had been instructed to advance no more money; and that letter was timed to arrive just as the Duchesse de Maufrigneuse was in the utmost perplexity, and the Comte d'Esgrignon consumed by the sense of a poverty as dreadful as it was cunningly hidden. The wretched young man was exerting all his ingenuity to seem as if he were wealthy!

Now in the letter which informed the victim that in future the Kellers would make no further advances without security, there was a tolerably wide space left between the forms of an exaggerated respect and the signature. It was quite easy to tear off the best part of the letter and convert it into a bill of exchange for any amount. The diabolical missive had even been inclosed in an envelope, so that the other side of the sheet was blank. When it arrived, Victurnien was writhing in the lowest depths of despair. After two years of the most prosperous, sensual, thoughtless, and luxurious life, he found himself face to face with the most inexorable poverty; it was an absolute impossibility to procure money. There had been some throes of crisis before the journey came to an end. With the duchess' help he had managed to extort various sums from bankers; but it had been with the greatest difficulty, and, moreover, those very amounts were about to start up again before him as overdue bills of exchange in all their rigor, with a stern summons to pay from the Bank of France and the commercial court. All through the enjoyments of those last weeks the unhappy boy had felt the point of the commander's sword; at every supper-party he heard, like Don Juan, the heavy tread of the statue outside upon the stairs. He felt an unaccountable creeping of the flesh, a warning that the sirocco of debt is nigh at hand. He reckoned on chance. For five years he had never turned up a blank in the lottery; his purse had always been replenished. After Chesnel had come du Croisier (he told himself); after du Croisier surely another gold mine would pour out its wealth. And beside, he was winning great sums at play; his luck at play had saved him several unpleasant steps already; and often a wild hope sent him to the Salon des Étrangers only to lose his winnings afterward at whist at the club. His life for the past two months had been like the immortal finale of Mozart's " Don Giovanni ; '' and of a truth, if a young man has come to such a plight as Victurnien's, that finale is enough to make him shudder. Can anything better prove the enormous power of music than that sublime rendering of the disorder and confusion arising out of a life wholly given up to sensual indulgence? that fearful picture of a deliberate effort to shut out the thought of debts and duels, deceit and evil luck? In that music Mozart disputes the palm with Molière. The terrific finale, with its glow, its power, its despair and laughter, its grisly spectres and elfish women, centres about the prodigal's last effort made in the after-supper heat of wine, the frantic struggle which ends the drama. Victurnien was living through this infernal poem, and alone. He saw visions of himself—a friendless, solitary outcast, reading the words carved on the stone, the last words on the last page of the book that had held him spellbound—THE END !

Yes; for him all would be at an end, and that soon. Already he saw the cold, ironical eyes which his associates would turn upon him, and their amusement over his downfall. Some of them he knew were playing high on that gambling-table kept open all day long at the Bourse, or in private houses, at the clubs, and anywhere and everywhere in Paris; but not one of these men could spare a banknote to save an intimate. There was no help for it—Chesnel must be ruined. He had devoured Chesnel's living.

He sat with the duchess in their box at the Italiens, the whole house envying them their happiness; and while he smiled at her, all the Furies were tearing at his heart. Indeed, to give some idea of the depths of doubt, despair, and incredulity in which the boy was groveling; he who so clung to life—the life which the angel had made so fair—who so loved it that he would have stooped to baseness merely to live; he, the pleasure-loving scapegrace, the degenerate d'Esgrignon, had even taken out his pistols, had gone so far as to think of suicide. He who would never have brooked the appearance of an insult was abusing himself in language which no man is likely to hear except from himself.

He left du Croisier's letter laying open on the bed. Joséphin had brought it in at nine o'clock. Victurnien's furniture had been seized, but he slept none the less. After he came back from the opera, he and the duchess had gone to a voluptuous retreat, where they often spent a few hours together after the most brilliant court balls and evening parties and gayeties. Appearances were very cleverly saved. Their love-nest was a garret like any other to all appearance; Mme.

de Maufrigneuse was obliged to bow her head with its court feathers or the wreath of flowers to enter the doorway; but within all the peris of the East had made the chamber fair. And now that the count was on the brink of ruin, he had longed to bid farewell to the dainty nest, which he had built to realize a day-dream worthy of his angel. Presently adversity would break the enchanted eggs; there would be no brood of white doves, no brilliant tropical birds, no more of the thousand bright-winged fancies which hover above our heads even to the last days of our lives. Alas! alas! in three days he must be gone; his bills had fallen into the hands of the money-lenders, the law proceedings had reached the last stage.

An evil thought crossed his brain. He would fly with the duchess; they would live in some undiscovered nook in the wilds of North or South America; but—he would fly with a fortune, and leave his creditors to confront their bills. To carry out the plan, he had only to cut off the lower portion of that letter with du Croisier's signature, and to fill in the figures to turn it into a bill, and present it to the Kellers. There was a dreadful struggle with temptation; tears were shed, but the honor of the family triumphed, subject to one condition. Victurnien wanted to be sure of his beautiful Diane; he would do nothing unless she should consent to their flight. So he went to the duchess in the Rue Faubourg Saint-Honoré, and found her in coquettish morning dress, which cost as much in thought as in money, a fit dress in which to begin to play the part of Angel at eleven o'clock in the morning.

Mme. de Maufrigneuse was somewhat pensive. Cares of a similar kind were gnawing her mind; but she took them gallantly. Of all the various feminine organizations classified by physiologists, there is one that has something indescribably terrible about it. Such women combine strength of soul and clear insight, with a faculty for prompt decision, and a recklessness, or rather resolution, in a crisis which would shake a man's nerves. And these powers lie out of sight beneath an appearance of the most graceful helplessness. Such women only among womankind afford examples of a phenomenon which Buffon recognized in men alone, to wit, the union, or rather the disunion, of two different natures in one human being. Other women are wholly women ; wholly tender, wholly devoted, wholly mothers, completely null and completely tiresome ; nerves and brain and blood are all in harmony ; but the duchess, and others like her, are capable of rising to the highest heights of feeling, or of showing the most selfish insensibility. It is one of the glories of Molière that he has given us a wonderful portrait of such a woman, from one point of view only, in that greatest of his full-length figures—Célimène ; Célimène is the typical aristocratic woman, as Figaro, the second edition of Panurge, represents the people.

So the duchess, being overwhelmed with debt, laid it upon herself to give no more than a moment's thought to the avalanche of cares, and to take her resolution once and for all ; Napoleon could take up or lay down the burden of his thoughts in precisely the same way. The duchess possessed the faculty of standing aloof from herself ; she could look on as a spectator at the crash when it came, instead of submitting to be buried beneath. This was certainly great, but repulsive in a woman. When she awoke in the morning she collected her thoughts ; and by the time she had begun to dress she had looked at the danger in its fullest extent and faced the possibilities of terrific downfall. She pondered. Should she take refuge in a foreign country? Or should she go to the King and declare her debts to him? Or again, should she fascinate a du Tillet or a Nucingen, and gamble on the Stock Exchange to pay her creditors? The city man would find the money ; he would be intelligent enough to bring her nothing but the profits, without so much as mentioning the losses, a piece of delicacy which would gloss all over. The catastrophe, and these various ways of averting it, had all been reviewed quite coolly, calmly, and without trepidation.

As a naturalist takes up some king of butterflies and fastens him down on cotton-wool with a pin, so Mme. de Maufrigneuse had plucked love out of her heart while she pondered the necessity of the moment, and was quite ready to replace the beautiful passion on its immaculate setting so soon as her duchess' coronet was safe. *She* knew none of the hesitation which Cardinal Richelieu hid from all the world but Père Joseph ; none of the doubts that Napoleon kept at first entirely to himself. " Either the one or the other," she told herself.

She was sitting by the fire, giving orders for her toilet for a drive in the Bois if the weather should be fine, when Victurnien came in.

The Comte d'Esgrignon, with all his stifled capacity, his so keen intellect, was in exactly the state which might have been looked for in the woman. His heart was beating violently, the perspiration broke out over him as he stood in his dandy's trappings ; he was afraid as yet to lay a hand on the cornerstone which upheld the pyramid of his life with Diane. So much it cost him to know the truth. The cleverest men are fain to deceive themselves on one or two points if the truth once known is likely to humiliate them in their own eyes, and damage themselves with themselves. Victurnien forced his own irresolution into the field by committing himself.

"What is the matter with you ?" Diane de Maufrigneuse had said at once, at the sight of her beloved Victurnien's face.

"Why, dear Diane, I am in such utter perplexity ; a man gone to the bottom and at his last gasp is happy in comparison."

"Pshaw ! it is nothing," said she ; "you are a child. Let us see now ; tell me about it."

"I am hopelessly in debt. I have come to the end of my tether."

"Is that all?" said she, smiling at him. "Money matters can always be arranged somehow or other; nothing is irretrievable except disasters in love."

Victurnien's mind being set at rest by this swift comprehension of his position, he unrolled the bright-colored web of his life for the last two years and a half; but it was the seamy side of it which he displayed with something of genius, and still more of wit, to his Diane. He told his tale with the inspiration of the moment, which fails no one in great crises; he had sufficient artistic skill to set it off by a varnish of delicate scorn for men and things. It was an aristocrat who spoke. And the duchess listened as she could listen.

One knee was raised, for she sat with her foot on a stool. She rested her elbow on her knee and leaned her face on her hand so that her fingers closed daintily over her shapely chin. Her eyes never left his; but thoughts by myriads flitted under the blue surface, like gleams of stormy light between two clouds. Her forehead was calm, her mouth gravely intent; grave with love; her lips were knotted fast by Victurnien's lips. To have her listening thus was to believe that a divine love flowed from her heart. Wherefore, when the count had proposed flight to this soul, so closely knit to his own, he could not help crying:

"You are an angel!"

The fair Maufrigneuse made silent answer; but she had not spoken as yet.

"Good, very good," she said at last. (She had not given herself up to the love expressed in her face; her mind had been entirely absorbed by deep-laid schemes which she kept to herself.) "But *that* is not the question, dear." (The "angel" was only "that" by this time.) "Let us think of your affairs. Yes, we will go, and the sooner the better. Arrange it all; I will follow you. It is glorious to leave Paris and the world behind. I will set about my preparations in such a way that no one can suspect anything."

I will follow you ! Just so Mlle. Mars might have spoken those words to send a thrill through two thousand listening men and women. When a Duchesse de Maufrigneuse offers, in such words, to make such a sacrifice to love, she has paid her debt. How should Victurnien speak of sordid details after that ? He could so much the better hide his schemes, because Diane was particularly careful not to inquire into them. She was now, and always, as De Marsay said, an invited guest at a banquet wreathed with roses, a banquet which mankind, as in duty bound, made ready for her.

Victurnien would not go till the promise had been sealed. He must draw courage from his happiness before he could bring himself to do a deed on which, as he inwardly told himself, people would be certain to put a bad construction. Still (and this was the thought that decided him) he counted on his aunt and father to hush up the affair ; he even counted on Chesnel. Chesnel would think of one more compromise. Beside, "this business," as he called it in his thoughts, was the only way of raising money on the family estate. With three hundred thousand francs, he and Diane would lead a happy life hidden in some palace in Venice ; and there they would forget the world. They went through their romance in advance.

Next day Victurnien made out a bill for three hundred thousand francs, and took it to the Kellers. The Kellers advanced the money, for du Croisier happened to have a balance at the time ; but they wrote to let him know that he must not draw again on them without giving them notice. Du Croisier, much astonished, asked for a statement of accounts. It was sent. Everything was explained. The day of his vengeance had arrived.

When Victurnien had drawn "his" money, he took it to
16

Mme. de Maufrigneuse.   She locked up the banknotes in
her desk, and proposed to bid the world farewell by going to
the opera to see it for the last time.   Victurnien was thoughtful,
absent, and uneasy.   He was beginning to reflect.   He thought
that his seat in the duchess' box might cost him dear; that
perhaps, when he had put the three hundred thousand francs
in safety, it would be better to travel post, to fall at Chesnel's
feet, and tell him all.   But, before they left the opera-house,
the duchess, in spite of herself, gave Victurnien an adorable
glance, her eyes were shining with the desire to go back once
more to bid farewell to the nest which she loved so much.
And boy that he was, he lost a night.

The next day, at three o'clock, he was back again at the
Hôtel de Maufrigneuse; he had come to take the duchess'
orders for that night's escape.   And, "Why should we go?"
asked she; "I have thought it all out.   The Vicomtesse de
Beauséant and the Duchesse de Langeais disappeared.   If I go
too, it will be something quite commonplace.   We will brave
the storm.   It will be a far finer thing to do.   I am sure of
success."   Victurnien's eyes dazzled; he felt as if his skin
were dissolving and the blood oozing out all over him.

"What is the matter with you?" cried the fair Diane,
noticing a hesitation which a woman never forgives.   Your
truly adroit lover will hasten to agree with any fancy that
Woman may take into her head, and suggest reasons for doing
otherwise, while leaving her free exercise of her right to
change her mind, her intentions, and sentiments generally as
often as she pleases.   Victurnien was angry for the first time,
angry with the wrath of a weak man of poetic temperament;
it was a storm of rain and lightning flashes, but no thunder
followed.   The angel on whose faith he had risked more than
his life, the honor of his ancient house, was being very roughly
handled.

"So," said she, "we have come to this after eighteen
months of tenderness!   You are unkind, very unkind.   Go

away !—I do not want to see you again.   I thought that you loved me.   You do not.''

"*I do not love you ?* " repeated he, thunderstruck by the reproach.

" No, monsieur.''

"And yet——" he cried.   "Ah! if you but knew what I have just done for your sake ! ''

"And how have you done so much for me, monsieur?   As if a man ought not to do anything for a woman that has done so much for him.''

" You are not worthy to know it ! '' Victurnien cried in a passion of anger.

" Oh ! ''

After that sublime " Oh ! '' Diane bowed her head on her hand and sat, still, cold, and implacable as angels naturally may be expected to do, seeing that they share none of the passions of humanity.   At the sight of the woman he loved in this terrible attitude, Victurnien forgot his danger.   Had he not just that moment wronged the most angelic creature on earth?   He longed for forgiveness, he threw himself before her, he kissed her feet, he pleaded, he wept.   Two whole hours the unhappy young man spent in all kinds of follies, only to meet the same cold face, while the great silent tears, dropping one by one, were dried as soon as they fell lest the unworthy lover should try to wipe them away.   The duchess was acting a great agony, one of those hours which stamp the woman who passes through them as something august and sacred.

Two more hours went by.   By this time the count had gained possession of Diane's hand ; it felt cold and spiritless. The beautiful hand, with all the treasures in its grasp, might have been supple wood ; there was nothing of Diane in it ; he had taken it, it had not been given to him.   As for Victurnien, the spirit had ebbed out of his frame, he had ceased to think. He would not have seen the sun in heaven.   What was to be done? What course should he take? What resolution should he make? The man who can keep his head in such circumstances must be made of the same stuff as the convict who spent the night in robbing the Bibliothèque Royale of its gold medals, and repaired to his honest brother in the morning with a request to melt down the plunder. "What is to be done?" cried the brother. "Make me some coffee," replied the thief. Victurnien sank into a bewildered stupor, darkness settled down over his brain. Visions of past rapture flitted across the misty gloom like the figures that Raphael painted against a black background; to these he must bid farewell. Inexorable and disdainful, the duchess played with the tip of her scarf. She looked in irritation at Victurnien from time to time; she coquetted with memories, she spoke to her lover of his rivals as if anger had finally decided her to prefer one of them to a man who could so change in one moment after twenty-eight months of love.

"Ah! that charming young Félix de Vandenesse, so faithful as he was to Madame de Mortsauf, would never have permitted himself such a scene! He can love, can de Vandenesse! De Marsay, that terrible de Marsay, such a tiger as every one thought him, was rough with other men; but, like all strong men, he kept his gentleness for women. Montriveau trampled the Duchesse de Langeais under foot, as Othello killed Desdemona, in a burst of fury which at any rate proved the extravagance of his love. It was not like a paltry squabble. There was rapture in being so crushed. Little, fair-haired, slim, and slender men loved to torment women; they could only reign over poor, weak creatures; it pleased them to have some ground for believing that they were men. The tyranny of love was their one chance of asserting their power. She did not know why she had put herself at the mercy of fair hair. Such men as de Marsay, Montriveau, and Vandenesse, dark-haired and well grown, had a ray of sunlight in their eyes."

It was a storm of epigrams. Her speeches, like bullets, came hissing past his ears. Every word that Diane hurled at him was triple-barbed ; she humiliated, stung, and wounded him with an art that was all her own, as half a score of savages can torture an enemy bound to a stake.

"You are mad !" he cried at last, at the end of his patience, and out he went in God knows what mood. He drove as if he had never handled the reins before, locked his wheels in the wheels of other vehicles, collided with the curb-stone in the Place Louis-Quinze, went he knew not whither. The horse, left to its own devices, made a bolt for the stable along the Quai d'Orsay ; but as he turned into the Rue de l'Université, Joséphin appeared to stop the runaway.

"You cannot go home, sir," the old man said, with a scared look on his honest face ; "they have come with a warrant to arrest you."

Victurnien thought that he was to be arrested on the criminal charge, albeit there had not been time for the public prosecutor to receive his instructions. He had forgotten the matter of the bills of exchange, which had been stirred up again for some days past in the form of orders to pay, brought by the officers of the court with accompaniments in the shape of bailiffs, men in possession, magistrates, commissaries, policemen, and other representatives of social order. Like most guilty creatures, Victurnien had forgotten everything but his crime.

"It is all over with me," he cried.

"No, Monsieur le Comte, drive as fast as you can to the Hôtel du Bon la Fontaine, in the Rue de Grenelle. Mademoiselle Armande is waiting there for you, the horses have been put in, she will take you with her."

Victurnien, in his trouble, caught like a drowning man at the branch that came to his hand ; he rushed off to the inn, reached the place, and flung his arms about his aunt. Mlle. Armande cried as if her heart would break ; any one might have thought that she had a share in her nephew's guilt. They stepped into the carriage. A few minutes later they were on the road to Brest, and Paris lay behind them. Victurnien uttered not a sound; he was paralyzed. And when aunt and nephew began to speak, they talked at cross purposes; Victurnien, still laboring under the unlucky misapprehension which flung him into Mlle. Armande's arms, was thinking of his forgery; his aunt had the debts and the bills on her mind.

"You know all, aunt," he had said.

"Poor boy, yes, but we are here. I am not going to scold you just yet. Take heart."

"I must hide somewhere."

"Perhaps—— Yes, it is a very good idea."

"Perhaps I might get into Chesnel's house without being seen if we timed ourselves to arrive in the middle of the night?"

"That will be best. We shall be better able to hide this from my brother. Poor angel! how unhappy he is!" said she, petting the unworthy child.

"Ah! now I begin to know what dishonor means; it has chilled my love."

"Unhappy boy; what bliss and what misery!" And Mlle. Armande drew his fevered face to her breast and kissed his forehead, cold and damp though it was, as the holy women might have kissed the brow of the dead Christ when they laid Him in His grave-clothes. Following out the excellent scheme suggested by the prodigal son, he was brought by night to the quiet house in the Rue du Bercail; but chance ordered it that by so doing he ran straight into the wolf's jaws, as the saying goes. That evening Chesnel had been making arrangements to sell his connection to M. Lepressoir's head-clerk. M. Lepressoir was the notary employed by the Liberals, just as Chesnel's practice lay among the aristocratic families. The young fellow's relatives were rich enough to pay Chesnel the considerable sum of a hundred thousand francs in cash.

Chesnel was rubbing his hands. "A hundred thousand francs will go a long way in buying up debts," he thought. "The young man is paying a high rate of interest on his loans. We will lock him up down here. I will go yonder myself and bring those curs to terms."

Chesnel, honest Chesnel, upright, worthy Chesnel, called his darling Comte Victurnien's creditors "curs."

Meanwhile his successor was making his way along the Rue du Bercail just as Mlle. Armande's traveling carriage turned into it. Any young man might be expected to feel some curiosity if he saw a traveling carriage stop at a notary's door in such a town and at such an hour of the night ; the young man in question was sufficiently inquisitive to stand in a doorway and watch.   He saw Mlle. Armande alight.

"Mademoiselle d'Esgrignon at this time of night !" said he to himself. "What can be going forward at the d'Esgrignons?"

At the sight of mademoiselle, Chesnel opened the door circumspectly and set down the light which he was carrying ; but when he looked out and saw Victurnien, Mlle. Armande's first whispered word made the whole thing plain to him.   He looked up and down the street ; it seemed quite deserted ; he beckoned, and the young count sprang out of the carriage and entered the courtyard. All was lost. Chesnel's successor had discovered Victurnien's hiding-place.

Victurnien was hurried into the house and installed in a room beyond Chesnel's private office.   No one could enter it except across the old man's dead body.

"Ah! Monsieur le Comte !" exclaimed Chesnel, notary no longer.

"Yes, monsieur," the count answered, understanding his old friend's exclamation.   "I did not listen to you ; and now I have fallen into the depths, and I must perish."

"No, no," the good man answered, looking triumphantly from Mlle. Armande to the count. "I have sold my connection. I have been working for a very long time now, and am thinking of retiring. By noon to-morrow I shall have a hundred thousand francs; many things can be settled with that. Mademoiselle, you are tired," he added; "go back to the carriage and go home and sleep. Business to-morrow."

"Is he safe?" returned she, looking at Victurnien.

"Yes,"

She kissed her nephew; a few tears fell on his forehead. Then she went.

"My good Chesnel," said the count, when they began to talk of business, "what are your hundred thousand francs in such a position as mine? You do not know the full extent of my troubles, I think."

Victurnien explained the situation. Chesnel was thunderstruck. But for the strength of his devotion, he would have succumbed to this blow. Tears streamed from the eyes that might well have had no tears left to shed. For a few moments he was a child again, for a few moments he was bereft of his senses; he stood like a man who should find his own house on fire, and through a window see the cradle ablaze and hear the hiss of the flames on his children's curls. He rose to his full height—*il se dressa en pied*, as Amyot would have said; he seemed to grow taller; he raised his withered hands and wrung them despairingly and wildly.

"If only your father may die and never know this, young man! To be a forger is enough; a parricide you must not be. Fly, you say? No. They would condemn you for contempt of court! Oh, wretched boy! Why did you not forge *my* signature? *I* would have paid. I should not have taken the bill to the public prosecutor. Now I can do nothing. You have brought me to a stand in the lowest pit in hell!—— Du Croisier! What will come of it? What is to be done? If you had killed a man, there might be some help for it.

But forgery—*forgery!* And time—the time is flying," he went on, shaking his fist toward the old clock. "You will want a sham passport now. One crime leads to another. First," he added, after a pause, "first of all we must save the house of d'Esgrignon."

"But the money is still in Madame de Maufrigneuse's keeping," exclaimed Victurnien.

"Ah!" exclaimed Chesnel. "Well, there is some hope left—a faint hope. Could we soften du Croisier, I wonder, or buy him over? He shall have all the lands if he likes. I will go to him; I will wake him and offer him all we have. Beside, it was not you who forged that bill; it was I. I will go to jail; I am too old for the hulks, they can only put me in prison."

"But the body of the bill is in my handwriting," objected Victurnien, without a sign of surprise at this reckless devotion.

"Idiot!—— that is, pardon, Monsieur le Comte. Joséphin should have been made to write it," the old notary cried wrathfully. "He is a good creature; he would have taken it all on his shoulders. But there is an end of it; the world is falling to pieces," the old man continued, sinking exhausted into a chair. "Du Croisier is a tiger; we must be careful not to rouse him. What time is it? Where is the draft? If it is at Paris, it might be bought back from the Kellers; they might accommodate us. Ah! but there are dangers on all sides; a single false step means ruin. Money is wanted in any case. But, there! nobody knows you are here, you must live buried away in the cellar if needs must. I will go at once to Paris as fast as I can; I can hear the mail-coach from Brest."

In a moment the old man recovered the faculties of his youth—his agility and vigor. He packed up clothes for the journey, took money, brought a six-pound loaf to the little room beyond the office, and turned the key on his child by adoption.

" Not a sound in here," he said; " no light at night; and stop here till I come back, or you will go to the hulks. Do you understand, Monsieur le Comte? Yes, *to the hulks!* if anybody in a town like this knows that you are here."

With that Chesnel went out, first telling his housekeeper to give out that he was ill, to allow no one to come into the house, to send everybody away, and to postpone business of every kind for three days. He wheedled the manager of the coach-office, made up a tale for his benefit—he had the makings of an ingenious novelist in him—and obtained a promise that if there should be a place, he should have it, passport or no passport, as well as a further promise to keep the hurried departure a secret. Luckily, the coach was empty when it arrived.

In the middle of the following night Chesnel was set down in Paris. At nine o'clock in the morning he waited on the Kellers, and learned that the fatal draft had returned to du Croisier three days since; but while obtaining this information, he in no way committed himself. Before he went away he inquired whether the draft could be recovered if the amount were refunded. François Keller's answer was to the effect that the document was du Croisier's property, and that it was entirely in his power to keep or return it. Then, in desperation, the old man went to the duchess.

Mme. de Maufrigneuse was not at home to any visitor at that hour. Chesnel, feeling that every moment was precious, sat down in the hall, wrote a few lines, and succeeded in sending them to the lady by dint of wheedling, fascinating, bribing, and commanding the most insolent and inaccessible servants in the world. The duchess was still in bed; but, to the great astonishment of her household, the old man in black knee-breeches, ribbed stockings, and shoes with buckles to them was shown into her room.

" What is it, monsieur?" she asked, posing in her disorder. " What does he want of me, ungrateful that he is?"

"It is this, Madame la Duchesse," the good man exclaimed, "you have a hundred thousand crowns belonging to us."

"Yes," began she. "What does it signify——?"

"The money was gained by a forgery, for which we are going to the hulks, a forgery which we committed for love of you," Chesnel said quickly. "How is it that you did not guess it, so clever as you are? Instead of scolding the boy, you ought to have had the truth out of him, and stopped him while there was time, and saved him."

At the first words the duchess understood; she felt ashamed of her behavior to so impassioned a lover, and afraid beside that she might be suspected of complicity. In her wish to prove that she had not touched the money left in her keeping, she lost all regard for appearances; and beside, it did not occur to her that a notary was a man. She flung off the eider-down quilt, sprang to her desk (flitting past the lawyer like an angel out of one of the vignettes which illustrate Lamartine's books), held out the notes, and went back in confusion to bed.

"You are an angel, madame." (She was to be an angel for all the world, it seemed.) "But this will not be the end of it. I count upon your influence to save us."

"To save you! I will do it or die! Love that will not shrink from a crime must be love, indeed. Is there a woman in the world for whom such a thing has been done? Poor boy! Come, do not lose time, dear Monsieur Chesnel; and count upon me as upon yourself."

"Madame la Duchesse! Madame la Duchesse!" It was all that he could say, so overcome was he. He cried, he could have danced; but he was afraid of losing his senses, and refrained.

"Between us, we will save him," she said, as he left the room.

Chesnel went straight to Joséphin. Joséphin unlocked the

young count's desk and writing-table. Very luckily, the
notary found letters which might be useful, letters from du
Croisier and the Kellers. Then he took a place in a diligence
which was just about to start; and, by dint of fees to the
postillions, the lumbering vehicle went as quickly as the
coach. His two fellow-passengers on the journey happened
to be in as great a hurry as he himself, and readily agreed to
take their meals in the carriage. Thus swept over the road,
the notary reached the Rue du Bercail, after three days of
absence, an hour before midnight. And yet he was too late.
He saw the gendarmes at the gate, crossed the threshold, and
met the young count in the courtyard. Victurnien had been
arrested. If Chesnel had had the power, he would, beyond a
doubt, have killed the officers and men; as it was, he could
only fall on Victurnien's neck.

"If I cannot hush this matter up, you must kill yourself before the indictment is made out," he whispered. But Victurnien had sunk into such stupor that he stared back uncom-
prehendingly.

"Kill myself?" he repeated.

"Yes. If your courage should fail, my boy, count upon
me," said Chesnel, squeezing Victurnien's hand.

In spite of his anguish of mind and tottering limbs, he
stood firmly planted, to watch the son of his heart, the Comte
d'Esgrignon, go out of the courtyard between two gendarmes,
with the commissary, the justice of the peace, and the clerk
of the court; and not until the figures had disappeared, and
the sound of footsteps had died away into silence, did he recover his firmness and presence of mind.

"You will catch cold, sir," Brigitte remonstrated.

"The devil take you!" cried her aroused and exasperated
master.

Never in the nine-and-twenty years that Brigitte had been
in his service had she heard such words from him! Her
candle fell out of her hands; but Chesnel neither heeded his

housekeeper's alarm nor heard her exclaim. He hurried off toward the Val-Noble.

"He is out of his mind," said she; "after all, it is no wonder. But where is he off to? I cannot possibly go after him. What will become of him? Suppose that he should drown himself!"

And Brigitte went to waken the head-clerk and send him to look along the river-bank; the river had a gloomy reputation just then, for there had lately been two cases of suicide—one a young man full of promise, and the other a girl, a victim of seduction. Chesnel went straight to the Hôtel du Croisier. There lay his only hope. The law requires that a charge of forgery must be brought by a private individual. It was still possible to withdraw if du Croisier chose to admit that there had been a misapprehension; and Chesnel had hopes, even then, of buying the man over.

M. and Mme. du Croisier had much more company than usual that evening. Only a few persons were in the secret. M. du Ronceret, president of the Tribunal; M. Sauvager, deputy public prosecutor; and M. du Coudrai, a registrar of mortgages, who had lost his post by voting on the wrong side, were the only persons who were supposed to know about it; but Mesdames du Ronceret and du Coudrai had told the news, in strict confidence, to one or two intimate friends, so that it had spread half over the semi-noble, semi-bourgeois assembly at M. du Croisier's. Everybody felt the gravity of the situation, but no one ventured to speak of it openly; and, moreover, Mme. du Croisier's attachment to the upper sphere was so well known that people scarcely dared to mention the disaster which had befallen the d'Esgrignons or to ask for particulars. The persons most interested were waiting till good Mme. du Croisier retired, for that lady always retreated to her room at the same hour to perform her religious exercises as far as possible out of her husband's sight.

Du Croisier's adherents, knowing the secret and the plans

of the great commercial power, looked round when the lady of the house disappeared; but there were still several persons present whose opinions or interests marked them out as untrustworthy, so they continued to play. About half-past eleven all had gone save intimates: M. Sauvager, M. Camusot, the examining magistrate, and his wife, M. and Mme. du Ronceret and their son Fabien, M. and Mme. du Coudrai, and Joseph Blondet, the eldest son of an old judge; ten persons in all.

It is told of Talleyrand that one fatal day, three hours after midnight, he suddenly interrupted a game of cards in the Duchesse de Luynes' house by laying down his watch on the table and asking the players whether the Prince de Condé had any child but the Duc d'Enghien.

"Why do you ask?" returned Mme. de Luynes, "when you know so well that he has not."

"Because if the prince has no other son, the House of Condé is now at an end."

There was a moment's pause, and they finished the game. President du Ronceret now did something very similar. Perhaps he had heard the anecdote; perhaps, in political life, little minds and great minds are apt to hit upon the same expression. He looked at his watch, and interrupted the game of boston with—

"At this moment Monsieur le Comte d'Esgrignon is arrested, and that house which has held its head so high is dishonored for ever."

"Then have you got hold of the boy?" du Coudrai cried gleefully.

Every one in the room, with the exception of the president, the deputy, and du Croisier, looked startled.

"He has just been arrested in Chesnel's house, where he was hiding," said the deputy public prosecutor, with the air of a capable but unappreciated public servant, who ought by rights to be minister of police. M. Sauvager, the deputy, was a thin, tall young man of five-and-twenty, with a lengthy olive-hued countenance, black frizzled hair, and deep-set eyes; the wide, dark rings beneath them were completed by the wrinkled purple eyelids above. With a nose like the beak of some bird of prey, a pinched mouth, and cheeks worn lean with study and hollowed by ambition, he was the very type of a second-rate personage on the lookout for something to turn up, and ready to do anything if so he might get on in the world, while keeping within the limitations of the possible and the forms of law. His pompous expression was an admirable indication of the time-serving eloquence to be expected of him. Chesnel's successor had discovered the young count's hiding-place to him, and he took great credit to himself for his penetration.

The news seemed to come as a shock to the examining magistrate, M. Camusot, who had granted the warrant of arrest on Sauvager's application, with no idea that it was to be executed so promptly. Camusot was short, fair, and fat already, though he was only thirty years old or thereabout; he had the flabby, livid look peculiar to officials who live shut up in their private study or in a court of justice; and his little, pale, yellow eyes were full of the suspicion which is often mistaken for shrewdness.

Mme. Camusot looked at her spouse, as who should say: "Was I not right?"

"Then the case will come on?" was Camusot's comment.

"Could you doubt it?" asked du Coudrai. "Now they have got the count, all is over."

"There is the jury," said Camusot. "In this case, Monsieur le Préfet is sure to take care that, after the challenges from the prosecution and the defense, the jury to a man will be for an acquittal. My advice would be to come to a compromise," he added, turning to du Croisier.

"Compromise!" echoed the president; "why, he is in the hands of justice."

"Acquitted or convicted, the Comte d'Esgrignon will be dishonored all the same," put in Sauvager.

"I am bringing an action,"* said du Croisier. "I shall have Dupin senior. We shall see how the d'Esgrignon family will escape out of his clutches."

"The d'Esgrignons will defend the case and have counsel from Paris; they will have Berryer," said Mme. Camusot. "You will have a Roland for your Oliver."

Du Croisier, M. Sauvager, and the President du Ronceret looked at Camusot, and one thought troubled their minds. The lady's tone, the way in which she flung her proverb in the faces of the eight conspirators against the house d'Esgrignon, caused them inward perturbation, which they dissembled as provincials can dissemble, by dint of lifelong practice in the shifts of a monastic existence. Little Mme. Camusot saw their change of countenance and subsequent composure when they scented opposition on the part of the examining magistrate. When her husband unveiled the thoughts in the back of his own mind, she had tried to plumb the depths of hate in du Croisier's adherents. She wanted to find out how du Croisier had gained over this deputy public prosecutor, who had acted so promptly and so directly in opposition to the views of the central power.

"In any case," continued she, "if celebrated counsel come down from Paris, there is a prospect of a very interesting session in the Court of Assize; but the matter will be snuffed out between the Tribunal and the Court of Appeal. It is only to be expected that the Government should do all that can be done, below the surface, to save a young man who comes of a great family, and has the Duchesse de Maufrigneuse for friend. So I do not think that we shall have 'a sensation at Landernau.'"

* A trial for an offense of this kind in France is an action brought by a private person (*partie civile*) to recover damages, and at the same time a criminal prosecution conducted on behalf of the Government.—Tr.

"How you go on, madame!" the president said sternly. "Can you suppose that the Court of First Instance will be influenced by considerations which have nothing to do with justice?"

"The event proves the contrary," she said meaningly, looking full at Sauvager and the president, who glanced coldly at her.

"Explain yourself, madame," said Sauvager. "You speak as if we had not done our duty."

"Madame Camusot meant nothing," interposed her husband.

"But has not Monsieur le Président just said something prejudicing a case which depends on the examination of the prisoner?" said she. "And the evidence is still to be taken, and the court has not given its decision?"

"We are not at the law-courts," the deputy public prosecutor replied tartly; "and beside, we know all that."

"But the public prosecutor knows nothing at all about it yet," returned she, with an ironical glance. "He will come back from the Chamber of Deputies in all haste. You have cut out his work for him, and he, no doubt, will speak for himself."

The deputy prosecutor knitted his thick bushy brows. Those interested read tardy scruples in his countenance. A great silence followed, broken by no sound but the dealing of the cards. M. and Mme. Camusot, sensible of a decided chill in the atmosphere, took their departure to leave the conspirators to talk at their ease.

"Camusot," the lady began in the street, "you went too far. Why lead those people to suspect that you will have no part in their schemes? They will play you some ugly trick."

"What can they do? I am the only examining magistrate."

"Cannot they slander you in whispers, and procure your dismissal?"

17

At that very moment Chesnel ran up against the couple. The old notary recognized the examining magistrate; and with the lucidity which comes of an experience of business, he saw that the fate of the d'Esgrignons lay in the hands of the young man before him.

"Ah, sir!" he exclaimed, "we shall soon need you badly. Just a word with you. Your pardon, madame," he added, as he drew Camusot aside.

Mme. Camusot, as a good conspirator, looked toward du Croisier's house, ready to break up the conversation if anybody appeared; but she thought, and thought rightly, that their enemies were busy discussing this unexpected turn which she had given to the affair. Chesnel meanwhile drew the magistrate into a dark corner under the wall, and lowered his voice for his companion's ear.

"If, sir, you are for the house d'Esgrignon," he said, "Madame la Duchesse de Maufrigneuse, the Prince de Cadignan, the Ducs de Navarreins and de Lenoncourt, the keeper of the seals, the chancellor, the King himself, will interest themselves in you. I have just come from Paris; I knew all about this; I went post-haste to explain everything at Court. We are counting on you, and I will keep your secret. If you are hostile, I shall go back to Paris to-morrow and lodge a complaint with the keeper of the seals that there is a suspicion of corruption. Several functionaries were at du Croisier's house to-night, and, no doubt, ate and drank there, contrary to law; and beside, they are friends of his."

Chesnel would have brought the Almighty to intervene if he had had the power. He did not wait for an answer; he left Camusot and fled like a deer toward du Croisier's house. Camusot, meanwhile, bidden to reveal the notary's confidences, was at once assailed with: "Was I not right, dear?" —a wifely formula used on all occasions, but rather more vehemently when the fair speaker is in the wrong. By the time they reached home Camusot had admitted the superiority of his partner in life, and appreciated his good fortune in belonging to her ; which confession, doubtless, was the prelude of a blissful night.

Chesnel met his foes in a body as they left du Croisier's house, and began to fear that du Croisier had gone to bed. In his position he was compelled to act quickly, and any delay was a misfortune.

"In the King's name!" he cried, as the manservant was closing the hall door. He had just brought the King on the scene for the benefit of an ambitious little official, and the word was still on his lips. He fretted and chafed while the door was unbarred ; then, swift as a thunderbolt, dashed into the antechamber, and spoke to the servant—

" A hundred crowns to you, young man, if you can wake Madame du Croisier and send her to me this instant. Tell her anything you like."

Chesnel grew cool and composed as he opened the door of the brightly lighted drawing-room, where du Croisier was striding up and down. For a moment the two men scanned each other, with hatred and enmity, twenty years' deep, in their eyes. One of the two had his foot on the heart of the house d'Esgrignon ; the other, with a lion's strength, came forward to pluck it away.

"Your humble servant, sir," said Chesnel. "Have you made the charge ? "

" Yes, sir."

"When was it made ? "

"Yesterday."

" Have any steps been taken since the warrant of arrest was issued ? "

" I believe so."

" I have come to treat with you."

" Justice must take its course, nothing can stop it, the arrest has been made."

" Never mind that, I am at your orders, at your feet."

The old man knelt before du Croisier, and stretched out his hands entreatingly.

"What do you want? Our lands, our castle? Take all; withdraw the charge; leave us nothing but life and honor. And over and beside all this, I will be your servant; command, and I will obey."

Du Croisier sat down in an easy-chair and left the old man to kneel.

"You are not vindictive," pleaded Chesnel; "you are good-hearted, you do not bear us such a grudge that you will not listen to terms. Before daylight the young man ought to be at liberty."

"The whole town knows that he has been arrested," returned du Croisier, enjoying his revenge.

"It is a great misfortune; but as there will neither be proofs nor trial, we can easily manage that."

Du Croisier reflected. He seemed to be struggling with self-interest; Chesnel thought that he had gained a hold on his enemy through the great motive of human action. At that supreme moment Mme. du Croisier appeared.

"Come here and help me to soften your dear husband, madame," said Chesnel, still on his knees. Mme. du Croisier made him rise with every sign of profound astonishment. Chesnel explained his errand; and when she knew it, the generous daughter of the stewards of the Ducs d'Alençon turned to du Croisier with tears in her eyes.

"Ah! monsieur, can you hesitate? The d'Esgrignons, the honor of the province!" she said.

"There is more in it than that!" exclaimed du Croisier, rising to begin his restless walk again.

"More? What more?" asked Maître Chesnel in sheer amazement.

"France is involved, Monsieur Chesnel. It is a question of the country, of the people, of giving my lords your nobles a lesson, and teaching them that there is such a thing as jus-

tice, and law, and a bourgeoisie—a lesser nobility as good as
they, and a match for them ! There shall be no more tram-
pling down half a score of wheat-fields for a single hare ; no
bringing shame on families by seducing unprotected girls ;
they shall not look down on others as good as they are, and
mock at them for ten whole years, without finding out at last
that these things swell into avalanches, and those avalanches
will fall and crush and bury my lords the nobles. You want
to go back to the old order of things. You want to tear up
the social compact, the Charter, in which our rights are set
forth——"

"And so ?"

"Is it not a sacred mission to open the people's eyes ?"
cried du Croisier. "Their eyes will be opened to the morality of your party when they see nobles going to be tried at the
Assize Court like Pierre and Jacques. They will say, then,
that small folk who keep their self-respect are as good as great
folk that bring shame on themselves. The Assize Court is a
light for all the world. Here, I am the champion of the people, the friend of law. You yourselves twice flung me on the
side of the people—once when you refused an alliance, twice
when you put me under the ban of your society. You are
reaping as you have sown."

If Chesnel was startled by this outburst, so no less was
Mme. du Croisier. To her this was a terrible revelation of
her husband's character, a new light not merely on the past
but on the future as well. Any capitulation on the part of
the colossus was apparently out of the question ; but Chesnel
in nowise retreated before the impossible.

"What, monsieur ?" said Mme. du Croisier. "Would
you not forgive ? Then you are not a Christian."

"I forgive as God forgives, madame, on certain conditions."

"And what are they ?" asked Chesnel, thinking that he
saw a ray of hope.

" The elections are coming on ; I want the votes at your disposal."

" You shall have them."

" I wish that we, my wife and I, should be received famil-iarly every evening, with an appearance of friendliness at any rate, by Monsieur le Marquis d'Esgrignon and his circle," continued du Croisier.

" I do not know how we are going to compass it, but you shall be received."

" I wish to have the family bound over by a surety of four hundred thousand francs, and by a written document stating the nature of the compromise, so as to keep a loaded cannon pointed at its heart."

" We agree," said Chesnel, without admitting that the three hundred thousand francs was in his possession ; " but the amount must be deposited with a third party and returned to the family after your election and repayment."

" No ; after the marriage of my grand-niece, Mademoiselle Duval. She will very likely have four million francs some day ; the reversion of our property (mine and my wife's) shall be settled upon her by her marriage-contract, and you shall arrange a match between her and the young count."

" Never ! "

" *Never !* " repeated du Croisier, quite intoxicated with triumph. " Good-night ! "

" Idiot that I am," thought Chesnel, " why did I shrink from a lie to such a man ? "

Du Croisier took himself off ; he was pleased with himself ; he had enjoyed Chesnel's humiliation ; he had held the des-tinies of a proud house, the representative of the aristocracy of the province, suspended in his hand ; he had set the print of his heel on the very heart of the d'Esgrignons ; and, finally, he had broken off the whole negotiation on the score of his wounded pride. He went up to his room, leaving his wife alone with Chesnel. In his intoxication, he saw his victory clear before him. He firmly believed that the three hundred thousand francs had been squandered; the d'Esgrignons must sell or mortgage all that they had to raise the money; the Assize Court was inevitable to his mind.

An affair of forgery can always be settled out of court in France if the missing amount is returned. The losers by the crime are usually well-to-do, and have no wish to blight an imprudent man's character. But du Croisier had no mind to slacken his hold until he knew what he was about. He meditated until he fell asleep on the magnificent manner in which his hopes would be fulfilled by way of the Assize Court or by marriage. The murmur of voices below, the lamentations of Chesnel and Mme. du Croisier, sounded sweet in his ears.

Mme. du Croisier shared Chesnel's views of the d'Esgrignons. She was a deeply religious woman, a Royalist attached to the noblesse; the interview had been in every way a cruel shock to her feelings. She, a stanch Royalist, had heard the roaring of that Liberalism which, in her director's opinion, wished to crush the church. The Left benches for her meant the popular upheaval and the scaffolds of 1793.

"What would your uncle, that sainted man who hears us, say to this?" exclaimed Chesnel. Mme. du Croisier made no reply, but the great tears rolled down her cheeks.

"You have already been the cause of one poor boy's death; his mother will go mourning all her days," continued Chesnel (he saw how his words told, but he would have struck harder and even broken this woman's heart to save Victurnien). "Do you want to kill Mademoiselle Armande, for she would not survive the dishonor of the house for a week? Do you wish to be the death of poor Chesnel, your old notary? For I shall kill the count in prison before they shall bring the charge against him, and take my own life afterward, before they shall try me for murder in an Assize Court."

"That is enough! that is enough, my friend? I would do

anything to put a stop to such an affair; but I never knew
Monsieur du Croisier's real character until a few minutes ago.
To you I can make the admission: there is nothing to be
done."

"But what if there is?"

"I would give half the blood in my veins that it were so,"
said she, finishing her sentence by a wistful shake of the
head.

As the First Consul, beaten on the field of Marengo till five
o'clock in the evening, by six o'clock saw the tide of battle
turned by Desaix's desperate attack and Kellermann's terrific
charge, so Chesnel in the midst of defeat saw the beginnings
of victory. No one but a Chesnel, an old notary, an ex-
steward of the manor, old Maître Sorbier's junior clerk, in the
sudden flash of lucidity which comes with despair, could rise
thus, high as a Napoleon; nay, higher. This was not Marengo,
it was Waterloo, and the Prussians had come up; Chesnel saw
this, and was determined to beat them off the field.

"Madame," he said, "remember that I have been your
man of business for twenty years; remember that if the
d'Esgrignons mean the honor of the province, you represent
the honor of the bourgeoisie; it rests with you, and you alone,
to save the ancient house. Now, answer me; are you going
to allow dishonor to fall on the shade of your dead uncle, on
the d'Esgrignons, on poor Chesnel? Do you want to kill
Mademoiselle Armande weeping yonder? Or do you wish to
expiate wrongs done to others by a deed which will rejoice
your ancestors, the stewards of the dukes of Alençon, and
bring comfort to the soul of our dear abbé. If he could rise
from his grave, he would command you to do this thing that
I beg of you upon my knees."

"What is it?" asked Mme. du Croisier.

"Well. Here are the hundred thousand crowns," said
Chesnel, drawing the bundles of notes from his pocket.
"Take them, and there will be an end of it."

"If that is all," she began, "and if no harm can come of it to my husband——"

"Nothing but good," Chesnel replied. "You are saving him from eternal punishment in hell, at the cost of a slight disappointment here below."

"He will not be compromised, will he?" she asked, looking into Chesnel's face.

Then Chesnel read the depths of the poor wife's mind. Mme. du Croisier was hesitating between her two creeds; between wifely obedience to her husband as laid down by the church, and obedience to the altar and the throne. Her husband, in her eyes, was acting wrongly, but she dared not blame him; she would fain save the d'Esgrignons, but she was loyal to her husband's interests.

"Not in the least," Chesnel answered; "your old notary swears it by the Holy Gospels——"

He had nothing left to lose for the d'Esgrignons but his soul; he risked it now by this horrible perjury, but Mme. du Croisier must be deceived, there was no other choice but death. Without losing a moment, he dictated a form of receipt by which Mme. du Croisier acknowledged payment of a hundred thousand crowns five days before the fatal letter of exchange appeared; for he recollected that du Croisier was away from home, superintending improvements on his wife's property at the time.

"Now swear to me that you will declare before the examining magistrate that you received the money on that date," he said, when Mme. du Croisier had taken the notes and he held the receipt in his hand.

"It will be a lie, will it not?"

"Venial sin," said Chesnel.

"I could not do it without consulting my director, Monsieur l'Abbé Couturier."

"Very well," said Chesnel, "will you be guided entirely by his advice in this affair?"

"I promise that."

"And you must not give the money to Monsieur du Croisier until you have been before the magistrate."

"No. Ah! God give me strength to appear in a court of justice and maintain a lie before men!"

Chesnel kissed Mme. du Croisier's hand, then stood upright and majestic as one of the prophets that Raphael painted in the Vatican.

"Your uncle's soul is thrilled with joy," he said; "you have wiped out for ever the wrong that you did by marrying an enemy of altar and throne"—words that made a lively impression on Mme. du Croisier's timorous mind.

Then Chesnel all at once bethought himself that he must make sure of the lady's director, the Abbé du Couturier. He knew how obstinately devout souls can work for the triumph of their views when once they come forward for their side, and wished to secure the concurrence of the church as early as possible. So he went to the Hôtel d'Esgrignon, roused up Mlle. Armande, gave her an account of that night's work, and sped her to fetch the bishop himself into the forefront of the battle.

"Ah, God in heaven! Thou must save the house d'Esgrignon!" he exclaimed, as he went slowly home again. "The affair is developing now into a fight in a court of law. We are face to face with men that have passions and interests of their own; we cannot get anything out of them. This du Croisier has taken advantage of the public prosecutor's absence; the public prosecutor is devoted to us, but since the opening of the Chambers he has gone to Paris. Now, what can they have done to get round his deputy? They have induced him to take up the charge without consulting his chief. This mystery must be looked into, and the ground surveyed to-morrow; and then, perhaps, when I have unraveled this web of theirs, I will go back to Paris to set great powers at work through Madame de Maufrigneuse."

So he reasoned, poor, aged, clear-sighted wrestler, before he lay down half dead with bearing the weight of so much emotion and fatigue. And yet, before he fell asleep, he ran a searching eye over the list of magistrates, taking all their secret ambitions into account, casting about for ways of influencing them, calculating his chances in the coming struggle. Chesnel's prolonged scrutiny of consciences, given in a condensed form, will perhaps serve as a picture of the judicial world in a country town.

Magistrates and officials generally are obliged to begin their career in the provinces; judicial ambition there ferments. At the outset every man looks toward Paris; they all aspire to shine in the vast theatre where great political causes come before the courts, and the higher branches of the legal profession are closely connected with the palpitating interests of society.

At this time the younger men were full of Royalist zeal against the enemies of the Bourbons. The most insignificant deputy official was dreaming of conducting a prosecution, and praying with all his might for one of those political cases which bring a man's zeal into prominence, draw the attention of the higher powers, and mean advancement for King's men. Was there a member of any official staff of prosecuting counsel who could hear of a Bonapartist conspiracy breaking out somewhere else without a feeling of envy? Where was the man that did not burn to discover a Caron, or a Berton, or a revolt of some sort? With reasons of State, and the necessity of diffusing the monarchical spirit throughout France as their basis, and a fierce ambition stirred up whenever party spirit ran high, these ardent politicians on their promotion were lucid, clear-sighted, and perspicacious. They kept up a vigorous detective system throughout the kingdom; they did the work of spies, and urged the nation along a pathway of obedience, from which it had no business to swerve.

Justice, thus informed with monarchical enthusiasm, atoned

for the errors of the ancient parliaments, and walked, perhaps, too ostentatiously hand in hand with religion. There was more zeal than discretion shown; but justice sinned not so much in the direction of Machiavellism as by giving too candid expression to its views, when those views appeared to be opposed to the general interests of a country which must be put safely out of reach of revolutions.

Officials of both complexions were to be found in the court in which young d'Esgrignon's fate depended. M. le Président du Ronceret and an elderly judge, Blondet by name, represented the section of functionaries shelved for good, and resigned to stay where they were; while the young and ambitious party comprised the examining magistrate, M. Camusot, and his deputy, M. Michu, appointed through the interest of the Cinq-Cygnes, and certain of promotion to the Court of Appeals of Paris at the first opportunity.

President du Ronceret held a permanent post; it was impossible to turn him out. The aristocratic party declined to give him what he considered to be his due, socially speaking; so he declared for the bourgeoisie, glossed over his disappointment with the name of independence, and failed to realize that his opinions condemned him to remain a president of a court of first instance for the rest of his life. Once started on this track, the sequence of events led du Ronceret to place his hopes of advancement on the triumph of du Croisier and the Left. He was in no better odor at the prefecture than at the Court-Royal. He was compelled to keep on good terms with the authorities; the Liberals distrusted him, consequently he belonged to neither party. He was obliged to resign his chances of election to du Croisier, he exercised no influence, and played a secondary part. The false position reacted on his character; he was soured and discontented; he was tired of political ambiguity, and privately had made up his mind to come forward openly as leader of the Liberal party, and so to strike ahead of du Croisier. His behavior in the d'Esgrignon affair was the first step in this direction. To begin with, he was an admirable representative of that section of the middle-classes which allows its petty passions to obscure the wider interests of the country; a class of crotchety politicians, upholding the government one day and opposing it the next, compromising every cause and helping none; helpless after they have done the mischief till they set about brewing more; unwilling to face their own incompetence, thwarting authority while professing to serve it. With a compound of arrogance and humility they demand of the people more submission than kings expect, and fret their souls because those above them are not brought down to their level, as if greatness could be little, as if power existed without force.

President du Ronceret was a tall, spare man with a receding forehead and scanty, auburn hair. He was wall-eyed, his complexion was blotched, his lips thin and hard, his scarcely audible voice came out like the husky wheezings of asthma. He had for a wife a great, solemn, clumsy creature, tricked out in the most ridiculous fashion, and outrageously over-dressed. Mme. la Présidente gave herself the airs of a queen; she wore vivid colors, and always appeared at balls adorned with the turban, dear to the British female, and lovingly cultivated in out-of-the-way districts in France. Each of the pair had an income of four or five thousand francs, which, with the president's salary, reached a total of some twelve thousand. In spite of a decided tendency to parsimony, vanity required that they should receive one evening in the week. Du Croisier might import modern luxury into the town, M. and Mme. du Ronceret were faithful to the old traditions. They had always lived in the old-fashioned house belonging to Mme. du Ronceret, and had made no changes in it since their marriage. The house stood between a garden and a courtyard. The gray old gable end, with one window in each story, gave upon the road. High walls inclosed the garden and the yard, but the space taken up beneath them in

the garden by a walk shaded with chestnut trees was filled in
the yard by a row of outbuildings. An old rust-devoured
iron gate in the garden wall balanced the yard gateway, a
huge, double-leaved carriage entrance with a buttress on
either side, and a mighty shell on the top. The same shell
was repeated over the house-door.

The whole place was gloomy, close, and airless. The row
of iron-grated openings in the opposite wall, as you entered,
reminded you of prison windows. Every passer-by could
look in through the railings to see how the garden grew ; the
flowers in the little square borders never seemed to thrive
there.

The drawing-room on the first floor was lighted by a single
window on the side of the street and a French window above
a flight of steps, which gave upon the garden. The dining-
room on the other side of the great antechamber, with its
windows also looking out into the garden, was exactly the
same size as the drawing-room, and all three apartments were
in harmony with the general air of gloom. It wearied your
eyes to look at the ceilings all divided up by huge painted
cross-beams and adorned with a feeble lozenge pattern or a
rosette in the middle. The paint was old, startling in tint,
and begrimed with smoke. The sun had faded the heavy
silk curtains in the drawing-room ; the old-fashioned Beau-
vais tapestry which covered the white-painted furniture had
lost all its color with wear. A Louis Quinze clock on the
mantel stood between two extravagant, branched sconces
filled with yellow wax candles, which the presidente only
lighted on occasions when the old-fashioned rock-crystal
chandelier emerged from its green wrapper. Three card-
tables, covered with threadbare baize, and a backgammon
box, sufficed for the recreations of the company ; and Mme.
du Ronceret treated them to such refreshments as cider,
chestnuts, pastry puffs, glasses of *eau sucrée*, and home-made
orangeade. For some time past she had made a practice of

giving a party once a fortnight, when tea and some pitiable attempts at pastry appeared to grace the occasion.

Once a quarter the du Roncerets gave a grand three-course dinner, which made a great sensation in the town, a dinner served up on execrable ware, but prepared with the science for which the provincial cook is remarkable.   It was a Gargantuan repast, which lasted for six whole hours, and by abundance the president tried to vie with du Croisier's elegance.

And so du Ronceret's life and its accessories were just what might have been expected from his character and his false position.   He felt dissatisfied at home without precisely knowing what was the matter; but he dared not go to any expense to change existing conditions, and was only too glad to put by seven or eight thousand francs every year, so as to leave his son Fabien a handsome private fortune.   Fabien du Ronceret had no mind for the magistracy, the bar, or the civil service, and his pronounced turn for doing nothing drove his parent to despair.

On this head there was rivalry between the president and the vice-president, old M. Blondet.   M. Blondet, for a long time past, had been sedulously cultivating an acquaintance between his son and the Blandureau family.   The Blandureaus were well-to-do linen manufacturers, with an only daughter, and it was on this daughter that the president had fixed his choice of a wife for Fabien.   Now, Joseph Blondet's marriage with Mlle. Blandureau depended on his nomination to the post which his father, old Blondet, hoped to obtain for him when he himself should retire.   But President du Ronceret, in underhand ways, was thwarting the old man's plans, and working indirectly upon the Blandureaus.   Indeed, if it had not been for this affair of young d'Esgrignon's, the astute president might have cut them out, father and son, for their rivals were very much richer.

Before the Revolution broke out, Blondet senior had been a barrister; afterward he became the public accuser, and one

of the mildest of those formidable functionaries.   Goodman
Blondet, as they used to call him, deadened the force of the
new doctrines by acquiescing in them all, and putting none
of them in practice.   He had been obliged to send one or
two nobles to prison ; but his further proceedings were marked
with such deliberation, that he brought them through to the
9th Thermidor with a dexterity which won respect for him on
all sides.   As a matter of fact, Goodman Blondet ought to
have been president of the Tribunal, but when the courts of
law were reorganized he had been set aside ; Napoleon's aversion from Republicans was apt to reappear in the smallest
appointments under his government.   The qualification of
ex-public accuser, written in the margin of the list against
Blondet's name, set the Emperor inquiring of Cambacérès
whether there might not be some scion of an ancient parliamentary stock to appoint instead.   The consequence was that
du Ronceret, whose father had been a councilor of parliament,
was nominated to the presidency ; but, the Emperor's repugnance notwithstanding, Cambacérès allowed Blondet to remain
on the bench, saying that the old barrister was one of the best
juri-consuls in France.

Blondet's talents, his knowledge of the old law of the land
and subsequent legislation, should by rights have brought him
far in his profession ; but he had this much in common with
some few great spirits : he entertained a prodigious contempt
for his own special knowledge, and reserved all his preten-
tions, leisure, and capacity for a second pursuit unconnected
with the law.   To this pursuit he gave his almost exclusive
attention.   The good man was passionately fond of garden-
ing.   He was in correspondence with some of the most celebrated amateurs ; it was his ambition to create new species ;
he took an interest in botanical discoveries, and lived, in
short, in the world of flowers.   Like all florists, he had a
predilection for one particular plant ; the *pelargonium* was his
especial favorite.   The court, the cases that came before it,

and his outward life were as nothing to him compared with the inward life of fancies and abundant emotions which the old man led. He fell more and more in love with his flower-seraglio; and the pains which he bestowed on his garden, the sweet round of the labors of the months, held Goodman Blondet fast in his greenhouse. But for that hobby he would have been a deputy under the Empire, and shone conspicuous beyond a doubt in the Corps Legislatif.

His marriage was the second cause of his obscurity. As a man of forty, he was rash enough to marry a girl of eighteen, by whom he had a son named Joseph in the first year of their marriage. Three years afterward Mme. Blondet, then the prettiest woman in the town, inspired in the prefect of the department a passion which ended only with her death. The prefect was the father of her second son, Émile; the whole town knew this, old Blondet himself knew it. The wife who might have roused her husband's ambition, who might have won him away from his flowers, positively encouraged the judge in his botanical tastes. She no more cared to leave the place than the prefect cared to leave his prefecture so long as his mistress lived.

Blondet felt himself unequal at his age to a contest with a young wife. He sought consolation in his greenhouse, and engaged a very pretty servant-maid to assist him to tend his ever-changing bevy of beauties. So while the judge potted, pricked out, watered, layered, slipped, blended, and induced his flowers to break, Mme. Blondet spent his substance on the dress and finery in which she shone at the prefecture. One interest alone had power to draw her away from the tender care of a romantic affection which the town came to admire in the end; and this interest was Émile's education. The child of love was a bright and pretty boy, while Joseph was no less heavy and plain-featured. The old judge, blinded by paternal affection, loved Joseph as his wife loved Émile.

For a dozen years M. Blondet bore his lot with perfect
18

resignation.   He shut his eyes to his wife's intrigue with a
dignified, well-bred composure, quite in the style of an eighteenth-century great lord; but, like all men with a taste for a
quiet life, he could cherish a profound dislike, and he hated
the younger son.   When his wife died, therefore, in 1818, he
turned the intruder out of the house, and packed him off to
Paris to study law on an allowance of twelve hundred francs
for all resource, nor could any cry of distress extract another
penny from his purse.   Émile Blondet would have gone
under if it had not been for his real father.

M. Blondet's house was one of the prettiest in the town.   It
stood almost opposite the prefecture, with a neat little court
in front.   A row of old-fashioned iron railings between two
brickwork piers inclosed it from the street; and a low wall,
also of brick, with a second row of railings along the top, connected the piers with the neighboring house.   The little court,
a space about sixty feet in width by one hundred and twenty
in length, was cut in two by a brick pathway which ran from
the gate to the house door between a border on either side.
Those borders were always renewed; at every season of the
year they exhibited a successful show of blossom, to the
admiration of the public.   All along the back of the garden-
beds a quantity of climbing plants grew up and covered the
walls of the neighboring houses with a magnificent mantle;
the brickwork piers were hidden in clusters of honeysuckle;
and, to crown all, in a couple of terra-cotta vases at the summit, a pair of acclimatized cacti displayed to the astonished
eyes of the ignorant those thick leaves bristling with spiny
defenses which seem to be due to some plant disease.

It was a plain-looking house, built of brick, with brickwork
arches above the windows, and bright green Venetian blinds
to make it gay.   Through the glass door you could look
straight across the house to the opposite glass door, at the end
of a long passage, and down the central alley in the garden
beyond; while through the windows of the dining-room and

THE JEALOUSIES OF A COUNTRY TOWN.   275

drawing-room, which extended, like the hall, from back to front of the house, you could often catch further glimpses of the flower-beds in a garden of about two acres in extent. Seen from the road, the brickwork harmonized with the fresh flowers and shrubs, for two centuries had overlaid it with mosses, and green and russet tints. No one could pass through the town without falling in love with a house with such charming surroundings, so covered with flowers and mosses to the roof-ridge, where two pigeons of glazed crockery-ware were perched by way of ornament.

M. Blondet possessed an income of about four thousand livres derived from land, beside the old house in the town. He meant to avenge his wrongs legitimately enough. He would leave his house, his lands, his seat on the bench to his son Joseph, and the whole town knew what he meant to do. He had made a will in that son's favor; he had gone as far as the Code will permit a man to go in the way of disinheriting one child to benefit another; and what was more, he had been putting by money for the past fifteen years to enable his lout of a son to buy back from Émile that portion of his father's estate which could not legally be taken away from him.

Émile Blondet, thus turned adrift, had contrived to gain distinction in Paris, but so far it was rather a name than a practical result. Émile's indolence, recklessnness, and happy-go-lucky ways drove his real father to despair; and when that father died, a half-ruined man, turned out of office by one of the political reactions so frequent under the Restoration, it was with a mind uneasy as to the future of a man endowed with the most brilliant qualities.

Émile Blondet found support in a friendship with a Mlle. de Troisville, whom he had known before her marriage with the Comte de Montcornet. His mother was living when the Troisvilles came back after the emigration; she was related to the family, distantly it is true, but the connection was close enough to allow her to introduce Émile to the house. She, poor woman, foresaw the future. She knew that when she died her son would lose both mother and father, a thought which made death doubly bitter, so she tried to interest others in him. She encouraged the liking that sprang up between Émile and the eldest daughter of the house of Troisville ; but while the liking was exceedingly strong on the young lady's part, a marriage was out of the question. It was a romance on the pattern of " Paul and Virginia." Mme. Blondet did what she could to teach her son to look to the Troisvilles, to found a lasting attachment on a children's game of " make-be-lieve" love, which was bound to end as boy-and-girl romances usually do. When Mlle. de Troisville's marriage with General Montcornet was announced, Mme. Blondet, a dying woman, went to the bride and solemnly implored her never to abandon Émile, and to use her influence for him in society in Paris, whither the general's fortune summoned her to shine.

Luckily for Émile, he was able to make his own way. He made his appearance, at the age of twenty, as one of the masters of modern literature ; and met with no less success in the society into which he was launched by the father who at first could afford to bear the expense of the young man's extravagance. Perhaps Émile's precocious celebrity and the good figure that he made strengthened the bonds of his friend-ship with the countess. Perhaps Mme. de Montcornet, with the Russian blood in her veins (her mother was the daughter of the Princess Scherbelloff), might have cast off the friend of her childhood if he had been a poor man struggling with all his might among the difficulties which beset a man of letters in Paris ; but by the time that the real strain of Émile's adventurous life began, their attachment was unalterable on either side. He was looked upon as one of the leading lights of journalism when young d'Esgrignon met him at his first supper-party in Paris ; his acknowledged position in the world of letters was very high, and he towered above his reputation.

Goodman Blondet had not the faintest conception of the power which the Constitutional Government had given to the press; nobody ventured to talk in his presence of the son of whom he refused to hear. And so it came to pass that he knew nothing of Émile whom he had cursed and Émile's greatness.

Old Blondet's integrity was as deeply rooted in him as his passion for flowers; he knew nothing but law and botany. He would have interviews with litigants, listen to them, chat with them, and show them his flowers; he would accept rare seeds from them; but once on the bench, no judge on earth was more impartial. Indeed, his manner of proceeding was so well known that litigants never went near him except to hand over some document which might enlighten him in the performance of his duty, and nobody tried to throw dust in his eyes. With his learning, his lights, and his way of holding his real talents cheap, he was so indispensable to President du Ronceret, that, matrimonial schemes apart, that functionary would have done all that he could, in an underhand way, to prevent the vice-president from retiring in favor of his son. If the learned old man left the bench, the president would be utterly unable to do without him.

Goodman Blondet did not know that it was in Émile's power to fulfill all his wishes in a few hours. The simplicity of his life was worthy of one of Plutarch's men. In the evening he looked over his cases; next morning he worked among his flowers; and all day long he gave decisions on the bench. The pretty maid-servant, now of ripe age and wrinkled like an Easter pippin, looked after the house, and they lived according to the established customs of the strictest parsimony. Mlle. Cadot always carried the keys of her cupboards and fruit-loft about with her. She was indefatigable. She went to market herself, she cooked and dusted and swept, and never missed mass of a morning. To give some idea of the domestic life of the household, it will be enough to remark that the father and son never ate fruit till it was beginning to spoil, because Mlle. Cadot always brought out anything that would not keep. No one in the house ever tasted the luxury of new bread, and all the fast days in the kalendar were punctually observed. The gardener was put on rations like a soldier; the elderly Valideh always kept an eye upon him. And she, for her part, was so deferentially treated, that she took her meals with the family, and in consequence was continually trotting to and fro between the kitchen and the parlor at breakfast and dinner time.

Mlle. Blandureau's parents had consented to her marriage with Joseph Blondet upon one condition—the penniless and briefless barrister must be an assistant judge. So, with the desire of fitting his son to fill the position, old M. Blondet racked his brains to hammer the law into his son's head by dint of lessons, so as to make a cut-and-dried lawyer of him. As for Blondet junior, he spent almost every evening at the Blandureaus' house, to which also young Fabien du Ronceret had been admitted since his return, without raising the slightest suspicion in the minds of father or son.

Everything in this life of theirs was measured by an accuracy worthy of Gerard Dow's " Money Changer;" not a grain of salt too much, not a single profit foregone; but the economical principles by which it was regulated were relaxed in favor of the greenhouse and garden. " The garden was the master's craze," Mlle. Cadot used to say. The master's blind fondness for Joseph was not a craze in her eyes; she shared the father's predilection; she pampered Joseph; she darned his stockings; and would have been better pleased if the money spent on the garden had been put by for Joseph's benefit.

That garden was kept in marvelous order by a single man; the paths, covered with river-sand, continually turned over with the rake, meandered among the borders full of the rarest flowers. Here were all kinds of color and scent, here were lizards on the walls, legions of little flower-pots standing out in the sun, regiments of forks and hoes, and a host of innocent things, a combination of pleasant results to justify the gardener's charming hobby.

At the end of the greenhouse the judge had set up a grand stand, an amphitheatre of benches to hold some five or six thousand pelargoniums in pots—a splendid and famous show. People came to see his geraniums in flower, not only from the neighborhood, but even from the departments round about. The Empress Marie Louise, passing through the town, had honored the curiously kept greenhouse with a visit; so much was she impressed with the sight that she spoke of it to Napoleon, and the old judge received the cross of the Legion of Honor. But as the learned gardener never mingled in society at all, and went nowhere except to the Blandureaus, he had no suspicion of the president's underhand manœuvres; and others who could see the president's intentions were far too much afraid of him to interfere or to warn the inoffensive Blondets.

As for Michu, that young man with his powerful connections gave much more thought to making himself agreeable to the women in the upper social circles to which he was introduced by the Cinq-Cygnes, than to the extremely simple business of a provincial Tribunal. With his independent means (he had an income of twelve thousand livres), he was courted by mothers of daughters, and led a frivolous life. He did just enough at the Tribunal to satisfy his conscience, much as a schoolboy does his exercises, saying ditto on all occasions, with a "Yes, dear president." But underneath the appearance of indifference lurked the unusual powers of the Paris law student who had distinguished himself as one of the staff of prosecuting counsel before he came to the provinces. He was accustomed to taking broad views of things; he could do rapidly what the president and Blondet could only do after much thinking, and very often solved knotty points for them. In delicate conjunctures the president and vice-president took counsel with their junior, confided thorny questions to him, and never failed to wonder at the readiness with which he brought back a task in which old Blondet found nothing to criticise.   Michu was sure of the influence of the most crabbed aristocrats, and he was young and rich; he lived, therefore, above the level of departmental intrigues and pettinesses.   He was an indispensable man at picnics, he frisked with young ladies and paid court to their mothers, he danced at balls, he gambled like a capitalist.   In short, he played his part of young lawyer of fashion to admiration; without, at the same time, compromising his dignity, which he knew how to assert at the right moment like a man of spirit.   He won golden opinions by the manner in which he threw himself into provincial ways, without criticising them; and for these reasons, every one endeavored to make his time of exile endurable.

The public prosecutor was a lawyer of the highest ability; he had taken the plunge into political life, and was one of the most distinguished speakers on the ministerialist benches. The president stood in awe of him; if he had not been away in Paris at the time, no steps would have been taken against Victurnien; his dexterity, his experience of business, would have prevented the whole affair.   At that moment, however, he was in the Chamber of Deputies, and the president and du Croisier had taken advantage of his absence to weave their plot, calculating, with a certain ingenuity, that if once the law stepped in, and the matter was noised abroad, things would have gone too far to be remedied.

As a matter of fact, no staff of prosecuting counsel in any Tribunal, at that particular time, would have taken up a charge of forgery against the eldest son of one of the noblest houses in France without going into the case at great length, and a special reference, in all probability, to the attorney-general.   In such a case as this, the authorities and the Government would have tried endless ways of compromising and hushing up an affair which might send an imprudent

young man to the hulks.   They would very likely have done
the same for a Liberal family in a prominent position, so long
as the Liberals were not too openly hostile to the throne and
the altar.   So du Croisier's charge and the young count's
arrest had not been very easy to manage.   The president and
du Croisier had compassed their ends in the following manner:

M. Sauvager, a young Royalist barrister, had reached the
position of deputy public prosecutor by dint of subservience
to the Ministry.   In the absence of his chief he was head of
the staff of counsel for prosecution, and, consequently, it fell
to him to take up the charge made by du Croisier.   Sauvager
was a self-made man ; he had nothing but his stipend ; and
for that reason the authorities reckoned upon some one who
had everything to gain by devotion.   The president now exploited the position.   No sooner was the document with the
alleged forgery in du Croisier's hands, than Mme. la Présidente du Ronceret, prompted by her spouse, had a long conversation with M. Sauvager.   In the course of it she pointed
out the uncertainties of a career in the *magistrature debout*
compared with the *magistrature assise*, and the advantages of
the bench over the bar ; she showed how a freak on the part
of some official, or a single false step, might ruin a man's
career.

"If you are conscientious and give your conclusions
against the powers that be, you are lost," continued she.
"Now, at this moment, you might turn your position to
account to make a fine match that would put you above unlucky chances for the rest of your life ; you may marry a wife
with fortune sufficient to land you on the bench, in the
magistrature assise.   There is a fine chance for you.   Monsieur du Croisier will never have any children ; everybody
knows why.   His money, and his wife's as well, will go to his
niece, Mademoiselle Duval.   Monsieur Duval is an iron-
master, his purse is tolerably filled, to begin with, and his
father is still alive, and has a little property beside.   The

father and son have a million of francs between them; they will double it with du Croisier's help, for du Croisier has business connections among great capitalists and manufacturers in Paris.   Monsieur and Madame Duval the younger would be certain to give their daughter to a suitor brought forward by du Croisier, for he is sure to leave two fortunes to his niece; and, in all probability, he will settle the reversion of his wife's property upon Mademoiselle Duval in the marriage-contract, for Madame du Croisier has no kin.   You know how du Croisier hates the d'Esgrignons.   Do him a service, be his man, take up this charge of forgery which he is going to make against young d'Esgrignon, and follow up the proceedings at once without consulting the public prosecutor at Paris.   And, then, pray heaven that the Ministry dismisses you for doing your office impartially, in spite of the powers that be; for if they do, your fortune is made !   You will have a charming wife and thirty thousand francs a year with her, to say nothing of four millions of expectations in ten years' time.''

In two evenings Sauvager was talked over.   Both he and the president kept the affair a secret from old Blondet, from Michu, and from the second member of the staff of prosecuting counsel.   Feeling sure of Blondet's impartiality on a question of fact, the president made certain of a majority without counting Camusot.   And now Camusot's unexpected defection had thrown everything out.   What the president wanted was a committal for trial before the public prosecutor got warning.   How if Camusot or the second counsel for the prosecution should send word to Paris?

And here some portion of Camusot's private history may perhaps explain how it came to pass that Chesnel took it for granted that the examining magistrate would be on the d'Esgrignons' side, and how he had the boldness to tamper in the open street with that representative of justice.

Camusot's father, a well-known silk mercer in the Rue des

Bourdonnais, was ambitious for the only son of his first marriage, and brought him up to the law.   When Camusot junior
took a wife, he gained with her the influence of an usher of
the royal cabinet, back-stairs influence, it is true, but still
sufficient, since it had brought him his first appointment as
justice of the peace, and the second as examining magistrate.
At the time of his marriage, his father only settled an income
of six thousand francs upon him (the amount of his mother's
fortune, which he could legally claim), and as Mlle. Thirion
brought him no more than twenty thousand francs as her
portion, the young couple knew the hardships of hidden poverty.   The salary of a provincial justice of the peace does not
exceed fifteen hundred francs, while an examining magistrate's
stipend is augmented by something like a thousand francs, because his position entails expenses and extra work.   The post,
therefore, is much coveted, though it is not permanent, and
the work is heavy, and that was why Mme. Camusot had just
scolded her husband for allowing the president to read his
thoughts.

Marie-Cécile-Amélie Thirion, after three years of marriage,
perceived the blessing of heaven upon it in the regularity of
two auspicious events—the births of a girl and a boy ; but she
prayed to be less blessed in future.   A few more of such blessings would turn straitened means into distress.   M. Camusot's
father's money was not likely to come to them for a long
time ; and, rich as he was, he would scarcely leave more than
eight or ten thousand francs a year to each of his children,
four in number, for he had been married twice.   And beside,
by the time that all "expectations," as matchmakers call
them, were realized, would not the magistrate have children
of his own to settle in life ?   Any one can imagine the situation for a little woman with plenty of sense and determination,
and Mme. Camusot was such a woman.   She did not refrain
from meddling in matters judicial.   She had far too strong a
sense of the gravity of a false step in her husband's career.

She was the only child of an old servant of Louis XVIII.,
a valet who had followed his master in his wanderings in
Italy, Courland, and England, till after the Restoration the
King rewarded him with the one place that he could fill at
Court, and made him usher by rotation to the royal cabinet.
So in Amélie's home there had been, as it were, a sort of reflection of the Court.   Thirion used to tell her about the
lords, and ministers, and great men whom he announced and
introduced and saw passing to and fro.   The girl, brought up
at the gates of the Tuileries, had caught some tincture of the
maxims practiced there, and adopted the dogma of passive
obedience to authority.   She had sagely judged that her husband, by ranging himself on the side of the d'Esgrignons,
would find favor with Mme. la Duchesse de Maufrigneuse,
and with two powerful families on whose influence with the
King the Sieur Thirion could depend at an opportune moment.
Camusot might get an appointment at the first opportunity
within the jurisdiction of Paris, and afterward at Paris itself.
That promotion, dreamed of and longed for at every moment,
was certain to have a salary of six thousand francs attached to
it, as well as the alleviation of living in her own father's
house, or under the Camusots' roof, and all the advantages of
a father's fortune on either side.   If the adage : " Out of sight
is out of mind," holds good of most women, it is particularly
true where family feeling or royal or ministerial patronage is
concerned.   The personal attendants of kings prosper at all
times; you take an interest in a man, be it only a man in
livery, if you see him every day.

Mme. Camusot, regarding herself as a bird of passage, had
taken a little house in the Rue du Cygne.   Furnished lodg-
ings there were none ; the town was not enough of a thorough-
fare, and the Camusots could not afford to live at an inn, like
M. Michu.   So the fair Parisian had no choice for it but to
take such furniture as she could find ; and as she paid a very
moderate rent, the house was remarkably ugly, albeit a certain

quaintness of detail was not wanting. It was built against a neighboring house in such a fashion that the side, with only one window in each story, gave upon the street, and the front looked out upon a yard where rose-bushes and buckthorn were growing along the wall on either side. On the farther side, opposite the house, stood a shed, a roof over two brick arches. A little wicket-gate gave entrance into the gloomy place (made gloomier still by the great walnut tree which grew in the yard), and a double flight of steps, with an elaborately wrought but rust-eaten handrail, led to the house-door. Inside the house there were two rooms on each floor. The dining-room occupied that part of the first floor nearest the street, and the kitchen lay on the other side of a narrow passage almost wholly taken up by the wooden staircase. Of the two second-floor rooms, one did duty as the magistrate's study, the other as a bedroom, while the nursery and the servants' bedroom stood above in the attics. There were no ceilings in the house; the cross-beams were simply whitewashed and the spaces plastered over. Both rooms on the second floor and the dining-room below were wainscoted and adorned with the labyrinthine designs which taxed the patience of the eighteenth-century carpenter; but the carving had been painted a dingy gray most depressing to behold.

The magistrate's study looked as though it belonged to a provincial lawyer; it contained a big desk, a mahogany arm-chair, a law student's books, and shabby belongings transported from Paris. Mme. Camusot's room was more of a native product; it boasted a blue-and-white scheme of decoration, a carpet, and that anomalous kind of furniture which appears to be in the fashion, while it is simply some style that has failed in Paris. As to the dining-room, it was nothing but an ordinary provincial dining-room, bare and chilly, with a damp, faded paper on the walls.

In this shabby room, with nothing to see but the walnut tree, the dark leaves growing against the walls, and the almost deserted road beyond them, a somewhat lively and frivolous woman, accustomed to the amusements and stir of Paris, used to sit all day long, day after day, and for the most part of the time alone, though she received tiresome and inane visits which led her to think her loneliness preferable to empty tittle-tattle. If she permitted herself the slightest gleam of intelligence, it gave rise to interminable comment and embittered her condition. She occupied herself a good deal with her children, not so much from taste as for the sake of an interest in her almost solitary life, and exercised her mind on the only subjects which she could find ; to wit, the intrigues which went on around her, the ways of provincials, and the ambitions shut in by their narrow horizons. So she very soon fathomed mysteries of which her husband had no idea. As she sat at her window with a piece of intermittent embroidery work in her fingers, she did not see her wood-shed full of faggots nor the servant busy at the wash-tub ; she was looking out upon Paris, Paris where everything is pleasure, everything is full of life. She dreamed of Paris gayeties, and shed tears because she must abide in this dull prison of a country town. She was disconsolate because she lived in a peaceful district, where no conspiracy, no great affair would ever occur. She saw herself doomed to sit under the shadow of the walnut tree for some time to come.

Mme. Camusot was a little, plump, fresh, fair-haired woman, with a very prominent forehead, a mouth which receded, and a turned-up chin, a type of countenance which is passable in youth, but looks old before the time. Her bright, quick eyes expressed her innocent desire to get on in the world, and the envy born of her present inferior position, with rather too much candor ; but still they lighted up her commonplace face and set it off with a certain energy of feeling, which success was certain to extinguish in later life. At that time she used to give a good deal of time and thought to her dresses, inventing trimmings and embroidering them ; she planned out her costumes with the maid whom she had brought with her from Paris, and so maintained the reputation of Parisiennes in the provinces. Her caustic tongue was dreaded; she was not beloved. In that keen, investigating spirit peculiar to unoccupied women who are driven to find some occupation for empty days, she had pondered the president's private opinions, until at length she discovered what he meant to do, and for some time past she had advised Camusot to declare war. The young count's affair was an excellent opportunity. Was it not obviously Camusot's part to make a stepping-stone of this criminal case by favoring the d'Esgrignons, a family with power of a very different kind from the power of the du Croisier party.

"Sauvager will never marry Mademoiselle Duval. They are dangling her before him, but he will be the dupe of those Machiavels in the Val-Noble to whom he is going to sacrifice his position. Camusot, this affair, so unfortunate as it is for the d'Esgrignons, so insidiously brought on by the president for du Croisier's benefit, will turn out well for nobody but *you*," she had said, as they went in.

The shrewd Parisienne had likewise guessed the president's underhand manœuvres with the Blandureaus, and his object in baffling old Blondet's efforts, but she saw nothing to be gained by opening the eyes of father or son to the perils of the situation; she was enjoying the beginning of the comedy; she knew about the proposals made by Chesnel's successor on behalf of Fabien du Ronceret, but she did not suspect how important that secret might be to her. If she or her husband were threatened by the president, Mme. Camusot could threaten too, in her turn, to call the amateur gardener's attention to a scheme for carrying off the flower which he meant to transplant into his home.

Chesnel had not penetrated, like Mme. Camusot, into the means by which Sauvager had been won over; but by dint of looking into the various lives and interests of the men grouped about the lilies of the Tribunal, he knew that he could count upon the public prosecutor, upon Camusot, and M. Michu. Two judges for the d'Esgrignons would paralyze the rest. And, finally, Chesnel knew old Blondet well enough to feel sure that if he ever swerved from impartiality, it would be for the sake of the work of his whole lifetime—to secure his son's appointment.   So Chesnel slept, full of confidence, on the resolve to go to M. Blondet and offer to realize his so long-cherished hopes, while he opened his eyes to President du Ronceret's treachery.   Blondet won over, he would take a peremptory tone with the examining magistrate, to whom he hoped to prove that, if Victurnien was not blameless, he had been merely imprudent; the whole thing should be shown in the light of a boy's thoughtless escapade.

But Chesnel slept neither soundly nor for long.   Before dawn he was awakened by his housekeeper.   The most be-witching person in this history, the most adorable youth on the face of the globe, Mme. la Duchesse de Maufrigneuse her-self, in man's attire, had driven alone from Paris in a calèche, and was waiting to see him.

"I have come to save him or to die with him," said she, addressing the notary, who thought that he was dreaming. "I have brought a hundred thousand francs, given me by his majesty out of his private purse, to buy Victurnien's innocence, if his adversary can be bribed.   If we fail utterly, I have brought poison to snatch him away before anything takes place, before even the indictment is drawn up.   But we shall not fail.   I have sent word to the public prosecutor; he is on the road behind me; he could not travel in my calèche, be-cause he wished to take the instructions of the keeper of the seals."

Chesnel rose to the occasion and played up to the duchess; he wrapped himself in his dressing-gown, fell at her feet and kissed them, not without asking her pardon for forgetting him-self in his joy.

"We are saved!" cried he; and gave orders to Brigitte to see that Mme. la Duchesse had all that she needed after traveling post all night. He appealed to the fair Diane's spirit, by making her see that it was absolutely necessary that she should visit the examining magistrate before daylight, lest any one should discover the secret, or so much as imagine that the Duchesse de Maufrigneuse had come.

"And have I not a passport in due form?" quoth she, displaying a sheet of paper, wherein she was described as M. le Vicomte Félix de Vandenesse, master of requests, and his majesty's private secretary. "And do I not play my man's part well?" she added, running her fingers through her wig *à la Titus*, and twirling her riding switch.

"Oh! Madame la Duchesse, you are an angel!" cried Chesnel, with tears in his eyes. (She was destined always to be an angel, even in man's attire.) "Button up your greatcoat, muffle yourself up to the eyes in your traveling cloak, take my arm, and let us go as quickly as possible to Camusot's house before anybody can meet us."

"Then am I going to see a man called Camusot?" she asked.

"With a nose to match his name,"* assented old Maître Chesnel.

The old notary felt his heart dead within him, but he thought it none the less necessary to humor the duchess, to laugh when she laughed, and shed tears when she wept; groaning in spirit, all the same, over the feminine frivolity which could find matter for a jest while setting about a matter so serious. What would he not have done to save the count? While Chesnel dressed, Mme. de Maufrigneuse sipped the cup of coffee and cream which Brigitte brought her, and agreed with herself that provincial women cooks are superior to the Parisian *chefs*, who despise the little details which make all the difference to an epicure. Thanks to Chesnel's taste for

* *Camus*, flat-nosed.

19

delicate fare, Brigitte was found prepared to set an excellent meal before the duchess.

Chesnel and his charming companion set out for M. and Mme. Camusot's house.

"Ah! so there is a Madame Camusot?" said the duchess. "Then the affair may be managed."

"And so much the more readily, because the lady is visibly enough tired of living among us provincials; she comes from Paris," said Chesnel.

"Then we must have no secrets from her?"

"You will judge how much to tell or to conceal," Chesnel replied humbly. "I am sure that she will be greatly flattered to be the Duchesse de Maufrigneuse's hostess; you will be obliged to stay in her house until nightfall, I expect, unless you find it inconvenient to remain."

"Is this Madame Camusot a good-looking woman?" asked the duchess, with a coxcomb's air.

"She is certainly a bit of a queen in her own house," he made reply.

"Then she is sure to meddle in court-house affairs," returned the duchess. "Nowhere but in France, my dear Monsieur Chesnel, do you see women so much wedded to their husbands that they are wedded to their husbands' professions, work, or business as well. In Italy, England, and Germany, women make it a point of honor to leave men to fight their own battles; they shut their eyes to their husbands' work as perseveringly as our French citizens' wives do all that in them lies to understand the position of their joint-stock partnership; is not that what you call it in your legal language? Frenchwomen are so incredibly jealous in the conduct of their married life that they insist on knowing everything; and that is how, in the least difficulty, you feel the wife's hand in the business; the Frenchwoman advises, guides, and warns her husband. And, truth to tell, the man is none the worse off. In England, if a married man is put in prison for debt for twenty-four hours, his wife will be jealous and make a scene when he comes back."

"Here we are, without meeting a soul on the way," said Chesnel. "You are the more sure of complete ascendency here, Madame la Duchesse, since Madame Camusot's father is one Thirion, usher of the royal cabinet."

"And the King never thought of that!" exclaimed the duchess. "He thinks of nothing! Thirion introduced us, the Prince de Cadignan, Monsieur de Vandenesse, and me! We shall have it all our own way in this house. Settle everything with Monsieur Camusot while I talk to his wife."

The maid, who was washing and dressing the children, showed the visitors into the little fireless dining-room.

"Take that card to your mistress," said the duchess, lowering her voice for the woman's ear; "nobody else is to see it. If you are discreet, child, you shall not lose by it."

At the sound of a woman's voice, and the sight of the handsome young man's face, the maid looked thunderstruck.

"Wake Monsieur Camusot," said Chesnel, "and tell him that I am waiting to see him on important business," and she departed upstairs forthwith.

A few minutes later, Mme. Camusot, in her dressing-gown, sprang downstairs and brought the handsome stranger into her room. She had pushed Camusot out of bed and into his study with all his clothes, bidding him dress himself at once and wait there. The transformation scene had been brought about by a bit of pasteboard with the words MADAME LA DUCHESSE DE MAUFRIGNEUSE engraved upon it. A daughter of the usher of the royal cabinet took in the whole situation at once.

"Well!" exclaimed the maidservant, left with Chesnel in the dining-room, "would not any one think that a thunderbolt had dropped in among us? The master is dressing in his study; you may go upstairs."

"Not a word of all this, mind," said Chesnel.

Now that he was conscious of the support of a great lady

who had the King's consent (by word of mouth) to the measures about to be taken for rescuing the Comte d'Esgrignon, he spoke with an air of authority which served his cause much better with Camusot than the humility with which he would otherwise have approached him.

"Sir," said he, "the words let fall last evening may have surprised you, but they are serious. The house d'Esgrignon counts upon you for the proper conduct of investigations from which it must issue without a spot."

"I shall pass over anything in your remarks, sir, which must be offensive to me personally and obnoxious to justice; for your position with regard to the d'Esgrignons excuses you up to a certain point, but——"

"Pardon me, sir, if I interrupt you," said Chesnel. "I have just spoken aloud the things which your superiors are thinking and dare not avow; though what those things are any intelligent man can guess, and you are an intelligent man. Grant that the young man had acted imprudently, can you suppose that the sight of a d'Esgrignon dragged into an Assize Court can be gratifying to the King, the Court, or the Ministry? Is it to the interest of the kingdom, or of the country, that historic houses should fall? Is not the existence of a great aristocracy, consecrated by time, a guarantee of that Equality which is the catchword of the Opposition at this moment? Well and good; now not only has there not been the slightest imprudence, but we are innocent victims caught in a trap."

"I am curious to know how," said the examining magistrate.

"For the last two years, the Sieur du Croisier has regularly allowed Monsieur le Comte d'Esgrignon to draw upon him for very large sums," said Chesnel. "We are going to produce drafts for more than a hundred thousand crowns, which he continually met; the amounts being remitted by me—bear that well in mind—either before or after the bills fell due.

Monsieur le Comte d'Esgrignon is in a position to produce a receipt for the sum paid by him, before this bill, this alleged forgery, was drawn. Can you fail to see in that case that this charge is a piece of spite and party feeling? And a charge brought against the heir of a great house by one of the most dangerous enemies of the throne and altar, what is it but an odious slander? There has been no more forgery in this affair than there has been in my office. Summon Madame du Croisier, who knows nothing as yet of the charge of forgery; she will declare to you that I brought the money and paid it over to her, so that in her husband's absence she might remit the amount for which he has not asked her. Examine du Croisier on the point; he will tell you that he knows nothing of my payment to Madame du Croisier."

"You may make such assertions as these, sir, in Monsieur d'Esgrignon's salon, or in any other house where people know nothing of business, and they may be believed; but no examining magistrate, unless he is a driveling idiot, can imagine that a woman like Madame du Croisier, so submissive as she is to her husband, has a hundred thousand crowns lying in her desk at this moment, without saying a word to him; nor yet that an old notary would not have advised Monsieur du Croisier of the deposit on his return to town."

"The old notary, sir, had gone to Paris to put a stop to the young man's extravagance."

"I have not yet examined the Comte d'Esgrignon," Camusot began; "his answers will point out my duty."

"Is he in close custody?"

"Yes."

"Sir," said Chesnel, seeing danger ahead, "the examination can be made in our interests or against them. But there are two courses open to you: you can establish the fact on Madame du Croisier's deposition that the amount was deposited with her before the bill was drawn; or you can examine the unfortunate young man implicated in this affair, and he in his confusion may remember nothing and commit himself. You will decide which is the more credible—a slip of memory on the part of a woman in her ignorance of business, or a forgery committed by a d'Esgrignon.''

"All this is beside the point," began Camusot; "the question is, whether Monsieur le Comte d'Esgrignon has or has not used the lower half of a letter addressed to him by du Croisier as a bill of exchange."

" Eh! and so he might," a voice cried suddenly, as Madame Camusot broke in, followed by the handsome stranger, "so he might, when Monsieur Chesnel had advanced the money to meet the bill——''

She leaned over her husband.

" You will have the first vacant appointment as assistant judge at Paris, you are serving the King himself in this affair; I have proof of it; you will not be forgotten," she said, lowering her voice for his ear. " This young man that you see here is the Duchesse de Maufrigneuse; you must never have seen her, and do all that you can for the young count boldly."

"Gentlemen," said Camusot, "even if the preliminary examination is conducted to prove the young count's innocence, can I answer for the view the court may take? Monsieur Chesnel, and you also, my sweet, know what Monsieur le Président wants."

"Tut, tut, tut!" said Mme. Camusot, "go yourself to Monsieur Michu this morning, and tell him that the count has been arrested; you will be two against two in that case, I will be bound. *Michu* comes from Paris, and you know that he is devoted to the noblesse. Good blood cannot lie."

At that very moment Mlle. Cadot's voice was heard in the doorway. She had brought a note, and was waiting for an answer. Camusot went out, and came back again to read the note aloud:

" M. le Vice-Président begs M. Camusot to sit in audience to-day and for the next few days, so that there may be a quorum during M. le Président's absence."

" Then there is an end of the preliminary examination ! " cried Mme. Camusot. " Did I not tell you, dear, that they would play you some ugly trick ? The president has gone off to slander you to the public prosecutor and the president of the Court-Royal. You will be changed before you can make the examination. Is that clear ? "

" You will stay, monsieur," said the duchess. " The public prosecutor is coming, I hope, in time."

" When the public prosecutor arrives," little Mme. Camusot said, with some heat, " he must find all over. Yes, my dear, yes," she added, looking full at her amazed husband. " Ah ! old hypocrite of a president, you are setting your wits against us ; you shall remember it ! You have a mind to help us to a dish of your own making, you shall have two served up to you by your humble servant Cécile-Amélie Thirion ! Poor old Blondet ! It is lucky for him that the president has taken this journey to turn us out, for now that great oaf of a Joseph Blondet will marry Mademoiselle Blandureau. I will let Father Blondet have some seeds in return. As for you, Camusot, go to Monsieur Michu's, while Madame la Duchesse and I will go to find old Blondet. You must expect to hear it said all over the town to-morrow that I took a walk with a lover this morning."

Mme. Camusot took the duchess' arm, and they went through the town by deserted streets to avoid any unpleasant adventure on the way to the old vice-president's house. Chesnel meanwhile conferred with the young count in prison ; Camusot had arranged a stolen interview. Cook-maids, servants, and the other early risers of a country town, seeing Mme. Camusot and the duchess taking their way through the back streets, took the young gentleman for an adorer from

Paris.   That evening, as Cécile-Amélie had said, the news of
her behavior was circulated about the town, and more than
one scandalous rumor was occasioned thereby.   Mme. Camusot and her supposed lover found old Blondet in his greenhouse.   He greeted his colleague's wife and her companion,
and gave the charming young man a keen, uneasy glance.

"I have the honor to introduce one of my husband's
cousins," said Mme. Camusot, bringing forward the duchess;
"he is one of the most distinguished horticulturists in Paris;
and as he cannot spend more than the one day with us, on
his way back from Brittany, and has heard of your flowers
and plants, I have taken the liberty of coming early."

"Oh, the gentleman is a horticulturist, is he?" said old
Blondet.

The duchess bowed.

"This is my coffee-plant," said Blondet, "and here is a
tea-plant."

"What can have taken Monsieur le Président away from
home?" put in Mme. Camusot.   "I will wager that his
absence concerns Monsieur Camusot."

"Exactly.   This, monsieur, is the queerest of all cacti,"
he continued, producing a flower-pot which appeared to con-
tain a piece of mildewed rattan;   "it comes from Australia.
You are very young, sir, to be a horticulturist."

"Dear Monsieur Blondet, never mind your flowers," said
Mme. Camusot.   "*You* are concerned, you and your hopes,
and your son's marriage with Mademoiselle Blandureau.   You
are duped by the president."

"Bah!" said old Blondet, with an incredulous air.

"Yes," retorted she.   "If you cultivated people a little
more and your flowers a little less, you would know that the
dowry and the hopes that you have sown, and watered, and
tilled, and weeded are on the point of being gathered now by
cunning hands."

"Madame!——"

"Oh, nobody in the town will have the courage to fly in the president's face and warn you. I, however, do not belong to the town, and, thanks to this obliging young man, I shall soon be going back to Paris; so I can inform you that Chesnel's successor has made formal proposals for Mademoiselle Claire Blandureau's hand on behalf of young du Ronceret, who is to have fifty thousand crowns from his parents. As for Fabien, he has made up his mind to receive a call to the bar, so as to gain an appointment as judge."

Old Blondet dropped the flower-pot which he had brought out for the duchess to see.

"Oh, my cactus! Oh, my son! and Mademoiselle Blandureau! Look here! the cactus flower is broken to pieces."

"No," Mme. Camusot answered, laughing; "everything can be put right. If you have a mind to see your son a judge in another month, we will tell you how you must set to work and——"

"Step this way, sir, and you will see my pelargoniums, an enchanting sight while they are in flower——" Then he added to Mme. Camusot, "Why did you speak of these matters while your cousin was present?"

"All depends upon him," replied Mme. Camusot. "Your son's appointment is lost for ever if you let fall a word about this young man."

"Bah!"

'The young man is a flower——"

"Ah!"

"He is the Duchesse de Maufrigneuse, sent here by his majesty to save young d'Esgrignon, whom they arrested yesterday on a charge of forgery brought against him by du Croisier. Madame la Duchesse has authority from the keeper of the seals; he will ratify any promises that she makes to each of——"

"My cactus is all right!" exclaimed Blondet, peering at his precious plant. "Go on; I am listening."

"Take counsel with Camusot and Michu to hush up the affair as soon as possible, and your son will get the appointment. It will come in time enough to baffle du Ronceret's underhand dealings with the Blandureaus. Your son will be something better than assistant judge; he will have Monsieur Camusot's post within the year. The public prosecutor will be here to-day. Monsieur Sauvager will be obliged to resign, I expect, after his conduct in this affair. At the court my husband will show you documents which completely exonerate the count and prove that the forgery was a trap of du Croisier's own setting."

Old Blondet went into the Olympic circus where his six thousand pelargoniums stood, and made his bow to the duchesse.

"Monsieur," said he, "if your wishes do not exceed the law, this thing may be done."

"Monsieur," returned the duchesse, "send in your resignation to Monsieur Chesnel to-morrow, and I will promise you that your son shall be appointed within the week; but you must not resign until you have had confirmation of my promise from the public prosecutor. You men of law will come to a better understanding among yourselves. Only let him know that the Duchesse de Maufrigneuse has pledged her word to you. And not a word as to my journey hither," she added.

The old judge kissed her hand and began recklessly to gather his best flowers for her.

"Can you think of it? Give them to madame," said the duchesse. "A young man would not have flowers about him when he had a pretty woman on his arm."

"Before you go down to the court," added Mme. Camusot, "ask Chesnel's successor about those proposals that he made in the name of Monsieur and Madame du Ronceret."

Old Blondet, quite overcome by this revelation of the president's duplicity, stood planted on his feet by the wicket-gate, looking after the two women as they hurried away through by-streets home again. The edifice raised so painfully during ten years for his beloved son was crumbling visibly before his eyes. Was it possible? He suspected some trick, and hurried away to Chesnel's successor.

At half-past nine, before the court was sitting, Vice-President Blondet, Camusot, and Michu met with remarkable punctuality in the council chamber. Blondet locked the door with some precautions when Camusot and Michu came in together.

"Well, M'sieur Vice-President," began Michu, "Monsieur Sauvager, without consulting the public prosecutor, has issued a warrant for the apprehension of one Comte d'Esgrignon, in order to serve a grudge borne against him by one du Croisier, an enemy of the King's government. It is a regular topsy-turvy affair. The president, for his part, goes away, and thereby puts a stop to the preliminary examination! And we know nothing of the matter. Do they, by any chance, mean to force our hand?"

"This is the first word I have heard of it," said the vice-president. He was furious with the president for stealing a march on him with the Blandureaus. Chesnel's successor, the du Roncerets' man, had just fallen into a snare set by the old judge; the truth was out, he knew the secret.

"It is lucky that we spoke to you about that matter, my dear master," said Camusot, "or you might have given up all hope of seating your son on the bench or of marrying him to Mademoiselle Blandureau."

"But it is no question of my son, nor of his marriage," said the vice-president; "we are talking of young Comte d'Esgrignon. Is he or is he not guilty?"

"It seems that Chesnel deposited the amount to meet the bill with Madame du Croisier," said Michu, "and a crime has been made of a mere irregularity. According to the charge, the count made use of the lower half of a letter bearing du Croisier's signature as a draft which he cashed at the Kellers'."

"An imprudent thing to do," was Camusot's comment.

"But why is du Croisier proceeding against him if the amount was paid in beforehand?" asked Vice-President Blondet.

"He does not know that the money was deposited with his wife; or he pretends that he does not know," said Camusot.

"It is a piece of provincial spite," said Michu.

"Still it looks like a forgery to me," said old Blondet.

No passion could obscure judicial clear-sightedness in him.

"Do you think so?" returned Camusot. "But, at the outset, supposing that the count had no business to draw upon du Croisier, there would still be no forgery of the signature; and the count believed that he had a right to draw on Croisier when Chesnel advised him that the money had been placed to his credit."

"Well, then, where is the forgery?" asked Blondet. "It is the intent to defraud which constitutes forgery in a civil action."

"Oh, it is clear, if you take du Croisier's version for truth, that the signature was diverted from its purpose to obtain a sum of money in spite of du Croisier's contrary injunction to his bankers," Camusot answered.

"Gentlemen," said Blondet, "this seems to me to be a mere trifle, a quibble. Suppose you had the money, I ought perhaps to have waited until I had your authorization; but I, Comte d'Esgrignon, was pressed for money, so I—— Come, come, your prosecution is a piece of revengeful spite. Forgery is defined by the law as an attempt to obtain any advantage which rightfully belongs to another. There is no forgery here, according to the letter of the Roman law, nor according to the spirit of modern jurisprudence (always from the point of view of a civil action, for we are not here concerned with the falsification of public or authentic documents). Between private individuals the essence of a forgery is the intent to defraud ; where is it in this case ?   In what times are we living, gentlemen ?   Here is the president going away to balk a preliminary examination which ought to be over by this time ! Until to-day I did not know Monsieur le Président, but he shall have the benefit of arrears ; from this time forth he shall draft his decisions himself.   You must set about this affair with all possible speed, Monsieur Camusot.''

" Yes,'' said Michu.   " In my opinion, instead of letting the young man out on bail, we ought to pull him out of this mess at once.   Everything turns on the examination of du Croisier and his wife.   You might summon them to appear while the court is sitting, Monsieur Camusot ; take down their depositions before four o'clock, send in your report to-night, and we will give our decision in the morning before the court sits.''

" We will settle what course to pursue while the barristers are pleading,'' said Vice-President Blondet, addressing Camusot.

And with that the three judges put on their robes and went into court.

At noon Mlle. Armande and the bishop reached the Hôtel d'Esgrignon ; Chesnel and M. Couturier were there to meet them.   There was a sufficiently short conference between the prelate and Mme. du Croisier's director, and the latter set out at once to visit his charge.

At eleven o'clock that morning du Croisier received a summons to appear in the examining magistrate's office between one and two in the afternoon.   Thither he betook himself, consumed by well-founded suspicions.   It was impossible that the president should have foreseen the arrival of the Duchesse de Maufrigneuse upon the scene, the return of the public prosecutor, and the hasty confabulation of his learned brethren ; so he had omitted to trace out a plan for du Croisier's guidance in the event of the preliminary examination taking place. Neither of the pair imagined that the proceedings would be hurried on in this way. Du Croisier obeyed the summons at once; he wanted to know how M. Camusot was disposed to act. So he was compelled to answer the questions put to him. Camusot addressed him in summary fashion with the six following inquiries:

"Was the signature on the bill alleged to be a forgery in your handwriting? Had you previously done business with Monsieur le Comte d'Esgrignon? Was not Monsieur le Comte d'Esgrignon in the habit of drawing upon you, with or without advice? Did you not write a letter authorizing Monsieur d'Esgrignon to rely upon you at any time? Had not Chesnel squared the account not once, but many times already? Were you not away from home when this took place?"

All these questions the banker answered in the affirmative. In spite of wordy explanations, the magistrate always brought him back to a "Yes" or "No." When the questions and answers had been alike resumed in the *procès-verbal*, the examining magistrate brought out a final thunderbolt.

"Was du Croisier aware that the money destined to meet the bill had been deposited with him, du Croisier, according to Chesnel's declaration, and a letter of advice sent by the said Chesnel to the Comte d'Esgrignon, five days before the date of the bill?"

That last question frightened du Croisier. He asked what was meant by it, and whether he was supposed to be the defendant and M. le Comte d'Esgrignon the plaintiff? He called the magistrate's attention to the fact that if the money had been deposited with him, there was no ground for the action.

"Justice is seeking information," said the magistrate, as he dismissed the witness, but not before he had taken down du Croisier's last observation.

"But the money, sir——"

"The money is at your house."

Chesnel, likewise summoned, came forward to explain the matter. The truth of his assertions was borne out by Mme. du Croisier's deposition. The count had already been examined. Prompted by Chesnel, he produced du Croisier's first letter, in which he begged the count to draw upon him without the insulting formality of depositing the amount beforehand. The Comte d'Esgrignon next brought out a letter in Chesnel's handwriting, by which the notary advised him of the deposit of a hundred thousand crowns with M. du Croisier. With such primary facts as these to bring forward as evidence, the young count's innocence was bound to emerge triumphantly from a court of law.

Du Croisier went home from the court, his face white with rage, and the foam of repressed fury on his lips. His wife was sitting by the fireside in the drawing-room at work upon a pair of slippers for him. She trembled when she looked into his face, but her mind was made up.

"Madame," he stammered out, "what deposition is this that you made before the magistrate? You have dishonored, ruined, and betrayed me!"

"I have saved you, monsieur," answered she. "If some day you will have the honor of connecting yourself with the d'Esgrignons by marrying your niece to the count, it will be entirely owing to my conduct to-day."

"A miracle!" cried he. "Balaam's ass has spoken. Nothing will astonish me after this. And where are the hundred thousand crowns which (so Monsieur Camusot tells me) are here in my house?"

"Here they are," said she, pulling out a bundle of banknotes from beneath the cushions of her settee. "I have not committed mortal sin by declaring that Monsieur Chesnel gave them into my keeping."

"While I was away?"

"You were not here."

"Will you swear that to me on your salvation?"

"I swear it," she said composedly.

"Then why did you say nothing to me about it?" demanded he.

"I was wrong there," said his wife; "but my mistake was all for your good. Your niece will be Marquise d'Esgrignon some of these days, and you will perhaps be a deputy, if you behave well in this deplorable business. You have gone too far; you must find out how to get back again."

Du Croisier, under stress of painful agitation, strode up and down his drawing-room; while his wife, in no less agitation, awaited the result of this exercise. Du Croisier at length rang the bell.

"I am not at home to any one to-night," he said, when the man appeared; "shut the gates; and if any one calls, tell them that your mistress and I have gone into the country. We shall start directly after dinner, and dinner must be half an hour earlier than usual."

The great news was discussed that evening in every drawing-room; little storekeepers, working people, beggars, the noblesse, the merchant class—the whole town, in short, was talking of the Comte d'Esgrignon's arrest on a charge of forgery. The Comte d'Esgrignon would be tried in the Assize Court; he would be condemned and branded. Most of those who cared for the honor of the family denied the fact. At nightfall Chesnel went to Mme. Camusot and escorted the stranger to the Hôtel d'Esgrignon. Poor Mlle. Armande was expecting him; she led the fair duchess to her own room, which she had given up to her, for his lordship the bishop occupied Victurnien's chamber; and, left alone with her guest, the noble woman glanced at the duchess with most piteous eyes.

"You owed help, indeed, madame, to the poor boy who ruined himself for your sake," she said; "the boy to whom we are all of us sacrificing ourselves."

The duchess had already made a woman's survey of Mlle. d'Esgrignon's room; the cold, bare, comfortless chamber, that might have been a nun's cell, was like a picture of the life of the heroic woman before her. The duchess saw it all —past, present, and future—with rising emotion, felt the incongruity of her presence, and could not keep back the falling tears that made answer for her.

But in Mlle. Armande the Christian overcame Victurnien's aunt. "Ah, I was wrong; forgive me, Madame la Duchesse; you did not know how poor we were, and my nephew was incapable of the admission. And beside, now that I see you, I can understand all—even the crime!"

And Mlle. Armande, withered and thin and white, but beautiful as those tall, austere slender figures which German art alone can paint, had tears, too, in her eyes.

"Do not fear, dear angel?" the duchess said at last; "he is safe."

"Yes, but honor?—and his career? Chesnel told me; the King knows the truth."

"We will think of a way of repairing the evil," said the duchess.

Mlle. Armande went downstairs to the salon, and found the Collection of Antiquities complete to a man. Every one of them had come, partly to do honor to the bishop, partly to rally round the marquis; but Chesnel, posted in the antechamber, warned each new arrival to say no word of the affair, that the aged marquis might never know that such a thing had been. The loyal Frank was quite capable of killing his son or du Croisier; for either the one or the other must have been guilty of death in his eyes. It chanced, strangely enough, that he talked more of Victurnien than usual; he was glad that his son had gone back to Paris. The King would give Victurnien a place before very long; the King was interesting himself at last in the d'Esgrignons. And his friends, their hearts dead within them, praised Victurnien's conduct to the

20

skies.   Mlle. Armande prepared the way for her nephew's sudden appearance among them by remarking to her brother that Victurnien would be sure to come to see them, and that he must be even then on his way.

"Bah!" said the marquis, standing with his back to the hearth, "if he is doing well where he is, he ought to stay there, and not to be thinking of the joy it would give his old father to see him again.   The King's service has the first claim."

Scarcely one of those present heard the words without a shudder.   Justice might give over a d'Esgrignon to the executioner's branding-iron.   There was a dreadful pause.   The old Marquise de Castéran could not keep back a tear that stole down over her rouge, and turned her half-palsied head away to hide it.

Next day at noon, in the sunny weather, a whole excited population was dispersed in groups along the high street, which ran through the heart of the town, and nothing was talked of but the great affair.   Was the count in prison or was he not? All at once the Comte d'Esgrignon's well-known tilbury was seen driving down the Rue Saint-Blaise; it had evidently come from the prefecture, the count himself was on the box-seat, and by his side sat a charming young man, whom nobody recognized.   The pair were laughing and talking and in great spirits.   They wore Bengal roses in their button-holes. Altogether, it was a theatrical surprise which words would fail to describe.

At ten o'clock the court had decided to dismiss the charge, stating their very sufficient reasons for setting the count at liberty, in a document which contained a thunderbolt for du Croisier, in the shape of an "Inasmuch" that gave the count the right to institute proceedings for libel.   Old Chesnel was walking up the Grande Rue, as if by accident, telling all who cared to hear him that du Croisier had set the most shameful snares for the d'Esgrignons' honor, and that it was entirely owing to the forbearance and magnanimity of the family that he was not prosecuted for slander.

On the evening of that famous day, after the Marquis d'Esgrignon had gone to bed, the count, Mlle. Armande, and the chevalier were left with the handsome young page, now about to return to Paris. The charming cavalier's sex could not be hidden from the chevalier, and he alone, beside the three officials and Mme. Camusot, knew that the duchess had been among them.

"The house is saved," began Chesnel, "but after this shock it will take a hundred years to rise again. The debts must be paid now; you must marry an heiress, Monsieur le Comte, there is nothing else left for you to do."

"And take her where you can find her," said the duchess.

"A second *mésalliance!*" exclaimed Mlle. Armande.

The duchess began to laugh.

"It is better to marry than to die," said she. As she spoke she drew from her waistcoat pocket a tiny crystal phial that came from the court apothecary.

Mlle. Armande shrank away in horror. Old Chesnel took the fair Maufrigneuse's hand, and kissed it without permission.

"Are you all out of your minds here?" continued the duchess. "Do you really expect to live in the fifteenth century when the rest of the world has reached the nineteenth? My dear children, there is no noblesse nowadays; there is no aristocracy left! Napoleon's Code Civil made an end of the parchments, exactly as cannon made an end of feudal castles. When you have some money, you will be very much more of nobles than you are now. Marry anybody you please, Victurnien, you will raise your wife to your rank; that is the most substantial privilege left to the French noblesse. Did not Monsieur de Talleyrand marry Madame Grandt without compromising his position? Remember that Louis XIV. took the Widow Scarron for his wife."

"He did not marry her for her money," interposed Mlle. Armande.

"If the Comtesse d'Esgrignon were one du Croisier's niece, for instance, would you receive her?" asked Chesnel.

"Perhaps," replied the duchess; "but the King, beyond all doubt, would be very glad to see her. So you do not know what is going on in the world?" continued she, seeing the amazement in their faces. "Victurnien has been in Paris; he knows how things go there. We had more influence under Napoleon. Marry Mademoiselle Duval, Victurnien; she will be just as much Marquise d'Esgrignon as I am Duchesse de Maufrigneuse."

"All is lost—even honor!" said the chevalier, with a wave of the hand.

"Farewell, Victurnien," said the duchess, kissing her lover on the forehead; "we shall not see each other again. Live on your lands; that is the best thing for you to do; the air of Paris is not at all good for you."

"Diane!" the young count cried despairingly.

"Monsieur, you forget yourself strangely," the duchess retorted coolly, as she laid aside her rôle of man and mistress, and became not merely an angel again, but a duchess, and not only a duchess, but Molière's Célimène.

The Duchesse de Maufrigneuse made a stately bow to these four personages, and drew from the chevalier his last tear of admiration at the service of *le beau sexe*.

"How like she is to the Princess Goritza!" he exclaimed in a low voice.

Diane had disappeared. The crack of the postillion's whip told Victurnien that the fair romance of his first love was over. While the peril lasted, Diane could still see her lover in the young count; but out of danger, she despised him for the weakling that he was.

Six months afterward, Camusot received the appointment

of assistant judge at Paris, and later he became an examining magistrate. Goodman Blondet was made a councilor to the Court-Royal; he held the post just long enough to secure a retiring pension, and then went back to live in his pretty little house. Joseph Blondet sat in his father's seat at the court till the end of his days; there was not the faintest chance of promotion for him, but he became Mlle. Blandureau's husband; and she, no doubt, is leading to-day, in the little flower-covered brick house, as dull a life as any carp in a marble basin. Michu and Camusot also received the cross of the Legion of Honor, while Blondet became an officer. As for M. Sauvager, deputy public prosecutor, he was sent to Corsica, to du Croisier's great relief; he had decidedly no mind to bestow his niece upon that functionary.

Du Croisier himself, urged by President du Ronceret, appealed from the finding of the Tribunal to the Court-Royal, and lost his cause. The Liberals throughout the department held that little d'Esgrignon was guilty; while the Royalists, on the other hand, told frightful stories of plots woven by "that abominable du Croisier" to compass his revenge. A duel was fought indeed; the hazard of arms favored du Croisier, the young count was dangerously wounded, and his antagonist maintained his words. This affair embittered the strife between the two parties; the Liberals brought it forward on all occasions. Meanwhile du Croisier never could carry his election, and saw no hope of marrying his niece to the count, especially after the duel.

A month after the decision of the Tribunal was confirmed in the Court-Royal, Chesnel died, exhausted by the dreadful strain, which had weakened and shaken him mentally and physically. He died in the hour of victory, like some old faithful hound that has brought the boar to bay, and gets his death on the tusks. He died as happily as might be, seeing that he left the great House all but ruined, and the heir in penury, bored to death by an idle life, and without a hope of establishing himself. That bitter thought and his own exhaustion, no doubt, hastened the old man's end. One great comfort came to him as he lay amid the wreck of so many hopes, sinking under the burden of so many cares—the old marquis, at his sister's entreaty, gave him back all the old friendship. The great lord came to the little house in the Rue du Bercail, and sat by his old servant's bedside, all unaware how much that servant had done and sacrificed for him. Chesnel sat upright and repeated Simeon's cry—*nunc dimittis.* The marquis allowed them to bury Chesnel in the castle chapel ; they laid him crosswise at the foot of the tomb which was waiting for the marquis himself, the last, in a sense, of the d'Esgrignons.

And so died one of the last representatives of that great and beautiful thing, Service ; giving to that often discredited word its original meaning, the relation between feudal lord and servitor. That relation, only to be found in some out-of-the-way province or among a few old servants of the King, did honor alike to a noblesse that could call forth such affection, and to a bourgeoisie that could conceive it. Such noble and magnificent devotion is no longer possible among us. Noble houses have no servitors left ; even as France has no longer a King, nor an hereditary peerage, nor lands that are bound irrevocably to a historic house, that the glorious names of a nation may be perpetuated. Chesnel was not merely one of the obscure great men of private life ; he was something more —he was a great fact. In his sustained self-devotion is there not something indefinably solemn and sublime, something that rises above the one beneficent deed, or the heroic height which is reached by a moment's supreme effort ? Chesnel's virtues belong essentially to the classes which stand between the poverty of the people on the one hand, and the greatness of the aristocracy on the other ; for these can combine homely burgher virtues with the heroic ideals of the noble, enlightening both by a solid education.

Victurnien was not well looked upon at Court; there was no more chance of a great match for him, nor a place. His majesty steadily refused to raise the d'Esgrignons to the peerage, the one royal favor which could rescue Victurnien from his wretched position. It was impossible that he should marry a bourgeoise heiress in his father's lifetime, so he was bound to live on shabbily under the paternal roof with memories of his two years of splendor in Paris, and the lost love of a great lady to bear him company. He grew moody and depressed, vegetating at home with a careworn aunt and a half broken-hearted father, who attributed his son's condition to a wasting malady. Chesnel was no longer there.

The marquis died in 1830. The great d'Esgrignon, with a following of all the less infirm noblesse from the Collection of Antiquities, went to wait upon Charles X. at Nonancourt; he paid his respects to his sovereign, and swelled the meagre train of the fallen king. It was an act of courage which seems simple enough to-day, but, in that time of enthusiastic revolt, it was heroism.

"The Gaul has conquered!" These were the marquis' last words.

By that time du Croisier's victory was complete. The new Marquis d'Esgrignon accepted Mlle. Duval as his wife a week after his old father's death. His bride brought him three millions of francs, for du Croisier and his wife settled the reversion of their fortunes upon her in the marriage-contract. Du Croisier took occasion to say during the ceremony that the d'Esgrignon family was the most honorable of all the ancient houses in France.

Some day the present Marquis d'Esgrignon will have an income of more than a hundred thousand crowns. You may see him in Paris, for he comes to town every winter and leads a jolly bachelor life, while he treats his wife with something more than the indifference of the *grand seigneur* of olden times; he takes no thought whatever for her.

"As for Mademoiselle d'Esgrignon," said Émile Blondet, to whom all the detail of the story is due, "if she is no longer like the divinely fair woman whom I saw by glimpses in my childhood, she is decidedly, at the age of sixty-seven, the most pathetic and interesting figure in the Collection of Antiquities. She queens it among them still. I saw her when I made my last journey to my native place in search of the necessary papers for my marriage. When my father knew whom it was that I had married, he was struck dumb with amazement; he had not a word to say until I told him that I was a prefect.

" 'You were born to it,' he said, with a smile.

"As I took a walk round the town, I met Mademoiselle Armande. She looked taller than ever. I looked at her, and thought of Marius among the ruins of Carthage. Had she not outlived her creed, and the beliefs that had been destroyed? She is a sad and silent woman, with nothing of her old beauty left except the eyes, that shine with an unearthly light. I watched her on her way to mass, with her book in her hand, and could not help thinking that she prayed God to take her out of the world."

LES JARDIES, *July*, 1837.

A MARRIAGE SETTLEMENT

(Le Contrat de Mariage).

TRANSLATED BY CLARA BELL.

To G. Rossini.

MONSIEUR DE MANERVILLE the elder was a worthy gentleman of Normandy, well known to the Maréchal de Richelieu, who arranged his marriage with one of the richest heiresses of Bordeaux at the time when the old duke held court in that city as governor of Guienne. The Norman gentleman sold the lands he owned in Bessin, and established himself as a Gascon, tempted to this step by the beauty of the estate of Lanstrac, a delightful residence belonging to his wife. Toward the end of Louis XV.'s reign, he purchased the post of major of the King's bodyguard, and lived till 1813, having happily survived the Revolution.

This was how: In the winter of 1790 he made a voyage to Martinique, where his wife had property, leaving the management of his estates in Gascony to a worthy notary's clerk named Mathias, who had some taint of the new ideas. On his return, the Comte de Manerville found his possessions safe and profitably managed. This shrewdness was the fruit of a graft of the Gascon on the Norman.

Madame de Manerville died in 1810. Her husband, having learned by the dissipations of his youth the importance of money, and, like many old men, ascribing to it a greater power in life than it possesses, became progressively thrifty, avaricious, and mean. Forgetting that stingy fathers make spendthrift sons, he allowed scarcely anything to his son, though he was an only child.

Paul de Manerville came home from college at Vendôme

(313)

toward the end of 1810, and for three years lived under his father's rule. The tyranny exercised by the old man of sixty-nine over his sole heir could not fail to affect a heart and character as yet unformed. Though he did not lack the physical courage which would seem to be in the air of Gascony, Paul dared not contend with his father, and lost the elasticity of resistance that gives rise to moral courage. His suppressed feelings were pent at the bottom of his heart, where he kept them long in reserve without daring to express them; thus, at a later time, when he felt that they were not in accordance with the maxims of the world, though he could think rightly, he could act wrongly. He would have fought at a word, while he quaked at the thought of sending away a servant; for his shyness found a field in any struggle which demanded persistent determination.

He was a prisoner in his father's old house, for he had not money enough to disport himself with the young men of the town; he envied them their amusements, but could not share them. The old gentleman took him out every evening in an antique vehicle, drawn by a pair of shabbily harnessed horses, attended by two antique and shabbily dressed menservants, into the society of a Royalist clique, consisting of the waifs of the nobility of the old Parlement and of the sword. These two bodies of magnates, uniting after the Revolution to resist Imperial influence, had by degrees become an aristocracy of landowners. Overpowered by the wealth and the shifting fortunes of a great seaport, this " Saint-Germain " suburb of Bordeaux responded with scorn to the magnificence of commerce and of the civil and military authorities.

His so monotonous existence might have killed the young man, but that his father's death delivered him from this tyranny at the time when it was becoming unendurable. Paul found that his father's avarice had accumulated a considerable fortune, and left him an estate in the most splendid possible order; but he had a horror of Bordeaux, and no love for

Lanstrac, where his father had always spent the summer and kept him out shooting from morning till night.

As soon as the legal business was completed, the young heir, eager for pleasure, invested his capital in securities, left the management of the land to old Mathias, his father's agent, and spent six years away from Bordeaux. Attaché at first to the embassy at Naples, he subsequently went as secretary to Madrid and London, thus making the tour of Europe. After gaining knowledge of the world, and dissipating a great many illusions, after spending all the money his father had saved, a moment came when Paul, to continue this dashing existence, had to draw on the revenues from his estate which the notary had saved for him. So, at this critical moment, struck by one of those impulses which are regarded as wisdom, he resolved to leave Paris, to return to Bordeaux, to manage his own affairs, to lead the life of a country gentleman, settling at Lanstrac and improving his estate—to marry, and one day to be elected deputy.

Paul was a count; titles were recovering their value in the matrimonial market; he could, and ought to marry well. Though many women wish to marry for a title, a great many more look for a husband who has an intimate acquaintance with life. And Paul—at a cost of seven hundred thousand francs, consumed in six years—had acquired this official knowledge, a qualification which cannot be sold, and which is worth more than a stockbroker's license ; which, indeed, demands long studies, an apprenticeship, examinations, acquaintances, friends, and enemies, a certain elegance of appearance, good manners, and a handsome, tripping name ; which brings with it success with women, duels, betting at races, many disappointments, dull hours, tiresome tasks, and indigestible pleasures.

In spite of lavish outlay, he had never been the fashion. In the burlesque army of the gay world, the man who is *the fashion* is the field-marshal of the forces, the merely elegant man is the lieutenant-general.   Still, Paul enjoyed his little reputation for elegance, and lived up to it.   His servants were well drilled, his carriages were approved, his suppers had some success, and his bachelor's den was one of the seven or eight which were a match in luxury for the finest houses in Paris.   But he had not broken a woman's heart ; he played without losing, nor had he extraordinarily brilliant luck ; he was too honest to be false to any one, even a girl of the streets ; he did not leave his love-letters about, nor keep a boxful for his friends to dip into while he was shaving or putting a collar on ; but, not wishing to damage his estates in Guienne, he had not the audacity that prompts a young man into startling speculations and attracts all eyes to watch him ; he borrowed of no one, and was so wrong-headed as to lend to friends, who cut him and never mentioned him again, either for good or evil.   He seemed to have worked out the sum of his extravagance.   The secret of his character lay in his father's tyranny, which had made him a sort of social hybrid.

One morning Paul de Manerville said to a friend of his named de Marsay, who has since become famous—

"My dear fellow, life has a meaning."

"You must be seven-and-twenty before you understand it," said de Marsay, laughing at him.

"Yes, I am seven-and-twenty, and for that very reason I mean to go and live at Lanstrac as a country gentleman.   At Bordeaux I shall have my father's old house, whither I shall send my Paris furniture, and I shall spend three months of every winter here in my rooms, which I shall not give up."

"And you will marry?"

"I shall marry."

"I am your friend, my worthy Paul, as you know," said de Marsay, after a moment's silence ; "well, be a good father and a good husband—and ridiculous for the rest of your days. If you could be happy being ridiculous, the matter would de-

serve consideration ; but you would not be happy. You have
not a strong enough hand to rule a household. I do you
every justice : you are a perfect horseman ; no one holds the
ribbons better, makes a horse plunge, or keeps his seat more
immovably. But, my dear boy, the paces of matrimony are
quite another thing. Why, I can see you led at a round pace
by Madame la Comtesse de Manerville, galloping, more often
than not much against your will, and presently thrown—thrown
into the ditch, and left there with both legs broken !

"Listen to me. You have still forty-odd thousand francs
a year in land in the Department of the Gironde. Take your
horses and your servants, and furnish your house in Bordeaux;
you will be King in Bordeaux, you will promulgate there the
decrees we pronounce in Paris, you will be the corresponding
agent of our follies. Well and good. Commit follies in your
provincial capital—nay, even absurdities. So much the better ; they may make you famous. But—do not marry.

"Who are the men who marry nowadays ? Tradesmen, to
increase their capital or to have a second hand at the plough ;
peasants, who, by having large families, manufacture their
own laborers ; stockbrokers or notaries, to get money to pay
for their licenses ; the miserable kings, to perpetuate their
miserable dynasties. We alone are free from the pack-saddle ;
why insist on loading yourself? In short, what do you marry
for ? You must account for such a step to your best friend.

"In the first place, if you should find an heiress as rich as
yourself, eighty thousand francs a year for two are not the
same thing as forty thousand for one, because you very soon
are three—and four if you have a child. Do you really feel
any affection for the foolish propagation of Manervilles, who
will never give you anything but trouble ? Do you not know
what the duties are of a father and mother ? Marriage, my
dear Paul, is the most foolish of social sacrifices ; our children
alone profit by it, and even they do not know its cost till their
horses are cropping the weeds that grow over our graves.

" Do you, for instance, regret your father, the tyrant who wrecked your young life? How do you propose to make your children love you? Your plans for their education, your care for their advantage, your severity, however necessary, will alienate their affection. Children love a lavish or weak father, but later they will despise him. You are stranded between aversion and contempt. You cannot be a good father for the wishing.

" Look round on our friends, and name one you would like for a son. We have known some who were a disgrace to their name. Children, my dear boy, are a commodity very difficult to keep sweet. Yours will be angels! No doubt!

" But have you ever measured the gulf that separates the life of a single man from that of a married one? Listen. As you are, you can say: 'I will never be ridiculous beyond a certain point; the public shall never think of me excepting as I choose that it should think.' Married, you will fall into depths of the ridiculous! Unmarried, you make your own happiness; you want it to-day, you do without it to-morrow: married, you take it as it comes, and the day you seek it you have to do without it. Married, you are an ass; you calculate marriage-portions, you talk about public and religious morality, you look upon young men as immoral and dangerous; in short, you are socially Academical. I have nothing but pity for you! An old bachelor, whose relations are waiting for his money, and who struggles with his latest breath to make an old nurse give him something to drink, is in paradise compared with a married man. I say nothing of all the annoying, irritating, provoking, aggravating, stultifying, worrying things that may come to hypnotize and paralyze your mind and tyrannize over your life, in the course of the petty warfare of two human beings always together, united for ever, who have bound themselves, vainly believing that they will agree; no, that would be to repeat Boileau's 'Satire,' and we know it by heart.

"I would forgive you the absurd notion if you would promise to marry like a grandee, to settle your fortune on your eldest son, to take advantage of the honeymoon stage to have two legitimate children, to give your wife a completely separate establishment, to meet her only in society, and never come home from a journey without announcing your return. Two hundred thousand francs a year are enough to do it on, and your antecedents allow of your achieving this by finding some rich Englishwoman hungering for a title. That aristocratic way of life is the only one that seems to me truly French; the only handsome one, commanding a wife's respect and regard; the only life that distinguishes us from the common herd; in short, the only one for which a young man should ever give up his single blessedness. In such an attitude the Comte de Manerville is an example to his age, he is superior to the general, and must be nothing less than a minister or an ambassador. He can never be ridiculous; he conquers the social advantages of a married man, and preserves the privileges of a bachelor."

"But, my good friend, I am not a de Marsay; I am, as you yourself do me the honor to express it, Paul de Manerville, neither more nor less, a good husband and father, deputy of the Centre, and perhaps some day a peer of the Upper House—altogether a very humble destiny. But I am diffident—and resigned."

"And your wife," said the merciless de Marsay, "will she be resigned?"

"My wife, my dear fellow, will do what I wish."

"Oh! my poor friend, have you not got beyond that point? Farewell, Paul. Henceforth you have forfeited my esteem. Still, one word more, for I cannot subscribe to your abdication in cold blood. Consider what is the strength of our position. If a single man had no more than six thousand francs a year, if his whole fortune lay in his reputation for elegance and the memory of his successes, well, even this

fantastic ghost has considerable value.   Life still affords some
chances for the bachelor 'off color.'   Yes, he may still
aspire to anything.   But marriage !   Paul, it is the 'Thus far
and no further' of social existence.   Once married, you can
never more be anything but what you are—unless your wife
condescends to take you in hand.''

"But you are always crushing me under your exceptional
theories ! '' cried Paul.   "I am tired of living for the benefit
of others—of keeping horses for display, of doing everything
with a view to 'what people will say,' of ruining myself for
fear that idiots should remark : 'Why, Paul has the same old
carriage !   What has he done with his money ?   Does he
squander it ?   Gamble on the Bourse ?   Not at all ; he is a
millionaire.   Madame So-and-so is madly in love with him.
He has just had a team of horses from England, the handsomest in Paris.   At Longchamps, every one remarked the
four-horse chaises of Monsieur de Marsay and Monsieur de
Manerville ; the cattle were magnificent.'   In short, the thousand idiotic remarks by which the mob of fools drives us.

"I am beginning to see that this life, in which we are
simply rolled along by others instead of walking on our feet,
wears us out and makes us old.   Believe me, my dear Henri,
I admire your powers, but I do not envy you.   You are capable of judging everything ; you can act and think as a statesman, you stand above general laws, received ideas, recognized
prejudices, accepted conventionalities; in fact, you get all
the benefits of a position in which I, for my part, should find
nothing but disaster.   Your cold and systematic deductions,
which are perhaps quite true, are, in the eyes of the vulgar,
appallingly immoral.   I belong to the vulgar.

"I must play the game by the rules of the society in which I
am compelled to live.   You can stand on the summit of human
things, on ice-peaks, and still have feelings ; I should freeze
there.   The life of the greatest number, of which I am very
frankly one, is made up of emotions such as I feel at present

in need of. The most popular lady's man often flirts with ten women at once, and wins the favor of none; and then, whatever his gifts, his practice, his knowledge of the world, a crisis may arise when he finds himself, as it were, jammed between two doors. For my part, I like the quiet and faithful intercourse of home; I want the life where a man always finds a woman at his side."

"Marriage is a little free and easy!" cried de Marsay.

Paul was not to be dashed, and went on—

"Laugh if you please; I shall be the happiest man in the world when my servant comes to say: 'Madame is waiting breakfast'—when, on coming home in the afternoon, I may find a heart——"

"You are still too frivolous, Paul! You are not moral enough yet for married life!"

"A heart to which I may confide my business and tell my secrets. I want to live with some being on terms of such intimacy that our affection may not depend on a YES or No, or on situations where the most engaging man may disappoint passion. In short, I am bold enough to become, as you say, a good husband and a good father! I am suited to domestic happiness, and prepared to submit to the conditions insisted on by society to set up a wife, a family——"

"You suggest the idea of a beehive. Go ahead, then. You will be a dupe all your days. You mean to marry, to have a wife to yourself? In other words, you want to solve, to your own advantage, the most difficult social problem presented in our day by town life as the French Revolution has left it, so you begin by isolation! And do you suppose that your wife will be content to forego the life you contemn? Will she, like you, be disgusted with it? If you do not want to endure the conjugal joys described by your sincere friend de Marsay, listen to my last advice. Remain unmarried for thirteen years longer, and enjoy yourself to the top of your bent; then, at forty, with your first fit of the gout, marry a

21

widow of six-and-thirty; thus you may be happy. If you take a maid to wife, you will die a madman !"

"Indeed! And tell me why?" cried Paul, somewhat nettled.

"My dear fellow," replied de Marsay, "Boileau's 'Satire on Women' is no more than a series of commonplace observations in verse. Why should women be faultless? Why deny them the heritage of the most obvious possession of human · nature? In my opinion, the problem of marriage no longer lies in the form in which that critic discerned it. Do you really suppose that, to command affection in marriage, as in love, it is enough for a husband to be a man? You who haunt boudoirs, have you none but fortunate experiences?

"Everything in our bachelor existence prepares a disastrous mistake for the man who marries without having deeply studied the human heart. In the golden days of youth, by a singular fact in our manners, a man always bestows pleasure, he triumphs over fascinated woman, and she submits to his wishes. The obstacles set up by law and feeling, and the natural coyness of woman, give rise to a common impulse on both sides, which deludes superficial men as to their future position in the married state where there are no obstacles to be overcome, where women endure rather than allow a man's advances, and repel them rather than invite them. The whole aspect of life is altered for us. The unmarried man, free from care and always the leader, has nothing to fear from a defeat. In married life a repulse is irreparable. Though a lover may make a mistress change her mind in his favor, such a rout, my dear boy, is Waterloo to a husband. A husband, like Napoleon, is bound to gain the victory; however often he may have won, the first defeat is his overthrow. The woman who is flattered by a lover's persistency, and proud of his wrath, calls them brutal in a husband. The lover may choose his ground and do what he will, the master has no such license, and his battlefield is always the same.

"Again, the struggle is the other way about. A wife is naturally inclined to refuse what she ought; a mistress is ready to give what she ought not.

"You who wish to marry (and who will do it), have you ever duly meditated on the Civil Code? I have never soiled my feet in that cave of commentary, that cockloft of gabble called the Law Schools; I never looked into the Code, but I see how it works in the living organism of the world. I am a lawyer, as a clinical professor is a doctor. The malady is not in books, it is in the patient. The Code, my friend, provides women with guardians, treats them as minors, as children. And how do we manage children? By fear. In that word, my dear Paul, you have the bit for the steed. Feel your pulse, and say: Can you disguise yourself as a tyrant; you who are so gentle, so friendly, so trusting; you whom at first I used to laugh at, and whom I now love well enough to initiate you into my science. Yes, this is part of a science to which the Germans have already given the name of anthropology.

"Oh! if I had not solved life by a measure of pleasure, if I had not an excessive antipathy for men who think instead of acting, if I did not despise the idiots who are so stupid as to believe that a book may live, when the sands of African deserts are composed of the ashes of I know not how many unknown Londons, Venices, Parises, and Romes now in dust, I would write a book on modern marriages and the influence of the Christian system; I would erect a beacon on the heap of sharp stones on which the votaries lie who devote themselves to the social *multiplicamini*. And yet—is the human race worth a quarter of an hour of my time? Is not the sole rational use of pen and ink to ensnare hearts by the writing of seductive love-letters!

"So you will introduce us to the Comtesse de Manerville?"

"Perhaps," said Paul.

"We shall still be friends," said de Marsay.

"Sure?" replied Paul.

"Be quite easy; we will be very polite to you, as the Maison Rouge were to the English at Fontenoy."

Though this conversation shook him, the Comte de Manerville set to work to carry out his plans, and returned to Bordeaux for the winter of 1821. The cost at which he restored and furnished his house did credit to the reputation for elegance that had preceded him. His old connections secured him an introduction to the Royalist circle of Bordeaux, to which, indeed, he belonged, alike by opinion, name, and fortune, and he soon became the leader of its fashion. His knowledge of life, good manners, and Parisian training enchanted the Saint-Germain suburb of Bordeaux. An old marquise applied to him an expression formerly current at Court to designate the flower of handsome youth, of the dandies of a past day, whose speech and style were law; she called him *la fleur des pois*—as who should say Sweet-pea. The Liberal faction took up the nickname, which they used in irony, and the Royalists as a compliment.

Paul de Manerville fulfilled with glory the requirements of the name. He was in the position of many a second-rate actor; as soon as the public vouchsafes some approval, they become almost good. Paul, quite at his ease, displayed the qualities of his defects. His banter was neither harsh nor bitter, his manners were not haughty; in his conversation with women, he expressed the respect they value without too much deference or too much familiarity. His dandyism was no more than an engaging care for his person; he was considerate of rank; he allowed a freedom to younger men which his Paris experience kept within due limits; though a master with the sword and pistol, he was liked for his feminine gentleness. He was one of those men who are made to accept rather than give happiness, to whom woman is a great factor in life, who need understanding and encouraging, and to whom a wife's love should play the part of Providence.

Though such a character as this gives rise to trouble in domestic life, it is charming and attractive in society. Paul was a success in the narrow provincial circle, where his character, in no respect strongly marked, was better appreciated than in Paris.

The decoration of his town-house, and the necessary restoration of the Lanstrac Castle, which he fitted up with English comfort and luxury, absorbed the capital his agent had saved during the past six years. Reduced, therefore, to his exact income of forty-odd thousand francs in stocks, he thought it wise to arrange his housekeeping so as to spend no more than this. By the time he had duly displayed his carriages and horses, and entertained the young men of position in the town, he perceived that provincial life necessitated marriage. Still too young to devote himself to the avaricious cares or speculative improvements in which provincial folk ultimately find employment, as required by the need for providing for their children, he ere long felt the want of the various amusements which become the vital habit of a Parisian.

At the same time, it was not a name to be perpetuated, an heir to whom to transmit his possessions, the position to be gained by having a house where the principal families of the neighborhood might meet, nor weariness of illicit connections, that proved to be the determining cause. He had on arriving fallen in love with the queen of Bordeaux society, the much-talked-of Mademoiselle Evangelista.

Early in the century a rich Spaniard named Evangelista had settled at Bordeaux, where good introductions, added to a fine fortune, had won him a footing in the drawing-rooms of the nobility. His wife had done much to preserve him in good odor amid this aristocracy, which would not, perhaps, have been so ready to receive him but that it could thus annoy the society next below it. Madame Evangelista, descended from the illustrious house of Casa-Real, connected with the Spanish monarchs, was a creole, and, like all women accustomed to

be served by slaves, she was a very fine lady, knew nothing of
the value of money, and indulged even her most extravagant
fancies, finding them always supplied by a husband who was
in love with her, and who was so generous as to conceal from
her all the machinery of money-making. The Spaniard, delighted to find that she could be happy at Bordeaux, where
his business required him to reside, bought a fine house, kept
it in good style, entertained splendidly, and showed excellent
taste in every respect. So, from 1800 till 1812, no one was
talked of in Bordeaux but Monsieur and Madame Evangelista.

The Spaniard died in 1813, leaving a widow of two-and-
thirty with an enormous fortune and the prettiest little
daughter in the world, at that time eleven years old, promising to become, as indeed she became, a very accomplished
person. Clever as Madame Evangelista might be, the Restoration altered her position ; the Royalist party sifted itself,
and several families left Bordeaux. Still, though her husband's head and hand were lacking to the management of the
business, for which she showed the inaptitude of a woman of
fashion and the indifference of the creole, she made no change
in her mode of living.

By the time when Paul de Manerville had made up his
mind to return to his native place, Mademoiselle Natalie
Evangelista was a remarkably beautiful girl, and apparently
the richest match in Bordeaux, where no one knew of the
gradual diminution of her mother's wealth ; for, to prolong
her reign, Madame Evangelista had spent vast sums of money.
Splendid entertainments and almost royal display had kept
up the public belief in the wealth of the house.

Natalie was nearly nineteen, no offer of marriage had as
yet come to her mother's ear. Accustomed to indulge all her
girlish fancies, Mademoiselle Evangelista had Indian shawls
and jewels, and lived amid such luxury as frightened the
speculative, in a land and at a time when the young are as
calculating as their parents. The fatal verdict: "Only a

prince could afford to marry Mademoiselle Evangelista," was a watchword in every drawing-room and boudoir. Mothers of families, dowagers with granddaughters to marry, and damsels jealous of the fair Natalie, whose unfailing elegance and tyrannous beauty were an annoyance to them, took care to add venom to this opinion by perfidious insinuations. When an eligible youth was heard to exclaim with rapturous admiration on Natalie's arrival at a ball—"Good heavens, what a beautiful creature!" "Yes," the mammas would reply, "but very expensive!" If some new-comer spoke of Mademoiselle Evangelista as charming, and opined that a man wanting a wife could not make a better choice—"Who would be bold enough," some one would ask, "to marry a girl to whom her mother allows a thousand francs a month for dress, who keeps horses and a lady's-maid, and wears lace? She has Mechlin lace on her dressing-gowns. What she pays for washing would keep a clerk in comfort. She has morning capes that cost six francs apiece to clean!"

Such speeches as these, constantly repeated by way of eulogium, extinguished the keenest desire a youth might feel to wed Mademoiselle Evangelista. The queen of every ball, surfeited with flattery, sure of smiles and admiration wherever she went, Natalie knew nothing of life. She lived as birds fly, as flowers bloom, finding every one about her ready to fulfill her least wish. She knew nothing of the price of things, nor of how money is acquired or kept. She very likely supposed that every house was furnished with cooks and coachmen, maids and menservants, just as a field produces fodder and trees yield fruit. To her the beggar, the pauper, the fallen tree, and the barren field were all the same thing. Cherished like a hope by her mother, fatigue never marred her pleasure; she pranced through the world like a courser on the steppes, a courser without either bridle or shoes.

Six months after Paul's arrival the upper circles of the town had brought about a meeting between "Sweet-pea" and the

queen of the ballroom.   The two flowers looked at each other
with apparent coldness, and thought each other charming.
Madame Evangelista, as being interested in this not unforeseen
meeting, read Paul's sentiments in his eyes, and said to herself:
"He will be my son-in-law;" while Paul said to himself, as
he looked at Natalie: "She will be my wife!"   The wealth of
the Evangelistas, proverbial in Bordeaux, remained in Paul's
memory as a tradition of his boyhood, the most indelible of
all such impressions.   And so pecuniary suitability was a foregone conclusion, without all the discussion and inquiry, which
are as horrible to shy as to proud natures.

When some persons tried to express to Paul the praise which
it was impossible to refuse to Natalie's manner and beauty and
wit, always ending with some of the bitterly mercenary reflections as to the future to which the expensive style of the household naturally gave rise, Pease-blossom replied with the disdain
that such provincialism deserves.   And this way of treating
the matter, which soon became known, silenced these remarks; for it was Paul who set the *ton* in ideas and speech
as much as in manners and appearance.   He had imported the
French development of the British stamp and its ice-bound
barriers, its Byronic irony, discontent with life, contempt for
sacred bonds, English plate and English wit, the scorn of old
provincial customs and old property; cigars, patent leather,
the pony, lemon-covered gloves, and the trot.   So that befell
Paul which had happened to no one before—no old dowager
or young maid tried to discourage him.

Madame Evangelista began by inviting him to several grand
dinners.   Could Sweet-pea remain absent from the entertainments to which the most fashionable young men of the town
were bidden?   In spite of Paul's affected coldness, which did
not deceive either the mother or the daughter, he found himself taking the first steps on the road to marriage.   When
Manerville passed in his tilbury or riding a good horse, other
young men would stop to watch him, and he could hear their

comments: "There's a lucky fellow; he is rich, he is handsome, and they say he is to marry Mademoiselle Evangelista. There are some people for whom the world seems to have been made!" If he happened to meet Madame Evangelista's carriage, he was proud of the peculiar graciousness with which the mother and daughter bowed to him.

Even if Paul had not been in love with Mademoiselle Natalie, the world would have married them whether or not. The world, which is the cause of no good thing, is implicated in many disasters; then, when it sees the evil hatching out that it has so maternally brooded, it denies it and avenges it. The upper society of Bordeaux, supposing Mademoiselle Evangelista to have a fortune of a million francs, handed her over to Paul without awaiting the consent of the parties concerned —as it often does.

So the affair was settled; the magnates of the tiptop Royalist circle, when the marriage was mentioned in their presence, made such civil speeches to Paul as flattered his vanity:

"Every one says you are to marry Mademoiselle Evangelista. You will do well to marry her; you will not find so handsome a wife anywhere, not even in Paris; she is elegant, pleasing, and allied through her mother with the Casa-Reals. You will be the most charming couple; you have the same tastes, the same views of life, and will keep the most agreeable house in Bordeaux. Your wife will only have to pack up her clothes and move in. In a case like yours a house ready to live in is as good as a settlement. And you are lucky to meet with a mother-in-law like Madame Evangelista. She is a clever woman, very attractive, and will be an important aid to you in the political career to which you ought now to aspire. She has sacrificed everything for her daughter, whom she worships; and Natalie will no doubt be a good wife, for she is loving to her mother. And then, everything must have an end."

"That is all very fine," was Paul's reply; for, in love

though he was, he wished to be free to choose, "but it must have a happy end."

Paul soon became a frequent visitor to Madame Evangelista, led there by the need to find employment for his idle hours, which he, more than other men, found it difficult to fill. There only in the town did he find the magnificence and luxury to which he had accustomed himself.

Madame Evangelista, at the age of forty, was handsome still, with the beauty of a grand sunset, which in summer crowns the close of a cloudless day. Her blameless reputation was an endless subject of discussion in the "sets" of Bordeaux society, and the curiosity of women was all the more alert, because the widow's appearance suggested the sort of temperament which makes Spanish and creole women notorious. She had black eyes and hair, the foot and figure of a Spaniard—the slender serpentine figure for which the Spaniards have a name. Her face, still beautiful, had the fascinating creole complexion, which can only be described by comparing it with white lawn over warm blood-color, so equably tinted is its fairness. Her forms were round, and attractive in the grace which combines the ease of indolence with vivacity, strength with extreme freedom. She was attractive, but imposing; she fascinated, but made no promises. Being tall, she could at will assume the port and dignity of a queen.

Men were ensnared by her conversation, as birds are by bird-lime, for she had by nature the spirit which necessity bestows on intriguers; she would go on from concession to concession, arming herself with what she gained to ask for something more, but always able to withdraw a thousand yards at a bound if she were asked for anything in return. She was ignorant of facts, but she had known the Courts of Spain and of Naples, the most famous persons of the two Americas, and various illustrious families of England and of the Continent, which gave her an amount of information superficially so wide that it seemed immense.

The mother and daughter were truly friends, apart from filial and maternal feeling. They suited each other, and their perpetual contact had never resulted in a jar. Thus many persons accounted for Madame Evangelista's self-sacrifice by her love for her daughter. However, though Natalie may have consoled her mother for her unalleviated widowhood, she was not perhaps its only motive. Madame Evangelista was said to have fallen in love with a man whom the second Restoration had reinstated in his title and peerage. This man, who would willingly have married her in 1814, had very decently thrown her over in 1816.

Now Madame Evangelista, apparently the best-hearted creature living, had in her nature one terrible quality which can be best expressed in Catherine de' Medici's motto, *Odiate e aspettate*—Hate and wait. Used always to be first, always to be obeyed, she resembled royal personages in being amiable, gentle, perfectly sweet and easy-going in daily life; but terrible, implacable, when offended in her pride as a woman, a Spaniard, and a Casa-Real. She never forgave. This woman believed in the power of her own hatred; she regarded it as an evil spell which hung over her enemies. This fateful influence she had cast over the man who had been false to her. Events which seemed to prove the efficacy of her *jettatura* confirmed her in her superstitious belief in it. Though he was a minister and a member of the Upper Chamber, ruin stole upon him, and he was utterly undone. His estate, his political and personal position—all was lost. One day Madame Evangelista was able to drive past him in her handsome carriage while he stood in the Champs Élysées, and to blight him with a look sparkling with the fires of triumph.

Madame Evangelista quickly read Paul's character and concealed her own. He was the very man she hoped for as a son-in-law, as the responsible editor of her influence and authority. He was related through his mother to the Maulincours; and the old Baronne de Maulincour, the friend of the Vidame de

Pamiers, lived in the heart of the Faubourg Saint-Germain. The grandson of the baronne, Auguste de Maulincour, had a brilliant position in society. Thus Paul would advantageously introduce the Evangelistas to the World of Paris. The widow had at rare intervals visited Paris under the Empire; she longed to shine in Paris under the Restoration. There only were the elements to be found of political success, the only form of fortune-making in which a woman of fashion can allow herself to coöperate.

Madame Evangelista, obliged by her husband's business to live in Bordeaux, had never liked it; she had a house there, and every one knows how many obligations fetter a woman's life under such circumstances; but she was tired of Bordeaux, she had exhausted its resources. She wished for a wider stage, as gamblers go where the play is highest. So, for her own benefit, she dreamed of high destinies for Paul. She intended to use her own cleverness and knowledge of life for her son-in-law's advancement, so as to enjoy the pleasures of power in his name. Many men are thus the screen of covert femi-nine ambitions. And, indeed, Madame Evangelista had more than one motive for wishing to govern her daughter's hus-band.

Paul was, of course, captivated by the lady, all the more certainly because she seemed not to wish to influence him in any way. She used her ascendency to magnify herself, to magnify her daughter, and to give enhanced value to every-thing about her, so as to have the upper hand from the first with the man in whom she saw the means of continuing her aristocratic connection.

And Paul valued himself the more highly for this apprecia-tion of the mother and daughter. He fancied himself wittier than he was, when he found that his remarks and his slightest jests were responded to by Mademoiselle Evangelista, who smiled or looked up intelligently, and by her mother, whose flattery always seemed to be involuntary. The two women were so frankly kind, he felt so sure of pleasing them, they drove him so cleverly by the guiding thread of his conceit, that, before long, he spent most of his time at their house.

Within a year of his arrival Count Paul, without having declared his intentions, was so attentive to Natalie that he was universally understood to be courting her. Neither mother nor daughter seemed to think of marriage. Mademoiselle Evangelista did not depart from the reserve of a fine lady who knows how to be charming and converse agreeably without allowing the slightest advance toward intimacy. This self-respect, rare among provincial folk, attracted Paul greatly. Shy men are often touchy, unexpected suggestions alarm them. They flee even from happiness if it comes with much display, and are ready to accept unhappiness if it comes in a modest form, surrounded by gentle shades. Hence Paul, seeing that Madame Evangelista made no effort to entrap him, ensnared himself. The Spanish lady captivated him finally one evening by saying that at a certain age a superior woman, like a man, found that ambition took the place of the feelings of earlier years.

"That woman," thought Paul, as he went away, "would be capable of getting me some good embassy before I could even be elected deputy."

The man who, under any circumstances, fails to look at everything or at every idea from all sides, to examine them under all aspects, is inefficient and weak, and consequently in danger. Paul at this moment was an optimist; he saw advantages in every contingency, and never remembered that an ambitious mother-in-law may become a tyrant. So every evening as he went home he pictured himself as married, he bewitched himself, and unconsciously shod himself with the slippers of matrimony. He had enjoyed his liberty too long to regret it; he was tired of single life, which could show him nothing new, and of which he now saw only the discomforts; whereas, though the difficulties of marriage sometimes occurred to him, he far more often contemplated its pleasures; the prospect was new to him.

"Married life," said he to himself, "is hard only on the poorer classes. Half its troubles vanish before wealth."

So every day some hopeful suggestion added to the list of advantages which he saw in this union.

"However high I may rise in life, Natalie will always be equal to her position," he would say to himself, "and that is no small merit in a wife. How many men of the Empire have I seen suffering torment from their wives! Is it not an important element of happiness never to feel one's pride or vanity rubbed the wrong way by the companion one has chosen? A man can never be utterly wretched with a well-bred woman; she never makes him contemptible, and she may be of use. Natalie will be a perfect mistress of a drawing-room."

He even endeavored to study Mademoiselle Evangelista in a way that would not compromise his ultimate decision in his own eyes, for his friend de Marsay's terrible speech rang in his ears now and again. But, in the first place, those who are accustomed to luxury have a tone of simplicity that is very deceptive. They scorn it, they use it habitually, it is the means and not the object of their lives. Paul, as he saw that these ladies' lives were so similar to his own, never for an instant imagined that they concealed any conceivable source of ruin. And then, though there are a few general rules for mitigating the worries of married life, there are none to enable us to guess or foresee them.

When troubles arise between two beings who have undertaken to make life happy and easy each for the other, they are based on the friction produced by an incessant intimacy which does not arise between two persons before marriage, and never can arise till the laws and habits of French life are changed. Two beings on the eve of joining their lives always deceive each other; but the deception is innocent and involuntary.

Each, of course, stands in the best light; they are rivals as to which makes the most promising show, and at that time form a favorable idea of themselves up to which they cannot afterward come. Real life, like a changeable day, consists more often of the gray, dull hours when Nature is overcast than of the brilliant intervals when the sun gives glory and joy to the fields. Young people look only at the fine days. Subsequently they ascribe the inevitable troubles of life to matrimony, for there is in man a tendency to seek the cause of his griefs in things or persons immediately at hand.

To discover in Mademoiselle Evangelista's demeanor or countenance, in her words or her gestures, any indication that might reveal the quota of imperfection inherent in her character, Paul would have needed not merely the science of Lavater and of Gall, but another kind of knowledge for which no code of formulas exists, the personal intuition of the observer, which requires almost universal knowledge. Like all girls, Natalie's countenance was impenetrable. The deep, serene peace given by sculptors to the virgin heads intended to personify Justice, Innocence, all the divinities who dwell above earthly agitations—this perfect calm is the greatest charm of a girlish face, it is the sign-manual of her purity; nothing has stirred her, no repressed passion, no betrayed affection has cast a shade on the placidity of her features; and if it is assumed, the girl has ceased to exist. Living always inseparable from her mother, Natalie, like every Spanish woman, had had none but religious teaching, and some few lessons of a mother to her daughter which might be useful for her part in life. Hence her calm expression was natural; but it was a veil, in which the woman was shrouded as a butterfly is in the chrysalis.

At the same time, a man skilled in the use of the scalpel of analysis might have discerned in Natalie some revelation of the difficulties her character might present in the conflict of married or social life. Her really wonderful beauty was marked by excessive regularity of features, in perfect harmony with the proportions of her head and figure. Such perfection does not promise well for the intellect, and there are few exceptions to this rule. Superior qualities show in some slight imperfections of form which become exquisitely attractive, points of light where antagonistic feelings sparkle and rivet the eye. Perfect harmony indicates the coldness of a compound nature.

Natalie had a round figure, a sign of strength, but also an infallible evidence of self-will often reaching the pitch of obstinacy in women whose mind is neither keen nor broad. Her hands, like those of a Greek statue, confirmed the forecast of her face and form by showing a love of unreasoning dominion. Will for will's sake. Her eyebrows met in the middle, which, according to observers, indicates a jealous disposition. The jealousy of noble souls becomes emulation and leads to great things; that of mean minds turns to hatred. Her mother's motto, *Odiate e aspettate*, was hers in all its strength. Her eyes looked black, but were in fact dark hazel-brown, and contrasted with her hair of that russet hue, so highly prized by the Romans, and known in English as auburn, the usual color of the hair in the children of two black-haired parents like Monsieur and Madame Evangelista. Her delicately white skin added infinitely to the charm of this contrast of colors in hair and eyes, but this refinement was purely superficial; for whenever the lines of a face have not a peculiar soft roundness, whatever the refinement and delicacy of the details, do not look for any especial charms of mind. These flowers of delusive youth presently fade, and you are surprised after the lapse of a few years to detect hardness, sternness, where you once admired the elegance of lofty qualities.

There was something august in Natalie's features; still, her chin was rather heavy—a painter would have said thick in *impasto*, an expression descriptive of a type that shows preëxisting sentiments of which the violence does not declare itself till middle life. Her mouth, a little sunk in her face, showed the arrogance no less expressed in her hand, her chin, her eyebrows, and her stately shape. Finally, a last sign which alone might have warned the judgment of a connoisseur, Natalie's pure and fascinating voice had a metallic ring. However gently the brazen instrument was handled, however tenderly the vibrations were sent through the curves of the horn, that voice proclaimed a nature like that of the Duke of Alva, from whom the Casa-Reals were collaterally descended. All these indications pointed to passions, violent but not tender, to sudden infatuations, irreconcilable hatred, a certain wit without intellect, and the craving to rule, inherent in persons who feel themselves below the pretensions.

These faults, the outcome of race and constitution, some-times compensated for by the impulsions of generous blood, were hidden in Natalie as ore is hidden in the mine, and would only be brought to the surface by the rough treatment and shocks to which character is subjected in the world. At present the sweetness and freshness of youth, the elegance of her manners, her saintly ignorance, and the grace of girl-hood, tinged her features with the delicate veneer that ever deceives superficial observers.

How should Paul, who loved as a man does when love is seconded by desire, foresee in a girl of this temper, whose beauty dazzled him, the woman as she would be at thirty, when shrewder observers might have been deceived by appearances? If happiness were difficult to find in married life, with this girl it would not be impossible. Some fine qualities shone through her defects. In the hand of a skillful master any good quality may be made to stifle faults, especially in a girl who can love.

But to make so stern a metal ductile, the iron fist of which de Marsay had spoken was needed. The Paris dandy was right. Fear, inspired by love, is an infallible tool for dealing

22

with a woman's spirit. Those who fear, love ; and fear is more nearly akin to love than to hatred. Would Paul have the coolness, the judgment, the firmness needed in the contest of which no wife should be allowed to have a suspicion? And, again, did Natalie love Paul?

Natalie, like most girls, mistook for love the first impulses of instinct and liking that Paul's appearance stirred in her, knowing nothing of the meaning of marriage or of house-wifery. To her the Comte de Manerville, who had seen diplomatic service at every court in Europe, one of the most fashionable men of Paris, could not be an ordinary man de-void of moral strength, with a mixture of bravery and shyness, energetic perhaps in adversity, but defenseless against the foes that poison happiness. Would she develop tact enough to discern Paul's good qualities among his superficial defects? Would she not magnify these and forget those, after the manner of young wives who know nothing of life?

At a certain age a woman will overlook vice in the man who spares her petty annoyances, while she regards such an-noyances as misfortunes. What conciliatory influence and what experience would cement and enlighten this young couple? Would not Paul and his wife imagine that love was all-in-all, when they were only at the stage of affectionate grimacing in which young wives indulge at the beginning of their life, and of the compliments a husband pays on their return from a ball while he still has the courtesy of admi-ration?

In such a situation would not Paul succumb to his wife's tyranny instead of asserting his authority? Would he be able to say " No ? " All was danger for a weak man in cir-cumstances where a strong one might perhaps have run some risk.

The subject of this study is not the transition of an unmar-ried to a married man—a picture which, broadly treated, would not lack the interest which the innermost storm of our feelings must lend to the commonest facts of life. The events and ideas which culminated in Paul's marriage to Mademoiselle Evangelista are an introduction to the work, and only intended as a study to the great comedy which is the prologue to every married life. Hitherto this passage has been neglected by dramatic writers, though it offers fresh resources to their wit.

This prologue, which decided Paul's future life, and to which Madame Evangelista looked forward with terror, was the discussion to which the marriage-settlements give rise in every family, whether of the nobility or of the middle-class; for human passions are quite as strongly agitated by small interests as by great ones. These dramas, played out in the presence of the notary, are all more or less like this one, and its real interest will be less in these pages than in the memory of most married people.

Early in the winter of 1822 Paul de Manerville, through the intervention of his grand-aunt, Madame la Baronne de Maulincour, asked the hand of Mademoiselle Evangelista. Though the baroness usually spent no more than two months in Médoc, she remained on this occasion till the end of October to be of use to her grand-nephew in this matter, and play the part of a mother. After laying the overtures before Madame Evangelista, the experienced old lady came to report to Paul on the results of this step.

"My boy," said she, "I have settled the matter. In discussing money matters I discovered that Madame Evangelista gives her daughter nothing. Mademoiselle Natalie marries with but her barest rights. Marry, my dear; men who have a name and estates to transmit must sooner or later end by marriage. I should like to see my dear Auguste do the same.

"You can get married without me, I have nothing to bestow on you but my blessing, and old women of my age have no business at weddings. I shall return to Paris to-morrow.

When you introduce your wife to society, I shall see her much more comfortably than I can here. If you had not your house in Paris, you would have found a home with me. I should have been delighted to arrange my third-floor rooms to suit you."

"Dear aunt," said Paul, "I thank you very warmly. But what do you mean by saying her mother gives her nothing, and that she marries only with her bare rights?"

"Her mother, my dear boy, is a very knowing hand, who is taking advantage of the girl's beauty to make terms and give you no more than what she cannot keep back—the father's fortune. We old folk, you know, think a deal deal of 'How much has he? How much has she?' I advise you to give strict instructions to your notary. The marriage-contract, my child, is a sacred duty. If your father and mother had not made their bed well, you might now be without sheets. You will have children—they are the usual result of marriage —so you are bound to think of this. Call in Maître Mathias, our old notary."

Madame de Maulincour left Paul plunged in perplexity. His mother-in-law was a knowing hand! He must discuss and defend his interests in the marriage-contract! Who, then, proposed to attack them? So he took his aunt's advice and intrusted the matter of settlements to Maître Mathias.

Still, he could not help thinking of the anticipated discussion. And it was not without much trepidation that he went to see Madame Evangelista with a view to announcing his intentions. Like all timid people, he was afraid lest he should betray the distrust suggested by his aunt, which he thought nothing less than insulting. To avoid the slightest friction with so imposing a personage as his future mother-in-law seemed, he fell back on the circumlocutions natural to those who dare not face a difficulty.

"Madame, you know what an old family notary is like," said he, when Natalie was absent for a minute. "Mine is a worthy old man, who would be deeply aggrieved if I did not place my marriage-contract in his hands——"

"But, my dear fellow," said Madame Evangelista, interrupting him, "are not marriage-contracts always settled through the notaries on each side?"

During the interval while Paul sat pondering, not daring to open the matter, Madame Evangelista had been wondering, "What is he thinking about?" for women have a great power of reading thought from the play of feature. And she could guess at the great-aunt's hints from the embarrassed gaze and agitated tone which betrayed Paul's mental disturbance.

"At last," thought she, "the decisive moment has come; the crisis is at hand; what will be the end of it? My notary," she went on, after a pause, " is Maître Solonet, and yours is Maître Mathias; I will ask them both to dinner to-morrow, and they can settle the matter between them. Is it not their business to conciliate our interests without our meddling, as it is that of the cook to feed us well?"

"Why, of course," said he, with a little sigh of relief.

By a strange inversion of parts, Paul, who was blameless, quaked, while Madame Evangelista, though dreadfully anxious, appeared calm. The widow owed her daughter the third of the fortune left by Monsieur Evangelista, twelve hundred thousand francs, and was quite unable to pay it, even if she stripped herself of all her possessions. She would be at her son-in-law's mercy. Though she might override Paul alone, would Paul, enlightened by his lawyer, agree to any compromise as to the account of her stewardship? If he withdrew, all Bordeaux would know the reason, and it would be impossible for Natalie to marry. The mother who wished to secure her daughter's happiness, the woman who from the hour of her birth had lived in honor, foresaw the day when she must be dishonored.

Like those great generals who would fain wipe out of their lives the moment when they were cowards at heart, she wished

she could score out that day from the days of her life. And
certainly some of her hairs turned white in the course of the
night when, face to face with this difficulty, she bitterly
blamed herself for her want of care.

In the first place, she was obliged to confide in her lawyer,
whom she sent for to attend her as soon as she was up. She
had to confess a secret vexation which she had never admitted
even to herself, for she had walked on to the verge of the
precipice, trusting to one of those chances that never happen.
And a feeling was born in her soul, a little animus against
Paul that was not yet hatred, nor aversion, nor in any way
evil—but, was not he the antagonistic party in this family
suit? Was he not, unwittingly, an innocent enemy who
must be defeated? And who could ever love any one he had
duped?

Compelled to deceive, the Spanish woman resolved, like
any woman, to show her superiority in a contest of which the
entire success could alone wipe out the discredit. In the
silence of the night she excused herself by a line of argument
in which her pride had the upper hand. Had not Natalie
benefited by her lavishness? Had her conduct ever been
actuated by one of the base and ignoble motives that degrade
the soul? She could not keep accounts—well, was that a sin,
a crime? Was not a man only too lucky to win such a wife
as Natalie? Was not the treasure she had preserved for him
worth a discharge in full? Did not many a man pay for the
woman he loved by making great sacrifices? And why should
he do more for a courtesan than for a wife? Beside, Paul was
a commonplace, incapable being; she would support him by
the resources of her own cleverness; she would help him to
make his way in the world; he would owe his position to her;
would not this amply pay the debt? He would be a fool to
hesitate? And for a few thousand francs more or less? It
would be disgraceful!

"If I am not at once successful," said she to herself, "I

leave Bordeaux. I can still secure a good match for Natalie by realizing all that is left—the house, my diamonds, and the furniture, giving her all but an annuity for myself."

When a strongly tempered spirit plans a retreat, as Richelieu did at Brouage, and schemes for a splendid finale, this alternative becomes a fulcrum which helps the schemer to triumph. This escape, in case of failure, reassured Madame Evangelista, who went to sleep, indeed, full of confidence in her second in this duel. She trusted greatly to the aid of the cleverest notary in Bordeaux, Maître Solonet, a young man of seven-and-twenty, a member of the Legion of Honor as the reward of having contributed actively to the restoration of the Bourbons. Proud and delighted to be admitted to an acquaintance with Madame Evangelista, less as a lawyer than as belonging to the Royalist party in Bordeaux, Solonet cherished for her sunset beauty one of those passions which such women as Madame Evangelista ignore while they are flattered by them, and which even the prudish allow to float in their wake. Solonet lived in an attitude of vanity full of respect and seemly attentions. This young man arrived next morning with the zeal of a slave, and was admitted to the widow's bedroom, where he found her coquettishly dressed in a most becoming wrapper.

"Now," said she, "can I trust to your reticence and entire devotion in the discussion which is to take place this evening? Of course, you can guess that my daughter's marriage-contract is in question."

The young lawyer was profuse in protestations.

"For the facts, then," said she.

"I am all attention," he replied, with a look of concentration.

Madame Evangelista stated the case without any finesse.

"My dear madame, all this matters not," said Maître Solonet, assuming an important air when his client had laid the exact figures before him. "How have you dealt with Mon-

sieur de Manerville ? The moral attitude is of greater consequence than any questions of law or finance."

Madame Evangelista robed herself in dignity; the young
notary was delighted to learn that to this day his client, in
her treatment of Paul, had preserved the strictest distance ;
half out of real pride and half out of unconscious self-interest,
she had always behaved to the Comte de Manerville as though
he were her inferior, and it would be an honor for him to
marry Mademoiselle Evangelista. Neither she nor her daughter
could be suspected of interested motives ; their feelings were
evidently free from meanness; if Paul should raise the least
difficulty on the money question, they had every right to
withdraw to an immeasurable distance—in fact, she had a
complete ascendency over her would-be son-in-law.

"This being the case," said Solonet, "what is the utmost
concession you are inclined to make ?"

"The least possible," said she, laughing.

"A woman's answer !" replied Solonet. "Madame, do
you really wish to see Mademoiselle Natalie married ?"

"Yes."

"And you want a discharge for the eleven hundred and
fifty-six thousand francs you will owe her in accordance with
the account rendered of your guardianship ?"

"Exactly !"

"How much do you wish to reserve ?"

"At least thirty thousand francs a year."

"So we must conquer or perish ?"

"Yes."

"Well, I will consider the ways and means of achieving
that end, for we must be very dexterous and husband our
resources. I will give you a few hints on arriving ; act on
them exactly, and I can confidently predict complete success.
Is Count Paul in love with Mademoiselle Natalie ?" he asked
as he rose.

"He worships her."

"That is not enough. Is he so anxious to have her as his wife that he will pass over any little pecuniary difficulties?"

"Yes."

"That is what I call having personal property in a daughter!" exclaimed the notary. "Make her look her best this evening," he added, with a cunning twinkle.

"We have a perfect dress for her."

"The dress for the contract, in my opinion, is half the settlements," said Solonet.

This last argument struck Madame Evangelista as so cogent that she insisted on helping her daughter to dress, partly to superintend the toilet, but also to secure her as an innocent accomplice in her financial plot. And her daughter, with her hair like la Sévigné's, and a white cashmere dress with rose-colored bows, seemed to her handsome enough to assure the victory.

When the maid had left them, and Madame Evangelista was sure that nobody was within hearing, she arranged her daughter's curls as a preliminary.

"My dear child, are you sincerely attached to Monsieur de Manerville?" said she in a steady voice.

The mother and daughter exchanged a strangely meaning glance.

"Why, my little mother, should you ask to-day rather than yesterday? Why have you allowed me to imagine a doubt?"

"If it were to part you from me for ever, would you marry him all the same?"

"I could give him up without dying of grief."

"Then you do not love him, my dear," said the mother, kissing her daughter's forehead.

"But why, my dear mamma, are you playing the grand inquisitor?"

"I wanted to see if you cared to be married without being madly in love with your husband."

"I like him."

"You are right ; he is a count, and, between us, he shall be made peer of France.　But there will be difficulties."

"Difficulties between people who care for each other ?　No ! This Sweet-pea, my mother, is too well planted there," and she pointed to her heart with a pretty gesture, "to make the smallest objection ; I am sure of that."

"But if it were not so ? "

"I should utterly forget him."

"Well said !　You are a Casa-Real.　But though he is madly in love with you, if certain matters were discussed which do not immediately concern him, but which he would have to make the best of for your sake and mine, Natalie, eh ? If, without proceeding in the least too far, a little graciousness of manner might turn the scale ?　A mere nothing, you know, a word ?　Men are like that—they can resist sound argument and yield to a glance."

"I understand !　A little touch just to make Favorite leap the gate," said Natalie with a flourish as if she were whipping a horse.

"My darling, I do not wish you to do anything approaching to invitation.　We have traditions of old Castilian pride which will never allow us to go too far.　The count will be informed of my situation."

"What situation ? "

"You would not understand if I told you.　Well, if after seeing you in all your beauty his eye should betray the slightest hesitancy—and I shall watch him—at that instant I should break the whole thing off; I should turn everything into money, leave Bordeaux, and go to Douai, to the Claes, who, after all, are related to us through the Temnincks.　Then I would find a French peer for your husband, even if I had to take refuge in a convent and give you my whole fortune."

"My dear mother, what can I do to hinder such misfortunes ? " said Natalie.

"I never saw you lovelier, my child ! Be a little purposely attractive, and all will be well."

Madame Evangelista left Natalie pensive, and went to achieve a toilet which allowed her to stand a comparison with her daughter. If Natalie was to fascinate Paul, must not she herself fire the enthusiasm of her champion Solonet ?

The mother and daughter were armed for conquest when Paul arrived with the bouquet which for some months past had been his daily offering to Natalie. Then they sat chatting while awaiting the lawyers.

This day was to Paul the first skirmish in the long and weary warfare of married life. It is necessary, therefore, to review the forces on either side, to place the belligerents, and to define the field on which they are to do battle.

To second him in a struggle of which he did not in the least appreciate the consequences, Paul had nobody but his old lawyer Mathias. They were each to be surprised unarmed by an unexpected manœuvre, driven by an enemy whose plans were laid, and compelled to act without having time for reflection. What man but would have failed even with Cujas and Barthole to back him ? How should he fear perfidy when everything seemed so simple and natural ?

What could Mathias do single-handed against Madame Evangelista, Solonet, and Natalie, especially when his client was a lover who would go over to the enemy as soon as his happiness should seem to be imperiled ? Paul was already entangling himself by making the pretty speeches customary with lovers, to which his passion gave an emphasis of immense value in the eyes of Madame Evangelista, who was leading him on to commit himself.

The matrimonial *condottieri* (mercenary soldiers), who were about to do battle for their clients, and whose personal prowess would prove decisive in this solemn contest—the two notaries —represented the old and the new schools, the old and the new style of notary.

Maître Mathias was a worthy old man of sixty-nine, proud of twenty years' practice in his office. His broad, gouty feet were shod in shoes with silver buckles, and were an absurd finish to legs so thin, with such prominent knee-bones, that when he crossed his feet they looked like the cross-bones on a tombstone. His lean thighs, lost in baggy, black knee-breeches with silver buckles, seemed to bend under the weight of a burly stomach and the round shoulders characteristic of men who live in an office; a huge ball, always clothed in a green coat with square-cut skirts, which no one remembered ever to have seen new. His hair, tightly combed back and powdered, was tied in a rat's-tail that always tucked itself away between the collar of his coat and that of his flowered white vest. With his bullet head, his face as red as a vine-leaf, his blue eyes, trumpet-nose, thick lips, and double-chin, the dear little man, wherever he went, aroused the laughter so liberally bestowed by the French on the grotesque creations which Nature sometimes allows herself and Art thinks it funny to exaggerate, calling them caricatures.

But in Maître Mathias the mind had triumped over the body, the qualities of the soul had vanquished the eccentricity of his appearance. Most of the townsfolk treated him with friendly respect and deference full of esteem. The notary's voice won all hearts by the eloquent ring of honesty. His only cunning consisted in going straight to the point, over-setting every evil thought by the directness of his questions. His sharply observant eye, and his long experience of business, gave him that spirit of divination which allowed him to read consciences and discern the most secret thoughts. Though grave and quiet in business, this patriarch had the cheerfulness of our ancestors. He might, one felt, risk a song at table, accept and keep up family customs, celebrate anniversaries and birthdays, whether of grandparents or children, and burn the Christmas log with due ceremony; he loved to give New Year's gifts, to invent surprises, and bring

out Easter eggs; he believed, no doubt, in the duties of a
godfather, and would never neglect any old-time custom that
gave color to life of yore.

Maître Mathias was a noble and a respectable survival of
the notaries, obscure men of honor, of whom no receipt was
asked for millions, and who returned them in the same bags,
tied with the same string; who fulfilled every trust to the
letter, drew up inventories for probate with decent feeling,
took a paternal interest in their clients' affairs, put a bar
sometimes in the way of a spendthrift, and were the deposi-
tories of family secrets; in short, one of those notaries who
considered themselves responsible for blunders in their deeds,
and who gave time and thought to them. Never, in the whole
of his career as a notary, had one of his clients to complain of
a bad investment, of a mortgage ill-chosen or carelessly managed. His wealth, slowly but honestly acquired, had been
accumulated through thirty years of industry and economy.
He had found places for fourteen of his clerks. Religious and
generous in secret, Mathias was always to be found where
good was to be done without reward. He was an acting
member of the Board of Asylums and the Charitable Com-
mittee, and the largest subscriber to the voluntary taxes for
relief of unexpected disaster, or the establishment of some
useful institution. Thus, neither he nor his wife had a carriage; his word was sacred; he had as much money deposited
in his cellar as lay at the bank; he was known as "Good
Monsieur Mathias;" and when he died, three thousand persons followed him to the grave.

Solonet was the youthful notary who comes in humming a
tune, who affects an airy manner, and declares that business
may be done quite as efficiently with a laugh as with a serious
countenance; the notary who is a captain in the National
Guard, who does not like to be known for a lawyer, and aims
at the cross of the Legion of Honor, who keeps his carriage
and leaves the correcting of his deeds to his clerks; the notary

who goes to balls and to the play, who buys pictures and plays *écarté*, who has a cash drawer into which he pours deposit-money, repaying in notes what he receives in gold ; the notary who keeps pace with the times and risks his capital in doubtful investments, who speculates, hoping to retire with an income of thirty thousand francs after ten years in his office ; the notary whose acumen is the outcome of duplicity, and who is feared by many as an accomplice in possession of their secrets ; the notary who regards his official position as a means of marrying some blue-stocking heiress.

When the fair and elegant Solonet—all curled and scented, booted like a lover of the Vaudeville, and dressed like a dandy whose most important business is a duel—entered the room before his older colleague, who walked slowly from a touch of the gout, the two were the living representatives of one of the caricatures entitled "Then and Now," which had great success under the Empire.

Though Madame and Mademoiselle Evangelista, to whom "Good Monsieur Mathias" was a stranger, at first felt a slight inclination to laugh, they were at once touched by the perfect grace of his greeting. The worthy man's speech was full of the amenity that an amiable old man can infuse both into what he says and the manner of saying it.

The younger man, with his frothy sparkle, was at once thrown into the shade. Mathias showed his superior breeding by the measured respect of his address to Paul. Without humiliating his white hairs, he recognized the young man's rank, while appreciating the fact that certain honors are due to old age, and that all such social rights are interdependent. Solonet's bow and "How d'ye do?" were, on the contrary, the utterance of perfect equality, which could not fail to offend the susceptibilities of a man of the world, and to make himself ridiculous in the eyes of a man of rank.

The young notary, by a somewhat familiar gesture, invited Madame Evangelista to speak with him in a window-recess.

For some few minutes they spoke in whispers, laughing now and then, no doubt to mislead the others as to the importance of the conversation, in which Maître Solonet communicated the plan of battle to the lady in command.

"And could you really," said he in conclusion, "make up your mind to sell your house?"

"Undoubtedly!" said she.

Madame Evangelista did not choose to tell her lawyer her reasons for such heroism, as he thought it, for Solonet's zeal might have cooled if he had known that his client meant to leave Bordeaux. She had not even said so to Paul, not wishing to alarm him prematurely by the extent of the circumvallations needed for the first outworks of a political position.

After dinner the plenipotentiaries left the lovers with Madame Evangelista, and went into an adjoining room to discuss business. Thus two dramas were being enacted: by the chimney-corner in the drawing-room a love scene in which life smiled bright and happy; in the study a serious duologue, in which interest was laid bare, and already played the part it always fills under the most flowery, cloudless, and summer-like aspects of life.

"My dear sir, the deed will be in your hands; I know what I owe to my senior." Mathias bowed gravely. "But," Solonet went on, unfolding a rough draft, of no use whatever, that a clerk had written out, "as we are the weaker party, as we are the spinster, I have drafted the articles to save you the trouble. We propose to marry with all our rights on a footing of possession in common, an unqualified settlement of all estate, real and personal, each on the other in case of decease without issue; or, if issue survive them, a settlement of one-quarter on the surviving parent, and a life-interest in one-quarter more. The sum thrown into common stock to be one-quarter of the estate of each contracting party, the survivor to have all furniture and movables without exception and duty free. It is all as plain as day."

" Ta, ta, ta, ta," said Mathias, " I do not do business as you would sing a ballad. What have you to show?"

" What on your side?" asked Solonet.

" We have to settle," said Mathias, " the estate of Lanstrac, producing twenty-three thousand francs a year in rents, to say nothing of produce in kind: *Item :* the farms of le Grassol and le Guadet, each let for three thousand six hundred francs. *Item :* the vineyards of Bellerose, yielding on an average sixteen thousand—together forty-six thousand two hundred francs a year. *Item :* a family mansion at Bordeaux, assessed at nine hundred. *Item :* a fine house in Paris, with a forecourt and garden, Rue de la Pépinière, assessed at fifteen hundred. These properties, of which I hold the title-deeds, we inherit from our parents, excepting the house in Paris acquired by purchase. We have also to include the furniture of the two houses and of the castle at Lanstrac, valued at four hundred and fifty thousand francs. There you have the table, the cloth, and the first course. Now what have you for the second course and the dessert?"

" Our rights and expectations," said Solonet.

" Specify, my dear sir," replied Mathias. " What have you to show? Where is the valuation made at Monsieur Evangelista's death? Show me your valuations, and the investments you hold. Where is your capital—if you have any? Where is your land—if you have land? Show me your guardian's accounts, and tell us what your mother gives or promises to give you."

" Is Monsieur le Comte de Manerville in love with Mademoiselle Evangelista?"

" He means to marry her if everything proves suitable," said the old notary. " I am not a child; this is a matter of business and not of sentiment."

" The business will fall through if you have no sentiment— and generous sentiment; and this is why," said Solonet. " We had no valuation made after our husband's death.

Spanish, and a creole, we knew nothing of French law. And we were too deeply grieved to think of the petty formalities which absorb colder hearts. It is a matter of public notoriety that the deceased gentleman adored his wife, and that we were plunged in woe. Though we had a probate and a kind of valuation on a general estimate, you may thank the surrogate guardian for that, who called upon us to make a statement and settle a sum upon our daughter as best we might just at a time when we were obliged to sell out of the English Funds to an enormous amount which we wished to reinvest in Paris at double the interest."

"Come, do not talk nonsense to me. There are means of checking these amounts. How much did you pay in succession duties? The figure will be enough to verify the amounts. Go to the facts. Tell us plainly how much you had, and what is left. And then, if we are too desperately in love, we shall see."

"Well, if you are marrying for money, you may make your bow at once. We may lay claim to more than a million francs; but our mother has nothing of it left but this house and furniture and four hundred odd thousand francs, invested in 1817 in five per cents., and bringing in forty thousand francs a year."

"How then do you keep up a style costing a hundred thousand?" cried Mathias in dismay.

"Our daughter has cost us vast sums. Beside, we like display. And, finally, all your jeremiads will not bring back two sous of it."

"Mademoiselle Natalie might have been very handsomely brought up on the fifty thousand francs a year that belonged to her without rushing into ruin. And if you ate with such an appetite as a girl, what will you not devour when you become a wife?"

"Let us go then," said Solonet. "The handsomest girl alive is bound to spend more than she has."

23

"I will go and speak two words to my client," said the older lawyer.

"Go, go," thought Maître Solonet. "Go, old Father Cassandra, and tell your client we have not a centime." For, in the silence of his private office, he had strategically disposed of his masses, formed his arguments in columns, fixed the turning-points of the discussion, and prepared the critical moment when the antagonistic parties, thinking all was lost, would jump at a compromise which would be the triumph of his client.

The flowing dress with pink ribbons, the ringlets *à la Sévigné*, Natalie's small foot, her insinuating looks, her slender hand, constantly engaged in rearranging the curls which did not need it—all the tricks of a girl showing off, as a peacock spreads its tail in the sun—had brought Paul to the point at which her mother wished to see him. He was crazy with admiration, as crazy as a schoolboy for a courtesan ; his looks, an unfailing thermometer of the mind, marked the frenzy of passion which leads a man to commit a thousand follies.

"Natalie is so beautiful," he whispered to Madame Evangelista, "that I can understand the madness which drives us to pay for pleasure by death."

The lady tossed her head.

"A lover's words !" she replied. "My husband never made me such fine speeches ; but he married me penniless, and never in thirteen years gave me an instant's pain."

"Is that a hint for me ?" said Paul, smiling.

"You know how truly I care for you, dear boy," said she, pressing his hand. "Beside, do you not think I must love you well to be willing to give you my Natalie ?"

"To give me ! To give me !" cried the girl, laughing and waving a fan of Indian feathers. "What are you whispering about ?"

"I," said Paul, "was saying how well I love you—since the proprieties forbid my expressing my hopes to you."

" Why ? "

" I am afraid of myself."

" Oh ! you are too clever not to know how to set the gems of flattery. Would you like me to tell you what I think of you ? Well, you seem to me to have more wit than a man in love should show. To be Sweet-pea and at the same time very clever," said she, looking down, " seems to me an unfair advantage. A man ought to choose between the two. I, too, am afraid."

" Of what ? "

" We will not talk like this. Do not you think, mother, that there is danger in such a conversation when the contract is not yet signed ? "

" But it will be," said Paul.

" I should very much like to know what Achilles and Nestor are saying to each other," said Natalie, with a glance of child-like curiosity at the door of the adjoining room.

" They are discussing our children, our death, and I know not what trifles beside," said Paul. " They are counting out our crown-pieces, to tell us whether we may have five horses in the stable. And they are considering certain deeds of gift, but I have forestalled them there."

" How ? " said Natalie.

" Have I not given you myself wholly and all I have ? " said he, looking at the girl, who was handsomer than ever as the blush brought up by her pleasure at this reply mounted to her cheeks.

" Mother, how am I to repay such generosity ? "

" My dear child, is not your life before you ? If you make him happy every day, is not that a gift of inexhaustible treasures ? I had no other fortune."

" Do you like Lanstrac ? " asked Paul.

" How can I fail to like anything that is yours ? " said she. " And I should like to see your house."

" Our house," said Paul. " You want to see whether I

have anticipated your tastes, if you can be happy there? Your mother has made your husband's task a hard one; you have always been so happy; but when love is infinite, nothing is impossible."

"Dear children," said Madame Evangelista, "do you think you can remain in Bordeaux during the early days of your marriage? If you feel bold enough to face the world that knows you, watches you, criticises you—well and good! But if you both have that coyness which dwells in the soul and finds no utterance, we will go to Paris, where the life of a young couple is lost in the torrent. There only can you live like lovers without fear of ridicule."

"You are right, mother; I had not thought of it. But I shall hardly have time to get the house ready. I will write this evening to de Marsay, a friend on whom I can rely, to hurry on the workmen."

At the very moment when, like all young men who are accustomed to gratify their wishes without any preliminary reflection, Paul was recklessly pledging himself to the expenses of a residence in Paris, Maître Mathias came into the room and signed to his client to come and speak with him.

"What is it, my good friend?" said Paul, allowing himself to be led aside.

"Monsieur le Comte," said the worthy man, "the lady has not a sou. My advice is to put off this discussion till another day to give you the opportunity of acting with propriety."

"Monsieur Paul," said Natalie, "I also should like a private word with you."

Though Madame Evangelista's face was calm, no Jew in the Dark Ages ever suffered greater martyrdom in his caldron of boiling oil than she in her violet velvet dress. Solonet had pledged himself to the marriage, but she knew not by what means and conditions he meant to succeed, and she endured the most dreadful anguish of alternative courses. She

really owed her triumph, perhaps, to her daughter's disobedi-
ence.

Natalie had put her own interpretation on her mother's
words, for she could not fail to see her uneasiness.   When she
perceived the effect of her advances, her mind was torn by a
thousand contradictory thoughts.   Without criticising her
mother, she felt half ashamed of this manœuvring, of which
the result was obviously to be some definite advantage.   Then
she was seized by a very intelligible sort of jealous curiosity.
She wanted to ascertain whether Paul loved her well enough
to overlook the difficulties her mother had alluded to, and of
which the existence was proved by Maître Mathias' cloudy
brow.   These feelings prompted her to an impulse of honesty
which, in fact, became her well.   The blackest perfidy would
have been less dangerous than her innocence was.

"Paul," said she in an undertone, and it was the first time
she had addressed him by his name, "if some difficulties of
money matters could divide us, understand that I release you
from every pledge, and give you leave to ascribe to me all the
blame that could arise from such a separation."

She spoke with such perfect dignity in the expression of her
generosity that Paul believed in her disinterestedness and
her ignorance of the fact which the notary had just communicated to him; he pressed the girl's hand, kissing it like
a man to whom love is far dearer than money.

Natalie left the room.

"Bless me ! Monsieur le Comte, you are committing great
follies," growled the old notary, rejoining his client.

But Paul stood pensive ; he had expected to have an income
of about a hundred thousand francs by uniting his fortune
and Natalie's ; and however blindly in love a man may be,
he does not drop without a pang from a hundred thousand to
forty-six thousand francs a year when he marries a woman
accustomed to every luxury.

"My daughter then is gone," said Madame Evangelista,

advancing with royal dignity to where Paul and the notary were standing. " Can you not tell me what is going on ! "

" Madame," said Mathias, dismayed by Paul's silence, and forced to break the ice, " an impediment—a delay——"

On this, Maître Solonet came out of the inner room and interrupted his senior with a speech that restored Paul to life. Overwhelmed by the recollection of his own devoted speeches and lover-like attitude, Paul knew not how to withdraw or to modify them; he only longed to fling himself into some yawning gulf.

" There is a way of releasing Madame Evangelista from her debt to her daughter," said the young lawyer with airy ease. " Madame Evangelista holds securities for forty thousand francs yearly in five per cents.; the capital will soon be at par, if not higher ; we may call it eight hundred thousand francs. This house and garden are worth certainly two hundred thousand. Granting this, madame may, under the marriage-contract, transfer the securities and title-deeds to her daughter, reserving only the life-interest, for I cannot suppose that the count wishes to leave his mother-in-law penniless. Though madame has spent her own fortune, she will thus restore her daughter's, all but a trifling sum."

" Women are most unfortunate when they do not understand business," said Madame Evangelista. " I have securities and title-deeds? What in the world are they?"

Paul was enraptured as he heard this proposal. The old lawyer, seeing the snare spread and his client with one foot already caught in it, stood petrified, saying to himself—

" I believe we are being tricked ! "

" If madame takes my advice, she will at least secure peace," the younger man went on. " If she sacrifices herself, at least she will not be worried by the young people. Who can foresee who will live or die? Monsieur le Comte will then sign a release for the whole sum due to Mademoiselle Evangelista out of her father's fortune."

Mathias could not conceal the wrath that sparkled in his eyes and crimsoned his face.

"A sum of——?" he asked, trembling with indignation.

"Of one million one hundred and fifty-six thousand francs, according to the deed——"

"Why do you not ask Monsieur le Comte *hic et nunc* (here and now) to renounce all claims on his wife's fortune?" said Mathias. "It would be more straightforward. Well, Monsieur le Comte de Manerville's ruin shall not be accomplished under my eyes. I beg to withdraw."

He went a step toward the door, to show his client that the matter was really serious. But he turned back, and, addressing Madame Evangelista, he said—

"Do not suppose, madame, that I imagine you to be in collusion with my colleague in his ideas. I believe you to be an honest woman—a fine lady, who knows nothing of business."

"Thank you, my dear sir!" retorted Solonet.

"You know that there is no question of offense among lawyers," said Mathias. "But at least, madame, let me explain to you the upshot of this bargain. You are still young enough and handsome enough to marry again. Oh, dear me!" he went on, in reply to a gesture of the lady's, "who can answer for the future?"

"I never thought, monsieur," said she, "that after seven years of widowhood in the prime of life, and after refusing some splendid offers for my daughter's sake, I should, at nine-and-thirty, be thought capable of such madness. If we were not discussing business, I should regard such a speech as an impertinence."

"Would it not be a greater impertinence to assume that you could not remarry?"

"Can and will are very different words," said Solonet, with a gallant flourish.

"Well," said Mathias, "we need not talk about your marrying. You may—and we all hope you will—live for five-and-forty years yet. Now, since you are to retain your life-interest in the income left by Monsieur Evangelista as long as you live, must your children dine with Duke Humphrey?"*

"What is the meaning of it all?" said the widow. "Who is Duke Humphrey, and what is life-interest?"

Solonet, a speaker of elegance and taste, began to laugh.

"I will translate," said the old man: "If your children wish to be prudent, they will think of the future. To think of the future means to save half one's income, supposing there are no more than two children, who must first have a good education, and then a handsome marriage-portion. Thus, your daughter and her husband will be reduced to living on twenty thousand francs a year when they have each been accustomed to spend fifty thousand while unmarried. And even that is nothing. My client will be expected to hand over to his children in due course eleven hundred thousand francs as their share of their mother's fortune, and he will never have received any of it if his wife should die and madame survive her—which is quite possible. In all conscience, is not this to throw himself into the Gironde, tied hand and foot? You wish to see Mademoiselle Natalie made happy? If she loves her husband—which no lawyer allows himself to doubt—she will share his troubles. Madame, I foresee enough to make her die of grief, for she will be miserably poor. Yes, madame, miserably poor; for it is poverty to those who require a hundred thousand francs a year to be reduced to twenty thousand. If love should lead Monsieur le Comte into extravagance, his wife would reduce him to beggary by claiming her share in the event of any disaster.

"I am arguing for your sake, for theirs, for that of their children—for all parties."

"The good man has certainly delivered a broadside," thought Solonet, with a glance at his client, as much as to say: "Come on!"

* To go hungry.

"There is a way of reconciling all these interests," replied Madame Evangelista calmly. "I may reserve only such a small allowance as may enable me to go into a convent, and you will become at once possessed of all my property. I will renounce the world if my death to it will secure my daughter's happiness."

"Madame," said the old man, "let us take time for mature consideration of the steps that may smooth away all difficulties."

"Bless me, my dear sir," cried Madame Evangelista, who foresaw that by delay she would be lost, "all has been considered. I did not know what marriage meant in France; I am a Spanish creole. I did not know that before I could see my daughter married I had to make sure how many days longer God would grant me to live, that my child would be wronged by my living, that I have no business to be alive or ever to have lived!

"When my husband married me I had nothing but my name and myself. My name was to him a treasure beside which his wealth paled. What fortune can compare with a great name? My fortune was my beauty, virtue, happy temper, birth, and breeding. Can money buy these gifts? If Natalie's father could hear this discussion, his magnanimous spirit would be grieved forever and his happiness would be marred in paradise. I spent millions of francs, foolishly I daresay, without his ever frowning even. Since his death I have been economical and thrifty by comparison with the life he liked me to lead. Let this end it! Monsieur de Manerville is so dejected that I——"

No words can represent the confusion and excitement produced by this exclamation "end it!" It is enough to say that these four well-bred persons all talked at once.

"In Spain you marry Spanish fashion, as you will; but in France you marry French fashion—rationally, and as you can," said Mathias.

"Ah, madame," Paul began, rousing himself from his stupor, "you are mistaken in my feelings——"

"This is not a question of feelings," said the old man, anxious to stop his client; "this is business affecting three generations. Was it we who made away with the missing millions—we, who merely ask to clear up the difficulties of which we are innocent?"

"Let us marry without further haggling," said the wily Maître Solonet.

"Haggling! Haggling! Do you call it haggling to defend the interests of the children and of their father and mother?" cried Mathias.

"Yes," Paul went on, addressing his mother-in-law, "I deplore the recklessness of my youth, which now hinders my closing this discussion with a word, as much as you deplore your ignorance of business matters and involuntary extravagance. God be my witness that at this moment I am not thinking of myself; a quiet life at Lanstrac has no terrors for me; but Mademoiselle Natalie would have to give up her tastes and habits. That would alter our whole existence."

"But where did Evangelista find his millions?" said the widow.

"Monsieur Evangelista was a man of business, he played the great game of commerce, he loaded ships and made considerable sums; we are a landed proprietor, our capital is sunk, and our income more or less fixed," the old lawyer replied.

"Still, there is a way out of the difficulty," said Solonet, speaking in a high-pitched key, and silencing the other three by attracting their attention and their eyes.

The young man was like a dexterous coachman who, holding the reins of a four-in-hand, amuses himself by lashing and, at the same time, holding in the team. He spurred their passions and soothed them by turns, making Paul foam in his harness, for to him life and happiness were in the balance;

and his client as well, for she did not see her way through the intricacies of the dispute.

"Madame Evangelista may, this very day, hand over the securities in the five per cents., and sell this house. Sold in lots, it will fetch three hundred thousand francs. Madame will pay you one hundred and fifty thousand francs. Thus, madame will pay down nine hundred and fifty thousand francs at once. Though this is not all she owes her daughter, can you find many fortunes to match it in France?"

"Well and good," said Mathias; "but what is madame to live on?"

At this question, which implied assent, Solonet said within himself—

"Oh, ho! old fox, so you are caught."

"Madame?" he said aloud. "Madame will keep the fifty thousand crowns left of the price of the house. That sum, added to the sale of her furniture, can be invested in an annuity, and will give her twenty thousand francs a year. Monsieur le Comte will arrange for her to live with him. Lanstrac is a large place. You have a good house in Paris," he went on, addressing Paul, "so madame your mother-in-law can live with you wherever you are. A widow who, having no house to keep up, has twenty thousand francs a year, is better off than madame was when she was mistress of all her fortune. Madame Evangelista has no one to care for but her daughter; Monsieur le Comte also stands alone; your heirs are in the distant future, there is no fear of conflicting interests.

"A son-in-law and a mother-in-law under such circumstances always join to form one household. Madame Evangelista will make up for the deficit of capital by paying a quota out of her annuity which will help toward the housekeeping. We know her to be too generous, too large-minded, to live as a charge on her children.

"Thus, you may live happy and united with a hundred thousand francs a year to spend—a sufficient income, surely,

Monsieur le Comte, to afford you, in any country, all the comforts of life and the indulgence of your fancies. And, believe me, young married people often feel the need of a third in the household. Now, I ask you, what third can be more suitable than an affectionate, good mother?"

Paul, as he listened to Solonet, thought he heard the voice of an angel. He looked at Mathias to see if he did not share his admiration for Solonet's fervid eloquence: for he did not know that, under the assumed enthusiasm of impassioned words, notaries, like attorneys, hide the cold and unremitting alertness of the diplomatist.

"A pretty paradise!" said the old man.

Bewildered by his client's delight, Mathias sat down on an ottoman, resting his head on one hand, lost in evidently grieved meditations. He knew too well the ponderous phrases in which men of business purposely shroud their tricks, and he was not the man to be duped by them. He stole a glance at his fellow-notary and at Madame Evangelista, who went on talking to Paul, and he tried to detect some indications of the plot of which the elaborate design was beginning to be perceptible.

"Monsieur," said Paul to Solonet, "I have to thank you for the care you have devoted to the conciliation of our interests. This arrangement solves all difficulties more happily than I had dared to hope—that is to say, if it suits you, madame," he added, turning to Madame Evangelista, "for I will have nothing to say to any plan that is not equally satisfactory to you."

"I?" said she. "Whatever will make my children happy will delight me. Do not consider me at all."

"But that must not be," said Paul eagerly. "If your comfort and dignity were not secured, Natalie and I would be more distressed about it than you yourself could be."

"Do not be uneasy on that score, Monsieur le Comte," said Solonet.

"Ah!" thought Maître Mathias, "they mean to make him kiss the rod before they scourge him."

"Be quite easy," Solonet went on; "there is such a spirit of speculation in Bordeaux just now that investments for annuities are to be made on very advantageous terms. After handing over to you the fifty thousand crowns due to you on the sale of the house and furniture, I believe I may guarantee to madame a residue of two hundred thousand francs. This I undertake to invest in an annuity on a first mortgage on an estate worth a million, and to get ten per cent., twenty-five thousand francs a year. Thus we should unite two very nearly equal fortunes. Mademoiselle Natalie will bring forty thousand francs a year in five per cents. and a hundred and fifty thousand francs in money, which will yield seven thousand francs a year: total, forty-seven as against your forty-six thousand."

"That is quite plain," said Paul.

As he ended his speech, Solonet had cast a side-long glance at his client, not unseen by Mathias, and which was as much as to say:

"Bring up your reserves."

"Why!" cried Madame Evangelista in a tone of joy that seemed quite genuine, "I can give Natalie my diamonds; they must be worth at least a hundred thousand francs."

"We can have them valued," said Solonet, "and this entirely alters the case. Nothing, then, can hinder Monsieur le Comte from giving a discharge in full for the sums due to Mademoiselle Natalie as her share of her father's fortune, or the betrothed couple from taking the guardian's accounts as passed, at the reading of the contract. If madame, with truly Spanish magnificence, despoils herself to fulfill her obligations within a hundred thousand francs of the sum-total, it is but fair to release her."

"Nothing could be fairer," said Paul. "I am only overpowered by so much generosity."

"Is not my daughter my second self?" said Madame Evangelista.

Maître Mathias detected an expression of joy on Madame Evangelista's face when she saw the difficulties so nearly set aside; and this, and the sudden recollection of the diamonds, brought out like fresh troops, confirmed all his suspicions.

"The scene was planned between them," thought he, "as gamblers pack the cards when some pigeon is to be rooked. So the poor boy I have known from his cradle is to be plucked alive by a mother-in-law, done brown by love, and ruined by his wife? After taking such care of his fine estate, am I to see it gobbled up in a single evening? Three and a half millions mortgaged, in fact, to guarantee eleven hundred thousand francs of her portion, which these two women will make him throw away."

As he thus discerned in Madame Evangelista's soul a scheme which was not dishonest or criminal—which was not thieving, or cheating, or swindling—which was not based on any evil or blamable feeling, but yet contained the germ of every crime, Maître Mathias was neither shocked nor generously indignant. He was not a misanthrope; he was an old lawyer, inured by his business to the keen self-interest of men of the world, to their ingenious treachery, more deadly than a bold highway murder committed by some poor devil who is guillotined with due solemnity. In the higher ranks these passages of arms, these diplomatic discussions, are like the little dark corners into which every kind of filth is shot.

Maître Mathias, very sorry for his client, cast a long look into the future, and saw no hope of good.

"Well, we must take the field with the same weapons," said he to himself, "and beat them on their own ground."

At this juncture Paul, Solonet, and Madame Evangelista, dismayed by the old man's silence, were feeling the necessity of this stern censor's approbation to sanction these arrangements, and all three looked at him.

" Well, my dear sir, and what do you think of this?'' asked
Paul.

" This is what I think,'' replied the uncompromising and
conscientious old man, " you are not rich enough to commit
such princely follies. The estate of Lanstrac, valued at three
per cent., is worth one million of francs, including the furniture; the farms of le Grassol and le Guadet, with the vineyards of Bellerose, are worth another million; your two
residences and furniture a third million. To meet these three
millions, yielding an income of forty-seven thousand two
hundred francs, Mademoiselle Natalie shows eight hundred
thousand francs in the Funds, and let us say one hundred thousand francs' worth of diamonds—at a hypothetical valuation!
Also, one hundred and fifty thousand francs in cash—one
million and fifty thousand francs in all. Then, in the face of
these facts, my friend here triumphantly asserts that we are
uniting equal fortunes! He requires us to stand indebted in
a hundred thousand francs to our children, since we are to
give the lady a discharge in full, by taking the guardian's
accounts as passed, for a sum of eleven hundred and fifty-six
thousand francs, while receiving only one million and fifty
thousand !

"You can listen to this nonsense with a lover's rapture;
and do you suppose that old Mathias, who is not in love, will
forget his arithmetic and fail to appreciate the difference
between landed estate of enormous value as capital, and of
increasing value, and the income derivable from money in
securities which are liable to fluctuations in value and diminution of interest? I am old enough to have seen land improve
and funds fall. You called me in, Monsieur le Comte, to
stipulate for your interests; allow me to protect them or dismiss me.''

"If monsieur looks for a fortune of which the capital is a
match for his own,'' said Solonet, " we have nothing like
three millions and a half; that is self-evident. If you can

show these overpowering millions, we have but our one poor little million to offer—a mere trifle! three times as much as the dower of an archduchess of Austria. Bonaparte received two hundred and fifty thousand francs when he married Marie Louise.''

''Marie Louise ruined Napoleon,'' said Maître Mathias in a growl.

Natalie's mother understood the bearing of this speech.

''If my sacrifices are in vain,'' she exclaimed, ''I decline to carry such a discussion any further; I trust to the count's discretion, and renounce the honor of his proposals for my daughter.''

After the manœuvres planned by the young notary this battle of conflicting interests had reached the point where the victory ought to have rested with Madame Evangelista. The mother-in-law had opened her heart, abandoned her possessions, and was almost released. The intending husband was bound to accept the conditions laid down beforehand by the collusion of Maître Solonet and his client, or sin against every law of generosity, and be false to his love.

Like the hand of a clock moved by the works, Paul came duly to the point.

''What, madame,'' cried he, ''you could undo in one moment——''

''Why, monsieur, to whom do I owe my duty? To my daughter. When she is one-and-twenty she will pass my accounts and release me. She will have a million francs, and can, if she pleases, choose among the sons of the peers of France. Is she not the daughter of a Casa-Real?''

''Madame is quite justified. Why should she be worse off to-day than she will be fourteen months hence? Do not rob her of the benefits of her position,'' said Solonet.

''Mathias,'' said Paul, with deep grief, ''there are two ways of being ruined—and at this moment you have undone me!''

He went toward the old lawyer, no doubt intending to order that the contract should be at once drawn up. Mathias forefended this disaster by a glance which seemed to say, "Wait!" He saw tears in Paul's eyes—tears of shame at the tenor of this debate, and at the peremptory tone in which Madame Evangelista had thrown him over—and he checked them by a start, the start of Archimedes, successful in his search, crying EUREKA!

The words "Peer of France" had flashed light on his mind like a torch in a cavern.

At this instant Natalie reappeared, as lovely as the dawn, and said with an innocent air:

"Am I in the way?"

"Strangely in the way, my child!" replied her mother, with cruel bitterness.

"Come, dear Natalie," said Paul, taking her hand and leading her to a chair by the fire, "everything is settled!" for he could not endure to think that his hopes were overthrown.

And Mathias eagerly put in:

"Yes, everything can yet be settled."

Like a general who in one move baffles the tactics of the enemy, the old lawyer had had a vision of the Genius that watches over notaries, unfolding before him in legal script a conception that might save the future prospects of Paul and of his children. Maître Solonet knew of no other issue from these irreconcilable difficulties than the determination to which the young count had been led by love, and by this storm of contending feelings and interests; so he was excessively surprised by his senior's remark.

Curious to know what remedy Maître Mathias had to suggest for a state of things which must have seemed to him past all hope, he asked him:

"What have you to propose?"

24

"Natalie, my dear child, leave us," said Madame Evan-gelista.

"Mademoiselle is not *de trop*," replied Maître Mathias, with a smile. "I speak as much for her as for Monsieur le Comte."

There was a solemn silence, each one in great excitement awaiting the old man's speech with the utmost curiosity.

"In our day," Mathias went on after a pause, "the notary's profession has changed in many ways. In our day political revolutions affect the future prospects of families, and this used not to be the case. Formerly life ran in fixed grooves, ranks were clearly defined——"

"We are not here to listen to a lecture on political economy, but to arrange a marriage-contract," said Solonet, with a flippant impatience, and interrupting the old man.

"I beg you to allow me to speak in my turn," said Mathias.

Solonet took his seat on the ottoman, saying to Madame Evangelista in an undertone—

"Now you will learn what we lawyers mean by rigma-role."

"Notaries are consequently obliged to watch the course of politics, since they now are intimately concerned with private affairs. To give you an instance: Formerly noble families had inalienable fortunes, but the Revolution overthrew them; the present system tends to reconstructing such fortunes," said the old man, indulging somewhat in the twaddle of the *tabellionaris boa constrictor*. "Now, Monsieur le Comte, in virtue of his name, his talents, and his wealth, is evidently destined to sit some day in the lower Chamber; destiny may perhaps lead him to the upper and hereditary Chamber; and, as we know, he has every qualification that may justify our prognostics. Are you not of my opinion, madame?" said he to the widow.

"You have anticipated my dearest hope," said she.

" Manerville must be a peer of France, or I shall die of grief."

"All that may tend to that end——?" said Maître Mathias, appealing to the mother-in-law with a look of frank good-humor.

"Answers to my dearest wish," she put in.

" Well, then," said Mathias, " is not this marriage a fitting opportunity for creating an entail? Such a foundation will most certainly be an argument in the eyes of the present government for the nomination of my client when a batch of peers is created. Monsieur le Comte will, of course, dedicate to this purpose the estate of Lanstrac, worth about a million. I do not ask that mademoiselle should contribute an equal sum ; that would not be fair ; but we may take eight hundred thousand francs of her money for the purpose. I know of two estates for sale at this moment, bordering on the lands of Lanstrac, in which those eight hundred thousand francs, to be sunk in real estate, may be invested at four and a half per cent. The Paris house ought also to be included in the entail. The surplus of the two fortunes, wisely managed, will amply suffice to provide for the younger children. If the contracting parties can agree as to these details, Monsieur de Manerville may then pass your guardian's accounts and be chargeable for the balance. I will consent."

"*Questa coda non è di questo gatto !*" (this tail does not fit that cat) exclaimed Madame Evangelista, looking at her sponsor, Solonet, and pointing to Maître Mathias.

" There is something behind all this," said Solonet in an undertone.

"And what is all this muddle for?" Paul asked of Mathias, going with him into the adjoining room.

" To save you from ruin," said the old notary in a whisper. " You are quite bent on marrying a girl—and her mother— who have made away with two millions of francs in seven years ; you are accepting a debt of more than a hundred thou-

sand francs to your children, to whom you will some day have
to hand over eleven hundred and fifty-six thousand francs on
their mother's behalf, when you are receiving hardly a million.
You run the risk of seeing your whole fortune melt away in
five years, leaving you as bare as St. John the Baptist, while
you will remain the debtor in enormous sums to your wife and
her representatives. If you choose to embark in that boat, go
on, Monsieur le Comte; but at least allow your old friend to
save the house of Manerville."

"But how will this save it?" asked Paul.

"Listen, Monsieur le Comte; you are very much in love?"

"Yes," replied Paul.

"A man in love is about as secret as a cannon-shot; I will
tell you nothing! If you were to repeat things, your marriage might come to nothing, so I place your love under the
protection of my silence. You trust to my fidelity?"

"What a question!"

"Well, then, let me tell you that Madame Evangelista,
her notary, and her daughter were playing a trick on us all
through, and are more than clever. By heaven, what sharp
practice!"

"Natalie?" cried Paul.

"Well, I will not swear to that," said the old man. "You
want her—take her! But I wish this marriage might fall
through without the smallest blame to you!"

"Why?"

"That girl would beggar Peru. Beside, she rides like a
circus-rider; she is what you may call emancipated. Women
of that sort make bad wives."

Paul pressed his old friend's hand and replied with a little
fatuous smile.

"Don't be alarmed. And for the moment, what must
I do?"

"Stand firm to these conditions; they will consent, for the
bargain does not damage their interests. And beside, all

Madame Evangelista wants is to get her daughter married; I have seen her hand; do not trust her."

Paul returned to the drawing-room, where he found the widow talking in low tones to Solonet, just as he had been talking to Mathias. Natalie, left out of this mysterious conference, was playing with a screen. Somewhat out of countenance, she was wondering: "What absurdity keeps me from all knowledge of my own concerns?"

The younger lawyer was taking in the general outlines and remote effects of a stipulation based on the personal pride of the parties concerned, into which his client had blindly rushed. But though Mathias was now nothing else but a notary, Solonet was still to some degree a man, and carried some juvenile conceit into his dealings. It often happens that personal vanity makes a young lawyer forgetful of his client's interests. Under these circumstances, Maître Solonet, who would not allow the widow to think that Nestor was beating Achilles, was advising her to conclude the matter at once on these lines. Little did he care for the ultimate fulfillment of the contract; to him victory meant the release of Madame Evangelista with an assured income, and the marriage of Natalie.

"All Bordeaux will know that you have settled about eleven hundred thousand francs on your daughter, and that you still have twenty-five thousand francs a year," said Solonet in the lady's ear. "I had not hoped for such a brilliant result."

"But," said she, "explain to me why the creation of an entail should so immediately have stilled the storm."

"Distrust of you and your daughter. An entailed estate is inalienable: neither husband nor wife can touch it."

"That is a positive insult."

"Oh, no. We call that foresight. The good man caught you in a snare. If you refuse the entail, he will say: 'Then you want to squander my client's fortune;' whereas, if he creates an entail, it is out of all risk, just as if the couple were married under the provisions of the trust."

Solonet silenced his own scruples by reflecting—

"These stipulations will only take effect in the remote future, and by that time Madame Evangelista will be dead and buried."

She, for her part, was satisfied with Solonet's explanation; she had entire confidence in him.   She was perfectly ignorant of the law; she saw her daughter married, and that was all she asked for the nonce; she was delighted at their success. And so, as Mathias suspected, neither Solonet nor Madame Evangelista as yet understood the full extent of his plan, which had incontrovertible reasons to support it.

"Well, then, Monsieur Mathias," said the widow, "everything is satisfactory."

"Madame, if you and Monsieur le Comte agree to these conditions, you should exchange pledges.   It is fully understood by you both, is it not," he went on, "that the marriage takes place only on condition of the creation of an entail, including the estate of Lanstrac and the house in the Rue de la Pépinière, both belonging to the intending husband; *item :* eight hundred thousand francs deducted in money from the portion of the intending wife to be invested in land?   Forgive me, madame, for repeating this; a solemn and positive pledge is necessary in such a case.   The formation of an entail requires many formalities—it must be registered in Chancery and receive the royal signature; and we ought to proceed at once to the purchase of the lands, so as to include them in the schedule of property which the royal patent renders inalienable.   In many families a document would be required; but, as between you, verbal consent will no doubt be sufficient. Do you both consent?"

"Yes," said Madame Evangelista.

"Yes," said Paul.

"And how about me?" asked Natalie, laughing.

"You, mademoiselle, are a minor," replied Solonet, "and that need not distress you!"

It was then agreed that Maître Mathias should draw up the contract, and Maître Solonet audit the guardian's accounts, and that all the papers should be signed, in agreement with the law, a day or two before the wedding.

After a few civilities the lawyers rose.

"It is raining, Mathias; shall I take you home? I have my cab here," said Solonet.

"My carriage is at your service," said Paul, preparing to accompany the good man.

"I will not rob you of a minute," said the old man; "I will accept my friend's offer."

"Well," said Achilles to Nestor, as the carriage rolled on its way, "you have been truly patriarchal. Those young people would, no doubt, have ruined themselves."

"I was uneasy about the future," said Mathias, not betraying the real motive of his proposal.

At this moment the two lawyers were like two actors who shake hands behind the scenes after playing on the stage a scene of hatred and provocation.

"But is it not my business," said Solonet, who was thinking of technicalities, "to purchase the lands of which you speak? Is it not our money that is to be invested?"

"How can you include Mademoiselle Evangelista's land in an entail created by the Comte de Manerville?" asked Mathias.

"That difficulty can be settled in Chancery," said Solonet.

"But I am the seller's notary as well as the buyer's," replied Mathias. "Beside, Monsieur de Manerville can purchase in his own name. When it comes to paying, we can state the use of the wife's portion."

"You have an answer for everything, my worthy senior," said Solonet, laughing. "You have been grand this evening, and you have beaten us."

"Well, for an old fellow unprepared for your batteries loaded with grape-shot, it was not so bad, eh?"

"Ah, ha!" laughed Solonet.

The odious contest in which the happiness of a family had been so narrowly risked was to them no more than a matter of legal polemics. "We have not gone through forty years of chicanery for nothing," said Mathias. "Solonet," he added, "I am a good-natured fellow; you may be present at the sale and purchase of the lands to be added to the estate."

"Thank you, my good friend! You will find me at your service in case of need."

While the two notaries were thus peaceably going on their way, with no emotion beyond a little dryness of the throat, Paul and Madame Evangelista were suffering from the nervous trepidation, the fluttering about the heart, the spasm of brain and spine, to which persons of strong passions are prone after a scene when their interests or their feelings have been severely attacked. In Madame Evangelista these mutterings of the dispersing storm were aggravated by a terrible thought, a lurid gleam that needed explanation.

"Has not Maître Mathias overthrown my six months' labors?" she wondered. "Has he not destroyed my influence over Paul by filling him with base suspicions during their conference in the inner room?"

She stood in front of the fireplace, her elbow resting on the corner of the mantelpiece, lost in thought.

When the outer gate closed behind the notary's carriage, she turned to her son-in-law, eager to settle her doubts.

"This has been the most terrible day of my life," cried Paul, really glad to see the end of all these difficulties. "I know no tougher customer than old Mathias. God grant his wishes and make me peer of France! Dear Natalie, I desire it more for your sake than for my own. You are my sole ambition. I live in and for you."

On hearing these words spoken from the heart, and especially as she looked into Paul's clear eyes, whose look was as free from any concealment as his open brow, Madame Evangelista's joy was complete. She blamed herself for the somewhat sharp terms in which she had tried to spur her son-in-law, and in the triumph of success determined to make all smooth for the future. Her face was calm again, and her eyes expressed the sweet friendliness that made her so attractive as she replied—

" I may truly say the same. And perhaps, my dear boy, my Spanish temper carried me further than my heart intended. Be always what you are—as good as gold ! And owe me no grudge for a few ill-considered words. Give me your hand, let——"

Paul was overwhelmed ; he blamed himself in a thousand things, and embraced Madame Evangelista.

" Dear Paul," said she with emotion, " why could not those two scriveners arrange matters without us, since it has all come right in the end ? "

" But then," said Paul, " I should not have known how noble and generous you could be."

" Well said, Paul ! " cried Natalie, taking his hand.

" We have several little matters to settle yet, my dear boy," said Madame Evangelista. " My daughter and I are superior to the follies of which some people think so much. For instance, Natalie will need no diamonds—I give her mine."

" Oh ! my dear mother, do you suppose I should accept them ? " cried Natalie.

" Yes, my child, they are a condition of the contract."

" I will not have them ! I will never marry ! " said Natalie vehemently. " Keep what my father gave you with so much pleasure. How can Monsieur Paul demand——? "

" Be silent, dear child," said her mother, her eyes filling with tears ; " my ignorance of business requires far more than that."

" What ? "

" I must sell this house to pay you what I owe you."

"What can you owe to me," said the girl—"to me, who owe my life to you? Can I ever repay you? On the contrary, if my marriage is to cost you the smallest sacrifice, I will never marry!"

"You are but a child!"

"My dear Natalie," said Paul, "you must understand that it is neither I, nor you, nor your mother who insists on these sacrifices, but the children——"

"But if I do not marry," she interrupted.

"Then you do not love me?" said Paul.

"Come, silly child," said her mother; "do you suppose that a marriage-contract is a house of cards to be blown down at your pleasure? Poor ignorant darling, you do not know what trouble we have been at to create an entailed estate for your eldest son. Do not throw us back into the troubles from which we have escaped."

"But why ruin my mother?" said Natalie to Paul.

"Why are you so rich?" he said, with a smile.

"Do not discuss the matter too far, my children; you are not married yet," said Madame Evangelista. "Paul," she went on, "Natalie needs no wedding-gifts, no jewels, no trousseau; she has everything in profusion. Save the money you would have spent in presents to secure to yourselves some permanent home luxuries. There is nothing to my mind so foolishly vulgar as the expenditure of a hundred thousand francs in a *corbeille*,* of which nothing is left at last but an old white satin-covered trunk. Five thousand francs a year, on the other hand, as pin-money, save a young wife many small cares, and are hers for life. And indeed you will want the money of the *corbeille* to refurnish your house in Paris this winter. We will come back to Lanstrac in the spring; Solonet will have settled all our affairs in the course of the winter."

* The bridegroom's presents of lace, jewels, and apparel constitute the *corbeille* or "basket."

"Then all is well," said Paul, at the height of happiness.

"And I shall see Paris!" cried Natalie, in a tone that might indeed have alarmed a de Marsay.

"If that is quite settled, I will write to de Marsay to secure a box for the winter season at the Italian opera."

"You are most nice! I dared not ask it of you," said Natalie. "Marriage is a delightful institution if it gives husbands the power of guessing their wives' wishes."

"That is precisely what it is," said Paul. "But it is midnight—I must go."

"Why so early this evening?" said Madame Evangelista, who was lavish of the attentions to which men are so keenly alive.

Though the whole business had been conducted on terms of the most refined politeness, the effect of this clashing of interests had sown a germ of distrust and hostility between the lady and her son-in-law, ready to develop at the first spark of anger, or under the heat of a too strong display of feeling.

In most families the question of settlements and allowances under the marriage-contract is prone to give rise to these primitive conflicts, stirred up by wounded pride or injured feelings, by some reluctance to make any sacrifice, or the desire to minimize it. When a difficulty arises, must there not be a conqueror and a conquered? The parents of the plighted couple try to bring the affair to a happy issue; in their eyes it is a purely commercial transaction, allowing all the tricks, the profits, and the deceptions of trade. As a rule, the husband only is initiated into the secret of the transaction, and the young wife remains, as did Natalie, ignorant of the stipulations which make her rich or poor.

Paul, as he went home, reflected that, thanks to his lawyer's ingenuity, his fortune was almost certainly secured against ruin. If Madame Evangelista lived with her daughter, the household would have more than a hundred thousand francs

a year for ordinary expenses.   Thus his hopes of a happy life
would be realized.

"My mother-in-law seems to me a very good sort of
woman," he reflected, still under the influence of the wheedling ways by which Madame Evangelista had succeeded in
dissipating the clouds raised by the discussion.   "Mathias is
mistaken.   These lawyers are strange beings; they poison
everything.   The mischief was made by that contentious little
Solonet, who wanted to be clever."

While Paul, as he went to bed, was recapitulating the advantages he had won in the course of the evening, Madame
Evangelista was no less confident of having gained the victory.

"Well, darling mother, are you satisfied?" said Natalie,
following her mother into her bedroom.

"Yes, my love, everything has succeeded as I wished, and
I feel a weight taken off my shoulders, which crushed me this
morning.   Paul is really an excellent fellow.   Dear boy!
Yes, we can certainly give him a delightful life.   You will
make him happy, and I will take care of his political prospects.   The Spanish ambassador is an old friend of mine.   I
will renew my acquaintance with him and with several other
persons.   We shall soon be in the heart of politics, and all
will be well with us.   The pleasure for you, dear children;
for me the later and more serious occupations of life—the
game of ambition.

"Do not be alarmed at my selling this house; do you suppose we should ever return to Bordeaux?   To Lanstrac—yes.
But we shall spend every winter in Paris, where our true interests now lie.   Well, Natalie, was what I asked you so difficult to do?"

"My dear mother, I was ashamed at moments."

"Solonet advises me to buy an annuity with the price of
the house," said Madame Evangelista, "but I must make
some other arrangement.   I will not deprive you of one sou
of my capital."

"You were all very angry, I saw," said Natalie. "How was the storm appeased?"

"By the offer of my diamonds," replied her mother. "Solonet was in the right. How cleverly he managed the business! But fetch my jewel-box, Natalie. I never seriously inquired what those diamonds were worth. When I said a hundred thousand francs, it was absurd. Did not Madame de Gyas declare that the necklace and earrings your father gave me on the day of our wedding were alone worth as much? My poor husband was so lavish! And then the family diamond given by Philip II. to the Duke of Alva, and left to me by my aunt—the Discreto—was, I believe, valued then at four thousand quadruples."

Natalie brought out and laid on her mother's dressing-table pearl necklaces, sets of jewels, gold bracelets, gems of every kind, piling them up with the inexpressible satisfaction that rejoices the heart of some women at the sight of these valuables, with which, according to the Talmud, the fallen angels tempted the daughters of men, bringing up from the bowels of the earth these blossoms of celestial fires.

"Certainly," said Madame Evangelista, "although I know nothing of precious stones but how to accept them and wear them, it seems to me that these must be worth a great deal of money. And then, if we all live together, I can sell my plate, which is worth thirty thousand francs at the mere value of the silver. I remember when we brought it from Lima that was the valuation at the Custom House here. Solonet is right. I will send for Élie Magus. The Jew will tell me the value of these stones. I may perhaps escape sinking the rest of my capital in an annuity."

"What a beautiful string of pearls?" said Natalie, admiringly.

"I hope he will give you that if he loves you. Indeed, he ought to have all the stones reset and make them a present to you. The diamonds are yours by settlement. Well, good-night, my darling.   After such a fatiguing day, we both need sleep.''

The woman of fashion, the creole, the fine lady, incapable of understanding the conditions of a contract that was not yet drawn up, fell asleep in full content at seeing her daughter the wife of a man she could so easily manage, who would leave them to be on equal terms the mistresses of his house, and whose fortune, combined with their own, would allow of their living in the way to which they were accustomed.   Even after paying up her daughter, for whose whole fortune she was to receive a discharge, Madame Evangelista would still have enough to live upon.

" How absurd I was to be so worried!" said she to herself.   " I wish the marriage was over and done with.''

So Madame Evangelista, Paul, Natalie, and the two lawyers were all delighted with the results of this first meeting.   The *Te Deum* was sung in both camps—a perilous state of things! The moment must come when the vanquished would no longer be deluded.   To Madame Evangelista her son-in-law was conquered.

Next morning Élie Magus came to the widow's house, supposing, from the rumors current as to Mademoiselle Natalie's approaching marriage to Count Paul, that they wanted to purchase diamonds.   What, then, was his surprise on learning that he was wanted to make a more or less official valuation of the mother-in-law's jewels.   The Jewish instinct, added to a few insidious questions, led him to conclude that the value was to be included in the property under the marriage-contract.

As the stones were not for sale, he priced them as a merchant selling to a private purchaser.   Experts alone know Indian diamonds from those of Brazil.   The stones from Golconda and Vizapur are distinguishable by a whiteness and clear brilliancy which the others have not, their hue being yellower, and this depreciates their selling value. Madame Evangelista's necklace and earrings, being entirely composed of Asiatic stones, were valued by Élie Magus at two hundred and fifty thousand francs. As to the Discreto, it was, he said, one of the finest diamonds extant in private hands, and was worth a hundred thousand francs.

On hearing these figures, which showed her how liberal her husband had been, Madame Evangelista asked whether she could have that sum at once."

"If you wish to sell them, madame," said the Jew, "I can only give you seventy thousand francs for the single stone, and a hundred and sixty thousand for the necklace and earrings."

"And why such a reduction?" asked Madame Evangelista in surprise.

"Madame," said he, "the finer the jewels, the longer we have to keep them. The opportunities for sale are rare in proportion to the greater value of the diamonds. As the dealer cannot afford to lose the interest on his money, the recoupment for that interest, added to the risks of rise and fall in the market, accounts for the difference between the selling and purchasing value. For twenty years you have been losing the interest of three hundred thousand francs. If you have worn your diamonds ten times a year, it has cost you a thousand crowns each time. How many handsome dresses you might have had for a thousand crowns! Persons who keep their diamonds are fools; however, happily for us, ladies do not understand these calculations."

"I am much obliged to you for having explained them to me; I will profit by the lesson."

"Then you want to sell?" cried the Jew eagerly.

"What are the rest worth?" said Madame Evangelista.

The Jew examined the gold of the settings, held the pearls to the light, turned over the rubies, the tiaras, brooches, bracelets, clasps, and chains, and mumbled out—

"There are several Portuguese diamonds brought from Brazil. I cannot give more than a hundred thousand francs for the lot. But sold to a customer," he added, "they would fetch more than fifty thousand crowns."

"We will keep them," said the lady.

"You are wrong," replied Élie Magus. "With the income of the sum now sunk in them, in five years you could buy others just as fine, and still have the capital."

This rather singular interview was soon known, and confirmed the rumors to which the discussion of the contract had given rise. In a provincial town everything is known. The servants of the house, having heard loud voices, supposed the dispute to have been warmer than it was; their gossip with other people's servants spread far and wide, and from the lower depths came up to the masters. The attention of the upper and citizen circles was concentrated on the marriage of two persons of equal wealth. Everybody, great and small, talked the matter over, and within a week the strangest reports were afloat in Bordeaux. Madame Evangelista was selling her house, so she must be ruined. She had offered her diamonds to Élie Magus. Nothing was yet final between her and the Comte de Manerville. Would the marriage ever come off? Some said Yes; others said No. The two lawyers, on being questioned, denied these calumnies, and said that the difficulties were purely technical, arising from the formalities of creating an entail.

But when public opinion has rushed down an incline, it is very difficult to get it up again. Though Paul went every day to Madame Evangelista's, and in spite of the assertions of the two notaries, the insinuated slander held its own. Several young ladies, and their mothers or their aunts, aggrieved by a match of which they or their families had dreamed for themselves, could no more forgive Madame Evangelista for her good-luck than an author forgives his friend for a success. Some were only too glad to be avenged for the twenty years of luxury and splendor by which the Spaniards had crushed their vanities. A bigwig at the prefecture declared that the two notaries and the two parties concerned could say no more, nor behave otherwise, if the rupture were complete. The time it took to settle the entail confirmed the suspicions of the citizens of Bordeaux.

"They will sit by the chimney-corner all the winter; then, in the spring, they will go to some watering-place; and in the course of the year we shall hear that the match is broken off."

"You will see," said one set, "in order to save the credit of both parties, the obstacles will not have arisen on either side; there will be some demur in Chancery, some hitch discovered by the lawyers to hinder the entail."

"Madame Evangelista," said the others, "has been living at a rate that would have exhausted the mines of Valenciana. Then, when pay-day came round there was nothing to be found."

What a capital opportunity for calculating the handsome widow's expenditure, so as to prove her ruin to a demonstration! Rumor ran so high that bets were laid for and against the marriage. And, in accordance with the accepted rules of society, this tittle-tattle remained unknown to the interested parties. No one was sufficiently inimical to Paul or Madame Evangelista to attack them on the subject.

Paul had some business at Lanstrac and took advantage of it to make up a shooting-party, inviting some of the young men of the town as a sort of farewell to his bachelor life. This shooting-party was regarded by society as a flagrant confirmation of its suspicions.

At this juncture Madame de Gyas, who had a daughter to marry, thought it well to sound her way, and to rejoice sadly over the checkmate offered to Madame Evangelista. Natalie and her mother were not a little astonished to see the marquise's badly assumed distress, and asked her if anything had annoyed her.

25

"Why," said she, "can you be ignorant of the reports current in Bordeaux? Though I feel sure that they are false, I have come to ascertain the truth and put a stop to them, at any rate in my own circle of friends. To be the dupe or the accomplice of such a misapprehension is to be in a false position, in which no true friend can endure to remain."

"But what in the world is happening?" asked the mother and daughter.

Madame de Gyas then had the pleasure of repeating everybody's comments, not sparing her intimate friends a single dagger-thrust. Natalie and her mother looked at each other and laughed; but they quite understood the purpose and motives of their friend's revelation. The Spanish lady revenged herself much as Célimène did on Arsinoé.

"My dear—you who know what provincial life is—you must know of what a mother is capable when she has a daughter on her hands who does not marry, for lack of a fortune and a lover, of beauty and talent—for lack of everything sometimes! She would rob a diligence, she would commit murder, waylay a man at a street corner, and give herself away a hundred times, if she were worth giving. There are plenty such in Bordeaux, who are ready, no doubt, to attribute to us their thoughts and actions. Naturalists have described the manners and customs of many fierce animals, but they have overlooked the mother and daughter in quest of a husband. They are hyænas who, as the Psalmist has it, seek whom they may devour, and who add to the nature of the wild beast the intelligence of man and the genius of woman.

"That such little Bordeaux spiders as Mademoiselle de Belor, Mademoiselle de Trans, and their like, who have spread their nets for so long without seeing a fly, or hearing the least hum of wings near them—that they should be furious I understand, and I forgive them their venomous tattle. But that you, who have a title and money, who are not in the least provincial, who have a clever and accomplished daughter, pretty and free to pick and choose—that you, so far above everybody here by your Parisian elegance, should have taken such a tone, is really a matter of astonishment. Am I expected to account to the public for the matrimonial stipulations which our men of business have considered necessary under the political conditions which will govern my son-in-law's existence? Is the mania for public discussion to invade the privacy of family life? Ought I to have invited the fathers and mothers of your province, under sealed covers, to come and vote on the articles of our marriage-contract?"

A torrent of epigrams was poured out on Bordeaux.

Madame Evangelista was about to leave the town ; she could afford to criticise her friends and enemies, to caricature them, and lash them at will, having nothing to fear from them. So she gave vent to all the remarks she had stored up, the revenges she had postponed, and her surprise that any one should deny the existence of the sun at noonday.

" Really, my dear," said the Marquise de Gyas, "Monsieur de Manerville's visit to Lanstrac, these parties to young men— under such circumstances——"

" Really, my dear," retorted the fine lady, interrupting her, "can you suppose that we care for the trumpery proprieties of a middle-class marriage? Am I to keep Count Paul in leading-strings, as if he would run away? Do you think he needs watching by the police? Need we fear his being spirited away by some Bordeaux conspiracy?"

" Believe me, my, dear friend, you give me infinite pleasure——"

The marquise was cut short in her speech by the manservant announcing Paul. Like all lovers, Paul had thought it delightful to ride eight leagues in order to spend an hour with Natalie. He had left his friends to their sport, and came in, booted and spurred, his whip in his hand.

" Dear Paul," said Natalie, " you have no idea how effectually you are answering madame at this moment."

When Paul heard the calumnies that were rife in Bordeaux, he laughed instead of being angry.

"The good people have heard, no doubt, that there will be none of the gay and uproarious doings usual in the country, no midday ceremony in church, and they are furious. Well, dear mother," said he, kissing Madame Evangelista's hand, "we will fling a ball at their heads on the day when the contract is signed, as a fête is thrown to the mob in the square of the Champs Élysées, and give our good friends the painful pleasure of such a signing as is rarely seen in a provincial city!"

This incident was of great importance. Madame Evangelista invited all Bordeaux on the occasion, and expressed her intention of displaying in this final entertainment a magnificence that should give the lie unmistakably to silly and false reports. She was thus solemnly pledged to the world to carry through this marriage.

The preparations for this ball went on for forty days, and it was known as the "evening of the camellias," there were such immense numbers of these flowers on the stairs, in the anteroom, and in the great supper-room. The time agreed with the necessary delay for the preliminary formalities of the marriage, and the steps taken in Paris for the settlement of the entail. The lands adjoining Lanstrac were purchased, the banns were published, and doubts were dispelled. Friends and foes had nothing left to think about but the preparation of their dresses for the great occasion.

The time taken up by these details overlaid the difficulties raised at the first meeting, and carried away into oblivion the words and retorts of the stormy altercation that had arisen over the question of the settlements. Neither Paul nor his mother-in-law thought any more of the matter. Was it not, as Madame Evangelista had said, the lawyers' business? But who is there that has not known, in the rush of a busy phase of life, what it is to be suddenly startled by the voice of memory, speaking too late, and recalling some important fact, some imminent danger?

On the morning of the day when the contract was to be signed, one of these will-o'-the-wisps of the brain flashed upon Madame Evangelista between sleeping and waking. The phrase spoken by herself at the moment when Mathias agreed to Solonet's proposal was, as it were, shouted in her ear: *Questa coda non è di questo gatto.* In spite of her ignorance of business, Madame Evangelista said to herself: "If that sharp old lawyer is satisfied, it is at the expense of one or other of the parties." And the damaged interest was certainly not on Paul's side, as she had hoped. Was it her daughter's fortune, then, that was to pay the costs of the war? She resolved to make full inquiries as to the tenor of the bargain, though she did not consider what she could do in the event of finding her own interests too seriously compromised.

The events of this day had so serious an influence on Paul's married life that it is necessary to give some account of the external details which have their effect on every mind.

As the house was forthwith to be sold, the Comte de Manerville's mother-in-law had hesitated at no expense. The forecourt was graveled, covered in with a tent, and filled with shrubs, though it was winter. The camellias, which were talked of from Dax to Angoulême, decked the stairs and vestibules. A wall had been removed to enlarge the supper-room and ballroom. Bordeaux, splendid with the luxury of many a colonial fortune, eagerly anticipated a fairy scene. By eight o'clock, when the business was drawing to a close, the populace, curious to see the ladies' dresses, formed a hedge on each side of the gateway. Thus the heady atmosphere of a great festivity excited all concerned at the moment of signing the contract. At the very crisis the little lamps fixed on yew-trees were already lighted, and the rumbling of the first carriages came up from the forecourt.

The two lawyers had dined with the bride and bridegroom and the mother-in-law. Mathias' head-clerk, who was to see the contract signed by certain of the guests in the course of the evening, and to take care that it was not read, was also one of the party.

The reader will rack his memory in vain—no dress, no woman was ever to compare with Natalie's beauty in her satin and lace, her hair beautifully dressed in a mass of curls falling about her neck ; she was like a flower in its natural setting of foliage.

Madame Evangelista, in a cherry-colored velvet, cleverly designed to set off the brilliancy of her eyes, her complexion, and her hair, with all the beauty of a woman of forty, wore her pearl necklace clasped with the famous Discreto, to give the lie to slander.

Fully to understand the scene, it is necessary to remark that Paul and Natalie sat by the fire on a little sofa, and never listened to one word of the guardian's accounts. One as much a child as the other, both equally happy, he in his hopes, she in her expectant curiosity, seeing life one calm blue heaven, rich, young, and in love, they never ceased whispering in each other's ears. Paul, already regarding his passion as legalized, amused himself with kissing the tips of Natalie's fingers, or just touching her snowy shoulders or her hair, hiding the raptures of these illicit joys from every eye. Natalie was playing with a fan of peacock feathers, a gift from Paul —a luckless omen in love, if we may accept the superstitious belief of some countries, as fatal as that of scissors, or any other cutting instrument, which is based, no doubt, on some association with the mythological Fates.

Madame Evangelista, sitting by the notaries, paid the closest attention to the reading of the two documents. After hearing the schedule of her accounts, very learnedly drawn out by Solonet, which showed a reduction of the three millions and some hundred thousand francs left by Monsieur Evangelista, to the famous eleven hundred and fifty-six thousand francs constituting Natalie's portion, she called out to the young couple—

"Come, listen, children ; this is your marriage-contract."

The clerk drank a glass of *eau de sucré*—sugared water ; Solonet and Mathias blew their noses ; Paul and Natalie looked at the four personages, listened to the preamble, and then began to talk together again. The statements of revenues ; the settlement of the whole estate on either party in the event of the other's death without issue ; the bequest, according to law, of one-quarter of the whole property absolutely to the wife, and of the interest of one-quarter more, however many children should survive ; the schedule of the property held in common ; the gift of the diamonds on the wife's part, and of the books and horses on the husband's—all passed without remark. Then came the settlement for the entail. And when everything had been read, and there was nothing to be done but to sign, Madame Evangelista asked what would be the effect of the entail.

"The entailed estate, madame, is inalienable ; it is property separated from the general estate of the married pair, and reserved for the eldest son of the house from generation to generation, without his being thereby deprived of his share of the rest of the property."

"And what are the consequences to my daughter?" she asked. Maître Mathias, incapable of disguising the truth, made reply—

"Madame, the entail being an inheritance derived from both fortunes, if the wife should be the first to die, and leaves one or several children, one of them a boy, Monsieur le Comte de Manerville will account to them for no more than three hundred and fifty-six thousand francs, from which he will deduct his one absolute fourth, and the fourth part of the interest of the residue. Thus their claim on him is reduced to about a hundred and sixty thousand francs independently of his share of profits on the common stock, the sums he could claim, etc. In the contrary case, if he should die first, leaving a son or sons, Madame de Manerville would be entitled to no more than three hundred and fifty-six thousand francs, to her share of all of Monsieur de Manerville's estate that is not included in the entail, to the restitution of her diamonds, and her portion of the common stock."

The results of Maître Mathias' profound policy were now amply evident.

"My daughter is ruined," said Evangelista in a low voice. The lawyers both heard her exclamation.

"Is it ruin," said Maître Mathias in an undertone, "to establish an indestructible fortune for her family in the future?"

As he saw the expression of his client's face, the younger notary thought it necessary to state the sum of the disaster in figures.

"We wanted to get three hundred thousand francs out of them, and they have evidently succeeded in getting eight hundred thousand out of us; the balance to their advantage on the contract is a loss of four hundred thousand francs to us for the benefit of the children. We must break it off or go on," he added to Madame Evangelista.

No words could describe the silence, though brief, that ensued. Mathias triumphantly awaited the signature of the two persons who had hoped to plunder his client. Natalie, incapable of understanding that she was bereft of half of her fortune, and Paul, not knowing that the house of Manerville was acquiring it, sat laughing and talking as before. Solonet and Madame Evangelista looked at each other, he concealing his indifference, she disguising a myriad angry feelings.

After suffering from terrible remorse, and regarding Paul as the cause of her dishonesty, the widow had made up her mind to certain discreditable manœuvres to cast the blunders of her guardianship on his shoulders, making him her victim. And now, in an instant, she had discovered that, instead of triumphing, she was overthrown, and that the real victim was her daughter. Thus guilty to no purpose, she was the dupe of an honest old man, whose esteem she had doubtless sacrificed. Was it not her own secret conduct that had inspired the stipulations insisted on by Mathias?

Hideous thought! Mathias had, doubtless, told Paul.

If he had not yet spoken, as soon as the contract should be signed that old wolf would warn his client of the dangers he had run and escaped, if it were only to gather the praises to which everybody is open. Would he not put him on his guard against a woman so astute as to have joined such an ignoble conspiracy? Would he not undermine the influence she had acquired over her son-in-law? And weak natures, once warned, turn obstinate, and never reconsider the circumstances.

So all was lost!

On the day when the discussion was opened, she had trusted to Paul's feebleness and the impossibility of his retreating after advancing so far. And now it was she who had tied her own hands. Paul, three months since, would not have had many obstacles to surmount to break off the marriage; now, all Bordeaux knew that the lawyers had, two months ago, smoothed away every difficulty. The banns were published; the wedding was fixed for the next day but one. The friends of both families, all the town were arriving, dressed for the ball—how could she announce a postponement? The cause of the rupture would become known, the unblemished honesty of Maître Mathias would gain credence, his story would be believed in preference to hers. The laugh would be against the Evangelistas, of whom so many were envious. She must yield!

These painfully accurate reflections fell on Madame Evangelista like a waterspout and crushed her brain. Though she maintained a diplomatic impassibility, her chin showed the nervous jerking by which Catherine II. betrayed her fury one day when, sitting on her throne and surrounded by her Court,

she was defied by the young King of Sweden under almost
similar circumstances. Solonet noted the spasmodic movement
of the muscles that proclaimed a mortal hatred, a storm without a sound or a lightning-flash; and in fact, at that moment,
the widow had sworn such hatred of her son-in-law, such an
implacable feud as the Arabs have left the germs of in the
atmosphere of Spain.

"Monsieur," said she to her notary, "you called this a
rigmarole—it seems to me that nothing can be clearer."

"Madame, allow me——"

"Monsieur," she went on, without listening to Solonet, "if
you did not understand the upshot of this bargain at the time
of our former discussion, it is at least extraordinary that you
should not have perceived it in the retirement of your study.
It cannot be from incapacity."

The young man led her into the adjoining room, saying to
himself—

"More than a thousand crowns are due to me for the
schedule of accounts, and a thousand more for the contract;
six thousand francs I can make over the sale of the house—
fifteen thousand francs in all. We must keep our temper."

He shut the door, gave Madame Evangelista the cold look
of a man of business, guessing the feelings that agitated her,
and said—

"Madame, how, when I have perhaps overstepped in your
behalf the due limits of finesse, can you repay my devotion by
such a speech?"

"But, monsieur——"

"Madame, I did not, it is true, fully estimate the amount
of our surrender; but if you do not care to have Count Paul
for your son-in-law, are you obliged to agree? The contract
is not signed. Give your ball and postpone the signing. It
is better to take in all Bordeaux than to be taken in yourself."

"And what excuse can I make to all the world—already
prejudiced against us—to account for this delay?"

"A blunder in Paris, a document missing," said Solonet.

" But the land that has been purchased ? "

" Monsieur de Manerville will find plenty of matches with money."

" He! Oh, he will lose nothing ; we are losing everything on our side."

" You," said Solonet, " may have a count, a better bargain, if the title is the great point of this match in your eyes."

" No, no ; we cannot throw our honor overboard in that fashion ! I am caught in a trap, monsieur. All Bordeaux would ring with it to-morrow. We have solemnly pledged ourselves."

" You wish Mademoiselle Natalie to be happy ? " asked Solonet.

" That is the chief thing."

" In France," said the lawyer, " does not being happy mean being mistress of the hearth ? She will lead that nincompoop Manerville by the nose. He is so stupid that he has seen nothing. Even if he should distrust you, he will still believe in his wife. And are not you and his wife one ? Count Paul's fate still lies in your hands."

" If you should be speaking truly, I do not know what I could refuse you ! " she exclaimed, with delight that glowed in her eyes.

" Come in again, then, madame," said Solonet, understanding his client. " But, above all, listen to what I say; you may regard me as incapable afterward if you please."

" My dear friend," said the young lawyer to Mathias, as he re-entered the room, " for all your skill you have failed to foresee the contingency of Monsieur de Manerville's death without issue, or, again, that of his leaving none but daughters. In either of those cases the entail would give rise to lawsuits with other Manervilles, for plently would crop up, do not doubt it for a moment. It strikes me, therefore, as desirable to stipulate that in the former case the entailed property should

be included in the general estate settled by each on either,
and in the second that the entail should be canceled as null
and void.   It is an agreement solely affecting the intending
wife."

"The clause seems to me perfectly fair," said Mathias.
"As to its ratification, Monsieur le Comte will make the
necessary arrangements with the Court of Chancery, no
doubt, if requisite."

The younger notary took a pen and wrote in on the margin
this ominous clause, to which Paul and Natalie paid no attention.   Madame Evangelista sat with downcast eyes while it
was read by Maître Mathias.

" Now to sign," said the mother.

The strong voice which she controlled betrayed vehement
excitement.   She had just said to herself—

" No, my daughter shall not be ruined—but he shall!   My
daughter shall have his name, title, and fortune.   If Natalie
should ever discover that she does not love her husband, if
some day she should love another man more passionately—
Paul will be exiled from France, and my daughter will be free,
happy, and rich."

Though Maître Mathias was expert in the analysis of
interests, he had no skill in analyzing human passions.   He
accepted the lady's speech as an honorable surrender, instead
of seeing that it was a declaration of war.   While Solonet
and his clerk took care that Natalie signed in full at the foot
of every document—a business that required some time—
Mathias took Paul aside and explained to him the bearing of
the clauses which he had introduced to save him from inevitable ruin.

"You have a mortgage on this house for a hundred and
fifty thousand francs," he said in conclusion, "and we fore-
close to-morrow.   I have at my office the securities in the
Funds, which I have taken care to place in your wife's name.
Everything is quite regular.   But the contract includes a

receipt for the sum represented by the diamonds; ask for them. Business is business. Diamonds are just now going up in the market; they may go down again. Your purchase of the lands of Auzac and Saint-Froult justifies you in turning everything into money so as not to touch your wife's income. So, no false pride, Monsieur le Comte. The first payment is to be made after the formalities are concluded; use the diamonds for that purpose; it amounts to two hundred thousand francs. You will have the mortgage value of this house for the second call, and the income on the entailed property will help you to pay off the remainder. If only you are firm enough to spend no more than fifty thousand francs for the first three years, you will recoup the two hundred thousand francs you now owe. If you plant vines on the hill-slopes of Saint-Froult, you may raise the returns to twenty-six thousand francs. Thus the entailed property, without including your house in Paris, will some day be worth fifty thousand francs a year—one of the finest estates I know of. And so you will have married very handsomely."

Paul pressed his old friend's hands with warm affection. The gesture did not escape Madame Evangelista, who came to hand the pen to Paul. Her suspicion was now certainty; she was convinced that Paul and Mathias had an understanding. Surges of blood, hot with rage and hatred, choked her heart. Paul was warned!

After ascertaining that every clause was duly signed, that the three contracting parties had initialed the bottom of every page with their usual sign-manual, Maître Mathias looked first at his client and then at Madame Evangelista, and observing that Paul did not ask for the diamonds, he said—

"I suppose there will be no question as to the delivery of the diamonds now that you are but one family?"

"It would, no doubt, be in order that Madame Evangelista should surrender them. Monsieur de Manerville has given his discharge for the balance of the trust values, and no one can tell who may die or live," said Maître Solonet, who thought this an opportunity for inciting his client against her son-in-law.

"Oh, my dear mother, it would be an affront to us if you did so!" cried Paul. *"Summum jus, summa injuria,* monsieur," said he to Solonet.

"And I, on my part," said she, her hostile temper regarding Mathias' indirect demand as an insult, "if you do not accept the jewels, will tear up the contract."

She went out of the room in one of those bloodthirsty furies which only long for the chance of wrecking everything, and which, when that is impossible, rise to the pitch of frenzy.

"In heaven's name, take them," whispered Natalie. "My mother is angry; I will find out why this evening, and will tell you; we will pacify her."

Madame Evangelista, quite pleased at this first stroke of policy, kept on her necklace and earrings. She brought the rest of the jewels, valued by Élie Magus at a hundred and fifty thousand francs. Maître Mathias and Solonet, though accustomed to handling family diamonds, exclaimed at the beauty of these jewels as they examined the contents of the cases.

"You will lose nothing of mademoiselle's fortune, Monsieur le Comte," said Solonet, and Paul reddened.

"Ay," said Mathias, "these jewels will certainly pay the first installment of the newly purchased land."

"And the expenses of the contract," said Solonet.

Hatred, like love, is fed on the merest trifles. Everything adds to it. Just as the one we love can do no wrong, the one we hate can do nothing right. Madame Evangelista scorned the hesitancy to which a natural reluctance gave rise in Paul as affected airs; while he, not knowing what to do with the jewel-cases, would have been glad to throw them out of the window. Madame Evangelista, seeing his embarrassment, fixed her eyes on him in a way which seemed to say: "Take them out of my sight!"

"My dear Natalie," said Paul to his fiancée, "put the jewels away yourself; they are yours; I make them a present to you."

Natalie put them into the drawers of a cabinet. At this instant the clatter of carriages and the voices of the guests waiting in the adjoining rooms required Natalie and her mother to appear among them. The rooms were immediately filled, and the ball began.

"Take advantage of the honeymoon to sell your diamonds," said the old notary to Paul, as he withdrew.

While waiting for the dancing to begin, everybody was discussing the marriage in lowered tones, some of the company expressing doubts as to the future prospects of the engaged couple.

"Is it quite settled?" said one of the magnates of the town to Madame Evangelista.

"We have had so many papers to read and hear read that we are late; but we may be excused," replied she.

"For my part, I heard nothing," said Natalie, taking Paul's hand to open the ball.

"Both those young people like extravagance, and it will not be the mother that will check them," said a dowager.

"But they have created an entail, I hear, of fifty thousand francs a year."

"Pooh!"

"I see that our good Maître Mathias has had a finger in the pie. And certainly, if that is the case, the worthy man will have done his best to save the future fortunes of the family."

"Natalie is too handsome not to be a desperate flirt. By the time she has been married two years, I will not answer for it that Manerville will not be miserable in his home," remarked a young wife.

"What, the peas will be 'snicked,' you think?" replied Maître Solonet.

" He needed no more than that tall pole," said a young lady.

" Does it not strike you that Madame Evangelista is not best pleased ? "

" Well, my dear, I have just been told that she has hardly twenty-five thousand francs a year, and what is that for her ? "

" Beggary, my dear."

" Yes, she has stripped herself for her daughter. Monsieur has been exacting——"

" Beyond conception ! " said Solonet. " But he is to be a peer of France. The Maulincours and the Vidame de Pamiers* will help him on ; he belongs to the Faubourg Saint-Germain."

" Oh, he visits there, that is all," said a lady, who had wanted him for her son-in-law. " Mademoiselle Evangelista, a merchant's daughter, will certainly not open the doors of the Chapter of Cologne to him."

" She is grand-niece to the Duc de Casa-Real."

" On the female side ! "

. All this tittle-tattle was soon exhausted. The gamblers sat down to cards, the young people danced, supper was served, and the turmoil of festivity was not silenced till morning, when the first streaks of dawn shone pale through the windows.

After taking leave of Paul, who was the last to leave, Madame Evangelista went up to her daughter's room, for her own had been demolished by the builder to enlarge the ballroom. Though Natalie and her mother were dying for sleep, they spoke a few words.

" Tell me, darling mother, what is the matter ? "

" My dear, I discovered this evening how far a mother's love may carry her. You know nothing of affairs, and you have no idea to what suspicions my honesty lies exposed.

* See "The Thirteen."

However, I have trodden my pride underfoot ; your happiness and our honor were at stake."

"As concerned the diamonds, you mean ? He wept over it, poor boy ! He would not take them ; I have them."

"Well, go to sleep, dearest child. We will talk business when we wake ; for we have business—and now there is a third to come between us," and she sighed.

"Indeed, dear mother, Paul will never stand in the way of our happiness," said Natalie, and she went to sleep.

"Poor child, she does not know that the man has ruined her ! "

Madame Evangelista was now seized in the grip of the first promptings of that avarice to which old folk at last fall a prey. She was determined to replace, for her daughter's benefit, the whole of the fortune left by her husband. She regarded her honor as pledged to this restitution. Her affection for Natalie made her in an instant as close a calculator in money matters as she had hitherto been a reckless spendthrift. She proposed to invest her capital in land after placing part of it in the State Funds, purchasable at that time for about eighty francs.

'A passion not infrequently produces a complete change of character ; the tattler turns diplomatic, the coward is suddenly brave. Hatred made the prodigal Madame Evangelista turn parsimonious. Money might help her in the schemes of revenge, as yet vague and ill-defined, which she proposed to elaborate. She went to sleep, saying to herself—

"To-morrow ! " and by an unexplained phenomenon, of which the effects are well known to philosophers, her brain during sleep worked out her idea, threw light on her plans, organized them, and hit on a way of ruling over Paul's life, devising a scheme which she began to work out on the very next day.

Though the excitement of the evening had driven away certain anxious thoughts which had now and again invaded

26

Paul, when he was alone once more and in bed they returned to torment him.

"It would seem," said he to himself, "that, but for that worthy Mathias, my mother-in-law would have taken me in. Is it credible? What interest could she have had in cheating me? Are we not to unite our incomes and live together? After all, what is there to be anxious about? In a few days Natalie will be my wife, our interests are clearly defined, nothing can sever us. On we go! At the same time, I will be on my guard. If Mathias should prove to be right—well, I am not obliged to marry my mother-in-law," and so thinking fell asleep.

In this second contest, Paul's future prospects had been entirely altered without his being aware of it. Of the two women he was marrying, far the cleverer had become his mortal enemy, and was bent on separating her own interests from his. Being incapable of appreciating the difference that the fact of her creole birth made between his mother-in-law's character and that of other women, he was still less able to measure her immense cleverness.

The creole woman is a being apart, deriving her intellect from Europe, and from the Tropics her vehemently illogical passions, while she is Indian in the apathetic indifference with which she accepts good or evil as it comes; a gracious nature too, but dangerous, as a child is when it is not kept in order. Like a child, this woman must have everything she wishes for, and at once; like a child, she would set a house on fire to boil an egg. In her flaccid every-day mood she thinks of nothing; when she is in a passion she thinks of everything. There is in her nature some touch of the perfidy caught from the negroes among whom she has lived from the cradle, but she is artless too, as they are. Like them, and like children, she can wish persistently for one thing with ever-growing intensity of desire, and brood over an idea till it hatches out. It is a nature strangely compounded of good and evil qualities;

and in Madame Evangelista it was strengthened by the Spanish temper, over which French manners had laid the polish of their veneer.

This nature, which had lain dormant in happiness for sixteen years, and had since found occupation in the frivolities of fashion, had discovered its own force under the first impulse of hatred, and flared up like a conflagration ; it had broken out at a stage in her life when a woman, bereft of what is dearest to her, craves some new material to feed the energies that are consuming her.

For three days longer Natalie would remain under her mother's influence. So Madame Evangelista, though vanquished, had still a day before her, the last her child would spend with her mother. By a single word the creole might color the lives of these two beings whose fate it was to walk hand in hand through the thickets and highways of Paris society—for Natalie had a blind belief in her mother. What far-reaching importance would a hint of advice have on a mind thus prepared ! The whole future might be modified by a sentence. No code, no human constitution, can forefend the moral crime of killing by a word. That is the weak point of social forms of justice. That is where the difference lies between the world of fashion and the people ; these are outspoken, those are hypocrites ; these snatch the knife, those use the poison of words and suggestions ; these are punished with death, those sin with impunity.

At about noon next day, Madame Evangelista was half sitting, half reclining on Natalie's bed. At this waking hour they were playing and petting each other with fond caresses, recalling the happy memories of their life together, during which no discord had troubled the harmony of their feelings, the agreement of their ideas, or the perfect union of their pleasures.

"Poor dear child," said the mother, shedding genuine tears, "I cannot bear to think that, after having had your own way all your life, to-morrow evening you will be bound to a man whom you must obey ! "

" Oh, my dear mother, as to obeying him ! " said Natalie, with a little willful nod expressive of pretty rebellion. " You laugh ! " she went on, " but my father always indulged your fancies. And why? Because he loved you. Shall not I be loved ? "

" Yes, Paul is in love with you. But if a married woman is not careful, nothing evaporates so quickly as conjugal affection. The influence a wife may preserve over her husband depends on the first steps in married life, and you will want good advice."

" But you will be with us."

" Perhaps, my dear child. Last evening, during the ball, I very seriously considered the risks of our being together. If my presence were to be disadvantageous to you, if the little details by which you must gradually confirm your authority as a wife should be ascribed to my influence, your home would become a hell. At the first frown on your husband's brow, should not I, so proud as I am, instantly quit the house? If I am to leave it sooner or later, in my opinion, I had better never enter it. I could not forgive your husband if he dis-united us.

" On the other hand, when you are the mistress, when your husband is to you what your father was to me, there will be less fear of any such misfortune. Although such a policy must be painful to a heart so young and tender as yours, it is indispensable for your happiness that you should be the abso-lute sovereign of your home."

" Why, then, dear mother, did you say I was to obey him ? "

" Dear little girl, to enable a woman to command, she must seem always to do what her husband wishes. If you did not know that, you might wreck your future life by an untimely rebellion. Paul is a weak man; he might come under the influence of a friend, nay, he might fall under the control of a woman, and you would feel the effects of their influence. Forefend such misfortunes by being mistress yourself. Will it not be better that you should govern him than that any one else should?"

"No doubt," said Natalie. "I could only aim at his happiness."

"And it certainly is my part, dear child, to think only of yours, and to endeavor that, in so serious a matter, you should not find yourself without a compass in the midst of the shoals you must navigate."

"But, my darling mother, are we not both of us firm enough to remain together under his roof without provoking the frowns you seem so much to dread? Paul is fond of you, mamma."

"Oh, he fears me more than he loves me. Watch him narrowly to-day when I tell him that I shall leave you to go to Paris without me, and, however carefully he may try to conceal his feelings, you will see his secret satisfaction in his face."

"But why?" said Natalie.

"Why, my child? I am like Saint-John-Chrysostom—I will tell him why, and before you."

"But since I am marrying him on the express condition that you and I are not to part?" said Natalie.

"Our separation has become necessary," Madame Evangelista replied. "Several considerations affect my future prospects. I am very poor. You will have a splendid life in Paris; I could not live with you suitably without exhausting the little possessions that remain to me; whereas, by living at Lanstrac, I can take care of your interests and reconstitute my own fortune by economy."

"You, mother! you economize?" cried Natalie, laughing. "Come, do not be a grandmother yet. What, would you part from me for such a reason as that? Dear mother, Paul may seem to you just a little stupid, but at least he is perfectly disinterested——''

"Well," replied Madame Evangelista, in a tone big with comment, which made Natalie's heart beat, "the discussion of the contract had made me suspicious and suggested some doubts to my mind. But do not be uneasy, dearest child," she went on, putting her arm round the girl's neck and clasping her closely, "I will not leave you alone for long. When my return to you can give him no umbrage, when Paul has learned to judge me truly, we will go back to our snug little life again, our evening chats——''

"Why, mother, can you live without your Ninie?" she asked, caressingly.

"Yes, my darling, because I shall be living for you. Will not my motherly heart be constantly rejoiced by the idea that I am contributing, as I ought, to your fortune and your husband's?"

"But, my dear, adorable mother, am I to be alone there with Paul? At once? Quite alone? What will become of me? What will happen? What ought I to do—or not to do?"

"Poor child, do you think I mean to desert you forthwith at the first battle? We will write to each other three times a week, like two lovers, and thus we shall always live in each other's heart. Nothing can happen to you that I shall not know, and I will protect you against all evil. And beside, it would be too ridiculous that I should not go to visit you; that would cast a reflection on your husband; I shall always spend a month or two with you in Paris——''

"Alone—alone with him, and at once!" cried Natalie in terror, interrupting her mother.

"Are you not to be his wife?"

"Yes, and I am quite content; but tell me at least how to behave. You, who did what you would with my father, know all about it, and I will obey you blindly."

Madame Evangelista kissed her daughter's forehead; she had been hoping and waiting for this request.

"My child, my advice must be adapted to the circumstances. Men are not all alike. The lion and the frog are less dissimilar than one man as compared with another, morally speaking. Do I know what will happen to you to-morrow? I can only give you general instructions as to your usual plan of conduct."

"Dearest mother, tell me at once all you know."

"In the first place, my dear child, the cause of ruin to married women who would gladly retain their husband's heart —and," she added, as a parenthesis, "to retain their affection and to rule the man are one and the same thing—well, the chief cause of matrimonial differences lies in the unbroken companionship, which did not subsist in former days, and which was introduced into this country with the mania for family life. Ever since the Revolution vulgar notions have invaded aristocratic households. This misfortune is attributable to one of their writers, Rousseau, a base heretic, who had none but reactionary ideas, and who—how I know not—argued out the most irrational conclusions. He asserted that all women have the same rights and the same faculties; that under the conditions of social life the laws of Nature must be obeyed—as if the wife of a Spanish Grandee—as if you or I—had anything in common with a woman of the people. And since then women of rank have nursed their own children, have brought up their daughters, and lived at home.

"Life has thus been made so complicated that happiness is almost impossible; for such an agreement of two characters as has enabled you and me to live together as friends is a rare exception. And perpetual friction is not less to be avoided between parents and children than between husband and wife. There are few natures in which love can survive in spite of omnipresence; that miracle is the prerogative of God.

"So place the barriers of society between you and Paul;
go to balls, to the opera, drive out in the morning, dine out
in the evening, pay visits; do not give Paul more than a few
minutes of your time. By this system you will never lose
your value in his eyes. When two beings have nothing but
sentiment to go through life on, they soon exhaust its resources, and ere long satiety and disgust ensue. Then, when
once the sentiment is blighted, what is to be done? Make no
mistake; when love is extinct, only indifference or contempt
ever fills its place. So be always fresh and new to him. If
he bores you—that may occur—at any rate, never bore him.
To submit to boredom on occasion is one of the conditions of
every form of power. You will have no occasion to vary your
happiness either by thrift in money matters or the management of a household; hence, if you do not lead your husband
to share your outside pleasures, if you do not amuse him, in
short, you will sink into the most crushing lethargy. Then
begins the spleen of love. But we always love those who
amuse us or make us happy. To give and to receive happiness are two systems of wifely conduct between which a gulf
lies."

"Dear mother, I am listening, but I do not understand."

"If you love Paul so blindly as to do everything he desires,
and if he makes you really happy, there is an end of it; you
will never be the mistress, and the wisest precepts in the world
will be of no use."

"That is rather clearer; but I learn the rule without knowing how to apply it," said Natalie, laughing. "Well, I have
the theory, and practice will follow."

"My poor Ninie," said her mother, dropping a sincere
tear as she thought of her daughter's marriage and pressed her
to her heart, "events will strengthen your memory. In short,
my Natalie," said she after a pause, during which they sat
clasped in a sympathetic embrace, "you will learn that each
of us, as a woman, has her destiny, just as every man has his

vocation. A woman is born to be a woman of fashion, the charming mistress of her house, just as a man is born to be a general or a poet. Your calling in life is to attract. And your education has fitted you for the world. In these days a woman ought to be brought up to grace a drawing-room, as of old she was brought up for the Gynæceum. You, child, were never made to be the mother of a family or a notable housekeeper.

"If you have children, I hope they will not come to spoil your figure as soon as you are married. Nothing can be more vulgar—and beside, it casts reflections on your husband's love for you. Well, if you have children two or three years hence, you will have nurses and tutors to bring them up. You must always be the great lady, representing the wealth and pleasures of the house ; but only show your superiority in such things as flatter men's vanity, and hide any superiority you may acquire in serious matters."

"You frighten me, mamma !" cried Natalie. "How am I ever to remember all your instructions? How am I, heedless and childish as I know I am, to reckon on results and always reflect before acting ?"

"My darling child, I am only telling you now what you would learn for yourself later, paying for experience by wretched mistakes, by misguided conduct, which would cause you many regrets and hamper your life."

"But how, then, am I to begin?" asked the handsome Natalie artlessly.

"Instinct will guide you," said her mother. "What Paul feels for you at this moment is far more desire than love ; for the love to which desire gives rise is hope, and that which follows its gratification is realization. There, my dear, lies your power, there is the heart of the question. What woman is not loved the day before marriage? Be still loved the day after, and you will be loved for life. Paul is weak; he will be easily formed by habit; if he yields once, he will yield al-

ways. A woman not yet won may insist on anything. Do
not commit the folly I have seen in so many wives, who, not
knowing the importance of the first hours of their sovereignty,
waste them in folly, in aimless absurdities. Make use of the
dominion given you by your husband's first passion to ac-
custom him to obey you. And to break him in, choose the
most unreasonable thing possible, so as to gauge the extent of
your power by the extent of his concession. What merit
would there be in making him agree to what is reasonable?
Would that be obeying you? 'Always take a bull by the
horns,' says a Castilian proverb. When once he sees the use-
lessness of his weapons and his strength, he is conquered. If
your husband commits a folly for your sake, you will master
him.''

"Good heavens ! But why ? ''

" Because, my child, marriage is for life, and a husband is
not like any other man. So never be so foolish as to give
way in anything whatever. Always be strictly reserved in
your speech and actions; you may even go to the point of
coldness, for that may be modified at pleasure, while there is
nothing beyond the most vehement expressions of love. A
husband, my dear, is the only man to whom a woman must
grant no license.

"And, after all, nothing is easier than to preserve your
dignity. The simple words, ' Your wife must not or cannot
do this thing or that,' is the great talisman. A woman's
whole life is wrapped up in ' I will not !—I cannot ! ' ' I
cannot ' is the irresistible appeal of weakness which succumbs,
weeps, and wins. ' I will not' is the last resort. It is the
crowning effort of feminine strength; it should never be used
but on great occasions. Success depends entirely on the way
in which a woman uses these two words, works on them, and
varies them.

" But there is a better method of rule than these, which
sometimes involve a contest. I, my child, governed by faith.

If your husband believes in you, you may do anything. To inspire him with this religion, you must convince him that you understand him. And do not think that this is such an easy matter. A woman can always prove that she loves a man, but it is more difficult to get him to confess that she has understood him. I must tell you everything, my child; for, to you, life with all its complications, a life in which two wills are to be reconciled and harmonized, will begin to-morrow. Do you realize the difficulty? The best way to bring two wills into agreement is to take care that there is but one in the house. People often say that a woman makes trouble for herself by this inversion of the parts; but, my dear, the wife is thus in a position to command events instead of submitting to them, and that single advantage counterbalances every possible disadvantage.''

Natalie kissed her mother's hands, on which she left her tears of gratitude. Like all women in whom physical passion does not fire the passion of the soul, she suddenly took in all the bearings of this lofty feminine policy. Still, like spoilt children who will never admit that they are beaten even by the soundest reasoning, but who reiterate their obstinate demands, she returned to the charge with one of those personal arguments that are suggested by the logical rectitude of children.

"My dear mother, a few days ago you said so much about the necessary arrangements for Paul's fortune, which you alone could manage; why have you changed your views in thus leaving us to ourselves?''

"I did not then know the extent of my indebtedness to you, nor how much I owed,'' replied her mother, who would not confess her secret. "Beside, in a year or two I can give you my answer.

"Now, Paul will be here directly. We must dress. Be as coaxing and sweet, you know, as you were that evening when we discussed that ill-starred contract, for to-day I am bent on saving a relic of the family, and on giving you a thing to which I am superstitiously attached."

"What is that?"

"The Discreto."

Paul appeared at about four o'clock. Though, when addressing his mother, he did his utmost to seem gracious, Madame Evangelista saw on his brow the clouds which his cogitations of the night and reflections on waking had gathered there.

"Mathias has told him," thought she, vowing that she would undo the old lawyer's work.

"My dear boy," she said, "you have left your diamonds in the cabinet drawer, and I honestly confess that I never want to see the things again which so nearly raised a storm between us. Beside, as Mathias remarked, they must be sold to provide for the first installment of payment on the lands you have purchased."

"The diamonds are not mine," rejoined Paul. "I gave them to Natalie, so that when you see her wear them you may never more remember the trouble they have caused you."

Madame Evangelista took Paul's hand and pressed it cordially, while restraining a sentimental tear.

"Listen, my dear, good children," said she, looking at Natalie and Paul. "If this is so, I will propose to make a bargain with you. I am obliged to sell my pearl necklace and earrings. Yes, Paul; I will not invest a centime in an annuity; I do not forget my duties to you. Well, I confess my weakness, but to sell the Discreto seems to me to portend disaster. To part with a diamond known to have belonged to Philip II., to have graced his royal hand—a historical gem which the Duke of Alva played with for ten years on the hilt of his sword—no, it shall never be. Élie Magus valued my necklace and earrings at a hundred-odd thousand francs; let us exchange them for the jewels I have handed over to you to cancel my debts to my daughter; you will gain a little, but what do I care; I am not grasping. And then, Paul, out of your savings you can have the pleasure of procuring a diadem or hairpins for Natalie, a diamond at a time. Instead of having one of those fancy sets, trinkets which are in fashion only among second-rate people, your wife will thus have magnificent stones that will give her real pleasure. If something must be sold, is it not better to get rid of these old-fashioned jewels, and keep the really fine things in the family?"

"But you, my dear mother," said Paul.

"I," replied Madame Evangelista, "I want nothing now. No, I am going to be your farm-bailiff at Lanstrac. Would it not be sheer folly to go to Paris just when I have to wind up my affairs here? I am going to be avaricious for my grand-children."

"Dear mother," said Paul, much touched, "ought I to accept this exchange without compensation?"

"Dear heaven! are you not my nearest and dearest? Do you think that I shall find no happiness when I sit by my fire and say to myself: ' Natalie is gone in splendor to-night to the Duchesse de Berri's ball. When she sees herself with my diamond at her throat, my earrings in her ears, she will have those little pleasures of self-satisfaction which add so much to a woman's enjoyment, and make her gay and attractive.' Nothing crushes a woman so much as the chafing of her vanity. I never saw a badly dressed woman look amiable and pleasant. Be honest, Paul! we enjoy much more through the one we love than in any pleasure of our own."

"What on earth was Mathias driving at?" thought Paul. "Well, mother," said he, in a low voice, "I accept."

"I am quite overpowered," said Natalie.

Just now Solonet came in with good news for his client. He had found two speculators of his acquaintance, builders, who were much tempted by the house, as the extent of the grounds afforded good building land.

"They are prepared to pay two hundred and fifty thousand francs," said he; "but if you are ready to sell, I could bring them up to three hundred thousand. You have two acres of garden."

"My husband paid two hundred thousand for the whole thing," said she, "so I agree; but you will not include the furniture or the mirrors."

"Ah, ha!" said Solonet, with a laugh, "you understand business."

"Alas! needs must," said she, with a sigh.

"I hear that a great many persons are coming to your midnight ceremony," said Solonet, who, finding himself in the way, bowed himself out.

Madame Evangelista went with him as far as the door of the outer drawing-room, and, seeing there was no fear of being overheard, said to him privately—

"I have now property representing two hundred and fifty thousand francs; if I get two hundred thousand francs for myself out of the price of the house, I can command a capital of four hundred and fifty thousand francs. I want to invest it to the best advantage, and I trust to you to do it. I shall most likely remain at Lanstrac."

The young lawyer kissed his client's hand with a bow of gratitude, for the widow's tone led him to believe that this alliance, strengthened by interest, might even go a little further.

"You may depend on me," said he. "I will find you trade investments, in which you will risk nothing, and make large profits."

"Well—till to-morrow," said she; "for you and Monsieur le Marquis de Gyas are going to sign for us."

"Why, dear mother, do you refuse to come with us to Paris?" asked Paul. "Natalie is as much vexed with me as if I were the cause of your determination."

"I have thought it well over, my children, and I should

be in your way. You would think yourselves obliged to include me as a third in everything you might do, and young
people have notions of their own which I might involuntarily
oppose. Go to Paris by yourselves. I do not propose to
exercise over the Comtesse de Manerville the mild dominion
I held over Natalie. I must leave her entirely to you. There
are habits which she and I share, you see, Paul, and which
must be broken. My influence must give way to yours. I
wish you to be attached to me; believe me, I have your interests at heart more than you think perhaps. Young husbands, sooner or later, are jealous of a wife's affection for her
mother. Perhaps they are right. When you are entirely
united, when love has amalgamated your souls into one—then,
my dear boy, you will have no fears of an adverse influence
when you see me under your roof.

"I know the world, men and things; I have seen many a
household rendered unhappy by the blind affection of a
mother who made herself intolerable, as much to her daughter
as to her son-in-law. The affection of old people is often
petty and vexatious; perhaps I should not succeed in effacing
myself. I am weak enough to think myself handsome still;
some flatterers try to persuade me that I am lovable, and I
might assume an inconvenient prominence. Let me make one
more sacrifice to your happiness. I have given you my fortune; well, now I surrender my last womanly vanities. Your
good father Mathias is growing old; he cannot look after
your estates. I will constitute myself your bailiff. I shall
make such occupation for myself as old folk must sooner or
later fall back on; then, when you need me, I will go to Paris
and help in your plans of ambition.

"Come, Paul, be honest; this arrangement is to your
mind? Answer."

Paul would not admit it, but he was very glad to be free.
The suspicions as to his mother-in-law's character, implanted
in his mind by the old notary, were dispelled by this conver-

sation, which Madame Evangelista continued to the same effect.

"My mother was right," thought Natalie, who was watching Paul's expression. "He is really glad to see me parted from her. But why?"

Was not this *Why?* the first query of suspicion, and did it not add considerable weight to her mother's instructions?

There are some natures who, on the strength of a single proof, can believe in friendship. In such folk as these the North wind blows away clouds as fast as the West wind brings them up; they are content with effects, and do not look for the causes. Paul's was one of these essentially confiding characters, devoid of ill-feeling, and no less devoid of foresight. His weakness was the outcome of kindness and a belief in goodness in others, far more than of want of strength of mind.

Natalie was pensive and sad; she did not know how to do without her mother. Paul, with the sort of fatuity that love can produce, laughed at his bride's melancholy mood, promising himself that the pleasures of married life and the excitement of Paris would dissipate it. It was with marked satisfaction that Madame Evangelista encouraged Paul in his confidence, for the first condition of revenge is dissimulation. Overt hatred is powerless.

The creole lady had made two long strides already. Her daughter had possession of splendid jewels which had cost Paul two hundred thousand francs, and to which he would, no doubt, add more. Then, she was leaving the two young people to themselves, with no guidance but unregulated love. Thus she had laid the foundations of revenge of which her daughter knew nothing, though sooner or later she would be accessory to it.

Now, would Natalie love Paul? This was as yet an unanswered question, of which the issue would modify Madame Evangelista's schemes; for she was too sincerely fond of her daughter not to be tender of her happiness. Thus Paul's future life depended on himself. If he could make his wife love him, he would be saved.

Finally, on the following night, after an evening spent with the four witnesses whom Madame Evangelista had invited to the lengthy dinner which followed the legal ceremony, at midnight the young couple and their friends attended mass by the light of blazing tapers in the presence of above a hundred curious spectators.

A wedding celebrated at night always seems of ill-omen; daylight is a symbol of life and enjoyment, and its happy augury is lacking. Ask the stanchest spirit the cause of this chill, why the dark vault depresses the nerves, why the sound of footsteps is so startling, why the cry of owls and bats is so strangely audible. Though there is no reason for alarm, every one quakes; darkness, the forecast of death, is crushing to the spirit.

Natalie, torn from her mother, was weeping. The girl was tormented by all the doubts which clutch the heart on the threshold of a new life, where, in spite of every promise of happiness, there are a thousand pitfalls for a woman's feet. She shivered with cold, and had to put on a cloak.

Madame Evangelista's manner and that of the young couple gave rise to comments among the elegant crowd that stood round the altar.

"Solonet tells me that the young people go off to Paris to-morrow morning alone."

"Madame Evangelista was to have gone to live with them."

"Count Paul has got rid of her?"

"What a mistake!" said the Marquise de Gyas. "The man who shuts his door on his mother-in-law opens it to a lover. Does he not know all that a mother is?"

"He has been very hard on Madame Evangelista. The poor woman has had to sell her house, and is going to live at Lanstrac."

27

"Natalie is very unhappy."

"Well, would you like to spend the day after your wedding on the highway?"

"It is very uncomfortable."

"I am glad I came," said another lady, "to convince myself of the necessity of surrounding a wedding with all the usual ceremonies and festivities, for this seems to me very cold and dismal.   Indeed, if I were to tell the whole truth," she whispered, leaning over to her neighbor, "it strikes me as altogether uncanny."

Madame Evangelista took Natalie in her own carriage to Count Paul's house.

"Well, mother, it is all over——"

"Remember my advice, and you will be happy.   Always be his wife, and not his mistress."

When Natalie had gone to her room, Madame Evangelista went through the little farce of throwing herself into her son-in-law's arms, and weeping on his shoulder.   It was the only provincial detail Madame Evangelista had allowed herself; but she had her reasons.   In the midst of her apparently wild and desperate tears and speeches, she extracted from Paul such concessions as a husband will always make.

The next day she saw the young people into their chaise, and accompanied them across the ferry over the Gironde. Natalie, in a word, had made her mother understand that if Paul had won in the game concerning the contract, her revenge was beginning.   Natalie had already reduced her husband to perfect obedience.

CONCLUSION.

Five years after this, one afternoon in November, the Comte Paul de Manerville, wrapped in a cloak, with a bowed head, mysteriously arrived at the house of Monsieur Mathias at Bordeaux.   The worthy man, too old now to attend business, had sold his connection, and was peacefully ending his days in one of his houses.

Important business had taken him out at the time when his visitor called; but his old housekeeper, warned of Paul's advent, showed him into the room that had belonged to Madame Mathias, who had died a year since.

Paul, tired out by a hurried journey, slept till late. The old man, on his return, came to look at his erstwhile client, and was satisfied to look at him lying asleep, as a mother looks at her child. Josette, the housekeeper, came in with her master and stood by the bedside, her hands on her hips.

"This day twelvemonth, Josette, when my dear wife breathed her last in this bed, I little thought of seeing Monsieur le Comte here looking like death."

"Poor gentleman! he groans in his sleep," said Josette.

The old lawyer made no reply but "*Sac à papier!*" an innocent oath, which, from him, always represented the despair of a man of business in the face of some insuperable dilemma.

"At any rate," thought he, "I have saved the freehold of Lanstrac, Auzac, Saint-Froult, and his town-house here."

Mathias counted on his fingers and exclaimed: "Five years! Yes, it is five years this very month since his old aunt, now deceased, the venerable Madame de Maulincour, asked on his behalf for the hand of that little crocodile in woman's skirts who has managed to ruin him—as I knew she would!"

After looking at the young man for some time, the good old man, now very gouty, went away, leaning on his stick, to walk slowly up and down his little garden. At nine o'clock supper was served, for the old man supped; and he was not a little surprised to see Paul come in with a calm brow and an unruffled expression, though perceptibly altered. Though at three-and-thirty the Comte de Manerville looked forty, the change was due solely to mental shocks; physically he was in good health. He went up to his old friend, took his hands, and pressed them affectionately, saying:

"Dear, good Maître Mathias! And you have had your troubles!"

"Mine were in the course of nature, Monsieur le Comte, but yours——"

"We will talk over mine presently at supper," replied de Manerville.

"If I had not a son high up in the law, and a married daughter," said the worthy man, "believe me, Monsieur le Comte, you would have found something more than bare hospitality from old Mathias. How is it that you have come to Bordeaux just at the time when you may read on every wall bills announcing the seizure and sale of the farms of le Grassol and le Guadet, of the vine-land of Bellerose and your house here? I cannot possibly express my grief on seeing those huge posters—I, who for forty years took as much care of your estates as if they were my own; I, who, when I was third clerk under Monsieur Chesneau, my predecessor, transacted the purchase for your mother, and in my young clerk's hand engrossed the deed of sale on parchment; I, who have the title-deeds safe in my successor's office; I, who made out all the accounts. Why, I remember you when so high——" and the old man held his hand two feet from the floor.

"After being a notary for more than forty years, to see my name printed as large as life in the face of Israel, in the announcement of the seizure and the disposal of the property —you cannot imagine the pain it gives me. As I go along the street and see the folk all reading those horrible yellow bills, I am as much ashamed as if my own ruin and honor were involved. And there are a pack of idiots who spell it all out at the top of their voices on purpose to attract idlers, and they add the most ridiculous comments."

"Are you not master of your own? Your father ran through two fortunes before making the one he left you, and you would not be a Manerville if you did not tread in his steps.

"And beside, the seizure of real property is foreseen in the Code, and provided for under a special *capitulum;* you are in a position recognized by law. If I were not a white-headed old man, only waiting for a nudge to push me into the grave, I would thrash the men who stand staring at such abominations—'At the suit of Madame Natalie Evangelista, wife of Paul François Joseph Comte de Manerville, of separate estate by the ruling of the lower Court of the Department of the Seine,' and so forth."

"Yes," said Paul, "and now separate in bed and board——"

"Indeed !" said the old man.

"Oh! against Natalie's will," said the count quickly. "I had to deceive her. She does not know that I am going away."

"Going away?"

"My passage is taken; I sail on the Belle-Amélie for Calcutta."

"In two days !" said Mathias. "Then we meet no more, Monsieur le Comte."

"You are but seventy-three, my dear Mathias, and you have the gout, an assurance of old age. When I come back I shall find you just where you are. Your sound brain and heart will be as good as ever ; you will help me to rebuild the ruined home. I mean to make a fine fortune in seven years. On my return I shall only be forty. At that age everything is still possible."

"You, Monsieur le Comte !" exclaimed Mathias, with a gesture of amazement. "You are going into trade ! What are you thinking of?"

"I am no longer Monsieur le Comte, dear Mathias. I have taken my passage in the name of Camille, a Christian name of my mother's. And I have some connections which may enable me to make a fortune in other ways. Trade will be my last resource. Also, I am starting with a large enough sum of money to allow of my tempting fortune on a grand scale."

"Where is that money?"

"A friend will send it to me."

The old man dropped his fork at the sound of the word *friend*, not out of irony or surprise; his face expressed his grief at finding Paul under the influence of a delusion, for his eye saw a void where the count perceived a solid plank.

"I have been in a notary's office more than fifty years," said he, "and I never knew a ruined man who had friends willing to lend him money."

"You do not know de Marsay. At this minute, while I speak to yóu, I am perfectly certain that he has sold out of the Funds if it was necessary, and to-morrow you will receive a bill of exchange for fifty thousand crowns."

"I only hope so. But then could not this friend have set your affairs straight? You could have lived quietly at Lanstrac for five or six years on Madame la Comtesse's income."

"And would an assignment have paid fifteen hundred thousand francs of debts, of which my wife's share was five hundred and fifty thousand?"

"And how, in four years, have you managed to owe fourteen hundred and fifty thousand francs?"

"Nothing can be plainer, my good friend. Did I not make the diamonds a present to my wife? Did I not spend the hundred and fifty thousand francs that came to us from the sale of Madame Evangelista's house in redecorating my house in Paris? Had I not to pay the price of the land we purchased, and of the legal business of my marriage-contract? Finally, had I not to sell Natalie's forty thousand francs a year in the Funds to pay for d'Auzac and Saint-Froult? We sold at 87, so I was in debt about two hundred thousand francs within a month of my marriage.

"An income was left of sixty-seven thousand francs, and we have regularly spent two hundred thousand francs a year beyond it. To these nine hundred thousand francs add certain money-lenders' interest, and you will easily find it a million."

"Brrrr," said the old lawyer. "And then?"

"Well, I wished at once to make up the set of jewels for my wife, of which she already had the pearl necklace and the Discreto clasp—a family jewel—and her mother's earrings. I paid a hundred thousand francs for a diadem of wheat-ears. There you see eleven hundred thousand francs. Then I owe my wife the whole of her fortune, amounting to three hundred and fifty-six thousand francs settled on her."

"But then," said Mathias, "if Madame la Comtesse had pledged her diamonds and you your securities, you would have, by my calculations, three hundred thousand with which to pacify your creditors——"

"When a man is down, Mathias; when his estates are loaded with mortgages; when his wife is the first creditor for her settlement; when, to crown all, he is exposed to having writs against him for notes of hand to the tune of a hundred thousand francs—to be paid off, I hope, by good prices at the sales—nothing can be done. And the cost of conveyancing!"

"Frightful!" said the lawyer.

"The distraint has happily taken the form of a voluntary sale, which will mitigate the flare."

"And you are selling Bellerose with the wines of 1825 in the cellars?"

"I cannot help myself."

"Bellerose is worth six hundred thousand francs."

"Natalie will buy it in by my advice."

"Sixteen thousand francs in ordinary years—and such a season as 1825! I will run Bellerose up to seven hundred thousand francs myself, and each of the farms up to a hundred and twenty thousand."

"So much the better; then I can clear myself if my house in the town fetches two hundred thousand."

"Solonet will pay a little more for it; he has a fancy for it. He is retiring on a hundred-odd thousand a year, which he has made in gambling in *trois-six*. He has sold his business for three hundred thousand francs, and is marrying a rich mulatto. Gods knows where she got her money, but they say she has millions. A notary gambling in *trois-six!* A notary marrying a mulatto! What times these are! It was he, they say, who looked after your mother-in-law's investments."

"She has greatly improved Lanstrac, and taken good care of the land; she has regularly paid her rent."

"I should never have believed her capable of behaving so."

"She is so kind and devoted. She always paid Natalie's debts when she came to spend three months in Paris."

"So she very well might, she lives on Lanstrac," said Mathias. "She! Turned thrifty! What a miracle! She has just bought the estate of Grainrouge, lying between Lanstrac and Grassol, so that if she prolongs the avenue from Lanstrac down to the high road you can drive a league and a half through your own grounds. She paid a hundred thousand francs down for Grainrouge, which is worth a thousand crowns a year in cash rents."

"She is still handsome," said Paul. "Country life keeps her young. I will not go to take leave of her; she would bleed herself for me."

"You would waste your time; she has gone to Paris. She probably arrived just as you left."

"She has, of course, heard of the sale of the land, and has rushed to my assistance. I have no right to complain of life. I am loved as well as any man can be in this world, loved by two women who vie with each other in their devotion to me. They were jealous of each other; the daughter reproached her mother for being too fond of me, and the mother found fault with her daughter for her extravagance. This affection has been my ruin. How can a man help gratifying the lightest wish of the woman he loves? How can he protect himself? And, on the other hand, how can he accept self-sacrifice? We could, to be sure, pay up with my fortune and come to live at Lanstrac—but I would rather go to India and make my fortune than tear Natalie from the life she loves. It was I myself who proposed to her a separation of goods. Women are angels who ought never to be mixed up with the business of life."

Old Mathias listened to Paul with an expression of surprise and doubt.

" You have no children ? " said he.

" Happily ! " replied Paul.

" Well, I view marriage in a different light," replied the old notary quite simply. " In my opinion, a wife ought to share her husband's lot for good or ill. I have heard that young married people who are too much like lovers have no families. Is pleasure then the only end of marriage? Is it not rather the happiness of family life? Still, you were but eight-and-twenty and the countess no more than twenty; it was excusable that you should think only of love-making. At the same time, the terms of your marriage-contract, and your name—you will think me grossly lawyer-like—required you to begin by having a fine handsome boy. Yes, Monsieur le Comte, and if you had daughters, you ought not to have stopped till you had a male heir to succeed you in the entail.

" Was Mademoiselle Evangelista delicate? Was there anything to fear for her in motherhood? You will say that is very old-fashioned and antiquated; but in noble families, Monsieur le Comte, a legitimate wife ought to have children and bring them up well. As the Duchesse de Sully said—the wife of the great Sully—a wife is not a means of pleasure, but the honor and virtue of the household."

"You do not know what women are, my dear Mathias," said Paul. "To be happy, a man must love his wife as she chooses to be loved. And is it not rather brutal to deprive a woman so early of her charms and spoil her beauty before she has really enjoyed it?"

"If you had had a family, the mother would have checked the wife's dissipation; she would more than likely have stayed at home——"

"If you were in the right, my good friend," said Paul, with a frown, "I should be still more unhappy. Do not aggravate my misery by moralizing over my ruin; let me depart without any after bitterness."

Next day Mathias received a bill payable at sight for a hundred and fifty thousand francs, signed by de Marsay.

"You see," said Paul, "he does not write me a word. Henri's is the most perfectly imperfect, the most unconventionally noble nature I have ever met with. If you could but know how superior this man—who is still young—rises above feeling and interest, and what a great politician he is, you, like me, would be amazed to find what a warm heart he has."

Mathias tried to reason Paul out of his purpose, but it was irrevocable, and justified by so many practical reasons, that the old notary made no further attempt to detain his client.

Rarely enough does a vessel in cargo sail punctually to the day; but by an accident disastrous to Paul, the wind being favorable, the Belle-Amélie was to sail on the morrow. At the moment of departure the landing-stage is always crowded with relations, friends, and idlers. Among these, as it happened, were several personally acquainted with Manerville. His ruin had made him as famous now as he had once been for his fortune, so there was a stir of curiosity. Every one had some remark to make.

The old man had escorted Paul to the wharf, and he must have suffered keenly as he heard some of the comments.

"Who would recognize in the man you see there with old Mathias the dandy who used to be called Sweet-pea, and who was the oracle of fashion here at Bordeaux five years since?"

"What, can that fat little man in an alpaca overcoat, looking like a coachman, be the Comte Paul de Manerville?"

"Yes, my dear, the man who married Mademoiselle Evangelista. There he is ruined, without a sou to his name, going to the Indies to look for the roc's egg."

"But how was he ruined? He was so rich!"

"Paris—women—the Bourse—gambling—display——"

"And beside," said another, "Manerville is a poor creature; he has no sense, as limp as wet-paper, allowing himself to be fleeced, and incapable of any decisive action. He was born to be ruined."

Paul shook his old friend's hand and took refuge on board. Mathias stood on the quay, looking at his old client, who leaned over the netting, defying the crowd with a look of scorn.

Just as the anchor was weighed, Paul saw that Mathias was signaling to him by waving his handkerchief. The old housekeeper had come in hot haste, and was standing by her master, who seemed greatly excited by some matter of importance. Paul persuaded the captain to wait a few minutes and send a boat to land, that he might know what the old lawyer wanted; he was signaling vigorously, evidently desiring him to disembark. Mathias, too infirm to go to the ship, gave two letters to one of the sailors who were in the boat.

"My good fellow," said the old notary, showing one of the letters to the sailor, "this letter, mark it well, make no mistake—this packet has just been delivered by a messenger who has ridden from Paris in thirty-five hours. Explain this clearly to Monsieur le Comte, do not forget. It might make him change his plans.''

'' And we should have to land him ? ''

''Yes,'' said the lawyer rashly.

The sailor in most parts of the world is a creature apart, professing the deepest contempt for all landlubbers. As to townsfolk, he cannot understand them ; he knows nothing about them ; he laughs them to scorn ; he cheats them if he can without direct dishonesty. This one, as it happened, was a man of Lower Brittany, who saw worthy old Mathias' instructions in only one light.

''Just so,'' he muttered, as he took his oar, ''land him again ! The captain is to lose a passenger ! If we listened to these landlubbers, we should spend our lives in pulling them between the ship and shore. Is he afraid his son will take cold ? ''

So the sailor gave Paul the letters without any message. On recognizing his wife's writing and de Marsay's, Paul imagined all that either of them could have to say to him ; and being determined not to risk being influenced by the offers that might be inspired by their regard, he put the letters in his pocket with apparent indifference.

''And that is the rubbish we are kept waiting for ! What nonsense ! '' said the sailor to the captain, in his broad Breton. '' If the matter were as important as that old guy declared, would Monsieur le Comte drop the papers into his scuppers ? ''

Paul, lost in the dismal reflections that come over the strongest man in such circumstances, gave himself up to melancholy, while he waved his hand to his old friend, and bade farewell to France, watching the fast-disappearing buildings of Bordeaux.

He presently sat down on a coil of rope, and there night found him, lost in meditation. Doubt came upon him as twilight fell ; he gazed anxiously into the future ; he could see nothing before him but perils and uncertainty, and wondered whether his courage might not fail him. He felt some vague alarm as he thought of Natalie left to herself; he repented of his decision, regretting Paris and his past life.

Then he fell a victim to sea-sickness. Every one knows the miseries of this condition, and one of the worst features of its sufferings is the total effacement of will that accompanies it. An inexplicable incapacity loosens all the bonds of vitality at the core; the mind refuses to act, and everything is a matter of total indifference—a mother can forget her child, a lover his mistress; the strongest man becomes a mere inert mass. Paul was carried to his berth, where he remained for three days, alternately violently ill, and plied with grog by the sailors, thinking of nothing or sleeping; then he went through a sort of convalescence and recovered his ordinary health.

On the morning when, finding himself better, he went for a walk on deck to breathe the sea-air of a more southern climate, on putting his hands in his pockets he felt his letters. He at once took them out to read them, and began by Natalie's. In order that the Comtesse de Manerville's letter may be fully understood, it is necessary first to give that written by Paul to his wife on leaving Paris.

PAUL DE MANERVILLE TO HIS WIFE.

"My best Beloved :—When you read this letter I shall be far from you, probably on the vessel that is to carry me to India, where I am going to repair my shattered fortune. I did not feel that I had the courage to tell you of my departure. I have deceived you; but was it not necessary? You would have pinched yourself to no purpose, you would have wished to sacrifice your own fortune. Dear Natalie, feel no remorse; I shall know no repentance. When I return with millions, I will imitate your father; I will lay them at your feet as he laid his at your mother's, and will say, 'It is all yours.'

"I love you to distraction, Natalie; and I can say so with-out fearing that you will make my avowal a pretext for exerting a power which only weak men dread. Yours was unlimited from the first day I ever saw you. My love alone has led me to disaster; my gradual ruin has brought me the delirious joys of the gambler. As my money diminished my happiness grew greater; each fraction of my wealth converted into some little gratification to you caused me heavenly rapture. I could have wished you to have more caprices than you ever had.

"I knew that I was marching to an abyss, but I went, my brow wreathed with joys and feelings unknown to vulgar souls. I acted like the lovers who shut themselves up for a year or two in a cottage by a lake, vowing to kill themselves after plunging into the ocean of happiness, dying in all the glory of their illusions and their passion. I have always thought such persons eminently rational. You have never known any-thing of my pleasures or of my sacrifices. And is there not exquisite enjoyment in concealing from the one we love the cost of the things she wishes for?

"I may tell you these secrets now. I shall be far indeed away when you hold this sheet loaded with my love. Though I forego the pleasure of your gratitude, I do not feel that clutch at my heart which would seize me if I tried to talk of these things. Alas, my dearest, there is deep self-interest in thus revealing the past. Is it not to add to the volume of our love in the future? Could it indeed ever need such a stimu-lus? Do we not feel that pure affection to which proof is needless, which scorns time and distance, and lives in its own strength?

"Ah! Natalie, I just now left the table where I am writing by the fire, and looked at you asleep, calm and trustful, in the attitude of a guileless child, your hand lying where I could take it. I left a tear on the pillow that has been the witness of our happiness. I leave you without a fear on the promise of that attitude; I leave you to win peace by winning a fortune so large that no anxiety may ever disturb our joys, and that you may satisfy your every wish. Neither you nor I could ever dispense with the luxuries of the life we lead. I am a man, and I have courage; mine alone be the task of amassing the fortune we require.

"You might perhaps think of following me ! I will not tell you the name of the ship, nor the port I sail from, nor the day I leave. A friend will tell you when it is too late.

"Natalie, my devotion to you is boundless; I love you as a mother loves her child, as a lover worships his mistress, with perfect disinterestedness. The work be mine, the enjoyment yours; mine the sufferings, yours the life of happiness. Amuse yourself; keep up all your habits of luxury; go to the Italiens, to the French opera, into society and to balls; I absolve you beforehand. But, dear angel, each time you come home to the nest where we have enjoyed the fruits that have ripened during our five years of love, remember your lover, think of me for a moment, and sleep in my heart. That is all I ask.

"I—my one, dear, constant thought—when, under scorching skies, working for our future, I find some obstacle to overcome, or when, tired out, I rest in the hope of my return—I shall think of you who are the beauty of my life. Yes, I shall try to live in you, telling myself that you have neither cares nor uneasiness. Just as life is divided into day and night, waking and sleeping, so I shall have my life of enchantment in Paris, my life of labors in India—a dream of anguish, a reality·of delight; I shall live so completely in what is real to you that my days will be the dream. I have my memories; canto by canto I shall recall the lovely poem of five years; I shall remember the days when you chose to be dazzling, when by some perfection of evening-dress or morning-wrapper you made yourself new in my eyes. I shall taste on my lips the flavor of our little feasts.

"Yes, dear angel, I am going like a man pledged to some high emprise when by success he is to win his mistress ! To me the past will be like the dreams of desire which anticipate realization, and which realization often disappoints. But you have always more than fulfilled them. And I shall return to find a new wife, for will not absence lend you fresh charms? Oh, my dear love, my Natalie, let me be a religion to you. Be always the child I have seen sleeping! If you were to betray my blind confidence—Natalie, you would not have to fear my anger, of that you may be sure; I should die without a word. But a woman does not deceive the husband who leaves her free, for women are never mean. She may cheat a tyrant; but she does not care for the easy treason which would deal a death-blow. No, I cannot imagine such a thing—forgive me for this cry, natural to a man.

"My dearest, you will see de Marsay; he is now the tenant holding our house, and he will leave you in it. This lease to him was necessary to avoid useless loss. My creditors, not understanding that payment is merely a question of time, might have seized the furniture and the amount of the rent of the house. Be good to de Marsay; I have the most perfect confidence in his abilities and in his honor. Make him your advocate and your adviser, your familiar. Whatever his engagements may be, he will always be at your service. I have instructed him to keep an eye on the liquidation of my debts; if he should advance a sum of which he presently needed the use, I trust to you to pay him. Remember I am not leaving you to de Marsay's guidance, but to your own; when I mention him, I do not force him upon you.

"Alas, I cannot begin to write on business matters; only an hour remains to me under the same roof with you. I count your breathing; I try to picture your thoughts from the occasional changes in your sleep, your breathing revives the flowery hours of our early love. At every throb of your heart mine goes forth to you with all its wealth, and I scatter over you the petals of the roses of my soul, as children strew them in front of the altars on Corpus Christi Day. I commend you to the memories I am pouring out on you ; I would, if I could, pour my life-blood into your veins that you might indeed be mine, that your heart might be my heart, your thoughts my thoughts, that I might be wholly in you ! And you utter a little murmur as if in reply !

." Be ever as calm and lovely as you are at this moment. I would I had the fabled power of which we hear in fairy tales, and could leave you thus to sleep during my absence, to wake you on my return with a kiss. What energy, what love, must I feel to leave you when I behold you thus. You are Spanish and religious; you will observe an oath taken even in your sleep when your unspoken word was believed in beyond a doubt.

" Farewell, my dearest. Your hapless Sweet-pea is swept away by the storm-wind ; but it will come back to you for ever on the wings of Fortune. Nay, dear Ninie, I will not say farewell, for you will always be with me. Will you not be the soul of my actions ? Will not the hope of bringing you such happiness as cannot be wrecked give spirit to my enterprise and guide all my steps ? Will you not always be present to me ? No, it will not be the tropical sun, but the fire of your eyes, that will light me on my way.

" Be as happy as a woman can be, bereft of her lover. I should have been glad to have a parting kiss, in which you were not merely passive ; but, my Ninie, my adored darling, I would not awaken you. When you awake you will find a tear on your brow; let it be a talisman. Think, oh, think of him who is perhaps to die for you, far away from you ; think of him less as your husband than as a lover who worships you and leaves you in God's keeping."

REPLY FROM THE COMTESSE DE MANERVILLE TO
HER HUSBAND.

" My Dearest :—What grief your letter has brought me ! Had you any right to form a decision which concerns us
28

equally without consulting me? Are you free? Do you not belong to me? And am I not half a creole? Why should I not follow you? You have shown me that I am no longer indispensable to you. What have I done, Paul, that you should rob me of my rights? What is to become of me alone in Paris? Poor dear, you assume the blame for any ill I may have done. But am I not partly to blame for this ruin? Has not my finery weighed heavily in the wrong scale? You are making me curse the happy, heedless life we have led these four years. To think of you as exiled for six years! Is it not enough to kill me? How can you make a fortune in six years? Will you ever come back? I was wiser than I knew when I so strenuously opposed the separate maintenance on which you and my mother so absolutely insisted. What did I tell you? That it would expose you to discredit, that it would ruin your credit! You had to be quite angry before I would give in.

"My dear Paul, you have never been so noble in my eyes as you are at this moment. Without a hint of despair, to set out to make a fortune! Only such a character, such energy as yours could take such a step. I kneel at your feet. A man who confesses to weakness in such perfect good faith, who restores his fortune from the same motive that has led him to waste it—for love, for an irresistible passion—oh, Paul, such a man is sublime! Go without fear, trample down every obstacle, and never doubt your Natalie, for it would be doubting yourself. My poor dear, you say you want to live in me? And shall not I always live in you? I shall not be here, but with you wherever you may be.

"Though your letter brought me cruel anguish, it filled me too with joy; in one minute I went through both extremes; for, seeing how much you love me, I was proud, too, to find that my love was appreciated. Sometimes I have fancied that I loved you more than you loved me; now I confess myself outdone; you may add that delightful superiority to the others you possess; but have I not many more reasons for loving? Your letter, the precious letter in which your whole soul is revealed, and which so plainly tells me that between you and me nothing is lost, will dwell on my heart during your absence, for your whole soul is in it; that letter is my glory!

"I am going to live with my mother at Lanstrac; I shall there be dead to the world, and shall save out of my income to pay off your debts. From this day forth, Paul, I am another woman; I take leave for ever of the world; I will not have a pleasure that you do not share.

"Beside, Paul, I am obliged to leave Paris and live in solitude. Dear boy, you have a twofold reason for making a fortune. If your courage needed a spur, you may now find another heart dwelling in your own. My dear, cannot you guess? We shall have a child. Your dearest hopes will be crowned, monsieur. I would not give you the deceptive joys which are heart-breaking; we have already had so much disappointment on that score, and I was afraid of having to withdraw the glad announcement. But now I am sure of what I am saying, and happy to cast a gleam of joy over your sorrow. This morning, suspecting no evil, I had gone to the Church of the Assumption to return thanks to God. How could I foresee disaster? Everything seemed to smile on me. As I came out of church, I met my mother; she had heard of your distress, and had come by post with all her savings, thirty thousand francs, hoping to be able to arrange matters. What a heart, Paul! I was quite happy; I came home to tell you the two pieces of good news while we breakfasted under the awning in the conservatory, and I had ordered all the dainties you like best.

"Augustine gave me your letter. A letter from you, when we had slept together! It was a tragedy in itself. I was seized with a shivering fit—then I read it—I read it in tears, and my mother too melted into tears. And a woman must love a man very much to cry over him, crying makes us so ugly. I was half-dead. So much love and so much courage! So much happiness and such great grief! To be unable to clasp you to my heart, my beloved, at the very moment when my admiration for your magnanimity most constrained me! What woman could withstand such a whirlwind of emotions? To think that you were far away when your hand on my heart would have comforted me; that you were not there to give me the look I love so well, to rejoice with me over the realization of our hopes; and I was not with you to soften your sorrow by the affection which made your loving Natalie so dear to you, and which can make you forget every annoyance, every grief!

"I wanted to be off to fly to your feet; but my mother pointed out that the Belle-Amélie is to sail to-morrow, that only the post could go fast enough to overtake you, and that it would be the height of folly to risk all our future happiness on a jolt. Though a mother already, I ordered horses, and my mother cheated me into the belief that they would be brought round. She acted wisely, for I was already unfit to move. I could not bear such a combination of violent agitations, and I fainted away. I am writing in bed, for I am ordered perfect rest for some months. Hitherto I have been a frivolous woman, now I mean to be the mother of a family. Providence is good to me, for a child to nurse and bring up can alone alleviate the sorrows of your absence. In it I shall find a second Paul to make much of. I shall thus publicly flaunt the love we have so carefully kept to ourselves. I shall tell the truth.

"My mother has already had occasion to contradict certain calumnies which are current as to your conduct. The two Vandenesses, Charles and Félix, had defended you stoutly, but your friend de Marsay makes game of everything; he laughs at your detractors instead of answering them. I do not like such levity in response to serious attacks. Are you not mistaken in him? However, I will obey and make a friend of him.

"Be quite easy, my dearest, with regard to anything that may affect your honor. Is it not mine?

"I am about to pledge my diamonds. My mother and I will strain every resource to pay off your debts and try to buy in the vine-land of Bellerose. My mother, who is as good a man of business as a regular accountant, blames you for not having been open with her. She would not then have purchased—thinking to give you pleasure—the estate of Grain-rouge, which cut in on your lands; and then she could have lent you a hundred and thirty thousand francs. She is in despair at the step you have taken, and is afraid you will suffer from the life in India. She entreats you to be temperate, and not to be led astray by the women! I laughed in her face. I am as sure of you as of myself. You will come back to me wealthy and faithful. I alone in the world know your womanly refinement and those secret feelings which make you an exquisite human flower, worthy of heaven. The Bordeaux folk had every reason to give you your pretty nickname. And who will take care of my delicate flower? My heart is racked by dreadful ideas. I, his wife, his Natalie, am here, when already perhaps he is suffering! I, so entirely one with you, may not share your troubles, your annoyances, your dangers? In whom can you confide? How can you live without the ear into which you whisper everything? Dear, sensitive plant, swept away by the gale, why should you be transplanted from the only soil in which your fragrance could ever be developed? I feel as if I had been alone for two centuries, and I am cold in Paris! And I have cried so long——

"The cause of your ruin! What a text for the meditations of a woman full of love! You have treated me like a child, to whom nothing is refused that it asks for; like a courtesan, for whom a spendthrift throws away his fortune. Your delicacy, as you style it, is an insult. Do you suppose that I cannot live without fine clothes, balls, operas, successes? Am I such a frivolous woman? Do you think me incapable of a serious thought, of contributing to your fortune as much as I ever contributed to your pleasures? If you were not so far away and ill at ease, you would here find a good scolding for your impertinence. Can you disparage your wife to such an extent? Bless me! What did I go out into society for? To flatter your vanity; it was for you I dressed, and you know it. If I had been wrong, I should be too cruelly punished; your absence is a bitter expiation for our domestic happiness. That happiness was too complete; it could not fail to be paid for by some great sorrow; and here it is! After such delights, so carefully screened from the eyes of the curious; after these constant festivities, varied only by the secret madness of our affection, there is no alternative but solitude. Solitude, my dear one, feeds great passions, and I long for it. What can I do in the world of fashion; to whom should I report my triumphs?

"Ah, to live at Lanstrac, on the estate laid out by your father, in the house you restored so luxuriously—to live there with your child, waiting for you, and sending forth to you night and morning the prayers of the mother and child, of the woman and the angel—will not that be half-happiness? Cannot you see the little hands folded in mine? Will you still remember, as I shall remember every evening, the happiness of which your dear letter reminds me? Oh, yes, for we love each other equally. I can no more doubt you than you could doubt me.

"What consolations can I offer you here, I, who am left desolate, crushed; I, who look forward to the next six years as a desert to be crossed? Well, I am not the most to be pitied, for will not that desert be cheered by our little one? Yes—a boy—I must give you a boy, must I not? So farewell, dearly beloved one, our thoughts and our love will ever follow you. The tears on my paper will tell you much that I cannot express, and take the kisses you will find left here, below my name, by your own

" NATALIE."

This letter threw Paul into a day-dream, caused no less by the rapture into which he was thrown by these expressions of love than by the reminiscences of happiness thus intentionally called up ; and he went over them all, one by one, to account for this promise of a child.

The happier a man is, the greater are his fears. In souls that are exclusively tender—and a tender nature is generally a little weak—jealousy and disquietude are usually in direct proportion to happiness and to its greatness. Strong souls are neither jealous nor easily frightened : jealousy is doubt, and fear is small-minded. Belief without limits is the leading attribute of a high-minded man ; if he is deceived—and strength as well as weakness may make him a dupe—his scorn serves him as a hatchet, and he cuts through everything. Such greatness is exceptional. Which of us has not known what it is to be deserted by the spirit that upholds this frail machine, and to hear only the unknown voice that denies everything ?

Paul, caught as it were in the toils of certain undeniable facts, doubted and believed both at once. Lost in thought, a prey to terrible but involuntary questionings, and yet struggling with the proofs of true affection and his belief in Natalie, he read this discursive epistle through twice, unable to come to any conclusion for or against his wife. Love may be as great in wordiness as in brevity of expression.

Thoroughly to understand Paul's frame of mind, he must be seen floating on the ocean as on the wide expanse of the past ; looking back on his life as on a cloudless sky, and coming back at last after whirlwinds of doubt to the pure, entire, and untarnished faith of a believer, of a Christian, of a lover convinced by the voice of his heart.

It is now not less necessary to give the letter to which
Henri de Marsay's was a reply.

COMTE PAUL DE MANERVILLE TO MONSIEUR LE MARQUIS
HENRI DE MARSAY.

"HENRI :—I am going to tell you one of the greatest things
a man can tell a friend : I am ruined. When you read this
I shall be starting from Bordeaux for Calcutta on board the
good ship Belle-Amélie. You will find in your notary's hands
a deed which only needs your signature to ratify it, in which
I let my house to you for six years on a hypothetical lease ;
you will write a letter counteracting it to my wife. I am
obliged to take this precaution in order that Natalie may remain in her own house without any fear of being turned out
of it. I also empower you to draw the income of the entailed
property for four years, as against a sum of a hundred and
fifty thousand francs that I will beg you to send by a bill,
drawn on some house in Bordeaux, to the order of Mathias.
My wife will give you her guarantee to enable you to draw
the income. If the revenue from the entail should repay you
sooner than I imagine, we can settle accounts on my return.
The sum I ask of you is indispensable to enable me to set out
to seek my fortune ; and, if I am not mistaken in you, I shall
receive it without delay at Bordeaux the day before I sail. I
have acted exactly as you would have acted in my place. I
have held out to the last moment without allowing any one to
suspect my position. Then, when the news of the seizure of
my saleable estates reached Paris, I had raised money by notes
of hand to the sum of a hundred thousand francs, to try
gambling. Some stroke of luck might reinstate me. I lost.

"How did I ruin myself? Voluntarily, my dear Henri.
From the very first day I saw that I could not go on in the
way I started. I knew what the consequence would be ; I
persisted in shutting my eyes, for I could not bear to say to
my wife : 'Let us leave Paris and go to live at Lanstrac.' I

have ruined myself for her, as a man ruins himself for a mistress, but knowing it.

"Between you and me, I am neither a simpleton nor weak. A simpleton does not allow himself to be governed, with his eyes open, by an absorbing passion; and a man who sets out to reconstitute his fortune in the Indies, instead of blowing his brains out, is a man of spirit. And so, my dear friend, as I care for wealth only for her sake, as I do not wish to be any man's dupe, and as I shall be absent six years, I place my wife in your keeping. You are enough the favorite of women to respect Natalie, and to give me the benefit of the honest friendship that binds us. I know of no better protector than you will be. I am leaving my wife childless; a lover would be a danger. You must know, my dear de Marsay, I love Natalie desperately, cringingly, and am not ashamed of it. I could, I believe, forgive her if she were unfaithful, not because I am certain that I could be revenged, if I were to die for it! but because I would kill myself to leave her happy if I myself could not make her happy.

"But what have I to fear? Natalie has for me that true regard, independent of love, which preserves love. I have treated her like a spoiled child. I found such perfect happiness in my sacrifices, one led so naturally to the other, that she would be a monster to betray me. Love deserves love.

"Alas! must I tell you the whole truth, my dear Henri? I have just written her a letter in which I have led her to believe that I am setting out full of hope, with a calm face; that I have not a doubt, no jealousy, no fears; such a letter as sons write to deceive a mother when they go forth to die. Good God! de Marsay, I had hell within me, I am the most miserable man on earth. You must hear my cries, my gnashings of the teeth. To you I confess the tears of a despairing lover. Sooner would I sweep the gutter under her window for six years, if it were possible, than return with millions after six years' absence. I suffer the utmost anguish; I shall go on from sorrow to sorrow till you shall have written me a line to say that you accept a charge which you alone in the world can fulfill and carry out.

"My dear de Marsay, I cannot live without that woman; she is air and sunshine to me. Take her under your ægis, keep her faithful to me—even against her will. Yes, I can still be happy with such half-happiness. Be her protector; I have no fear of you. Show her how vulgar it would be to deceive me; that it would make her like every other woman; that the really brilliant thing will be to remain faithful.

"She must still have money enough to carry on her easy and undisturbed life; but if she should want anything, if she should have a whim, be her banker—do not be afraid, I shall come home rich.

"After all, my alarms are vain, no doubt; Natalie is an angel of virtue. When Félix de Vandenesse fell desperately in love with her and allowed himself to pay her some attentions, I only had to point out the danger to Natalie, and she thanked me so affectionately that I was moved to tears. She said that it would be awkward for her reputation if a man suddenly disappeared from her house, but that she would find means to dismiss him; and she did, in fact, receive him very coldly, so that everything ended well. In four years we have never had any other subject of discussion, if a conversation as between friends can be called a discussion.

"Well, my dear Henri, I must say farewell like a man. The disaster has come. From whatever cause, there it is; I can but bow to it. Poverty and Natalie are two irreconcilable terms. And the balance of my debts and assets will be very nearly exact; no one will have anything of which to complain. Still, should some unforeseen circumstance threaten my honor, I trust in you.

"Finally, if any serious event should occur, you can write me under cover to the governor-general at Calcutta. I have friends in his household, and some one will take charge of any letters for me that may arrive from Europe. My dear friend, I hope to find you still the same on my return—a man who can make fun of everything, and who is, nevertheless, alive to the feelings of others when they are in harmony with the noble nature you feel in yourself.

"You can stay in Paris! At the moment when you read this I shall be crying, 'To Carthage!'"

THE MARQUIS HENRI DE MARSAY IN REPLY TO THE COMTE
PAUL DE MANERVILLE.

"And so, Monsieur le Comte, you have collapsed! Monsieur the Ambassador has turned turtle! Are these the fine things you were doing? Why, Paul, did you keep any secret from me? If you had said but one word, my dear old fellow, I could have thrown light on the matter.

"Your wife refuses her guarantee. That should be enough to unseal your eyes. And, if not, I would have you to know that your notes of hand have been protested at the suit of one Lécuyer, formerly head-clerk to one Solonet, a notary at Bordeaux. This sucking money-lender, having come from Gascony to try his hand at stock-jobbing, lends his name to screen your very honorable mother-in-law, the real creditor to whom you owe the hundred thousand francs, for which, it is said, she gave you seventy thousand. Compared to Madame Evangelista, Daddy Gobseck is soft flannel velvet, a soothing draught, a *meringue à la vanille* (a vanilla-cake), a fifth-act uncle. Your vineyard of Bellerose will be your wife's booty; her mother is to pay her the difference between the price it sells for and the sum-total of her claims. Madame Evangelista is to acquire le Gaudet and le Grassol, and the mortgages on your house at Bordeaux are all in her hands under the names of men of straw, found for her by that fellow Solonet. And in this way these two worthy women will secure an income of a hundred and twenty thousand francs, the amount derivable from your estates, added to thirty-odd thousand francs a year in the Funds which the dear, delightful hussies have secured.

"Your wife's guarantee was unnecessary. The aforenamed Lécuyer came this morning to offer me repayment of the money I have sent you in exchange for a formal transfer of my claims. The vintage of 1825, which your mother-in-law has safe in the cellars at Lanstrac, is enough to pay me off. So the two women have calculated that you would be at sea by this time; but I am writing by special messenger that this may reach you in time for you to follow the advice I proceed to give you.

"I made this Lécuyer talk; and from his lies, his statements, and his concealments, I have culled the clues that I needed to reconstruct the whole web of domestic conspiracy that has been working against you. This evening at the Spanish Embassy I shall pay my admiring compliments to your wife and her mother. I shall be most attentive to Madame Evangelista, I shall throw you over in the meanest way, I shall abuse you, but with extreme subtlety; anything strong would at once put this Mascarille in petticoats on the scent. What did you do that set her against you? That is what I mean to find out. If only you had had wit enough to make love to the mother before marrying the daughter, you would at this moment be a peer of France, Duc de Manerville, and ambassador to Madrid. If only you had sent for me at the time of your marriage! I could have taught you to know, to analyze, the two women you would have to fight, and by comparing our observations we should have hit on some good counsel. Was not I the only friend you had who would certainly honor your wife? Was I a man to be afraid of? But after these women had learned to judge me, they took fright and divided us. If you had not been so silly as to sulk with me, they could not have eaten you out of house and home.

"Your wife contributed largely to our coolness. She was talked over by her mother, to whom she wrote twice a week, and you never heeded it. I recognized my friend Paul as I heard this detail.

"Within a month I will be on such terms with your mother-in-law that she herself will tell me the reason for the Hispano-Italian *vendetta* she has evidently vowed on you—you, the best fellow in the world. Did she hate you before her daughter was in love with Félix de Vandenesse? or has she driven you to the Indies that her daughter may be free, as a woman is in France when completely separated from her husband? That is the problem.

"I can see you leaping and howling when you read that your wife is madly in love with Félix de Vandenesse. If I had not taken it into my head to make a tour in the East with Montriveau, Ronquerolles, and certain other jolly fellows of your acquaintance, I could have told you more about this intrigue, which was incipient when I left. I could then see the first sprouting seed of your catastrophe. What gentleman could be scurvy enough to open such a subject without some invitation, or dare to blow on a woman? Who could bear to break the witch's mirror in which a friend loves to contemplate the fairy scenes of a happy marriage? Are not such illusions the wealth of the heart? And was not your wife, my dear boy, in the widest sense of the word, a woman of the world? She thought of nothing but her success, her dress; she frequented the Bouffons, the opera, and balls; rose late, drove in the Bois, dined out or gave dinner-parties. Such a life seems to me to be to women what war is to men; the public sees only the victorious, and forgets the dead. Some delicate women die of this exhausting round; those who survive must have iron constitutions, and consequently very little heart and very strong stomachs. Herein lies the reason of the want of feeling, the cold atmosphere of drawing-room society. Nobler souls dwell in solitude; the tender and weak succumb. What are left are the boulders which keep the social ocean within bounds by enduring to be beaten and

rolled by the breakers without wearing out. Your wife was
made to withstand this life; she seemed inured to it; she was
always fresh and beautiful. To me the inference was obvious
—she did not love you, while you loved her to distraction.
To strike the spark of love in this flinty nature a man of iron
was required.

"After being caught by Lady Dudley, who could not keep
him (she is the wife of my real father), Félix was obviously
the man for Natalie. Nor was there any great difficulty in
guessing that your wife did not care for you. From indifference to aversion is but a step; and sooner or later, a discussion, a word, an act of authority on your part, a mere trifle,
would make your wife overleap it.

"I myself could have rehearsed the scene that took place
between you every night in her room. You have no child,
my boy. Does not that fact account for many things to an
observer? You, who were in love, could hardly discern the
coldness natural to a young woman whom you have trained to
the very point for Félix de Vandenesse. If you had discovered that your wife was cold-hearted, the stupid policy of
married life would have prompted you to regard it as the
reserve of innocence. Like all husbands, you fancied you
could preserve her virtue in a world where women whisper to
each other things that men dare not say, where all that a husband would never tell his wife is spoken and commented on
behind a fan, with laughter and banter, *à propos* to a trial or
an adventure. Though your wife liked the advantages of a
married life, she found the price a little heavy; the price, the
tax, was yourself!

"You, seeing none of these things, went on digging pits
and covering them with flowers, to use the time-honored
rhetorical figure. You calmly submitted to the rule which
governs the common run of men, and from which I had
wished to protect you.

"My dear boy, nothing was wanting to make you as great

an ass as any tradesman who is surprised when his wife deceives him; nothing but this outcry to me about your sacrifices and your love for Natalie: 'How ungrateful she would be to betray me; I have done this and that and the other, and I will do more yet, I will go to India for her sake——' etc., etc. My dear Paul, you have lived in Paris, and you have had the honor of the most intimate friendship of one Henri de Marsay, and you do not know the commonest things, the first principles of the working of the female mechanism, the alphabet of a woman's heart! You may slave yourself to death, you may go to Sainte-Pélagie, you may kill two-and-twenty men, give up seven mistresses, serve Laban, cross the desert, narrowly escape the hulks, cover yourself with disgrace; like Nelson, refuse to give battle because you must kiss Lady Hamilton's shoulder, or, like Bonaparte, fight old Wurmser, get yourself cut up on the bridge of Arcole, rave like Rolando, break a leg in splints to dance with a woman for five minutes! But, my dear boy, what has any of these things to do with her loving you? If love were taken as proven by such evidence, men would be too happy; a few such demonstrations at the moment when he wanted her would win the woman of his heart.

"Love, you stupid old Paul, is a belief like that in the immaculate conception of the Virgin. You have it, or you have it not. Of what avail are rivers of blood, or the mines of Potosi, or the greatest glory, to produce an involuntary and inexplicable feeling? Young men like you, who look for love to balance their outlay, seem to me base usurers. Our legal wives owe us children and virtue; but they do not owe love. Love is the consciousness of happiness given and received, and the certainty of giving and getting it; it is an ever-living attraction, constantly satisfied, and yet insatiable. On the day when Vandenesse stirred in your wife's heart the chord you had left untouched and virginal, your amorous flourishes, your outpourings of soul, and of money, ceased even to be remembered.   Your nights of happiness strewn with roses—fudge !   Your devotion—an offering of remorse !   Yourself—a victim to be slain on the altar !   Your previous life—a blank ! One impulse of love annihilated your treasures of passion, which were now but old iron.   He, Félix, has had her beauty, her devotion—for no return perhaps ; but, in love, belief is as good as reality.

" Your mother-in-law was naturally on the side of the lover against the husband ; secretly or confessedly she shut her eyes —or she opened them ; I do not know what she did, but she took her daughter's part against you.   For fifteen years I have observed society, and I never knew a mother who, under such circumstances, deserted her daughter.   Such indulgence is hereditary, from woman to woman.   And what man can blame them ?   Some lawyer, perhaps, responsible for the Civil Code, which saw only formulas where feelings were at stake.   The extravagance into which you were dragged by the career of a fashionable wife, the tendencies of an easy nature, and your vanity too, perhaps, supplied her with the opportunity of getting rid of you by an ingenious scheme of ruin.

"̣ From all this you will conclude, my good friend, that the charge you put upon me, and which I should have fulfilled all the more gloriously because it would have amused me, is, so to speak, null and void.   The evil I was to have hindered is done—*consummatum est.*   Forgive me for writing *à la de Marsay*, as you say, on matters which to you are so serious.   Far be it from me to cut capers on a friend's grave, as heirs do on that of an uncle.   But you write to me that you mean henceforth to be a man, and I take you at your word ; I treat you as a statesman, and not as a lover.

" Has not this mishap been to you like the brand on his shoulder that determines a convict on a systematic antagonism to society, and a revolt against it ?   You are hereby released from one care—marriage was your master, now it is your servant.   Paul, I am your friend in the fullest meaning of the word. If your brain had been bound in a circlet of brass, if you had earlier had the energy that has come to you too late, I could have proved my friendship by telling you things that would have enabled you to walk over human beings as on a carpet. But whenever we talked over the combinations to which I owed the faculty of amusing myself with a few friends in the heart of Parisian civilization, like a bull in a china shop; whenever I told you, under romantic disguises, some true adventure of my youth, you always regarded them as romances, and did not see their bearing. Hence, I could only think of you as a case of unrequited passion. Well, on my word of honor, in the existing circumstances, you have played the nobler part, and you have lost nothing, as you might imagine, in my opinion. Though I admire a great scoundrel, I esteem and like those who are taken in.

"*À propos* to the doctor who came to such a bad end, brought to the scaffold by his love for his mistress, I remember telling you the far more beautiful story of the unhappy lawyer who is still living on the hulks, I know not where, branded as a forger because he wanted to give his wife—again, an adored wife—thirty thousand francs a year, and the wife gave him up to justice in order to get rid of him and live with another gentleman. You cried shame, you and some others too who were supping with us. Well, my dear fellow, you are that lawyer—minus the hulks.

"Your friends do not spare you the discredit which, in our sphere of life, is equivalent to a sentence pronounced by the Bench. The Marquise de Listomère, the sister of the two Vandenesses, and all her following, in which little Rastignac is now enlisted—a young rascal who is coming to the front; Madame d'Aiglemont and all her set, among whom Charles de Vandenesse is regnant; the Lenoncourts, the Comtesse Féraud, Madame d'Espard, the Nucingens, the Spanish Embassy; in short, a whole section of the fashionable world, very cleverly prompted, heap mud upon your name. 'You

29

are a dissipated wretch, a gambler, a debauchee, and have
made away with your money in the stupidest way. Your wife
—an angel of virtue!—after paying your debts several times,
has just paid off a hundred thousand francs to redeem bills
you had drawn, though her fortune is apart from yours.
Happily, you have pronounced sentence on yourself by getting
out of the way. If you had gone on so, you would have reduced her to beggary, and she would have been a martyr to
conjugal devotion!' When a man rises to power, he has as
many virtues as will furnish an epitaph; if he falls into poverty, he has more vices than the prodigal son; you could never
imagine how many Don Juan vices are attributed to you now.
You gambled on the Bourse, you had licentious tastes, which
it cost you vast sums to indulge, and which are mentioned
with comments and jests that mystify the women. You paid
enormous interest to the money-lenders. The two Vandenesses
laugh as they tell a story of Gigonnet's selling you an ivory
man-of-war for six thousand francs, and buying it of your
manservant for five crowns only to sell it to you again, till you
solemnly smashed it on discovering that you might have a real
ship for the money it was costing you. The adventure occurred nine years ago, and Maxime de Trailles was the hero
of it; but it is thought to fit you so well, that Maxime has
lost the command of his frigate for good. In short, I cannot
tell you everything, for you have furnished forth a perfect
encyclopædia of tittle-tattle, to which every woman tries to
add. In this state of affairs, the most prudish are ready to
legitimize any consolation bestowed by *Comte* Félix de Vandenesse—for their father is dead at last, yesterday.

"Your wife is the great success of the hour. Yesterday
Madame de Camps was repeating all these stories to me at
the Italian opera. 'Don't talk to me,' said I, 'you none of
you know half the facts. Paul had robbed the Bank and
swindled the Treasury. He murdered Ezzelino, and caused
the death of three Medoras of the Rue Saint-Denis, and, be-

tween you and me, I believe him to be implicated in the doings of the Ten Thousand. His agent is the notorious Jacques Collin, whom the police have never been able to find since his last escape from the hulks ; Paul harbored him in his house. As you see, he is capable of any crime ; he is deceiving the Government. Now they have gone off together to see what they can do in India, and rob the Great Mogul.' Madame de Camps understood that a woman of such distinction as herself ought not to use her pretty lips as a Venetian lion's maw.

"Many persons, on hearing these tragi-comedies, refuse to believe them; they defend human nature and noble sentiments, and insist that these are fictions. My dear fellow, Talleyrand made this clever remark: 'Everything happens.' Certainly even stranger things than this domestic conspiracy happen under our eyes; but the world is so deeply interested in denying them, and in declaring that it is slandered, and beside, these great dramas are played so naturally, with a veneer of such perfect good taste, that I often have to wipe my eyeglass before I can see to the bottom of things. But I say once more, when a man is my friend with whom I have received the baptism of Champagne, and communion at the altar of Venus Commoda, when we have together been confirmed by the clawing fingers of the croupier, and when then my friend is in a false position, I would uproot twenty families to set him straight again.

"You must see that I have a real affection for you; have I ever to your knowledge written so long a letter as this is? So read with care all that follows.

"Alack ! Paul ; I must take to writing, I must get into the habit of jotting down the minutes for dispatches ; I am starting on a political career. Within five years I mean to have a minister's portfolio, or find myself an ambassador where I can stir public affairs round in my own way. There is an age when a man's fairest mistress is his country. I am joining

the ranks of those who mean to overthrow not merely the existing Ministry, but their whole system.   In fact, I am swim-
ming in the wake of a prince who halts only on one foot, and
whom I regard as a man of political genius, whose name is
growing great in history ; as complete a prince as a great
artist may be.   We are Ronquerolles, Montriveau, the Grandlieus, the Roche-Hugons, Sérizy, Féraud, and Granville,* all
united against the priestly party, as the silly party that is
represented by the ' Constitutionnel ' ingeniously calls it.   We
mean to upset the two Vandenesses, the Ducs de Lenoncourt,
de Navarreins, de Langeais, and de la Grande-Aumônerie.
To gain our end, we may go so far as to form a coalition with
Lafayette, the Orleanists, the Left—all men who must be got
rid of as soon as we have won the day, for to govern on their
principles is impossible ; and we are capable of anything for
the good of the country—and our own.

   "Personal questions as to the King's person are mere sentimental folly in these days ; they must be cleared away.   From
that point of view, the English, with their sort of Doge, are
more advanced than we are.   Politics have nothing to do with
that, my dear fellow.   Politics consist in giving the nation an
impetus by creating an oligarchy embodying a fixed theory
of government, and able to direct public affairs along a
straight path, instead of allowing the country to be pulled in
a thousand different directions, which is what has been
happening for the last forty years in our beautiful France—at
once so intelligent and so sottish, so wise and so foolish ; it
needs a system indeed, much more than men.   What are
individuals in this great question ?   If the end is a great one, if
the country may live happy and free from trouble, what do
the masses care for the profits of our stewardship, our fortune,
privileges, and pleasures ?

   "I am now standing firm on my feet.   I have at the present
moment a hundred and fifty thousand francs a year in the

* See "The Thirteen."

Three per Cents., and a reserve of two hundred thousand francs to repair damages. Even this does not seem to me very much ballast in the pocket of a man starting left foot foremost to scale the heights of power.

"A fortunate accident settled the question of my setting out on this career, which did not particularly smile on me, for you know my predilection for the life of the East. After thirty-five years of slumber, my highly respected mother woke up to the recollection that she had a son who might do her honor. Often when a vine-stock is eradicated, some years after shoots come up to the surface of the ground; well, my dear boy, my mother had almost torn me up by the roots from her heart, and I sprouted again in her head. At the age of fifty-eight, she thinks herself old enough to think no more of any men but her son. At this juncture she has met in some hot-water caldron, at I know not what baths, a delightful old maid—English, with two hundred and forty thousand francs a year; and, like a good mother, she has inspired her with an audacious ambition to become my wife. A maid of six-and-thirty, my word! Brought up in the strictest puritanical principles, a steady sitting hen, who maintains that unfaithful wives should be publicly burnt. 'Where will you find wood enough?' I asked her. I could have sent her to the devil, for two hundred and forty thousand francs a year are no equivalent for liberty, nor a fair price for my physical and moral worth and my prospects. But she is the sole heiress of a gouty old fellow, some London brewer, who within a calculable time will leave her a fortune equal at least to what the sweet creature has already. Added to these advantages, she has a red nose, the eyes of a dead goat, a waist that makes one fear lest she should break into three pieces if she falls down, and the coloring of a badly painted doll. But— she is delightfully economical; but—she will adore her husband, do what he will; but—she has the English gift: she will manage my house, my stables, my servants, my estates better than any steward. She has all the dignity of virtue; she holds herself as erect as a confidante on the stage of the Français; nothing will persuade me that she has not been impaled and the shaft broken off in her body. Miss Stevens is, however, fair enough to be not too unpleasing if I must positively marry her. But—and this to me is truly pathetic— she has the hands of a woman as immaculate as the sacred ark; they are so red that I have not yet hit on any way to whiten them that will not be too costly, and I have no idea how to fine down her fingers, which are like sausages. Yes; she evidently belongs to the brewhouse by her hands, and to the aristocracy by her money; but she is apt to affect the great lady a little too much, as do rich Englishwomen who want to be mistaken for them, and she displays her lobster-claws too freely.

"She has, however, as little intelligence as I could wish in a woman. If there were a stupider one to be found, I would set out to seek her. This girl, whose name is Dinah, will never criticise me; she will never contradict me; I shall be her Upper Chamber, her Lords and Commons. In short, Paul, she is indefeasible evidence of the English genius; she is a product of English mechanics brought to their highest pitch of perfection; she was undoubtedly made at Manchester, between the manufactory of Perry's pens and the workshops for steam-engines. It eats, it drinks, it walks, it may have children, take good care of them, and bring them up admirably, and it apes a woman so well that you would believe it real.

"When my mother introduced us, she had set up the machine so cleverly, had so carefully fitted the pegs, and oiled the wheels so thoroughly, that nothing jarred; then, when she saw I did not make a very wry face, she set the springs in motion, and the woman spoke. Finally, my mother uttered the decisive words: ' Miss Dinah Stevens spends no more than thirty thousand francs a year, and has been traveling for seven

years in order to economize.' So there is another image, and
that one is silver.

"Matters are so far advanced that the banns are to be published. We have got as far as 'My dear love.' Miss makes
eyes at me that might floor a porter. The settlements are
prepared. My fortune is not inquired into; Miss Stevens
devotes a portion of hers to creating an entail in landed estate,
bearing an income of two hundred and forty thousand francs,
and to the purchase of a house, likewise entailed. The settlement credited to me is of a million francs. She has nothing
to complain of. I leave her uncle's money untouched.

"The worthy brewer, who has helped to found the entail,
was near to bursting with joy when he heard that his niece was
to be a marquise. He would be capable of doing something
handsome for my eldest boy.

"I shall sell out of the Funds as soon as they are up to
eighty, and invest in land. Thus, in two years I may look to
get six hundred thousand francs a year out of real estate. So,
you see, Paul, I do not give my friends advice that I am not
ready to act upon.

"If you had but listened to me, you would have an English
wife, some nabob's daughter, who would leave you the freedom of a bachelor and the independence necessary for playing
the whist of ambition. I would concede my future wife to
you if you were not married already. But that cannot be
helped, and I am not the man to bid you chew the cud of the
past.

"All this preamble was needful to explain to you that for
the future my position in life will be such as a man needs if
he wants to play the great game of pitch-and-toss. I cannot
do without you, my friend. Instead of going to pickle in the
Indies, you will find it much simpler to swim in my convoy
in the waters of the Seine. Believe me, Paris is still the spot
where fortune crops up most freely. Potosi is situated in the
Rue Vivienne or the Rue de la Paix, the Place Vendôme, or

the Rue de la Rivoli. In every other country, manual labor, the sweat of the perspiring agent, marches and counter-marches, are indispensable to the accumulation of a fortune; here intelligence is sufficient. Here a man, even of modern talent, may discover a gold-mine as he puts on his slippers or picks his teeth after dinner, as he goes to bed or gets up in the morning. Find me a spot on earth where a good com-monplace idea brings in more money or is more immediately understood than it is here? If I climb to the top of the tree, am I the man to refuse you a hand, a word, a signature? Do not we young scamps need a friend we can rely on, if it were only to compromise him in our place and stead, to send him forth to die as a private, so as to save the general? Politics are impossible without a man of honor at hand, to whom everything may be said and done.

"This, then, is my advice to you. Let the Belle-Amélie sail without you; return here like a lightning flash, and I will arrange a duel for you with Félix de Vandenesse, in which you must fire first, and down with your man as dead as a pigeon. In France an outraged husband who kills his man is at once respectable and respected. No one ever makes game of him! Fear, my dear boy, is an element of social life, and a means of success for those whose eyes never fall before the gaze of any other man. I, who care no more for life than for a cup of ass' milk, and who never felt a qualm of fear, have observed the strange effects of that form of emotion on modern manners. Some dread the idea of losing the enjoyments to which they are fettered, others that of parting from some woman. The adventurous temper of past times, when a man threw away his life like a slipper, has ceased to exist. In many men courage is merely a clever speculation on the fear that may seize their adversary. None but the Poles now, in Europe, ever fight for the pleasure of it; they still cultivate the art for art's sake, and not as a matter of calculation. Kill Vandenesse, and your wife will tremble, your mother-in-law will tremble, the public will tremble; you will be rehabilitated, you will proclaim your frantic passion for your wife, every one will believe you, and you will be a hero. Such is France.

"I shall not stickle over a hundred thousand francs with you. You can pay your principal debts, and can prevent utter ruin by pledging your property on a time bargain with option of repurchase, for you will soon be in position that will allow you to pay off the mortgage before the time is up. Also, knowing your wife's character, you can henceforth rule her with a word. While you loved her you could not hold your own; now, having ceased to love her, your power will be irresistible. I shall have made your mother-in-law as supple as a glove; for what you have to do is to reinstate yourself with the hundred and fifty thousand francs those women have saved for themselves.

"So give up your self-exile, which always seems to me the charcoal-brasier of men of brains. If you run away, you leave slander mistress of the field. The gambler who goes home to fetch his money and comes back to the tables loses all. You must have your funds in your pocket. You appear to me to be seeking fresh reinforcements in the Indies. No good at all! We are two gamblers at the green table of politics; between you and me loans are a matter of course. So take post-horses, come to Paris, and begin a new game; with Henri de Marsay for a partner you will win, for Henri de Marsay knows what he wants and when to strike.

"This, you see, is where we stand. My real father is in the English Ministry. We shall have connections with Spain through the Evangelistas; for as soon as your mother-in-law and I have measured claws, we shall perceive that when devil meets devil there is nothing to be gained on either side. Montriveau is a lieutenant-general; he will certainly be war minister sooner or later, for his eloquence gives him much power in the Chamber. Ronquerolles is in the Ministry and on the Privy Council. Martial de la Roche-Hugon is appointed minister to Germany and made a peer of France, and he has brought us as an addition Marshal the Duc de Carigliano and all the 'rump' of the Empire, which so stupidly held on to the rear of the Restoration. Sérizy is leader of the State Council; he is indispensable there. Granville is master of the legal party; he has two sons on the Bench. The Grandlieus are in high favor at Court. Féraud is the soul of the Gondreville set, low intriguers who, I know not why, are always at the top. Thus supported, what have we to fear? We have a foot in every capital, an eye in every cabinet; we hem in the whole administration without their suspecting it.

"Is not the money question a mere trifle, nothing at all, when all this machinery is ready. And, above all, what is a woman? Will you never be anything but a schoolboy? What is life, my dear fellow, when it is wrapped up in a woman? A ship over which we have no command, which obeys a wild compass though it has indeed a lode-stone; which runs before every wind that blows, and in which the man really is a galley-slave, obedient not only to the law, but to every rule improvised by his driver, without the possibility of retaliation. Phaugh!

"I can understand that from passion, or the pleasure to be found in placing our power in a pair of white hands, a man should obey his wife—but when it comes to obeying Médor— then away with Angelica! The great secret of social alchemy, my dear sir, is to get the best of everything out of each stage of our life, to gather all its leaves in spring, all its flowers in summer, all its fruits in autumn. Now we—I and some boon companions—have enjoyed ourselves for twelve years, like musketeers, black, white, and red, refusing ourselves nothing, not even a filibustering expedition now and again; henceforth we mean to shake ripe plums off the tree, at an age when experience has ripened the harvest. Come, join us; you shall have a share of the pudding we mean to stir.

"Come, and you will find a friend wholly yours in the skin of   HENRI DE M."

At the moment when Paul de Manerville finished reading this letter, of which every sentence fell like a sledge-hammer on the tower of his hopes, his illusions, and his love, he was already beyond the Azores.   In the midst of this ruin, rage surged up in him—cold and impotent rage.

"What had I done to them?" he asked himself.

This question is the impulse of the simpleton, of the weak natures, which, as they see nothing, can foresee nothing.

"Henri, Henri!" he cried aloud.   "The one true friend!"

Many men would have gone mad.   Paul went to bed and slept the deep sleep which supervenes on immeasurable disaster; as Napoleon slept after the battle of Waterloo.

PARIS, *September–October,* 1835.